The
Rangers Are
Coming

By

Phil Walker

ISBN 13: 978-1-887982-02-3
ISBN 10: 1887982027

Dedication

For Autumn, child of light.
You were always on my mind
As I wrote this book,
The purity of your character never
Let me stray far from the soul of
The story as the words flowed.

Table of Contents

Foreword

For my entire life I've been absorbed by history. All kinds of history. It has always been a passion for me.

The whole idea of writing an alternative history story actually offended me for quite a while. Who was I to dream up a history all my own?

However, my continuous study of American history left me with an empty feeling. So many mistakes. So many missed opportunities. I began to wonder if the United States had the chance for a do-over, beginning in 1770, what would happen, especially if a group of people from 330 years in the future were there to help them along.

I pondered this notion for a very long time. Then one day I began writing. I didn't start at the beginning as you're supposed to. Big hunks of The Rangers Are Coming appeared in pieces as I addressed different elements of our history, almost as if I was writing separate stories. Eventually, the pieces began to fit together, and I had a much longer book than the one you have in your hands.

Pruning the big story down to something manageable was difficult. I kept the main elements of the Revolutionary War, slavery, the Civil War, and the acculturation of the Native Americans, plus many other actual events through modern times affecting our history.

I also used real characters from history and sprinkled them throughout the book. I viewed this as important. If the Patriots who created our nation had the benefit of seeing outcomes in the future, how would they react? What different choices would they make? The same applies to other global leaders of the 19th and 20th centuries.

The resulting story fascinated me. I began to prefer the history I created, to the history that actually was.

Ultimately, 'The Rangers Are Coming', became a total alternative history presentation with some astonishing outcomes, not only for the United States, but also for the entire world.

I don't want to say my imagination got the best of me. This is something you need to determine on your own. As you read the history I have created, I hope you smile and say, "if only it could have been that way."

Prologue

In the span of less than thirty years, The United States of America has reinvented itself.

It began with the remarkable Animal Park in Branson, Missouri, where the biblical prophecy by Isaiah in which the lion lay down with the lamb had actually come true. What was originally a very nice but unremarkable regional 1000-acre zoo suddenly made international headlines when all the animals began running free and living in peaceful co-existence with each other and the throngs of humans who rushed to Missouri to experience the sight for themselves.

It was a tremendous wake-up call. None could explain it, but there was doubt of its reality. For the millions who saw it with their own eyes, the transformation spread its influence across the country. The United States became a deeply Christian society.

Enormous political reforms were the result of this conversion as a dominant political party known as the New Revolution swept into every important elected office in the country. A renaissance of social changes came with the movement. The states and Congress ratified new amendments to the constitution setting term limits for the House of Representative and Senate, and dictating a balanced annual budget.

A drastic reduction in the bloated Federal bureaucracy occurred. A simple flat tax replaced the behemoth of the IRS. Federal regulations by the millions simply disappeared. The result was a tsunami of new businesses, new companies, and resurgence in enterprise producing an annual growth rate of the GDP to over 7 percent in less than five years. The trillions of dollars in Federal debt melted away. The space program got moving again and a manned mission to Mars was now just a few years away. The Department of Defense became a powerful, deadlier; force to provide security for the country.

Perhaps the most fundamental element of social life in America was the overhaul of the education system. No longer were students coming out of schools with mere fragments of education, but the schools from Kindergarten to Graduate schools were producing a bumper crop of smart, self-actuated, resourceful, and highly skilled students who quickly restored the United States to the premier education system in the world.

Church attendance for families was 90 percent. The divorce rate fell, as nuclear families became the standard for American life. The stability of the family resulted in a drastic drop in children born out of wedlock, crime, drug use, and homelessness. Abortion all but disappeared from society. People believed in God, and trusted His wisdom.

There was a smile on the face of America. From the point of view of the average citizen, community citizenship, generosity to the less fortunate, and a firm belief the blessings of God came, not from deeds, but from their hearts.

About the only persistent complaint anyone could think of, was they never seemed to win the lottery to actually visit the magical Park, and the perceived home of God.

However, success breeds envy, and envy bred resentment, and resentment caused unrest and hatred among others. The honeymoon of good will and global tranquility is ending. As America continued to glow, the rest of the world was growing decidedly unlovely.

Chapter 1
Too Good to Be True

Branson, Missouri, 2030

Jacob and Ali Martin were parents of three children. The two older boys were intelligent and levelheaded as their parents. Both of them graduated from the College of the Ozarks, plus graduate studies and other schools, Trinity Seminary in Chicago for Patrick, who was the oldest and had followed his father into the pulpit of the church, while Shane followed the family tradition of veterinary medicine.

The youngest member of the Martin family was a lovely blond-haired, blued-eyed beauty, who was the image of her mother in looks, and the equal of her father in piercing intellect. She was 22-year-old Arcadia. She also graduated ahead of time and with high honors from the College of the Ozarks. Afterwards, she seemed content to work in the Park.

Arcadia was a complete mystery to her parents. She was incredibly articulate when she needed to be, demonstrated a finely tuned mind her father appreciated, but was certain there were layer after layer underneath even he could not fathom, and Arcadia seldom showed.

The surface features were obvious. Arcadia had a near perfect photographic memory. She was fluent in Spanish, German, French, and Mandarin Chinese. She seemed to possess an ability to assemble a body of facts, however unconnected, and project them to a conclusion not obvious for months or even years. She was a happy, spirited, athletically gifted girl who attracted the opposite sex in droves. These did not last long, because the young men soon gave up because they were unable to keep up with her intellectually or, often athletically.

Perhaps most important of all, Arcadia loved God with all her heart and soul and viewed her life as an obligation to seek to follow His will on a daily basis. Her life choices were, filtered through God before they reached the ears of all the people who Arcadia touched.

The animals of the Park seemed to have a special connection to Arcadia. They flocked to her, and loved her. If it was possible for a wolverine to show affection, it happened when Arcadia was nearby.

More and more often, Arcadia's father, Jacob included her in meetings with the many high government officials who were frequent guests at the Park. He appreciated her understanding of the complexities involved in operating a country with 300 million people, and a world of six billion who wanted them all dead, or at least not nearly as blessed and happy.

One morning the phone rang. One the line was President Max Portner in his second in the White House, born and raised in Branson and a lifelong friend of the family.

"I understand, Max. Even when you give them everything you reasonably can, it's never enough." He pushed the button to allow Arcadia to hear the President's response.

"We have a million missionaries in the field and twice that working in the Peace Corps, all over the world. Many people are getting help and they appreciate it. The problem is every mullah in every mosque in the world is telling their congregations the only reason the United States is providing this aid is so they can convert every one of their faithful to Christianity. The problem is its working. The number of Muslims becoming Christians is growing. Some of the more radical Shia countries like Iran are executing the people they catch. It's a ghastly business."

"It's a good thing the Israelis' took out their nuclear facilities when they did. It set 'em back 30 years," said Jacob.

"Which is how long it's been," said Arcadia. "Mr. President, what does your intelligence community say about how close the Iranians are to getting up and running again?"

"We've flooded the country with agents. So has the Mosad. If they had anything really cooking, we would know it."

Arcadia wasn't satisfied, "Look it doesn't have to be big bombs on top of rockets. They have enough capacity, not destroyed, to put together a half a dozen smaller bombs. Any one of them could take out a whole city."

Portner laughed, "I should have you running the CIA, Arcadia. You think of every angle."

"Have they actually looked at the big picture," asked Arcadia?

"I guess I don't understand what you mean," said the President. "Arcadia, honey, I've known you all your life and I've learned you have better instincts than half the people who work for me every day. Is your hyper-trophied horse sense telling you something we've missed?"

"I beg your pardon, Mr. President," said Arcadia. "Please remember you're a native of Branson, and until you became President, were just Uncle Max to me. I didn't mean to question the way you're doing your job. As far as I'm concerned you've done a wonderful job."

Jacob sat back in his chair and lit his pipe. He knew his daughter kept up to date on current events from all over the world and frequently had insights others missed. He was interested in the analysis Arcadia seemed about to deliver to the President.

Max Portner was, indeed, one of the bright men produced by the New Revolution Party and their choice for President after the administrations of Paul Warfield and Chris Abernathy. He continued the policies begun by his predecessors. Under his leadership, he was able to take advantage of the advanced students coming out of the new school system and install them in critical places within the government. He now had the most efficient bureaucracy in the world. From top to bottom, he had the best first team of administrators and a bench of support people both deep and talented.

His emphasis was on two main fronts. First, he greatly expanded the teams of workers he put into the field around the world to provide aid and assistance to third world countries. Their expertise in farming, water systems, construction, and administration was making a big difference for millions of people. They were generally welcomed by nearly every country.

His second contribution was to organize the wide range of new products and innovations the U.S. was producing and exporting throughout the world. Modestly priced American products gave the country a competitive advantage over countries like China who still paid their workers a fraction of what Americans received. American products were so well built and turned out by automated systems they undercut the marketplace. U.S. exports were ten times their imports and the money flowing in had all but wiped out the Federal deficit during his administration.

The problem with providing all these services, products, and aid, was the Americans delivering them were motivated with a service to God and seeking to do His will. This made them natural missionaries and they weren't hesitant to share the "Good News" with people.

Wherever the work of Americans and American companies overlapped with countries, which had substantial Muslim populations, there were problems. A tragically large number of Americans died, for no other reason than the fact they existed as Christians.

Whenever the incidents were more than isolated or American property destroyed, the President reluctantly told the country receiving the aid; the United States would simply withdraw its people and services. Very often, the leadership of that country, particularly the poor third world nations sided with the Americans to keep the vital aid flowing. This infuriated the Muslim leaders who kept up a steady rant at every mosque, telling their faithful the hideous Christians were infidels who did not follow the truth faith of Allah, and killed immediately.

Arcadia knew all this, and believed a dangerous pattern was developing. "Mr. President, it's not just the Iranians you have to worry about. Our solid evangelism has caused Muslim nations to begin cooperating with each other. Furthermore, some of the non-Muslim nations, like China, with markets for their products declining, have a reason to give help to the Muslim nations. Unfortunately, you don't have enough resources to police the motivations and actions of every country with a grudge against us."

There was a long pause on the phone. Jacob spoke up, "Still with us Max?"

"Yes, unfortunately Arcadia is right. We have a very sophisticated intelligence system monitoring cell phone, email, and radio chatter on a global basis. We get regular reports from our agents all the time; the emerging picture is a little scary. We've increased our surveillance on all people, and products coming into the country. We intercept a lot of dangerous people and potentially deadly plots against the country, all the time. I even asked the CIA, FBI, and NSA to evaluate their success in stopping the threats and I can tell you I was a little disconcerted to learn the number is not 100 percent."

"So we are more vulnerable than the general public knows," asked Jacob?

"Correct," said Portner. "I'm afraid security will have to be one of the major policies for the near future."

"I know you hoped to reduce our military footprint in the world even more," said Jacob. "I'm sure it burns your soul, being such a devout Christian, to have to worry about such things."

"It does. Watching the country evolve over the past thirty years, I've always hoped our clear policy of providing aid instead of arms would finally be making a difference."

"It's making a difference all right," said Arcadia, "we're in greater danger now than ever."

When the conversation with the President was over, Arcadia went straight to the Emerald Cathedral to have a talk with God. The lovely cavern was unchanged and still regarded as the true heart of the sprawling Park. Arcadia felt closer to God here than anywhere else in the world, and came to pray and speak her thoughts to Jesus on a daily basis.

On this day, Arcadia had a deep sense of foreboding in her heart. The President only confirmed what she already knew and felt. "My Lord, I am concerned and confused. We truly seek to put our trust and our lives in your hands, and to praise and exalt you as the Master of the Universe. We serve you in the manner in which Jesus taught. We live in love with one another, and seek only the best for our fellow man. Having said this, our country is in greater danger today from the Enemy than ever before. I know your ways are not our ways, and your thoughts are not our thoughts. You live at a level incomprehensible to us poor humans. Still, I cannot believe you won't honor our worship and dedication to you. I know you have a plan for all lives, and I respect that, but Lord, I can't help but feel afraid for our future. I ask you to bring peace to my soul and hope to my heart, so I may continue to live according to your will. In the name of Christ Jesus, who is our greatest friend, Amen."

Chapter 2
The Conspiracy

Middle East - Dubai

The meeting convened in Dubai. A gathering of men from throughout the Islamic world would not attract much attention in such a place since it was an international destination attracting visitors from all over the world. The last thing the organizers of this meeting wanted was to draw attention from the hyper-alert American intelligence services.

Actually there were only a half dozen men, very carefully chosen men, meeting in secret to review the final planning of a scheme years in development. The men carefully arrived over a period of several days, so even though the individuals recorded as on the move by CIA operatives, the ultimate purpose of their being in Dubai would appear as nothing more than relatively minor Moslem leaders taking a few days off to enjoy the forbidden pleasures offered by the modern city.

The meeting began with a prayer from an Iranian mullah, "Mighty Allah, whose prophet on earth is Muhammad, the true authority of Heaven. May our jihad in your name be blessed and may the Great Satin of America and it's heresy of your truth be stricken and all of the infidels of that unholy land perish in the fires of destruction you have decreed us to unleash."

The Saudi representative began the discussion. "In the past thirty years, the United States has undergone a religious transformation and today the radical Christian, New Revolution Party controls the entire country. They've accomplished a great deal. They've led the world in the development of new technology and improved products of all kinds. Their universities are now the most effective seats of higher learning anywhere on the planet. The Americans have capitalized on all their own energy sources in oil, natural gas, and coal. They're virtually independent of any need to import foreign oil. What's more, they've developed a space-based solar array beaming energy to the country and rapidly replacing their need for any oil whatsoever. They have streamlined their government, and their economy is now expanding at no less than 7 percent a year with 10 percent being the projection in the next five years. They have virtually no debt, and full employment. Fortunately, the rest of the world still needs our oil, so production has not declined, but the price of oil has fallen drastically and is affecting the economy of the principal oil exporting countries."

"We already know all that," said the Egyptian delegate. "On the surface these developments can be applauded. The world's economy has dramatically improved as a result. However, along with the improved economy came a resurgence of religious zealotry on the part of the Americans. The Americans are exporting this fanatical dedication to nations everywhere. They publically say they're only interested in improving the lives of needy people and countries, but they're preaching their religion relentlessly. I'm ashamed to admit many Muslims, especially in countries benefitting the most from American aid, have turned their backs on the true faith, and embraced Christianity."

"How serious has the defection from Islam been," asked the Iranian representative?

"In countries where Islam is not the majority, it's been significant. The country of Tanzania, for example, was 40 percent Muslim ten years ago. Today that number is down to just over 10 percent."

"My brothers," said the Iranian mullah, "we cannot stand by and allow the Great Satan to threaten the true faith. They must be destroyed!"

"Which is the purpose of our meeting here today," said the Pakistani representative. "Iran's nuclear program was destroyed by the Israelis' 20 years ago, and the Americans have been very busy insuring it never recovers. However, there are other nuclear devises already in existence in other countries, such as ours. Of course, we could not actively launch these missiles at the U.S., no country could. The United States still has the largest nuclear arsenal in the world and would not hesitate to use it on any country attacking them."

"Our plan has been to acquire several nuclear weapons and smuggle them into the United States. It's taken us five years, but I am happy to report six such weapons are now inside the United States and ready for detonation."

"What are their locations," asked the Egyptian representative?"

"New York City, Washington, D.C., Chicago, Los Angeles, Houston and Denver, Colorado," said the Saudi representative.

"Why Denver," asked one of the others?"

"Because Denver is on the east side of the Rocky Mountains, and the radiation from the blast will blow across the entire center of the country."

"Our estimates are 50 million people will die immediately from the explosions and an additional 100 million people will die from radiation exposure in the following two weeks to a month."

"Goodbye to the Great Satan," cried the Iranian mullah. Allah Akbar!"

"Brothers," said the Saudi, "A week from today, we will strike."

Chapter 3
Disaster

Branson, Missouri

It was minutes before One O'clock in the afternoon in New York City on September 11, 2030. A van pulled into a parking garage in midtown Manhattan. At the same time, vans were also pulling into parking garages in Washington D.C., Chicago, Denver, Houston and Los Angeles.

The drivers of each van took out cell phones and waited quietly as the moments moved toward the top of the hour. As the phones reached the exact time, each of the drivers said in loud voices, "Allah, Akbar!", and entered a number in their phones. Simultaneously there were intensely bright lights signaling the detonation of each of the six nuclear bombs across America.

In Washington, the Capitol, White House, all the monuments, the Supreme Court, the FBI and every building within five miles of ground zero vaporized instantly and the blast blew down buildings for ten miles.

In Houston, a large crater formed at the site of the explosion, and the sea rushed in. The Johnson Space Center simply ceased to exist.

The Island of Manhattan became a heap of superheated rubble, as all the great buildings, museums, harbors, and the Statue of Liberty vanished in a few seconds.

In Chicago, the blast pushed the waters of Lake Michigan back hundreds of feet and when they returned, they were only washing over a steaming cauldron of devastation.

In Denver, the blast spread out from downtown, all the way to the Denver Tech Center. The campuses of the University of Denver, and the complex of buildings of the University of Colorado campus in

Denver, evaporated in an explosion of dust, heat, and burning fire.

In Los Angeles, the crowded freeways, the sprawling downtown, and the coastal communities were nothing more than huge piles of rubble.

Millions of Americans died instantly. The entire government, including legislators in both houses of Congress never knew what hit them. More millions died in Chicago, Denver, Houston and Los Angeles.

The men and women in the orbiting space station looked down and saw six enormous mushroom clouds spreading out over the country from the Atlantic to the Pacific Oceans.

It was a deathblow for America. She would never rise again.

In Branson, Missouri, far away from any of the deadly explosions, Arcadia Martin froze in her steps as she was walking near the central fountain of the Park. She had felt strangely ill at ease for several days. It was like waiting for the other shoe to drop. She sensed something terrible was about to happen, but she didn't know what it was. She prayed ceaselessly throughout each day for some clue from the Lord of the source of her worries.

Even now, she didn't know exactly what had happened. She just knew the source of her dread was now a fact. She ran into the tech center of the Park and saw row after row of monitors displaying only static. The Park system seemed to be operating normally and all those monitors showed peaceful scenes of people wandering through the Park and enjoying the animals.

Suddenly her phone rang. It was her father, Jacob. "Arcadia, several American cities have been struck by nuclear weapons. We're trying to sort it out now. Where are you?"

"In the tech center."

"Just wait there, I'll be there as quickly as I can."

Phones and alarms were now going off throughout the tech center. The staff on duty were answering the phones and tracing the source of the alarms before shutting them off. The big room was a beehive of activity. Arcadia turned to the master coordinator of all control room activities and said, "What are you hearing?"

"Nuclear explosions have gone off in at least three cities," he said. "So far we have identified New York City, Washington, D.C., and Chicago, but I think there are more. None of the television networks are broadcasting, but people are calling in from all over the country."

Jacob, the rest of the family, and most of the senior officials of the Park joined Arcadia in the tech center. For the next several hours they did everything, they could to understand the scope of the attack and to assess the damage, not just to cities, but also to human life.

As it happened, President Max Portner was in Branson, and not Washington, when the city exploded. He joined the group in the tech center and worked the phones for several hours, trying to get military leaders still alive assigned to positions and have them start bringing some command and control back to the chain of command.

Finally, as the sun was going down, he got up from his chair and called for everyone's attention. "We need to get all you Park and Community leaders together for a meeting in the big conference room. The rest of you keep on doing what you're doing and come tell me if anything big happens."

Portner led Jacob, Ali, both brothers, and the 12 directors of the Park into the conference room. Arcadia followed her father and sat next to him.

When everyone found places, Portner began his briefing, "It now appears six nuclear weapons were detonated. All of them were from bombs hidden in the cities. We had no missiles launched at us from anywhere in world. We've lost New York City, Washington, D.C., Chicago, Houston, Denver, and Los Angeles. We are estimating 50 million dead, and expect that number to rise to over 150 million in the next couple of weeks as people die from injuries and from radiation poisoning."

"We've lost our entire Federal government, almost all of Congress, most of the Cabinet, and everyone at the Pentagon is dead. All our big banks, the stock market, and the dozens of big corporations who had headquarters in New York are gone. The United Nations building and all the delegates died. I've established a new military headquarters at NORAD in Colorado Springs. They have reestablished operational control of the military, Army, Navy, and Air Force. Our nuclear arsenal is back under our control and I would be happy to use if I had any idea who was responsible for this."

Then he turned back to Jacob and said, "For a start, I appoint you Vice President, Jacob. We have to have a chain of command in case I get killed in the next few days."

Just then, a tech came rushing into the room. "There's a worldwide satellite feed coming in two minutes."

"Switch it in here," said the President.

Shortly a picture of an Islamic flag appeared on the screen and panned out to a table where six bearded men sat, some of them wearing cloaks of office as Muslim clerics. The man in the center chair, with dark eyes, heavy features, and a salt and pepper beard spoke.

"By this time, most of the world knows the Great Satan of the United States was struck a death blow by the will of Allah and his prophet Muhammad. At last the infidels who've defied the will of Allah for so long, who have tortured and bled the nations of Islam for endless years, will no longer be able to spread their lies, and abominations to the true faithful of the world. We declare Christianity dead. All Christians in the world will either declare their allegiance to Allah or lose their lives."

The group raised their fists in defiance and a sign of victory before the picture phased out.

Portner picked up a phone and talked to the tech center. "Find out where that signal originated, then arrange a global satellite link of our own. Call me back when you've made the connection to the link."

Moments passed and the people in the conference room were silent. Then a tech came into the room pushing a camera, which he sat up facing the President. "About a minute Mr. President, I'll give you a ten second countdown."

The President straightened his shirt and ran his hands through his hair. Then he sat up straight and looked directly into the camera, as the tech held his hand up counting down from five. A red light went on.

"This is President Maxwell Portner. It's not possible for me to express the outrage and the sorrow I feel at this moment. Six great American cities are now in ruins by nuclear weapons. For every American who is able to see or hear this broadcast, I pray to God your families and loved ones are safe, either with you, or with our Father in Heaven. We are damaged terribly, but we will rise to our feet and continue to worship God and praise His name."

"Let me caution anyone in the world who seeks to gain from our loss, the entire military command of the United States is intact and as deadly against our enemies as ever. I will caution, no I will warn, every leader in the world if any county launches a single missile of any kind, the United States will respond will all our weapons, all our missiles, all our planes at that country or any other country who dares to damage us further. The religion of Islam is a hateful, false, and repulsive lie. God does not honor you and He will punish you for your sins!"

Chapter 4
The Prayer Is Answered

The Emerald Cathedral

Arcadia wept. The meeting of the President and all his new advisors, along with video feeds from Cheyenne Mountain in Colorado Springs at the NORAD command center, and other remaining command centers, looked like it would go on for hours. It was too much to listen anymore, or see the ghastly pictures transmitted by satellites of the carnage standing astride the United States. She slipped out of her seat and left the room.

She went straight to the Emerald Cathedral, turning on a lantern, since night had long since fallen. She went to the center of the cavern where the pond stirred quietly, sitting down on one of the benches lining the walkway and surrounding the pond. With her face in her hands she sobbed, "Heavenly Father, you know I've always loved you and trusted you in all ways. Now this has happened. Please help me to understand."

"The problem with humans having free will is they're capable of committing great sins," said a soft voice.

Arcadia looked up and saw a man standing next to her. He was older, like a grandfather, but still with a strong oval face and soft, penetrating brown eyes. A smile filled his face.

Arcadia felt his voice take the sword from her hand. She hadn't realized how angry and vengeful she'd felt until the man spoke.

"I'm your guardian angel. I've looked over you for your entire life. You may call me David," he said as he sat down next to her. "You and I need to have a talk."

"I don't know what to say," said Arcadia, wiping her eyes.

"This is a day which we have dreaded for a long time," said

David.

"How could God have let it happen?" she cried.

"God did not let it happen," said David, "It happened because ultimately mankind determines its own destiny. That is the nature of Free Will. It is precariously God-like and despite everything that's occurred, He could not have stepped in and made it go away. The problem would not be solved, just postponed to occur again on another day, in another way."

"I don't understand."

"You are a true and honest believer, Arcadia, but until all people are like you, the carnage of today was inevitable."

David sat back against the bench and crossed his legs, putting his hands together as if he were settling in for a long conversation.

"Your father, Jacob, successfully used the Lord's gift of this Park to reinvent the United States and turn it into a truly good country, one He could honor. However, a large portion of the world doesn't really appreciate this success. America made enemies by its faithfulness to the true word of God. The result was today. It's a true tragedy and one that needs to be corrected."

"How does God intend to do that?" asked Arcadia, regaining her composure and focusing her mind on what her angel was saying.

"Let me put this is simply as I can," said David. "Time is like a river. If you stand next to the river, it will flow by. You know what's upstream because this is the past and you've lived it. Downstream is the future and unknown to you."

"What would happen if you could walk along the river, into the past and see all that has happened when you look back upstream?"

"You could see all of the bad things we have done," said Arcadia.

"That's right. Now what would happen if you were to build a dam across your river of time at the moment of the catastrophe and then started walking back upstream?"

"It would mean downstream would not be the future anymore, and you could tell everyone along the way what was wrong and change the outcome."

"Not just tell, but do. Otherwise you would end up like some kind of modern day Nostradamus who's not actually believed."

Arcadia smiled, "Great, let me walk up your time river a little way and stop those guys from detonating those bombs."

David chuckled, "Close in spirit, but wide of the mark. I'm afraid the problem is systemic. You'd need to set your sights a good deal down the river of time than that."

"How far?" asked Arcadia.

"Counting today, exactly 330 years."

Arcadia did the math and said, "That would be 1770!"

"I think five years is long enough to alter the outcome of the Revolutionary War."

Arcadia was totally confused, "Maybe you'd better tell me exactly what kind of an outcome you want."

"Imagine how you could change things by applying 2030 technology to 1770."

"To what end?" said Arcadia. She was past the shock of having a personal meeting with an angel, and was now concentrating on the concepts with her full mind.

"Here's the plan in a nutshell," said David. "The Lord will drop you off in 1770 with a few hundred good men with very special training, and modern equipment. George Washington defeats the British in one year, not eight, than proceeds to throw the British out of Canada, the Spanish out of Mexico and the Russians out of Alaska and you have a country to build from the Arctic Circle to the Isthmus of Panama.

"You help the founding fathers draft a constitution practically the same as you have today, but including the Bill of Rights, Term Limits, and Balanced Budgets. You make sure there's a true separation of church and state, but you insure the country is hard-wired with a reverence and worship of God."

"You snip slavery in the bud from the beginning, thereby avoiding the slaughter of the Civil War. You treat the Native Americans with respect and generosity, and avoid acculturating an entire people."

"You use the educational system you've built in the present day from the beginning, and you, bit by bit, release advanced technology to a country that will be the wonder of the world. In this way you will stay about a hundred years ahead of everyone else."

"Now here is the key point. You follow George Washington's advice to avoid foreign entanglements religiously. America is neutral, no matter what. The rest of the world can beat itself to pieces, but they can never attack the biggest, smartest, deadliest country in the world.

Particularly a country who shares its wealth freely."

"By the time we get to modern times, meaning today, the bombs will have never gone off, and America's evangelism will be gently guiding the world to a true Christian ethic."

"Simple," said Arcadia with doubt and disbelief in her voice.

"When you're finished with the job, The Lord will remove the dam and let the new future flow on. The old past will simply disappear."

Chapter 5
Laying Out the Plan

<u>Branson, Missouri</u>

"I think I can see a bunch of problems with all this," said Arcadia.

"You are special, Arcadia," said David. "You weren't born until your time had come and you have all the skills you need to do this task. Besides, Our Lord is with you, and won't let any harm come to you. Come on, Kid, who's ever gotten to do such an exciting job?"

Arcadia never knew how long the conversation with her guardian angel lasted. She did know she asked dozens of questions and didn't stop until the outline of the entire plan, all 330 years of it, were clear in her mind. She was particularly interested in how she was going to make the breakthrough with the very Founding Fathers she'd studied. They were among the most remarkable group of men to appear in one place and at the same time in history.

David counseled the principal players, Washington, Jefferson, Franklin, Madison, Adams, and Hamilton be brought into the conspiracy from the beginning, starting with telling them the truth about their future and proving it to them with a very comprehensive video, and some graphic demonstrations of what kinds of equipment would be brought to the party. He also said Arcadia would score a lot more points if she fixed Washington's teeth and cured Franklin's gout.

David left Arcadia sitting alone in the Emerald Cathedral. She went looking for her father. He and Ali had gone back to the bungalow after the meeting with the president and the staff had broken up. Arcadia came into the house and sat down heavily on one of big chairs.

"Dad and Mom, what if I were to tell you a story so fantastic you would never believe me, but which was true and I had to make you believe?"

"Our whole lives are a miracle," said Jacob, sitting down next to Ali on the couch across from Arcadia. "Why don't you just tell your story and we'll go from there?"

"OK," said Arcadia grimly, "I've just been speaking face to face to my guardian angel, speaking for God in the Emerald Cathedral."

Jacob's eyebrows went up a notch, but Ali just smiled and said, "It was really only a matter of time before God would make some kind of an appearance here. After all, it's His special place in the world, and you're a person who is after God's heart. Why don't you just start at the beginning and tell us everything?"

Arcadia began at the beginning and related the conversation, word for word in its entirety. It took her almost two hours to tell the whole story. Then she sat back and waited for her parents to react.

Jacob mused for a moment and then said, "It's really remarkable. God is going to give us all a chance for a Do-Over and the tool he's going to use to pull it off is you."

"What's your plan," asked her Mother?

"I got caught up in all the modern technology introductions and missed the more important first consideration," said Arcadia. "As David reminded me, we'll have plenty of time to phase in an educational system allowing for the development of advanced knowledge, know-how, equipment, tools, and expertise. However, we have to win the war and establish a government of the United States, before we do anything else. In order to do that, we can't wait for American Colonists to develop the means. Therefore, assuming I can get support from the President by telling them the entire plan, I'm going to build a military base near Washington's home at Mt. Vernon. We'll bring in the equipment, vehicles, weapons, supplies, and trainers to outfit a military force big enough to defeat the British Army in short order. I'll have to read up on it some, but my first estimate is we can do this with a reinforced brigade, about 4,000 men. Our core of personnel will be a company of the best soldiers we have. Add to that a support staff of doctors, political scientists, teachers, top research men, medical people, and some naval vessels, from this time, it will add up to three or four hundred people to become the core of the American Colonial Army."

"Where are you going to get your recruits," asked Jacob?

"From throughout all 13 colonies," said Arcadia. "We want the force to feel they are an American Army, without all the problems of being from any of the particular colonies. Unity and cooperation will be important parts of our training."

"So how is this going to work?"

"I'm going to bring the President and his staff in and brief them on this fantastic enterprise – I hope he believes me – and then we'll build our facility outside of Washington, away from the radiation danger. When everything is ready, David says God will transport the entire camp to 1770. That's when I make contact with George Washington at Mt. Vernon, gain his support, and get him to bring in the other Colonial leaders we'll need…Jefferson, Madison, Franklin, Adams, and Hamilton. Then I have to go through the whole process again with them, but my plan is to do it at our new facility, which I'm calling Fort Independence."

"You know, honey," said her mother. "Women weren't exactly at the top of the political heap in the 18th and 19th century. How do you intend to convince all these great men to follow your lead?"

"It won't be easy," said Arcadia, "However, I'm pretty good. Plus, I'll hold all the cards in finance, firepower, and technology."

"Where do we go from here," asked Jacob?

"I need a meeting with Uncle Max as soon as possible."

"I'll set that up for tomorrow. Now it looks like you're pretty tired. Why don't you turn in and we'll get this stupendous plan started first thing tomorrow."

"I am worn out," said Arcadia. "I'm on overload from today. Can we just say a prayer and then I'll go to bed."

"Heavenly Father," said Jacob, "We are overwhelmed with your majesty and tremble at your mighty hand. We thank you for the blessing you've given Arcadia by sending your angel and have him explain your plan. It's overwhelming for her and for all of us, but we know with you, anything is possible. Help us to follow your will and to lead Arcadia on the pathway you've set for her. In the name of Christ Jesus, our savior, Amen."

Arcadia kissed her parents good night and walked the pathway back up the hill to the family living quarters behind the sprawling Admin Center. She closed the door to her room and knelt by her bed.

"Dear Lord, I'm feeling a little unworthy of this big job you've given me. Please know I will do the best I can do, and please help me stay on the right path."

She changed into her pajamas and was asleep in minutes. She slept peacefully, but God was busy providing her with the knowledge and tools she would need to carry out the mission given her by His angel.

The sun was shining when Arcadia awoke the next morning. She glanced at her clock and saw that it was past eight. Quickly she got up and jumped into the shower. She brushed her teeth, combed her hair, sprinkled on a very modest bit of make-up, and dressed in jeans and a light Park sweatshirt.

As she came down the stairs, she found a crowd gathered in the dining room, having breakfast. Her brothers, mother and father, two or three of the senior directors of the Park and the President of the United States were all sitting around the table and actually rose from their places as she came in.

The President stepped over and gave Arcadia a hug. "I've always known you were a very special person. Now it looks like it will be you to carry out the mission of God to put everything right. Your folks told us all about your day yesterday and the job you're planning. I can't imagine what you're thinking or how you're going to do this, but I will tell you the entire resources of the country are yours to use in any fashion you need."

"Thanks Uncle Ma...Uh Mr. President. Sorry. You've been such a good friend for so long, I kind of forget who you are now."

"Just keep it Uncle Max, in private and I'll be happy with that," said the President.

"Have some breakfast, honey," said Arcadia's mother.

Arcadia had some eggs, toast, bacon, and coffee. In between bites, she fired off some questions to the President.

"I know we've taken a huge hit as a country, what's left?"

"A surprising amount," said the President. "The vast majority of our military is intact along with a great deal of our infrastructure. We're organizing all the remaining officials of government not killed to get our Federal structure running again. We've cordoned off the contaminated areas of the country and have all our medical people treating the injured and those who have suffered radiation poisoning.

We put our total losses at about 150 million people. However, we haven't detected any other active threats, either inside the country or among other nations. Apparently, they all believe we'll collapse on our own without any help from them. It looks like my threat of retaliation is keeping other countries from trying to cash in. I think we've bought ourselves some time to rebuild and to implement the Holy Mission you've been given. I must say you've taken on quite a job. Nevertheless, tell me what you need first."

"Just off the top of my head, I need to know the closest we can built a military headquarters safely to Mt. Vernon, Virginia. We need a cordoned off area with tall fences five miles square. The location needs to have an uncontaminated fresh water supply with a stream or waterfall where we can install generators to produce a lot of electricity. We should do these things right away.

"Next we have to recruit some specialists. We want people who can actually build a power plant from the ground up. We require people who can design and build a plant to produce steel. We need communications and computer experts who can design and tell us what we need to build a communication system. Micro-communications is the best. These people don't have to do the actual work, but be able to tell us how to build them and be able to teach others. This work is a little longer range. I want all these groups in place in about six months.

"The opening bell for the 'Do-Over' my angel talked to me about is 1770. That means we have to have a completely trained, operational, and fully equipped reinforced brigade of soldiers ready to do battle in five years. All I want us to supply, is the equipment, supplies, uniforms and a special list of weapons I'll give you. Then we need drill instructors to train our troops. All of the rank and file soldiers will be recruited colonists. The instructors will then become the cadre of officers to lead the men.

Next, we need money, lots of money. I assume the mint in San Francisco is still in operation. Have your people design new silver quarters with no markings to raise British suspicions. We'll use this money to pay our troops. They'll get a quarter a day, about eight dollars a month. One of the biggest problems with revolutionary soldiers was they never got paid regularly. This will solve the problem.

"Another big gripe the soldiers had was a lack of the supplies they needed to live day by day. We'll provide the food, the uniforms, the weapons, and quarters both at the Fort and in the field. Get your military men working on those problems.

"We need to have backing for the money we issue, so we need a gold reserve. Eventually Alexander Hamilton will establish a Federal Banking system. However, until he does, I want to store 500 million dollars in gold at our headquarters at Fort Independence. Security for that is up to you.

"The United States will be much larger than it is today. We'll be taking control of the entire North American continent, and Central America all the way to the Isthmus of Panama. This means several things. First, we have to take out the British Army in a hurry. Our new weapons and battle tactics should do the job, bloody as it will be. About all we have to conquer in Canada is Quebec. They failed in 1775 to do it, but we won't.

"Central America is a whole different problem. We have to beat the Spanish. Our ground forces can take and hold the land, but we need a little Navy to keep the British, French, and Spanish from sending reinforcements. What we need are about four nuclear powered destroyers, a nuclear submarine, and at least one nuclear powered cargo ship. We'll deploy them along the Atlantic and the Caribbean and blow away every military ship they send. We'll let all the commercial traffic sail right in and bring us the raw materials we're going to need initially and in the future. The American colonies have lots of goods to trade and I expect everyone will make a lot of money.

"The first ten years will be the hardest. We have to beat the major European powers and make sure they know we can't be defeated militarily, but are wide open for trade and immigration.

"We also need to avoid the eight years of the Articles of Confederation. My plan is to get our Constitution ratified while the Army is wiping out the Red Coats. By 1778, we need to have a national election that installs George Washington as the Father of His Country."

Everyone, especially the President, was feverishly taking notes while Arcadia spoke. When she paused, the people at the table looked up. She smiled, "That ought to be enough for you today. When you're finished, come back. There's more, lots more. There's nothing at stake here. Just saving the lives of 150 million Americans, revising history to make sure it can't happen again, and creating a better world according to the standards of God for the past, the present, and the future."

Arcadia watched as the people around the table, friends and family pursed their lips and shook their heads in determination. She knew all of them were counting on her to be the representative for God in this mighty effort, and that the chain of command was subtly changed. For better or worse, she was now the steward of two worlds.

Within a few days, President Portner was back to report all the many projects he'd set in motion. "I've put the San Francisco mint to designing our new silver quarters. They'll be able to start producing them in about a month. You didn't say how many you needed, so I ordered 20 million coins struck."

"That will probably not be enough," said Arcadia. "Better plan on 50 million."

"I had the Air Force fly a plane around Washington, the city itself is completely gone. The blast area goes out about five miles. The plane was equipped with instruments to measure airborne radiation. The prevailing winds near Washington are mostly east and north. I think we can build Fort Independence about five miles from Mt. Vernon. The Army is pretty good at putting up buildings that are permanent, but easy to construct. They estimate we can build the entire complex in six months. I'll have plans for you next week. I told them about the uniforms and they want to know how you want the soldiers equipped. Have you given any thought to that?"

"I've been studying that very subject," said Arcadia. The average height for Americans in 1750 was 5 foot 8 inches, so order the uniforms to fit. In addition, we need green camouflage uniforms and brown boots. We'll also need Kevlar body armament, and helmets. The basic weapon will be the AR-16. We need M-60 machine guns for each squad and LAW rocket launchers. Every soldier will have six grenades, a first aid kit, water bottle, 200 rounds of ammunition, and will carry packs for dry socks, clothes, and personal items. I want Seal Teams and Special Forces for my basic trainers, and no less than 20 men who are black belts in martial arts."

"What about the heavy stuff," asked the President?

"I think we can get by with a single battery of six 105 mm, artillery pieces. They are easy to move and have an effective range of about 7 miles. We want to make sure that in addition to the normal high explosive rounds, they have the controlled fragmentation anti-personnel rounds. We'll start with Bradley Fighting Vehicles as our principal armor. They'll be powerful enough to handle anything they run into and still small and easy to move on narrow roads and across open territory. Add about two dozen Humvees, along with 20 deuce and a half's."

"We also need overwhelming air support. I would say about 20 Black Hawks, a dozen or so heavy Huey's, about 20 big Chinooks, each equipped with front mounted mini-guns and rocket launchers, 10 four-man observation helicopters, at least a hundred drones, of all sizes. I also want at least one 787 jetliner in mothballs, a few single engine planes, and one, big C-130. We won't need those right away, but we need a model or two to reverse engineer when the time comes.

The President shook his head, "It sounds so strange to hear a 22 year woman rattling off the personnel and armaments for a military unit. However, I don't doubt or question anything you say, Arcadia. I know you've been working 20 hours a day in planning the full scope of this whole operation."

Arcadia shrugged, "It's true I didn't know any of these things a week ago. The trick is to keep the technology low enough not to overwhelm the capacity to learn and operate all this equipment by young men who think a single shot musket is state of the art. However, they must do the heavy lifting on their own. They have to feel they're the reasons they've won their freedom, no matter what kind of weapons they have."

"Well, you're doing a great job and we're proud of you."

"It's like playing three dimensional chess simultaneously on six different boards," groaned Arcadia.

"We've got our communications system back up and running for the most part," said the President. I'm able to speak to the nation whenever it seems necessary. I've confined all my messages to repairing the damage and directing relief efforts for the unaffected parts of country. What I have not done is to tell them anything about this bigger mission.

"What can you possibly say to give anyone relief from the crisis at hand?" said Arcadia. "No matter what reconstructions of time, are accomplished, it won't provide comfort for people suffering here and

- 27 -

now."

"Unfortunately, I'm sure you're right. I have to manage the crisis facing us right now."

"The thing to tell people is to take life one day at a time. The best news you can give them is that America is still fundamentally sound, and you are doing everything humanly possible to bring aid and relief as soon as possible. Moreover, it will calm everyone if you can assure them of their security from further attacks.

"When we are successful in what we are trying to do, the bombs will never have gone off and none of their friends and families will have died. However, no matter what, the future will be different from the one they remember, I think. Frankly, I have no idea how the Lord is planning to handle that. Maybe, He will readjust everyone's memories to the new realities. The best thing we have going for us is a nation filled with very good Christians. They're faithful and they trust in the wisdom and mercy of God. Having said that, Uncle Max, you need to hold on until the winds of time begin blowing in a new direction."

Chapter 6
The Stage Is Set

<u>Mains Neck, Virginia</u>

A helicopter made a couple of circuits of the facility before landing to let Arcadia see the layout of the Fort Independence. A tall fence surrounded the five square mile installation. A solid chain link fence filled with long aluminum strips to conceal the contents of the interior from the outside. A row of razor barbed wire covered the top of the 12-foot high fence. Guard towers dotted the perimeter. The chopper dropped down onto a landing pad at the airfield away from the center of the Fort. Arcadia, stepped out, flanked by several high-ranking military officers.

In the center of the Fort was a large building. It was both an assembly hall and also divided into sections to make classrooms by moving walls. Its capacity was 7,000 people. Flanking the Assembly building were two more buildings at each end. One was the Administration Center, and the other was a huge cafeteria and recreation center.

Surrounding the core buildings were wide, paved streets leading to a complex of two story barracks. Each building would house two hundred men and there were 35 such structures in rows around the Assembly building. Beyond the barracks were fields for training areas, a shooting range, workshops for all the equipment and more classrooms.

At the far end, in the center was the airfield with a dozen helicopters, large and small. In one corner was a building that housed the power plant of the fort, with electrical conductors fanning out to the camp. Outside the walls water poured from a tall waterfall diverted in two places and linked to massive generators.

All the power lines were underground. The military engineers assured Arcadia there was more than enough power to supply every conceivable need for the Fort.

In the other corner, huge tanks, holding diesel fuel also underground and an efficient refinery built on top. It would turn crude oil into fuel in a future time. For now, there was enough fuel stored to run all the engines of all the vehicles for more than a year.

Along the sides of the Fort were the garages for the Humvees, the Bradley light tanks and the battery of 105 mm artillery howitzers. The armory for all the ammunition for everything was in a reinforced concrete building near the big artillery guns.

All in all, it was a very compact and efficient fort. Arcadia was very satisfied to see the real thing from the plans she had approved.

"This way, ma'am" said one of the officers. He led her into the Admin Center and to the big conference room in the center of the building. It was full. No less than three dozen men and a few women were waiting for Arcadia. The codename used to refer to her, in communications, was "Lady Hawk."

She took her place at the head of the big table, flanked by her senior officers. She waved everybody to their seats and said, "Let's make it a practice to not stand for me when I come into a room, OK?"

"Sorry ma'am," said the Senior General Manny Compton, "We will obey every order you give us, except that one. Allow us to render the respect and honor all of us hold for you."

"All right, but let's keep the ma'am's down to about one a day. I'm Arcadia."

General Compton got to his feet, picked up a pointer, and activated the big screen at the front of the room. "As you can see, Arcadia, Fort Independence is complete. Everything we need to train and equip a Brigade is here. Our permanent party consists of my senior staff, 150 officers, and 500 non-commissioned men and women, who will become the cadre in the field for the men they train. At full strength, the brigade will have 150 combat platoons, an artillery battery, a mechanized arm of 12 Bradley tanks, 20 Humvees, and 60 helicopters that include 20 Blackhawks, 10 Super Huey's. 10 reconnaissance choppers and 20 Chinook ships that will hold 35 men or 15,000 pounds of equipment or supplies."

"The men we've selected as drill instructors are from the Army,

Navy, and Marines. They represent the most qualified men we have. They are highly proficient as instructors in weapons, martial arts, the humanities, and social issues. Believe me when I say they are the best of the best. Additionally, we have a medical unit of 50 doctors and nurses, and a complete medical facility. We also have political experts, technology, and engineering personnel for all our equipment. We have multiple spare parts for every piece of equipment at the Fort."

"Sounds to me you're already, raring to go, and wondering when I'm going to get off my butt and start doing a little politicking," said Arcadia with a smile.

"We await you're orders, ma'am," said the General.

"All right, the next part of the plan is to have a meeting with George Washington over at Mount Vernon. You do realize when we initiate the plan, the gate to our time today will transport everything here to 1770 and we'll really be on our own. We'll live or die by our planning and wits."

"We've decided the biggest shock value for my entrance will be by one of the scout choppers setting down right in front of Mt. Vernon, and then flying away quickly, leaving me alone. Our research shows Washington is in residence now and will be there for a while. My job is to enlist him as a co-conspirator of God's plan, and then bring in Jefferson, Adams, Franklin, and Madison. Once that's accomplished, and I am satisfied they will stay with the plan for the rest of their lives, I'll bring them all here for a look at the Fort. You have my gear ready to go?"

"The techs and directors have assembled the best history lesson you've ever seen. It's all on disc and ready to play from the laptop going with you. We are also giving you a big LED screen to show it on. We'll drop it off, along with your luggage when we take you in."

Arcadia took a deep breath. "All right everybody. We're going tomorrow."

When Arcadia woke the following morning, she knew she was no longer in the 21st Century. She thought there would be more of a noticeable shift, but it was just a surety in her own mind. She knew the Lord had moved. The quest had begun.

Chapter 7
Meeting Washington
Mount Vernon, Virginia, Spring, 1770

George Washington had just completed breakfast and given orders for the day's work to his staff, when he heard a strange sound. It was like a thumping, and it was getting louder. He got up from his desk and walked to the front door of his home.

As he opened the door and stepped out onto the veranda, he followed the noise and looked up. He saw a silver craft 200 feet up and coming straight down for the big circle that faced his home.

Others came running out to see what was going on. All stood rooted to their spot as the silver craft with a clear glass covering over the top of it and a whirling blur above the craft, sat down on the wide walkway and a door on the side opened. A man stepped out of the craft and put a suitcase, a large shoulder bag, and a very large rectangular bag on the ground. Then the man turned and put his hand out to help a young woman step out of the craft. As soon as he'd done this, he jumped back into the craft and with a whoosh; the strange object sprang from the ground and disappeared over the top of the mansion and out of sight. In seconds, it was quiet once more.

Washington looked at the woman. She was dressed in a shimmering silver/white gown-like dress, covered from her neck to the ground. There was a silver belt around her slim waist. She was very tall, quite attractive, had long flowing blond hair, and the most penetrating blue eyes he could ever remember seeing.

As he stepped forward, she slipped to her knees and held her hands in prayer. "Most gracious Heavenly Father, I ask you in the name of my Savior Jesus Christ to bless the mission you've given me and allow me to speak with the honorable Mr. Washington here at his home at Mount Vernon. Amen."

Then the woman smiled and strode forward with a pleasant smile, "Good Morning, Mr. Washington, my name is Arcadia. God has sent me on an important mission to speak privately with you. Will you allow me to come into your home?" She put out her hand, and Washington took it. Arcadia shook his hand firmly.

"What was that strange and mysterious craft in which you arrived," asked Washington?

"It's called a helicopter, Mr. Washington. It's only a tiny part of the wonders I've brought to show you. However, my message to you is vital to the cause of Liberty in these Colonies."

"Is that right?" said Washington. "I suppose you should come in and tell me more. Can I help you with your luggage?"

"Only the large, rectangular bag. It's quite fragile. Please don't drop it or allow it to hit your door frame."

Washington picked up the bag holding the LED screen by its strap and carefully carried it into the house, bowing as Arcadia went through the doorway first.

"You may set that against the wall. It will stand up and won't fall. Many thanks to you Mr. Washington. I was very much afraid you would not see me or allow me to explain my arrival and my purpose for being here."

"You seem to know me," said Washington, "Yet you have only said you are called Arcadia. Is that your Christian or Family name?"

"It is my only name, I hope you will use it."

"Very well, Arcadia," said Washington, "Perhaps you can explain your business here."

"You are George Washington, born February 22, 1732, in the new Gregorian calendar, implemented by the British this year. You were born into the provincial gentry of Colonial Virginia; your wealthy planter family owned tobacco plantations and slaves. Both your father and older brother died when you were young. However, mentoring by the powerful William Fairfax, both personally and professionally, gave you a career as a surveyor and soldier. Because of your leadership and intelligence, you quickly became a senior officer in the colonial forces during the first stages of the French and Indian War. Currently you live here at Mount Vernon with your wife, Martha.

Poor relations and injustices by the English Crown disturb you.

It's your belief the British rule of the 13 colonies be modified or actually dissolved. I am not a British Agent, Mr. Washington, and please note my first action was to pray to God he bless my mission he's assigned me to accomplish"

Washington was surprised, frightened, and impressed with the straightforward behavior of this strange woman. He said," You not only seem to know a great deal, but you also speak of matters seldom spoken in public."

"We are not in public, Mr. Washington; we are safe here at your home in Mount Vernon. I know a great many things, things you'll be very interested in learning. In fact, my story is so important; it will profoundly change your life."

Washington seemed on the verge of losing it when he said, "I don't know who you are, where you have come from, or what you represent. You speak of things considered treason in some circles. I think you should leave my house."

"Mr. Washington," said Arcadia evenly, "I more than understand your disquiet at this juncture, but let me ask you something. Don't you suspect my arrival here today in a vehicle you've never even imagined could suggest matters far more important than you can reasonably dismiss without more information?"

"What is it you want from me, Arcadia?"

"At this point, all I want is some of your time. Surely these mysterious occurrences warrant at least the courtesy of your time."

Washington sighed, "Very well, I will listen to your ranting's or fables, or the work of a demented mind."

Arcadia relaxed a little. She had her foot in the door. "Could we use your private office?"

Washington rose and said, "Come with me."

"Would you carry the LED screen for me again, please?"

Washington picked up the case and the two of them headed for the office he used. He shooed away the crowd of onlookers who had gathered.

When they were inside the office, Arcadia unzipped the case on the screen and set it on a table. Then she took out her shoulder bag and pulled out her laptop. She inserted the DVD disc and set the laptop to project onto the screen, adjusting the volume as she did so. She pulled the curtain of the window and the room grew darker. Then she pushed start and sat back.

The contents of the disc contained a comprehensive history of the world since before the Renaissance. The melodic voice of the narrator told of the plagues, the rise of the Protestant movement, a look at the history of Europe, the wars, the succession to the throne in the British Empire, and the colonization of the new world with the Puritans coming on the Mayflower looking for religious freedom. Arcadia knew Washington was familiar with all this history. She only showed it to demonstrate the authenticity of the information.

Washington stared in disbelief at the high definition color images and sound he was hearing, but he watched the content closely. The section ended with the Boston Massacre, which had occurred a month before in March.

Arcadia turned to Washington and said, "Would you agree I have correctly reported past history?"

"Very impressive," said Washington, "and your magic box is truly a wonder."

"Now Mr. Washington, let me show you some more history. This is history to me; however, for you it will represent the future."

She started the second section, which detailed the growing unrest in the colonies, the crackdown by the British and the brutal occupation of Boston. Then there was the formation of the Continental Congress where revolution first arose. Washington saw the adoption of the Declaration of Independence, saw him installed as the Commander in Chief of the Continental Army. For the next two hours, Washington watched in horror, the constant defeats of his army, their suffering, their victory in the Delaware crossing at Christmas, and ultimately the defeat of Cornwallis at Yorktown in 1781, with the assistance of the French.

"This is the true story of the Revolutionary War and the subsequent formation of the United States of America," said Arcadia.

"How could you possibly know all these things," asked Washington?

"How could I possibly have arrived at Mount Vernon in a helicopter?"

"Are you trying to tell me you are here from the future?"

"What possible other reason could there be? You saw the helicopter. You see this LED screen with perfect high definition color magically coming from this disc, out of this machine. Who else but a person from the future could possibly possess such technology?"

"To what purpose," asked Washington?

"Our purposes are the same. You will fight to have a United States. I am fighting to preserve a United States."

"You'd better tell me the whole truth," said Washington.

"You want it sugar-coated or right between the eyes?"

"Speak plainly, woman!" cried Washington.

"Very well. Here is the truth. I am from the year 2030. The United States suffered an attack with monstrous weapons. We have 150 million people dead. I prayed for understanding to this atrocity and an angel of the Lord appeared in the flesh before me. He says God choses for this event to be erased I must come back to this time and correct the errors of the past 330 years. It is God who is making this possible. No one can move in time, except God. My mission today is to show you the future of the United States right up to our current crisis and gain your support along with Adams, Jefferson, Franklin, Madison, and Hamilton to know the whole truth and convince your fellow countrymen to follow the correct course of history."

"I gather you have other ways of providing me with proof?"

"I wouldn't be here if I didn't. And the first thing I'm going to do to prove it is just for you."

"What would that be?"

"I'm going to give you a brand new set of real teeth, George."

Washington laughed for the first time, "That would be miraculous, indeed."

"I have another six hours of video for you to watch. You won't like it, but it's also the truth."

"Perhaps, we should have something to eat. Are you hungry?"

"I'm starved," said Arcadia. "It's already been a long day."

"Then come and we shall have our lunch," smiled Washington.

As the two of them were eating a lunch of sausages, bread, hard-boiled eggs, and some cheese, topped off with water laced with wine, Washington looked across the table at Arcadia. "Why do I believe you?"

"I think you are getting some help from God," said Arcadia with true sincerity. He knew this would be the hardest part. I believe he has put trust in your heart."

"Divine Providence," said Washington, "I believe in that. Something I have difficulty in comprehending is why your group in the future would send a woman."

"You will understand, Mr. Washington, the country will evolve over the centuries. However, the answer is found right here in this time. You will write, or rather Thomas Jefferson will write 'All men are created equal; that they are ordained by their Creator with certain inalienable rights; that among these are life, liberty and the pursuit of happiness. You must agree the use of the term 'men' is a metaphor for all humanity and includes by definition, women."

"In the broad interpretation of those words, very good words of great importance, I would have to agree women would also be included in that statement."

"I was selected to direct this huge operation for the simple reason the angel spoke to me. My father says the reason he believes is I am a person after God's own heart."

"Is that true?"

"I try to follow the advice of Paul, who says we should pray continuously, and as he writes in Romans 12, 'Do not conform any longer to the pattern of the world, but by transformed by the renewing of your mind'. If God sent Jesus to repeat history differently, who am I to question that? Frankly, I've no idea why He is doing it this way, but His Ways are not our ways, and His thoughts are not our thoughts."

"That was also well spoken," said Washington. "You say that you have more to show me on your magic lantern?"

"I do indeed, Sir," smiled Arcadia, "There are six full hours of video for you to see. It begins with the end of the war and struggle to form the United States. Then we have a second war with England as the country expands. The outcome of the problem of slavery you do not resolve in the formation of the country results, about 75 years from now, with a very destructive Civil War in which tragically 700,000 Americans die. You are going to see some pretty awful things. You will learn the truth of the good policy somebody writes in the future, which is the United States should avoid foreign entanglements."

"That sounds like good advice," said Washington, "Who said it?"

"You did, about 20 years from now."

Chapter 8
The Patriots Gather

Mount Vernon, Virginia

Washington shouted in anger, wept, and shook his head in disgust as he watched the following 330 years unfold on the screen. Arcadia knew the presentation was carefully prepared to elicit the greatest impact, and also to be very credible with exact dates and the actual footage of events when motion pictures became possible at the beginning of 20th century. He watched with wonder as the Park in which Isaiah' prophesy came true, and the country restored to a moral, God-centered civilization. He was horrified to see the result of this American transformation and the nuclear explosions wiping out the biggest cities and killing 150 million people.

When the video was finished, he was silent for a long time.

Arcadia sat quietly and let him process all he had seen.

Finally, he said, "God has given you a plan to prevent all of this carnage and destruction?"

"We are not certain about the rest of the world," said Arcadia, "but we believe much of this can be avoided by building a different United States."

"How do you intent to accomplish this?"

"I'm not going to do anything, except provide good counsel and the means to defeat the British in a hurry right now, all the real work will have to be done by you, and your colleagues, plus the men and women who will follow you in history."

"So," said Washington, "Assuming all you have said is true, and I am inclined to believe you more than ever now, what is the next step?"

"Send messengers immediately to Adams, Jefferson, Franklin, Madison, and Hamilton and ask them to come here as soon as they can. Tell them you have vital information to share and ask them to stop what they are doing and come to Mount Vernon."

"And then, what will happen," asked Washington?

"They will get the same briefing you got. Then they must make general decisions on how to proceed. I will then transport all of you to the installation we have built, not far from here and show you wonders beyond your scope of belief."

"I will send messengers with letters out in the morning," said Washington. "You will spend the night, of course."

"Absolutely not," Arcadia spoke with firm authority. "I have already taken a huge risk in spending the day with you. I should have worn a mask, along with my gloves, but I was afraid it would alarm you."

"Is something wrong?"

"Potentially. Over three centuries separate you and me. There's no telling, what kind of pathogens we have exposed each other too. The risk to me is less because of vaccinations against every disease we know about from this time, but there's no way of knowing if I have brought something lethal with me from my time that might infect you. It would be a tragedy if I gave you a 21st century disease that would kill you. It would make my mission much more difficult to accomplish. No, Sir, I'm leaving as soon as I can get a chopper in here to take me out.

She handed Washington an IPhone. "When all your guests have arrived, turn this on, by pushing this button and then enter the number one. I'll come back. Arcadia demonstrated by using the phone herself.

A man's figure appeared on the screen. "Ready for pickup."

"We'll be right there."

"I don't know how long it will take to assemble the men we need," said Arcadia, "Please do it as expeditiously as possible."

Moments later, the helicopter sat down on the space in front of the mansion. Arcadia bowed to Washington and said, "You can watch everything you've see today as many times as you like, just push start. Thank you, Mr. Washington and May God Bless you in the name of our Savior Jesus Christ."

With that, she hurried to the chopper and in seconds was gone.

Good to his word, Washington wrote long letters to each of the people Arcadia mentioned. He knew them all, of course, and he told them an extraordinary event was unfolding, and it was imperative all of them come immediately, no matter what their circumstances.

Young Thomas Jefferson was the first to arrive, since he had the shortest distance to come from Monticello. He pestered Washington endlessly. Once he had seen the equipment still in Washington's office, he insisted on seeing the video. Washington finally relented and Jefferson watched the entire program from start to finish, twice, before he commented.

"You have not said it, George, but in order for this magical equipment and all the information it contains to be here at all, would suggest your visitor comes from the future."

"To make it even more confounded," said Washington, "All of this was delivered by a tall, blond, and very attractive woman, named only Arcadia, who told me she was here because of a face to face encounter with an angel of the Lord."

"Amazing," said Jefferson "was there a hint of sorcery or dishonesty to what she said?"

"No," said Washington, "she was very frank, incredibly sincere, and her speech was sprinkled with strange words and expressions of the type that would be normal progression for English if it were to come from the future."

"And she invoked the name of God?"

"Several times and she swore an oath in the name of Christ all she was saying was true. You've seen the devastation she says the United States of the year 2030 suffered, and she was truly grieved over the loss of what she said was 150 million people. I can't explain it, but I think I actually believe her entire story."

"It was very wise to include a section of past history with names and dates we can confirm by our own studies," said Jefferson. "Some of these events are so obscure I don't recall them. I can however confirm them. It gives credence to all the future history presented on this remarkable apparatus."

Franklin, Madison, and Hamilton arrived together three days later, having come from Philadelphia. It took John Adams an additional week to arrive, since he had to travel the farthest from Boston. He came in complaining. He was as obnoxious and as abrasive as Washington remembered him to be.

Washington showed the video to the three. He found he was learning more each time he watched the future unfold and had to admit, there was certain credibility to it. Franklin immediately accepted the time travel story, and did everything he could to examine the equipment without actually damaging it.

Adams arrived late in the day, and the entire group watched the entire video together for the first time.

"Do you actually believe this story, Washington," asked Adams?

"I have no real reason not to," said Washington.

"A person from the future claiming to be on a mission from God?" he said, "That seems to me to be complete folly."

"I told Arcadia I would contact here as soon as you were all here.

I am to use this devise." Washington showed the others the IPhone.

"Shall we proceed?"

"If we can expose this fraud, I say, so much the sooner," said Adams.

The others nodded.

Washington turned on the phone and the screen lit up immediately. He pushed the button with the number one on it. There were pictures and music on the screen for a moment or two and then Arcadia's face came into focus on the screen. "Good evening, Mr. Washington. I gather all our fellow conspirators have arrived."

"They have indeed, Arcadia," said Washington.

"Have all of you seen the video?"

"John Adams arrived today and has just finished seeing it. The rest of us have seen it several times."

"So far all you have is my word and the video, but I can assure you what comes next will provide you with more proof of my sincerity. Are you gentlemen prepared to proceed?"

"I believe we have agreed we are," said Washington.

"Very well," said Arcadia. "Mr. Washington, you recall our conversation regarding the transmittal of disease when last we spoke?"

"I do."

"Then let me begin with an apology. Our first priority is to insure none of you contract any diseases present in the 21st century. Diseases for which we have developed immunity, but you have not. All of you are much too valuable to risk losing. Therefore, when you arrive at Fort Independence, the first thing is for all of you to undergo a physical examination and inoculation to vaccinate you against any diseases. It will not be overly uncomfortable, but it must be thorough. You will get your new teeth Mr. Washington, and we can treat the gout that plagues you, Mr. Franklin. There are also other advantages to modern medicine and I think I can promise you all will live long lives, well beyond that of your countrymen."

"We are in your hands Arcadia," said Washington taking charge.

"Then look for us at nine o'clock. Please avoid eating or drinking anything except water, and don't bother to dress, we will provide you with clothing."

Arcadia smiled brightly, "I am very grateful for your help gentlemen. Get a good night's sleep, and may the Lord bless each of you by the resurrected blood of Jesus Christ." She switched off.

The six Founding Fathers were left looking at each other.

Chapter 9
You Are In Command

Fort Independence, Virginia

The entire household was wide-awake at dawn and in an uproar. The events of the previous two weeks were told and retold down to the youngest slave.

Washington and the others were not sure what "not dressing" actually meant, so they were dressed in simple pants and shirts. Their pants were colonial and stopped just below the knees with long socks and shoes. The request to eat and drink nothing but water was observed.

At exactly nine o'clock, the sound of a rotor could be heard nearby. Soon a much larger craft in which Arcadia had arrived came into view and sat down on the big open area in front of the mansion, spraying dust everywhere. The engine idled down and the dust settled, even though the rotors continued to spin slowly. Arcadia was the first out of the craft. She was wearing the same shimmering white dress as before and was still wearing gloves. However, this time she had a white mask over her face. Three men wearing white, one-piece overalls and also wearing masks jumped off the chopper.

Arcadia stepped forward and shook hands with Washington and then each of the others, calling them by their names. Jefferson, clearly struck by Arcadia, bowed deeply.

"Mr. Washington, if you and your friends will go with my men, we have clothing into which we ask you to change. It's for you protection. The men had bundles of clothing in sealed plastic bags in their arms. Arcadia took Washington's arm and led him back into the house. The others followed.

While the men were changing, the men gathered up all the

equipment and took it back to the chopper. In a few minutes, the men came out the front door of the house. They were wearing light blue, one-piece zippered coveralls. Each of them had slipped on a pair of light gloves, and there was a baseball cap on each great head. Underneath they were wearing boxer shorts, and had white socks with white tennis shoes that were easily the most comfortable shoes any of the men had ever worn.

Arcadia smiled again and said, "If you will just climb aboard."

One by one, the men climbed the short stairs and into the helicopter. There were eight seats in the helicopter. Arcadia helped each man take a seat and showed him how to fasten his seat belt. The crew came aboard last and took the back two seats, while one of them went forward to join the pilot in the cockpit.

Arcadia picked up a pair of headphones with a microphone in front and put them on her head. She motioned the men to do the same. They fumbled a bit, but finally managed, hearing Arcadia's voice in their headset clearly.

"In the pouch in front of your seat you will find plastic bags. If you should feel sick from your first experience aloft, please don't miss the bag. Otherwise, just look out the windows and enjoy the flight."

They did not realize the chopper engine had roared to life and was preparing to lift them into the air. The headsets drowned out almost all the noise. Beautiful and soothing music was being piped into the headsets.

Suddenly they lifted from the ground, and were slowly lifting straight up. From Washington through Franklin, the group caught their breath and put their faces to the windows. The trees were below, the mansion was falling away, and the Potomac River came into view. The chopper turned slowly and went over the land that one day would be the Capital of the country, but now was just a radioactive heap. On this day, it was mostly marshy open land.

Arcadia laughed a little and pushed Washington's headset circuit. "Nice day to go flying, don't you think?"

"It's, it's magnificent," stammered Washington. He looked over his shoulder and saw Franklin and Jefferson enjoying the experience as much as he was. They grinned back at him in delight.

Arcadia told the pilot to take the scenic route back to the fort, but not to let the flight run longer than 15 minutes. She didn't want to take a chance one of the men would get airsick. For Adams, it was almost too late, but he held on.

Soon, Fort Independence came into view. With all the buildings laid out in their precise pattern, it was impressive. The helicopter came to ground at the small airdrome near the other helicopters. As they landed, an open top 10-seat carryall came driving up.

Arcadia pulled off her headsets, unclipped her seat belt, and signaled her passengers to do the same. She went down the aisle and helped the men to their feet and out of the chopper to the carryall. She asked all the men to take a seat and when they were all aboard, she jumped into the front seat, next to the driver, who took off down the main street to the spacious infirmary.

"This is where our doctors and technicians will give you a physical exam and vaccinate you for every disease we have names for," she said with a laugh. "I'll pick you up when the docs say they're finished."

The process was carefully planned. Each of the men had blood drawn, their blood pressure taken, got a full body CT scan, and each got a visit to the dental chair, where x-rays were taken. Then vaccination guns were used to deliver a wide array of serums for diseases. They also got flu sprays, and a shot of high potency vitamins. The men were very curious, but endured the procedures with silent patience from the men who were wearing masks on their faces.

Arcadia was notified when the exams finished and went to the infirmary. "Thanks for putting up with that," she said, "It's a great relief knowing you have all been vaccinated. The test results will be done in a few minutes, and then we will know what further steps to take to improve your health. If you will follow me, we'll go into a conference room."

She led them out of the infirmary and down a long hall before turning into a room containing a large conference table. Arcadia waved all the men to comfortable seats. She sat down at the head of the table.

"I would imagine all of you are still trying to catch your breath and collect your thoughts over what you've seen and experienced in the past two hours. I will try to answer any questions you may have."

Washington was the first to speak up. Flying in the air was an exhilarating experience, Arcadia. Now tell me, what is this place?

Seeing it from the air showed me a very large camp with many buildings and a lot of strange vehicles, but that doesn't tell me much."

"This is Fort Independence," said Arcadia, "it was built on this site, which is called Main Ness Historical refuge in my time. It is five miles square, 25 square miles. This is the headquarters and training facility for the United States Continental Army."

"Who is in command of this facility," asked Washington?

"You are, General," said Arcadia.

Chapter 10
I Think We Smell

<u>Fort Independence, Virginia</u>

"I beg your pardon," said Washington.

"Of course, we hope you will not give a lot of orders until your staff has an opportunity to brief you," said Arcadia.

"I have a staff?"

"All ready and eager to meet you."

"I don't understand."

"Think, General," said Arcadia, "and the rest of you too. Did you believe this is some kind of an elaborate hoax, or the ravings of a lunatic, or some kind of conspiracy against you by Satan? I can assure you nothing of the sort is true. The 13 colonies of America are only months away from beginning an active rebellion resulting in a war of Independence. You all watched the video showing the future. There must be some thoughts in your heads about that.

"I was horrified to see in just 90 years the United States would fight a Civil War over slavery," said Jefferson. "We must do something to prevent it."

"Correct," said Arcadia.

"Within two hundred years, the United States will be embroiled in what appears to be global wars fought in Europe," said Franklin. "We must avoid allowing ourselves to be drawn into that kind of conflict."

"Correct," said Arcadia.

"As near as I can tell, the United States gains its Independence from England and then wastes almost ten years with an unworkable government system before writing a real constitution to unify the country and become the law of the land," said Madison, "We need to eliminate this failure and begin with a proper government from the beginning."

"Correct," said Arcadia. "I'm happy to know you are actually the great men I've read about, and can face issues when confronted with the facts."

"All of this seems like some kind of nightmare, from which I will soon awaken," said John Adams.

"My United States is the one with the nightmare, and unless you men do something about it, we're never going to wake from it," said Arcadia sadly.

Just then, the door opened and doctors in white lab coats came into the room.

"Ah, the medical results are back," said Arcadia. "Gentlemen, if you will just go with your assigned doctor, they will give you a private medical evaluation. I assume you would like to keep your own medical information confidential."

The men filed out of the room, each with a doctor who had an IPad under his arm, headed toward private examination rooms. Arcadia watched them go and asked the chief physician, "Just give me the basics."

"We can give Washington a new set of teeth with tooth implants. Fortunately, his gums are still in decent shape. He'll be thrilled with the results. Franklin has arthritis; it is presenting itself right now as gout. We can fix that. We have a range of treatments to make him feel twenty years younger. Jefferson is in very good condition, as is Madison. Hamilton has gonorrhea. Adams has early Tuberculosis, which we think we can treat and control. All of them will see their health improve dramatically with proper diets, better hygiene, and regular vitamin supplements."

"They're probably hungry," said Arcadia, "have the kitchen send in a lunch to them all while you are treating them. Can you finish Washington's teeth in time for dinner?"

"No problem."

The men spent the rest of the day with the medical doctors. Part of the reason why it took so long was because the physicians were also providing some education on the rudiments of modern medicine. They saw the germs causing common diseases for the first time through projected images on big LED screens. The doctors were careful to say people needed to wash their hands often and take a shower every day, to protect them from germs that were everywhere.

Later in the day, the group was escorted by a man dressed in very unusual looking clothing to the living quarters of the leaders. Arcadia had used the design from her own home, only on a much larger scale. The rooms were large and comfortable suites with separate bedrooms and baths, built in a big square around a lovely garden covered with a plastic dome. The men stepped into the VIP quarters and were amazed at what they saw. Their guide showed them how everything worked in the rooms. The novelty of being able to flip a switch to get light or sound, or turn on the video screen with special programming, left the men speechless. Their guide was careful to show them the phones installed in the room. He said it was connected to the main headquarters and would be used to communicate messages back and forth. He demonstrated the phones by calling the com center and getting a ring back.

One of the most amazing appliances of the rooms was the toilets. Their guide explained the rudiments of modern plumbing, and was obligated to flush one several times to prove they worked.

He had to do the same demonstration with the shower. He reminded the men how the doctors emphasized a person should bathe on a daily basis. He showed them how the shower worked and the soap, shampoo, and conditioner dispensers.

In each closet was a small wardrobe of clothing. The guide said the coveralls they had worn all day were just to get them through the medical exams. Hanging in the closet were long pants, and long sleeved shirts, and two coats, for light and heavy wear, depending on the weather, there were two pairs of shoes on the closet floors. In the chest of drawers were socks, underwear, two sweaters, and a copy of the Bible. Arcadia had given this item a good deal of thought and chose a newer version of the Bible, instead of the King James Version.

When the escort answered all the many questions, he handed each man a wristwatch with a flexible band. He explained the time was the same as the clock on the nightstand, and dinner would be served at 7 PM. He said he would be back to guide the group to dinner. He suggested the men use the time until then to take a shower and dress in their choice of clothing from their wardrobes. He explained the weather was clear and sweaters and coats would not be necessary. Then he bowed, thanked the men sincerely for their patience, and left through the garden.

When they were alone, it was Washington who spoke first. "I know all this is as fantastic to you as it is to me. However, I do have new teeth and they feel wonderful."

"My gout is completely gone," said Franklin. "In fact, I must say I haven't felt so good for many years."

"Their science and technology is very advanced," said Jefferson. "Every time I turn around, there's a new wonder. It's beginning to look to me every word spoken by Arcadia and what we have seen on what they call their 'videos', may be the actual truth."

Washington glanced at his watch. It was 5:30 PM. "I suggest we each go to our rooms and follow our host's advice regarding bathing. I got the impression this is important, not only for hygiene, but also for body odor. I could not smell anything of the people we have encountered, but I did notice they seemed to be able to smell us, and not with pleasure."

For each of the famous men, their preparations were unique. However, not at all unpleasant. They all took Washington's lead and found the showers very enjoyable experiences. There was a list of instructions mounted on the wall, which told them what was inside the trays next to the sinks. They read the labels on the bottles, and strange substances flowed out of odd-looking containers. Each one of them figured out these were to be used to prevent underarm odor. There were also toothbrushes and toothpaste. Each man got the experience of their mouths feeling fresh and clean, from the rotating toothbrushes. They finished off by using the very efficient razors that shaved their faces with ease and not a single nick or cut, and then trying out the selection of three different aftershave lotions provided.

Then they put on clean boxer underwear, put on the long pants fitting them perfectly, as did the long sleeve shirts in several different colors. They put on clean socks and slipped their feet into very comfortable shoes of different colors than the white tennis shoes they had worn all day. None of them put their wigs back on. They smelled bad and it would clearly spoil the effect.

All were ready for dinner at 7 PM, when their escort returned to take them to the dining hall.

"You all look wonderful," said the man, and I can tell all of you have showered."

"Meaning, we no longer smell badly," smiled Washington.

"Exactly," said their escort, "follow me."

They walked down the street to a large building. Upon entering, they found they were being taken to a room separate from the main hall, where several hundred men were eating. Their entrance caused all the men to rise to their feet and applaud. The Colonial leaders smiled their best and waved at the men.

They continued into the room with a small stage at one end and a long table with six seats in front of it. Beyond were several rows of round tables set for six people, filled with men and a few women, with different outfits. The Colonials recognized several of the doctors, but the others were strangers and were dressed in the same strange outfit their guide had worn.

As they entered, all of the people in the room stopped talking and stood to their feet in quiet honor. They remained standing as the leaders were escorted to their table in front.

Chapter 11
The First Supper

<u>Fort Independence, Virginia</u>

Into the room came Arcadia, dressed in the same long white flowing robe-like dress as before. It shimmered in the light. She walked to the stage.

"The Apostle Paul wrote to Titus on Crete, 'For the grace of God that brings salvation has appeared to all men. It teaches us to say "No" to ungodliness and worldly passions, and to live self-controlled, upright, and Godly lives in this present age.' Arcadia smiled and said, "I'm not sure Paul could have imagined what this 'present age' means to us today, but he also said, 'to encourage the young men to be self-controlled. In everything, set them an example by doing what is good. In your teaching show integrity, seriousness, and soundness of speech that cannot be condemned, so that those who oppose you may be ashamed because they have nothing bad to say about us.'"

"In that spirit of our mission, let us pray" Arcadia fell to her knees and the Colonialists were surprised to see every other person in the room do the same.

"Heavenly Father, we come to you tonight with thanks for leading us through the first part of our mission successfully. We know the task assigned us will be long and hard. We ask your guidance and leadership as all of us surrender our personal emotions to your glorious will. We praise you for helping to bring our new friends and leaders here tonight. We ask a special blessing for each of them. Now bless this meal to our bodies, and give us the strength to continue according to the words of our savior Jesus Christ, whose sacrifice on the cross has given us salvation and the promise of eternal life in your Holy presence. Amen."

A chorus of "Amens" rang through the room and the men and

women of the company.

"Let us properly welcome the great men to whom we owe so much," said Arcadia. "Alexander Hamilton, the creator of our banking system." Hamilton rose to his feet with a confused look on his face, but bowed graciously at the big ovation.

"James Madison, author of the new constitution and insightful logic of the Federalist Papers."

"John Adams, the man whose great leadership drove the Continental Congress to declare we should have an American nation"

"Thomas Jefferson, author of the Declaration of Independence, and the man whose vision saw a manifest destiny for our country."

"Benjamin Franklin, scientist, inventor, statesman, and the voice of reason for all."

"Finally, George Washington, the Father of our country, the man who was considered the best man of all, even in the presence of these other great leaders, and the man who will assume command of Fort Independence at our first review tomorrow morning."

The applause was long and heartfelt.

Washington did not fail to notice how at least a half dozen of those who appeared to be senior leaders on their own, rushed to the stage to help Arcadia rise to her feet. Nor did he miss the singular applause and clear honor and respect all in the room had for the young woman with the long blond hair and bright blue eyes.

Jefferson saw it too. He leaned over to Washington and whispered. "She says you're in Command, but she is clearly the leader of this group. I suspect there's a great deal more to Arcadia than we suspect."

"I'm sure you're right," said Washington, "she's obviously very special and has the blessings of God. Besides, I'm quite taken by her powerful personality and obviously brilliant mind."

"She is also so beautiful, she takes your breath away," said Jefferson.

"Trust a young man to notice that," laughed Washington.

Dinner was served. Arcadia knew future meals would not be nearly so grand, but she carefully prepared for this first one. The salad came first with several types of lettuce, fresh vegetables, and a liberal sprinkling of Parmesan cheese. The dressing was delicious Italian vinaigrette. Fresh loaves of bread with special German butter came with salad.

For the main entrée, Arcadia served exotic Kobe beef, the world's finest filets, with béarnaise sauce on the side. There were perfectly whipped mashed potatoes with luxurious brown gravy and steaming fresh white asparagus. For dessert, a rich Swiss Chocolate cake with thick icing and whipped cream, and a side of coconut sherbet.

Arcadia sat in the center of the head table with three men on each side of her. She watched their expressions as they ate their meals, and washed it down with water with ice cubes in the glasses and the best Napa Valley Rose'. She could see the men regarded this meal as the finest they'd ever eaten. It did not take long for them to express exactly that opinion.

From speakers around the room flowed music. Some was familiar to the Colonials, and some of it was from Arcadia's time. It was all very tasteful and beautiful. The men remarked about that too, wondering where the orchestra was hidden.

When the meal was over and all had eaten, Arcadia rose to her feet. Instantly, the entire compliment of men and women snapped to attention. "Please by seated," said Arcadia.

"My brothers and sisters, tomorrow we begin the next Phase of our operation. It will start with a review of our current force level on the parade grounds. After that we'll begin our formal briefings for the Colonial leaders as to the facts as we see them, and the future as we see it. I hope you've all enjoyed your meal here tonight. Don't expect it to be as lavish from now on.

A waiter came forward and placed a small white cup in front of each of the Colonial leaders. There was a single pill in each cup. "Please swallow these pills gentlemen," said Arcadia, "they are the last medical treatment you'll receive today."

The men dutifully took the pills, not knowing they had just taken a sedative insuring each of them got a full night's sleep. Arcadia didn't want them tossing and turning in a strange place and not sleep. She motioned and six men, dressed in the strange uniforms with several shades of green imprinted in the cloth and tall, brown boots made of a rugged hide covering, stepped forward. "These men will guide you back to your quarters, answer any questions they can and make sure you're comfortable for the night. Your phones will ring at 6 am, which will give you an hour to shower, shave, and conduct your ablutions. We've provided clothing such as you see here for the General to wear tomorrow. The rest of you are civilians and can come, as you are dressed now. Breakfast is here at 7 am, and the review of your command is at 8 am. Until then, I thank you for your cooperation and promise many new wonders to come. Till the morning, I bid you a good night."

All stood as Arcadia left the room.

The aides led the Colonial leaders back to their rooms. The beds were turned down and pajamas with pants and shirt lay on the bed. Washington was shown the uniform for him to wear the following morning hanging in his closet. Each of the aides answered a number of questions regarding the facilities of the rooms. When all the Colonial leaders were settled, the aides left.

Washington got into bed. It was easily the most comfortable bed he'd ever known. He tried to think through the momentous day and speculate on what tomorrow would bring, but he found himself growing sleepier by the moment. Finally, he pushed the button on his light and the room went dark. He was asleep before he even knew it. It was the same for the others.

Chapter 12
Pass In Review

Fort Independence, Virginia

The phone rang in Washington's room at exactly six AM. He fumbled in the dark, pushed on the light and picked up the phone. "It's six o'clock, General," said the male voice at the other end. "Breakfast is at seven in the same place as last night. I will send someone to escort you." The phone clicked off.

Washington stretched and got out of bed. It seemed all old aches and pains were gone, and he did not have the throbbing in his mouth from the old ivory teeth. He jumped up, and went into the bathroom admiring his new teeth in the mirror for a moment. Then he proceeded to take a shower, enjoying it a great deal. He shaved, marveling at how easy it was and how close the shave was. He happily brushed his teeth. Then he added anti-perspirant, and a splash of cologne.

He went to the closet and pulled out the green fatigue uniform. It was fresh, and sharp with starch. There were two stars on the collar and a nametag sewn to his right pocket saying 'Washington' on the other pocket was sewn 'U.S. Army'. He put on the uniform. Then he slipped on the comfortable brown boots that went up past his ankles. There were a couple a stretchable cords inside the boots. He had no idea what they were for. He worked the belt, finding the clasp to be a green metal. He looked around for a hat and found a smart looking green beret in the closet. He slipped it on and looked at himself in the mirror. "So this is what the soldier of the future wears." He discovered the cloth was foreign to him. It was not cotton, but was light and comfortable and certainly seemed durable.

Just then, there was a knock at the door. He opened it and found his aide from the night before standing there, wearing the same uniform. The soldier snapped a smart salute, and said, "Good morning,

Sir, did you sleep well?"

"Very well, thank you," said Washington returning the salute with a kind of wave to his head.

"I see, sir, you found the blousing rubbers, but nobody showed you how to use them. Look at mine."

Washington saw how the bands were supposed to work and he put them around his legs, just above his boots and tucked his pants around them.

"Perfect, general," said the aide. "If you will just wait a second, I'll gather the rest of the group. He went down the row of doors, pounding on them. The five others came out, dressed as the night before, but very impressed with Washington's uniform.

"You look just like a true Commander in Chief," said Franklin.

Breakfast was eggs, cooked to order, bacon, sausage patties, pancakes, toast, and the best coffee any of the men had ever tasted.

Other soldiers, dressed in the green fatigues, came in and ate. All of them said a respectful good morning to the Colonials and "Good Morning, General" to Washington. Washington looked around and did not see Arcadia. He asked where she was.

"Arcadia went out with the recon chopper at dawn. She was hoping to contact some members of the Indian tribes who live nearby. She'll be back in time for your review."

"She's very active here, isn't she," said Madison.

"Our Arcadia is the heart and soul of our entire mission for God. Much of the planning you will hear today was written and designed by her. She's the smartest of us all, and there is not one person in this entire installation who would not give his life for her."

"You are not bothered by the fact she is a woman," asked Franklin?

"In our society, Mr. Franklin, women are completely equal with men. Many of our senior leaders are women."

Just before eight o'clock, Arcadia came bounding into the dining room. Gone was the white dress. Now she was dressed in green fatigues like most of the others. She wore a beret with a feather sticking out the side.

"Good Morning!" she said brightly, "ready to have a look at the hardware we've brought along to help you kick British Butt's?"

"We await your pleasure, Arcadia," said Washington. The others nodded.

"Then let's go." Arcadia headed for the door and the rest of the Colonials followed her. They walked past the big buildings in the center of the installation with the barracks surrounding them. Eventually they came to a wide-open parade ground with a reviewing stand built right in the center of one side. Arcadia led the Colonials up the stairs and Washington got a look at the formation below.

There were about 500 men and women, dressed in fatigues, drawn up in companies. Arcadia went to the microphone set in the center of the reviewing stand and barked the order, "Brigade! Attention!"

Instantly, the formation came into sharp focus and you could hear 500 sets of boots clicking together in unison. "Pass in Review!" ordered Arcadia.

Washington could hear supplemental orders being given within the ranks and each separate company began a complicated set of movements ending with a long line of companies in ranks marching across the parade ground and lined up across the back edge.

From the left side Washington saw a group of large green rolling machines driving in perfect unison. Twenty of these vehicles, the Humvees, drove in rows of two across the parade ground, turned at the corner, and came to a stop in a precise formation in front of the men. Next, 10 Bradley light tanks rolled across the parade ground in columns of two. They also made the turn at the end of the parade ground and ended up in a formation just in front of the Humvees. Then the artillery crossed in front of the reviewing stand. Six gleaming 105 mm Howitzers pulled by their own heavy trucks. They took their place in front of the Bradleys.

Now a whistle blew and the soldiers at the back of the formation marched to the corner of the parade ground, up its side, and marched perfectly in front of all the other equipment to make 10 precise formations in a row facing the reviewing stand.

Washington turned to Arcadia, "That was quite show."

"Does the parade ground still seem a little empty to you," asked Arcadia?

"There's still plenty of room, if that's what you mean."

"These are just the officers and trainers for our Colonial Army. When we next have a review, you will have an additional 3,000 soldiers of your own countrymen. The Colonial Army, one reinforced

Brigade."

"One Brigade?" said Washington. "The British will have 30,000 troops in their army."

"They are badly outnumbered," said Arcadia, "Not the Colonial Army, the British. When we're finished training you troops, one man will have the firepower of a regiment of Red Coats."

Arcadia went back to the microphone, "Well done! You are dismissed to continue your duties." The Brigade marched and drove off the parade ground in good order.

"OK, General, and the rest of you," said Arcadia, "let's go plan ourselves a future, starting with a war.

Chapter 13
Down to the Basics

<u>Fort Independence, Virginia</u>

The conference room in the Admin Center was full. Not only were the Colonials present, but also the senior commanders of all the components of the Brigade.

A professorial man, balding, with a round face and a smart goatee, stepped to the podium at the end of the conference table and in front of several big LED screens. His bright eyes twinkled with intelligence. "Gentlemen, let me introduce myself, I am Dr. Owen Wilkins, and I'm the Chairman of the Sociology Department at Harvard University. We didn't just cook up this plan overnight. Following Arcadia's encounter with her angel, she came out with a very long list of things we had to do in order wipe out the carnage in America today. Our biggest cities and half our population, about 150 million people are dead. Up until this time, the United States was the greatest power on the planet for almost a hundred years. The angel told Arcadia the only way to keep this from happening is to alter the past by coming to this time, 1770, in order to effect enough change to save our country and our people."

Wilkins pushed a button on a pad, and one of the screens came to life. "This is the current arrangements of countries in the world. The nuclear weapons detonated in the United States were almost certainly provided by this country." A red light highlighted Pakistan. "This country is Muslim. The other countries who are also Muslim and who contain the likely leaders in the attack are these." Iran, Iraq, Syria, Saudi Arabia, Egypt, Libya, Morocco, and Indonesia all went red. "The non-Muslim countries which would benefit the most from the destruction of the United States are China, and Russia." Orange lights highlighted these countries.

"Our premise to prevent the attack is really quite simple. We must make the United States so big, so powerful, so deadly, the rest of the world will not dare challenge us. I will also add the new United States will be a strictly neutral nation with no interest in anything but trade from the rest of the world. In fact, we'll lead the way in providing aid and assistance to struggling countries. However, our aid will never be in weapons. As an additional component of our supremacy, we intend to lead the world by decades in technology. We'll do this by having the greatest educational system on earth. With just a little help along the way, ordinary students of the country will be able to develop the kind of technology you are experiencing here. Trust me, you are only seeing a minute fraction of our capabilities."

Wilkins paused for effect, "While other countries are using letters to communicate with each other, we will have phone systems such as you used this morning. While others are studying better ways to build roads and bridges, we'll have a country crisscrossed with both. While other countries are working on ways to make better bombs with gunpowder, we'll be sending men to the moon. We'll be so far ahead of everyone else, countries will pay anything, do anything, to stay friends with us to receive even the smallest pieces of our technology."

Wilkins stepped aside. A man who was obviously, a clergyman came to the podium. "It's vital our country continue to worship God in a manner in which He will continue to honor and bless us. We couldn't care less about the doxology of the various churches as long as they all hold the core belief Jesus is the son of God and died, to atone for our sins. His resurrection made it possible for us to experience the love of God, follow His will in all ways, and experience entrance into the Kingdom of Heaven when our lives on earth have run its course. The key to this is in the manner in which we educate our children. We must have the finest schools from grade school to university, and all of them must teach its students to experience God in a very personal way."

"In about a hundred years, scientists are going to discover the Earth is about 4 billion years old. An immediate schism will develop between the scientists and theologians who question the first words of Genesis saying God created the Universe and Earth in six days. We would like you to know science will not kill God it will confirm him. I'm sure all you have heard the scripture, which says our ways are not God's ways, and our thoughts are not His thoughts. We now know part of what that means. Moses wrote the book of Genesis and quoted God directly. However, God was speaking of time as He measures it, and a day for God is billions of years long. Moses had no way of understanding that. He just wrote down what he heard. When we get to this particular crisis in America, we'll be ready to counter it, and God will continue, as always, the Master of the Universe."

Now it was Arcadia's turn at the podium. "All you've heard thus far is really only for effect. It's to let you know we have a really big plan spanning 330 years, and at every crisis point, we believe we have an answer for it. However, it doesn't solve the problem we have here and now. The British have to be defeated and it has to be done in short order." She pushed another button on her pad and a map of North America came up. "This is the United States as it exists today, with Canada to the north and Mexico and Central America to the south. Here is the new United States all the firepower you saw out there on the parade ground is going to give you." The map changed and showed a United States now including Canada, Alaska, Mexico, Central America, and all the islands in the Caribbean from the Bahamas to Aruba and from Cuba to the Cayman Islands.

"We will be the biggest country in world, all Christian, neutral, avoiding foreign entanglements, and virtually impregnable in 2030. At this point, God promises to release the gates blocking the river of time, and our creation will be real. Everything else will simply cease to exist. Our country is not attacked and 150 million people will not die."

Franklin was the first to respond, "How do you intend to turn a largely agrarian society into a massively industrialized nation this plan would certainly require."

"Two words, Ben," said Arcadia, "Steel and steam and you're going to do it. Beginning today, we're going to show you a new way of producing high quality steel. From that, you will be able to build huge plants to produce all the steel you'll need to build tracks on which to run steam driven locomotives. We are going to show you how to build them too. In your lifetime there will be a transcontinental railroad and a lot more besides."

"What are you going to use for a power source," asked Jefferson?

"Our man Franklin here has already figured it out...electricity. This entire camp runs on electricity from a modestly sized installation, generated by the waterfall outside the Fort. If you build larger generators, you can power the entire country."

"Where are we going to get the money to do all this," asked Hamilton?

"An excellent question and the reason you are part of this group. You are the financial genius. Your ideas of a central bank of the United States are correct."

Arcadia, motioned for the men waiting in the back of the room to come forward. They were carrying two big boxes and it took four men to do it. They set them down on the conference table in front of the Colonial leaders. Arcadia opened one box and took out a handful of coins. "We're going to pay your soldiers, one of these every day." She passed them out and the men could see they were silver coins

"This silver coin is called a quarter, because it is a quarter of a dollar, your principal unit of currency. They are marked only as being genuine silver to keep the British from noticing. The coin is worth about two British Shillings. Our soldiers will earn about 8 dollars a month, a very good wage for this age."

"But your dollars are worthless unless they are backed with something else of value. Therefore, we will use this." She opened the second box and lifted out a large gold bar. "This box has six gold bars in it. There are 1000 ounces in each bar. The British value gold at 19 dollars an ounce in the present day of 1770. Therefore, this bar is worth $19,000. Currently we are holding gold in a steel vault at Fort Independence with a value of 500 million dollars."

"Obviously money is not going to be a problem in financing the country," said Hamilton.

"But how do you expect to defeat the British Army with a single brigade of 3,000 men," asked Washington, "Let alone the idea of occupying the entire continent."

"Well general, you're going to have to learn some new battle tactics, but once you have, you'll be able to defeat the entire British force in a single engagement."

"What do we do when the British send their entire fleet and thousands of reinforcements?"

"They will never make it to an American Port," said Arcadia, "We're going to sink their ships."

"Amazing," said Washington.

"As a matter of fact, it's not the war with the British we are worried about, or the war with the French or the Spanish. The problem is the American people themselves. Events must unfold as history records it for the next six years. In that time, the people of this new country will have mostly developed an identity of their own and will support a break with England to establish an American nation. You don't have a majority who thinks that right now. Moreover, when the war with England is over, we need to have the real Constitution ready to go, with approval by all states. We won't waste ten years with the unworkable Articles of Confederation. This is going to be a tall order. The biggest obstacle will be convincing the southern states to give up slavery."

"How do you propose to do that," said John Adams speaking up for the first time, "Washington and Jefferson are from Virginia, and both of them hold slaves."

"All right," said Arcadia, "Let's deal with this right now. Why do you men hold slaves?"

"Cheap labor," said Jefferson, "I'm personally appalled by the idea of one man owning another, but it's simply a matter of economics. If we didn't have the manpower to work the fields we wouldn't show a profit on our crops."

"Do you provide housing, and food for your slaves?"

"Of course."

"How much money would you save if you didn't have the expense of feeding, housing, recapturing escaped slaves, the manpower to control your slave population, or the cost of buying more slaves?"

"I would have to do the numbers, but I doubt the difference would mean a profit."

"Well, we have done the numbers," said Arcadia. "If we were to found a company, purchase all your slaves, emancipate them, and then offer them a paid job to work in the same place they are currently living, don't you suppose most of them would take the offer of freedom AND a job for which they received money."

"Possibly," said Jefferson, "maybe even probably, but you still haven't solved the problem of room and board."

"Sell them their homes, set the price, and then let them make monthly payments against their wages. Our new company will open a grocery store and sell them whatever they need from their wages. The people will not have a lot of money left over at the end of the month, but they don't need much. However, the smart ones will save their money for things they want in the future. You should also open a school and teach them to write and read and do arithmetic. If you don't have to pay for the school because the state is supporting education with property taxes our company is giving to the state, you're still the hero. I'll tell you what. I'll purchase all your slaves with gold right now. You keep the considerable amount of money, and we'll come in and set up the exact system I've just described. At the end of a year, we'll run the books and see if our little company is making any money. I'm betting it will. You can use the example to convince all your other southern colleagues they can do the right thing, clear their consciences, and still make a profit."

"I will accept your offer," said Washington.

"I will too," said Jefferson.

John Adams jumped up enthusiastically, "That is the most innovative idea for eliminating slavery I've ever heard. I wish you the best of fortune with your new enterprise. May I congratulate you gentlemen for your noble gestures, and to you Arcadia.

Chapter 14
Sizing Up The Weapons

Fort Independence, Virginia

For George Washington it was a busy ten days. He was working at least 10 hours a day, but he'd never felt better. His new teeth took away so much discomfort from his life, but more, he was finding he had more endurance, his thinking was sharper, and his overall health was the best in years. The doctors checked him twice more, but these were simple blood tests to insure, no reactions to his full range of vaccinations were occurring.

The day after the major briefing, Washington met another General Officer, who introduced himself as Manny Compton. Compton was a very pleasant, but professional officer.

"General," said Compton, "in our army when we get promoted to General we normally speak to each other in private by our Christian names, mine's Manny. Would you object to me calling you George?"

"Not at all, Manny," said Washington, "we have much the same custom in our ranks."

"Great. Let me give you a little of my background. I am a graduate of the U.S. Military Academy, that's the Army College originally established on the Hudson River at West Point in 1789. I've been a professional soldier for 35 years. I'm a veteran of several American combat operations, and commanded a brigade for most of them. I'm also a graduate of the Army War College, where we study the latest combat tactics along with the long history of successful combat tactics going back 2,500 years. My job is to acquaint you with the capabilities of the equipment you will command. I've arranged an inspection for you, if it is convenient."

"By all means," said Washington, "I've been eager to see all the equipment we saw during the review, in action."

"Then let's start with a first-hand look at what we have."

Washington was growing more comfortable by the day in his new uniform. It was strong and very practical, with pockets and pouches located all over. He asked Manny about it.

"You're wearing the standard green camouflage fatigues. The uniform's design is to make you and your troops blend into the environment. In this part of the country that's mostly green trees so when you move into the forest the enemy has a hard time seeing you."

The two men walked out of the VIP quarters and jumped onto an ATV. "This vehicle is used for reconnaissance and advance patrolling. It will go over rough ground, and on a flat road can go 50 miles per hour. The power source is an internal combustion engine, as are all of our vehicles. They run on refined oil, known as diesel fuel."

They roared off down the road, headed for the motor pool. For Washington it was an exciting and exhilarating adventure.

Their first stop was at the garage housing the Humvees. Manny came to stop, and an enlisted man, a sergeant with a patch with three stripes up and three stripes down, came hurrying up. He saluted the Generals sharply. Washington was catching on to this acknowledgement of officers by the lower ranks, so his salute was a good deal crisper than it was the first time he saw it.

"Good morning, First Sergeant," said Compton. "This is General Washington, the Commander of the Colonial Army."

"Good Morning, sir," said the sergeant. Washington returned his salute and then shook hands with the man.

The Sergeant led the men over to the row of vehicles. The Sergeant rattled off the features of the vehicle. "This is the High Mobility Multipurpose Wheeled Vehicle, commonly known as the Humvee. It is a four-wheel drive military automobile carrying eight soldiers easily. It has a wide number of uses. All our Humvee's have 50 caliber machine guns mounted though the roof. With no heavy armor, they are capable of speeds of nearly 70 miles per hour and are designed to cross open country. They can ford a body of water not exceeding 2 and ½ feet, and are powered by a V-8 cylinder diesel engine."

The next stop was the Bradley Fighting Vehicles. Another sergeant was on duty to conduct the briefing. "General Washington,

The Bradley is designed to transport infantry or scouts with armor protection while providing covering fire to suppress enemy troops and armored vehicles. There are several Bradley variants, including the M2 Infantry Fighting Vehicle and the M3 Cavalry Fighting Vehicle. The M2 holds a crew of three: a commander, a gunner and a driver, as well as six fully equipped soldiers."

"The M2 model, which is what we have here, has primary armament of a 25 mm cannon which fires up to 200 rounds per minute and is accurate up to 2500 meters, It is also armed with a M240C machine gun mounted coaxially to the M242, with 2,200 rounds of 7.62 mm ammunition."

Washington looked at Compton, "I suppose you are going to explain what all these terms mean?"

"It will be a lot easier when we head out to the firing range and show you how all these weapons work," said Compton.

Next, they came to the artillery pieces. At least this was something Washington recognized, at least in principal. Nevertheless, he was astonished with the explanation by the Artillery sergeant.

"Sir, this is the M102 105 millimeter towed howitzer. It is a lightweight towed weapon providing direct support fire to light assault forces. It can be towed by a Humvee. It has a very low silhouette when firing and a roller tire attached to the tail assembly permits the weapon to be rotated 360 degrees. It weighs 3,000 pounds, has a maximum firing distance of about 7 miles, a crew of eight, and firing rate of 10 rounds per minute. It fires standard high explosive ammunition with a kill radius of 75 feet, or it can fire controlled fragmentation anti-personnel ammunition."

"Did you say this weapon can fire ten rounds per minute," asked Washington?

"Yes sir, for about the first three minutes. Its actual sustained rate of fire is three rounds per minute."

"I'm beginning to understand why Arcadia said we can defeat the British in no more than three engagements. I can hardly imagine this kind of firepower."

"Neither can the British," said Compton. "But come along and let me show you the real strength of your army, the individual soldier."

They walked out of the garage were a platoon of soldiers, stood at attention on the blacktop road. Compton motioned for the soldier standing in front of the formation to step forward.

"At ease, sergeant," said Compton. "We're going to show General Washington your standard issue weapons and equipment."

Compton removed the helmet and handed it to Washington. It was curved along the sides to provide protection for the ears. "These helmets are made from an artificial component called Kevlar. That makes them lighter, but they will stop most military bullets and especially British musket balls."

"You can see over the combat coat or shirt, our soldier is wearing body armor. It's also made of Kevlar and the British can't shoot through it. As you see, there are pockets and pouches all over the uniform. The belt is a two inch Kevlar, with rings to attach all sorts of things, like these extra ammo packs, a canteen, a first aid kit, and anything else we can think of that might improve the efficiency of the soldier."

"Surrender your weapon, Sergeant," said Compton. The soldier handed over his weapon immediately.

"This is the standard rifle of our trooper. It is the M-16A1. It fires a 5.56 millimeter round from magazines of 20 to 100 rounds. The rifle weighs about 8 pounds fully loaded. It fires either semi or fully automatically. It will fire about 50 rounds in ten seconds to an effective range of 500 yards. As you can see, this weapon has a modified addition. Think of it as a shotgun however the round it fires is actually a grenade accurate to about 200 meters with a kill radius of 15 feet."

Washington was silent. He was overwhelmed by what he saw and was beginning to believe the British Army didn't have a chance.

"It's time for us to go out to the firing range and see these weapons in action. I have sent out everything you've seen and they are ready for the demonstration."

The two jumped back into the ATV and drove out through the front gate of the Fort. Compton went straight ahead for about a mile and then turned onto a rough road ending on a bluff, overlooking a long valley becoming a big savannah. Just below the bluff were two Humvee's, a Bradley, and small squad of soldiers. Compton clamped a small headset with a single earphone and a tubular microphone that went in front of his mouth. He handed Washington a similar radio, helped him fit it over his head and then gave him a helmet.

Washington was surprised how compact and light it was. He heard Compton speaking into the mike, "OK, Captain, we're in place, run the exercise."

Compton pointed down the valley, to a group of targets, including a building, several large wagons, and a number of groups of upright silhouettes representing British troops. "First is the artillery, firing from the Fort about three miles away. The target is the largest group of figures on the right, at the back."

Washington could hear the report of a cannon firing from a long way away. Compton handed him a pair of binoculars and showed him how to focus on the large group of figures. Suddenly there was a large explosion over the top of the figures, followed by many smaller explosions among the figures. The entire group was literally shredded to pieces. Not one figure remained standing.

Next, the Bradley's moved forward. It stopped briefly about 500 yards from the building and the wagons before the main gun began firing. The building was blown into nothing but a portion of the foundation. The gun then turned on the wagons and blew them sky high in three quick shots. Meanwhile, the machine gun began firing at one of the groups of figures and mowed them all down in seconds.

Now it was the turn of the Humvees. They raced across the field at high speed with a soldier manning a 50-caliber machine gun from the top of the vehicle. Another group of figures splintered.

The soldiers split into two groups and slipped into the woods surrounding the field. Try as he might, Washington could not see them moving through the forest. There was just a blur, now and then, that appeared and then disappeared. There were two groups of about 20 figures each on the edge of field. Suddenly the soldiers came out of the forest and charged the groups. They were firing their weapons and there were thumps of explosions among the figures. In seconds, every figure was cut in half.

"That's the end of the demonstration, George," said Compton. Our job now is to recruit 3000 men, train them to operate all these weapons, and then figure out a way to lure the entire British force into the field so we can do to them what we just did to these cardboard figures."

Chapter 15
Emancipation

Fort Independence, Virginia

The Colonial leaders were working hard, very hard.

Franklin was busy learning the basics of a modern steel making process. The engineer in charge of building the working plant explained the fundamentals to the eager scientist.

"It's actually not all that complicated Mr. Franklin," said the engineer. "Of course there are many other improvements to the basic process I'm going to show you. In future years we can add these improvements and get better, cheaper steel."

"The key principle is removal of impurities from the iron by oxidation with air being blown through the molten iron. The oxidation also raises the temperature of the iron mass and keeps it molten. The oxidation process removes and skims off impurities such as silicon, manganese, and carbon in the form of oxides. These oxides either escape as gas or form a solid slag. When the molten steel is formed, it's poured out into ladles and then transferred into molds while the lighter slag is left behind. The conversion process called the "blow" is completed in only twenty minutes. During this period, the progress of the oxidation of the impurities is judged by the appearance of the flame issuing from the mouth of the converter. After the blow, the liquid metal is decarburized to the desired point and other alloying materials are added, depending on the desired product. This process will revolutionize steel manufacturing by decreasing its cost. Prices for steel will go down from £100 per long ton to £6–7 per long ton, along with greatly increasing the scale and speed of production of this vital raw material. The process also decreases the labor requirements for steel-making."

Franklin watched in awe as pig iron was heated in a huge

container, air blown by simple, but large bellows, increased the heat and most of the purities dissipated as gas. Then the whole vat was turned by a geared apparatus and poured into a mold. In less than two hours, the process produced nearly two miles of steel railroad tracks.

Franklin took the complete plans for the construction of a fairly sophisticated steam locomotive back to his room. He spent days studying the plans and making notes on how to build the first edition using steel molds to form the parts.

Madison and Adams were given the job of organizing both Continental Congresses and guiding the delegates through the Declaration of Independence, and the actual Constitution. Arcadia provided them a copy of the real constitution, amended, in her time, to incorporate the Bill of Rights, term limits for Congress, and the requirement for a balanced budget. Almost all of the other amendments, added over the last 330 years, were eliminated.

Hamilton was given a modern computer to use to study financial theory. He was able to see the outcome of his Federal Bank principle to produce an income flow to the Federal government rewarding enterprise and capitalism, while maintaining a strong middle class. The model he devised turned out to be a simple flat tax on all income with no loopholes or deductions.

For Jefferson it was a pleasant and stimulating mission. Arcadia decided not to waste any time in putting her slave emancipation plan into action. Although Jefferson would be needed to help the others with the Continental Congress, she believed she could set up the system, work out the bugs, and get the whole operation up and running in a few months. In addition, Jefferson had a large estate, 5000 acres and owned about 200 slaves. That was more than Washington and Arcadia believed she had a better chance to test her plan with the bigger slave population.

Jefferson wanted to make the 100-mile trip to Monticello by coach, but Arcadia nixed that. She couldn't afford to spend two extra weeks in travel and she didn't want to fan the flames of infatuation Jefferson was already showing. She was fond of Jefferson, but knew she could not afford any "foreign entanglements" of her own. In the end, Arcadia had Jefferson send a letter to his foreman to pick them up at a certain time on a certain day. The letter would take a week to arrive. Arcadia could fly with Jefferson and be in a roadhouse near

Monticello waiting for Jefferson's coach.

It worked out just that way. The two of them took the small chopper to a Roadhouse Jefferson knew, only a few miles from his home. Arcadia put the chopper down in a meadow, half a mile from the roadhouse and they walked in. Nobody noticed much, except being happy to see Jefferson and meet his enchanting companion.

This Monticello was not the Monticello of later times. Jefferson had only started building it less than two years before and the only part of the structure finished was the southern pavilion. However, Arcadia had her own room and many people to help her.

Jefferson was a lifelong opponent of slavery. He morally, religiously, and personally despised the practice, so he was delighted to hear somebody had a sensible idea about abolishing it without creating financial ruin.

The day after they arrived, Jefferson sent runners and called for a general gathering of all slaves on the front lawn of the property for the following Sunday, after church. Arcadia arranged for caterers to supply a sumptuous dinner. Jefferson put together long tables and benches. She spared no expense and made sure the meal would be several notches better than anything to which the slaves were accustomed.

On Sunday afternoon, 178 slaves, including their families arrived. Jefferson stood on a small podium and invited everyone to be seated for a meal. He announced a matter of great importance would be presented by his guest, who was providing the meal. Jefferson then waxed poetic about the greatness, intelligence, insight, and religious purity of Arcadia. He said she was the equal of any man, and deserved their most careful consideration.

The meal was a tremendous success and by the time every one couldn't eat another bite of the delicious food, were more than willing to listen to what Arcadia had to say.

She climbed onto the platform and said, "Let us pray. Heavenly Father, we thank you and praise you for your gift of life and the promise of eternal life in Heaven because of the sacrifice of our savior Jesus Christ, who was crucified for our sins, and then rose on the third day to bring a new world of salvation to all people. We know you love us, dear Father, help us to live according to your will. In Jesus name we pray, Amen."

"My brothers and sisters, I am here today to offer each of you a new life, the kind of life God intended for you. Slavery is an abomination of God, and must end!"

There was a hush and then a general roll of conversation among the slaves. Some of them actually cheered. Arcadia smiled in satisfaction and continued.

"None of you can read or write, but this does not mean you are ignorant. However, the proposal I am offering you today is difficult to understand since it's so new and revolutionary. I will attempt to be as clear as I can. Did everyone here understand what I just said? Raise your hands if you did." Nearly all the adults signaled they did.

"Very well let me begin with the most important thing I am offering you today...Freedom." There was a gasp through the crowd as she spoke the word. "I'm talking about real freedom, freedom from slavery, freedom from lives with no future, freedom for you and your children to choose the way you will live."

The crowd cheered and applauded, waiting eagerly for the rest of the story they knew must be coming.

"Here is what I propose. I will purchase all of you from Mr. Jefferson, today. My first act after doing this will be to emancipate every one of you. Now I'm sure some of you might want to leave in search of a better life, but I think most of you are wondering where will I live, how will I feed my children, how can I survive in a world such as this?

"You can join a new company I am establishing, as a free worker. As a worker, you will be paid a monthly wage for your work. I am free to offer your talents and skills as an employee of this company.

"This new company is called 'The Foundation' and will provide each of you with an opportunity to go to school, learn to read, write and do numbers, to learn new skills, to educate yourselves in such a way your skills could be sold to the highest bidder."

The crowd was halfway to its feet now, and growing more excited by the minute.

"It is my intention to make this offer to every slave holding household in America. The Foundation will grow and the opportunities for all men and women, black, white, brown, or yellow, will grow along with it.

"Now, there is something else you need to know. We have to start somewhere, and the somewhere is here at Monticello. As it happens, Mr. Jefferson is looking for workers, since he will no longer have any slaves. He agrees to hire all the workers I enlist in the Foundation. You don't need to worry about where you will go or how you will live. You can stay right here, as free people with a monthly wage."

"I have also purchased all the homes in which each of you live. I now offer to sell them to you, to own as property of your own. I will spread the payment for your home over a long time and let you pay the Foundation just a little bit of your monthly wage as payment for your new homes."

"I am also opening a store. It will have food and furniture, and clothing, and blankets for sale, and so much more. I will sell everything to you for not one penny more than I paid for it. Since I will have many stores, I'll be able to buy for less, so you will pay less.

At your home, you can still tend your gardens and make your food costs less. In the end, your monthly pay will go, partly to purchase property of your own, and partly to buy the things you need day by day. But for the wise people here, and I'm sure there are a lot, every month you will have a little money left over, to save so one day you will be able to pay cash money for something you would like to have."

"So let me ask you, will you live as you do now, or will you accept my offer to become an employee of The Foundation, where you will be free, educated, property owners who can look forward to a better tomorrow?"

The crowd rose as one and cheered their support. They crowded around Arcadia to touch her, to embrace her, to show her their love. Jefferson sat in a chair nearby with his arms crossed and a smile on his face.

Later that night, when everyone had finally gone home, and Arcadia and Jefferson were finally alone, Jefferson said, "You really got the people stirred up today. Freedom is a powerful incentive, but you went the extra steps to provide sense to their joy. I only hope you don't lose all your money on a doubtful enterprise."

"Look, Thomas, I'm not merely trying something out to see if it sticks to the wall. Some very smart people in my time devised this plan. We have the benefit of instruments doing millions of calculations per second. We ran the numbers on the slave economy. When you amortize the cost of what you pay for the slave over their useful life, provide housing, medical treatment, food and the costs of chasing, recovering and disposing of runaways, and a dozen other factors, we found out its actually costing you 10 dollars a month in 1770 to own a single slave. Your place here is a good average example for the rest of the South."

"You pay The Foundation 8 dollars a month for your new employees, the same wage as the soldiers. You save 2 dollars a month on what it's costing you now. We charge them $2.50 per month to buy their homes plus an additional dollar for education, for a total of $3.50. We estimate they will spend the same amount every month in the store for food and staples, which the Foundation keeps. That ought to leave them a whole dollar a month to save or spend. I'm going to save a lot of money by buying in bulk and will produce enough money to pay for people to run the stores. We think the rest will go for state and federal taxes, so it will be a wash. In twenty years, there will not be a single slave in America, all of them will have a proper education, and the result will be no Civil War. The total cost for us to buy 600,000 slaves, and operate the stores will be about $20 million. We think that's a cheap price to pay for buying a better future."

Jefferson shook his head in wonder, "Tell me, Arcadia, are all people in 2030 as smart as you, or are you the lucky exception who got the counsel of an angel?"

"Only the Lord knows the answer to that question."

Chapter 16
Progress Reports

Fort Independence, Virginia

Two months passed while Arcadia and Jefferson set up their new worker system at Monticello. Arcadia decided it was time for a review of their progress and a planning session of how to proceed. The Colonial Leaders and the senior staff gathered in the big conference room.

"I know you've all been busy," said Arcadia, after the opening prayer, "Each of you Colonial leaders is bursting to tell what you've accomplished, and we're eager to hear it. With your permission, I would like to begin with a report from Mr. Jefferson on our project at Monticello."

Jefferson stood up, "I admit I had serious doubts about Arcadia's plan to emancipate all my slaves and then hire them as employees to continue working at Monticello. I was sure once they got their emancipation documents, they would all be gone overnight. As it turned out, only six of some 200 former slaves actually left. The rest of them hired on at Arcadia's new company called, 'The Foundation' and she returned them to their old jobs on the plantation. Arcadia also bought all the homes I previously used to house the slaves. She made up a Deed of Trust for each home, including the adjoining land around them, and had each head of the family and their wives sign the document with their mark. She withholds a portion of their pay to make the payment on the property. Most of the notes are for a period of ten years."

"Then she opened a new store, called an Emporium, in a barn close to the main home. She stocked it with food, clothing, furniture, household items, and a whole range of other products. The employees come to the Emporium and buy the supplies they need to feed their families and buy other things. It's strictly a cash transaction."

"Next, she opened a school for the younger children, hired a teacher, and started educating the children to read, write, and do numbers. The school has 40 students."

"Arcadia paid me in gold for the purchase of the slaves and for the real estate, so I suddenly had a lot of cash on my hands. She proved to me it was costing 10 dollars a month to keep my slaves, but I only pay her 8 dollars a month, so I'm saving 2 dollars a month per person. It only took a month to prove she was right."

"Now here is the most important point. My former slaves are working harder than they ever worked before. We're getting a great many things done. Our free people are happy, thrifty, careful in their work, and life at Monticello is a dream. Arcadia demonstrated what it means to be an employee for The Foundation. In the first month, she sacked five people for loafing, stealing, fighting, and sent them packing. The people are learning freedom has its responsibilities. It's a privilege, not a right, to work for The Foundation."

"In my opinion, this model will work throughout the slave-holding south, and will allow us to abolish slavery in less than a generation. It was an amazing demonstration of an idea which would never have occurred to us."

The group applauded loudly.

"Thank you, Thomas," said Arcadia. "Now let's hear from Mr. Franklin on the progress he's made in bringing a true industrial revolution to America."

"Thank you, Arcadia," said Franklin coming to the podium. "The first thing I learned was a new way to produce, high quality, cheap steel. It will allow us to build steel bridges, steel buildings and many, many new things. The second thing I acquired where detailed plans for building a steam-powered locomotive...a train. We are using those plans right now to produce the steel components we need to build such a machine. Once we have a working model, we will be able to build the steam engines, construct cars for them to pull, produce steel rails, and construct a railroad system. With enough labor, plus the financial backing of our hosts, I estimate we can complete a rail link between Boston and Philadelphia in less than ten years."

"However, what I saw next is, by far, the most important modern development in the world. We have all come to take for granted the lights burning in our rooms and the other buildings. The source of the energy to make this magic occur is electricity, the same electricity we see every time there's a storm with lighting. Lighting is pure electricity. I've seen the method for harnessing this wonder and providing power of our own. Let me demonstrate my first example, which I built myself."

A soldier brought in a big wooden board and placed it on the table. There was a steel box on the board with a hand crank, and wires coming out of the box and connected to a two-inch thick spike of copper. It was mounted on a little track with springs on each end. In the center of the track was a group of metal rods dangling down from strings.

"Now watch this," said Franklin. He turned the crank of his box slowly, and the copper spike began to move, tapping a rod, and making a little chime. When the spike reached the spring, it bounced back. Franklin turned the crank faster and the copper spike went faster, hitting the chimes and bouncing back and forth between the springs. The room rang with the sound of chimes ringing.

"Inside this box, is an apparatus called a generator. It's a collection of copper coils and opposing magnets. When I turn the crank, I produce controlled lightning…electricity. The same electricity is lighting all these lights and cooling our rooms. The power does not have to come from a person. For Fort Independence, it's coming by capturing the water from a waterfall outside the Fort and running it through machines called dynamos, which turn the generator and make all this power. Our ability to produce electricity is virtually unlimited. We can power everything. I know how to do it, and I'm going to train some others to do it too."

After the applause died out, Arcadia said, "This technology will put the new United States ahead of the rest of the world by a hundred years. It's the key to a great economic expansion. You keep the secret of the power source, but produce an endless list of products we can sell all over the world."

"Now," continued Arcadia, "it's time to hear from our political experts and their progress in producing a functioning government."

John Adams and James Madison came forward. Madison began, "We didn't really have a big job, since our hosts were kind enough to provide us with a copy of what is known as the Articles of

Confederation ratified by all the colonies about ten years from now. The Articles envisioned a permanent confederation, but granted to Congress—the only federal institution—little power to finance itself or to ensure its resolutions are enforced. It had no president and no national court. The Federal government had no power to levy taxes, make trade agreements with foreign countries, or maintain an Army or Navy. Ultimately, the Articles were too weak to hold a fast-growing nation together, they did settle the western issue, as the states voluntarily turned over their lands to national control."

"So, in 1776, the Second Continental Congress will draft a Constitution, nearly identical to what was eventually written. Our new Constitution enumerates the important Bill of Rights of every citizen, as part of the document, plus limitations for terms of elected officials, and a mandate for a balanced budget. Arcadia says most of the problems in the past 50 years of her time were caused by the absence of these elements."

"The original Constitution was less than 4,500 words long, and established the law of the land for the next 300 years. The document worked very well for all the years until 2030. It's a document that will be copied by dozens of new countries in the future. Both Mr. Adams and I agree it's the best we could do."

Adams stepped forward and said, "Our plan is to introduce the new Constitution for ratification by the former colonies, at the Constitutional Convention in 1776, instead of the Articles of Confederation. We believe it will be approved because our interim Federal government will be so successful in defeating the British and expanding the United States to include all of North America, Mexico, Central America, and the Caribbean. In other words, we'll have a great deal of support and credibility with the people."

When the applause ran out again, Arcadia returned to the podium. "I know all of you Colonial leaders are wondering how we're going to accomplish this rather bold expansion, beginning with the defeat of the British, the most powerful country in the world at this time. The answer to those questions will be provided by the person all of you regard to be the best man of all, the true Father of our Country, George Washington.

Washington hugged Arcadia as he came to the podium. "My friends, I've spent the last two months learning modern battle tactics as applied to the new weaponry being provided to us. I can absolutely promise our defeat of the British Empire throughout North America and the Caribbean can be accomplished in under a year. Moreover, we will not require the aid of the French or the Spanish to accomplish this. In fact, we will drive both of those countries out of North America after we've finished with the British, and establish the United States as a new great power in the world.

"You simply cannot believe the weapons and capabilities we possess. I've seen and worked with almost all of it, and the simple fact is a single one of our new American soldiers will possess the firepower of an entire regiment in any other army. When we are finished educating and training the men we are about to recruit, they will be the best fighting force in the world.

"What's more, this army will not disappear when the war is over. We will maintain a permanent, all-volunteer, career military from now on. They will be well paid, dedicated, deeply religious, and incorruptible. They will be commanded by a civilian, the President of the United States."

"I have been absent for so long, George," said Jefferson, I suffer from ignorance. Can you tell me how and when you are going to assemble this collection of mighty warriors?"

"You haven't missed anything, Thomas," smiled Washington, "I haven't explained this part of our operation at all. Let me tell you what we are currently thinking."

"We are going to purchase ads in all the daily papers of the colonies and say this." He picked up the clicker and activated on of the screens. It flashed the message.

A Call to The Strong, The Few, The Proud!

A large Colonial Enterprise is now recruiting men and women between the ages of 18-22, for the adventure of a lifetime. Our purpose is to conduct the largest exploration of the North American continent in history. This will be a most dangerous job and your safety, while of paramount importance to us, is not guaranteed. However, you will see the greatest sights in the world and experience excitement only achieved with dedication and hard work. We offer excellent pay, full provisions, clothing, food and the best training to be found anywhere in the world. Only the most

physically fit need apply, however we will offer schooling in reading, writing, and mathematics for those who are not yet proficient. This is a full-time career commitment and only those who are willing to give a lifetime to this extraordinary opportunity should consider it. Your acceptance is strictly provisional on the completion of our rigorous enlistment requirements. We promise, if you do meet our standards, you will experience the greatest and most satisfying life God can provide. To apply: appear in person at 8 am, September 1 through 5, 1770, at the central post office in the Capital city of your colony.

"If we send this by special post riders today, there should be enough time for anyone who reads this and catches the fever of adventure to reach their Colonial capital on time. In any case, our men will be in the area for several days sifting through the candidates, so if some show up late, we can still get them in for a test."

"What is the test, George," asked Hamilton?

"General Compton is putting together the details with specially trained men who've done this kind of thing before. He assures me only the best will get through the net. Still, we expect to lose at least 35% during training to those who cannot stand the rigors of service or who do not, otherwise, measure up. We are looking for the best 3,000 men or women, we can find in the country."

"Do you really expect any women to show up?"

"If they do, they will have to run Arcadia's gauntlet. Have any of you ever seen her in action?"

"Not me," said Adams. "Is she especially skilled?"

Washington shook his head as if the memory was still a mystery to him, "I saw her take on five men, at the same time, in hand to hand combat, and beat them all...badly. She's the toughest, smartest, most lethal, open hand fighter I've ever seen."

The Post riders went out. General Compton called his best 13 drill sergeants, all Navy Seals, together. "Pick five men each for your teams," he said. "We've put together 13 sets of wagons that look like regular wagons, to go to each Colonial capital, but will ride much easier and go quicker than anything the colonials have. Each team will have three wagons. They are much bigger than normal wagons. Load them up with enough MRE rations, Gatorade, and coffee for 200 men for five days, plus all the equipment you see here, for the tests we've briefed you we are going to use. Make sure you get familiar with handling and taking care of four horse teams. Bring us back wagons loaded with some real men, you know what kind of people we need."

For anything extra you might need, including bribing officials, we are sending you out with a big supply of Spanish Gold coins. Make sure nobody takes it away from you."

"Funny," said another soldier. "What about weapons?"

"We can't risk sending much," said Compton. "You'll have big combat knives, some garroting wires, and for emergencies I'm throwing in some grenades and a few canisters of tear gas. We can't take a chance on other weapons of any kind. Our mission here relies on secrecy until the time comes to haul out the heavy stuff."

"If you're so worried about us causing a stir, then how come we're going dressed in combat fatigues?"

"That's to impress the recruits. You're bound to attract some notice, just handle it, and try not to kill anybody.

Chapter 17
The Recruits
<u>Concord, Massachusetts, Fall, 1770</u>
Robert Pierce came running up to the cottage. He pounded on the door and then opened it and went in.

"Robby Pierce!" said Harriet Grant, "What's so important you can't even wait for a body to open the door?"

"I'm sorry, Mizz Grant, I gotta see Willis right off."

"Well, he's down in the barn tossing hay."

"Thank you, Ma'am." Robert was out the door in an instant. He dashed across the heavy ground still damp from the overnight rain, and into the barn. "Willis, Willis, you here?"

A tall, young man stood up from behind a stall. He wasn't wearing a shirt and his powerful chest glistened with sweat. His blond hair was falling across his strong face. He pushed it back with his big hands. "What you having a fit about!"

"You know how we are always talking about heading out into the wilderness to find sport and adventure?"

"Not much chance for a couple of farm boys."

"Now there is," said Robby with a wide grin.

"What you talkin' about?"

"This!" said Robby, pulling a paper out of his back pocket. "It just came in the Boston Herald."

"What is it?"

"Here, I'll read it."

A Call to The Strong, The Few, The Proud!
A large Colonial Enterprise is now recruiting men and women between the ages of 18-22, for the adventure of a lifetime. Our purpose is to conduct the largest exploration of the North

American continent in history. This will be a most dangerous job and your safety, while of paramount importance to us, is not guaranteed. However, you will see the greatest sights in the world and experience the excitement only achieved with dedication and hard work. We offer excellent pay, full provisions, clothing, food and the best training to be found anywhere in the world. Only the most physically fit need apply, however we will offer schooling in reading, writing, and mathematics for those who are not qualified. This is a full-time career commitment and only those who are willing to give a lifetime to this extraordinary opportunity should consider it. Your acceptance is strictly provisional on the completion of our rigorous enlistment requirements. We promise, if you do meet our standards, the greatest and most satisfying life that God can provide. To apply: appear in person at 8 am on September 1 through 5 1770, at the central post office in the Capital city of your colony.

"Don't hardly sound real," said Willis.

"We can do this!" said Robby, "we are both strong as an ox. We got plenty of family for our Pa's to do the farming, we are both 19, right inside where it says we have to be, and both of us have never wanted to stay on the farm all our lives. We want something special for our lives. This is it!"

"September 1 is just two days away."

"We can catch the freight wagon to Boston tomorrow, and be at the Post Office on time come Friday morning."

There was trouble in both households that night as the young men made their cases for setting out to find a better life. When Robby got the grudging support of his father, if he promised to write and send home some of that "excellent pay" the ad mentioned. Robby promised and rushed out to run the mile to the Grant farm.

As he came in, he found Willis pleading with his crying mother. "You always said, you wanted the best for me, Ma. This ad says they will teach me to read and write, and do my numbers. I could use some more of that, the Lord knows."

"It also says this is a permanent career job. I may never see you again."

"Ah Ma, I won't be gone forever, and I promise to write when I can, after I learn my letters better."

"Did you come up with this Robby Pierce," said Mrs. Grant?

"I brung the ad, if'n that's what you mean Mizz Grant, but this is a chance for both of us to make somethin' of our selves. Please say yes, my folks already have done so."

The following morning, with just a change of clothes and a few personal things in a shoulder bag, the young men caught the freight wagon to Boston.

Boston was big and busy and hard to get around in, but the two, finally made their way to the main Boston Post Office and settled down to wait for morning. Robby spent a couple of pennies for a sack of apples, and they pulled a blanket out of their bags to stay warm against the building.

As the sun came up, the men stirred. It wasn't long before other young men began to arrive at the Post Office. By 7:30 there were at least 50 young men standing around waiting. Willis and Robby, said a few words to some of the others. Mostly, they seemed like local boys, but a fair number had come from at least as far as Concord and further.

At exactly 8 am, a wagon pulled up in the square facing the Post Office. Five men jumped down. They were very big men, only Willis was close to their size. Robby was a couple of inches shorter than all of them. The men from the wagon were dressed in very strange clothing. Their pants and shirt were patches of green. They looked like work clothes, but there was a very snappy look to them. They all wore very sharp looking green berets, and had brown boots going up past their ankles. Their pants turned under just above their boots. All five men looked incredibly fit and had lean, hard looks on their faces.

Five tables were quickly set up and a business-like tent went up over the tables, with a canvas sheet separating the interview areas. The leader of the group had a patch on both sleeves with brown stripes, three going up, and three going down.

He turned to the men gathered around and said, "Are you all here in response to our ad?" There was a murmur of agreement.

"Did all of you read the ad thoroughly and understand it? We want you to know if you qualify for training, you will be making a commitment with no set end date. It's a career choice. We believe you will find the experience to be the greatest of your life, beyond anything you can imagine. However, our training regimen is long, hard, and very physically challenging. You can quit anytime you like during training. In fact, we encourage it. We only want men who are serious, dedicated, and worthy of respect. The respect you will have to earn. Our training system requires you to follow orders immediately and without question, because we don't have the luxury of wasting time, and a great deal of what we do is dangerous. I need to tell you we expect to have at least one fatality during the training. Almost always, it's because a man was doing something he shouldn't have done, or didn't follow orders. This is your first chance to quit. If any one of you didn't like what I said, leave now."

A few men did walk off. Robby and Willis stood their ground. Willis as calm as ever and Robby with eyes shining,

"Alright," said the sergeant, "let's get started. I want five lines in front of these tables. In each line, arrange yourself according to height, with the shortest first."

The young men milled around a little. Robby and Willis got into the line in front of the sergeant who did the talking. Five or six men separated them because Willis was close to the rear of the line and Robby several spaces forward.

The line did not move quickly. Each man came into the tent alone and the man outside could not hear the conversation. The questionnaire was two pages long and the sergeant made careful notes.

When it was finally Robby's turn, he stepped into the tent and the sergeant waved him to a seat. "I'm First Sergeant Thomas Seacrest," he put his hand out and shook Robby's hand. It was hard and firm.

"What's your name?"

"Robert Pierce."

"Where do you live?"

"Concord, Massachusetts."

It went on that way for a while. Seacrest wanted to know about Robby's family, what they did for a living, how old he was, did he have any diseases or disabilities, was he brave, had he ever been in a fight, the questions went on and on.

Finally, Seacrest asked, "Robby, do you read your Bible and believe in God?"

"I've read the whole Bible several times, Sir, although I don't know it as well as some of my other friends."

"Do you remember the first few verses of Romans 12?"

"Do not conform to the ways of the world, but let your mind be transformed by the Holy Spirit?"

"Close enough," smiled the Sergeant. "Now tell me this, in light of Romans 12, what is your opinion of the British occupation of the American Colonies. You can tell me what you really believe, I'm not a British sympathizer."

"Well, sir, the British seem to think we're their servants and the colonies exist to make them money. We have no say in the way they do things. It's just not right."

"Do you believe the Colonies should break away from England and form an American nation."

"We talk about it all the time in Concord, but nobody really knows how we could do it."

"What if I told you there is a way and you can be a part of it?"

"I would be ready to do whatever I could."

"Fine, now go out and join the men standing near the steps of the Post Office. Just wait until we finish interviewing the entire group, and then we'll tell you what comes next."

Robby exited the tent and walked over to a crowd of young men. He estimated there were about thirty. Robby joined them. "Good afternoon, anybody have an idea of what comes next?"

"None of us know anything," said a young man who seemed a little older than Robby, "I was one of the first people to be interviewed, and I've been waiting here for hours. One of the fellows wearing those strange clothes left a while ago, so it slowed things down. The other two fellows are still talking to people"

Robby turned and looked at the line. It had gotten longer. "Some others must have come later."

"What did your man ask you?"

"He wanted to know where I was from, how old I was, everything about my family, whether or not I had any infirmities, and then he asked me to repeat a verse from the Bible. After that, he wanted to know what I thought of the British and whether I would be in favor of separating from England and making a new country. What did he ask you."

"Almost exactly the same things," said the young man. "Say, where are you from anyway?"

"My friend and I came in from Concord last night. My name is

Robby Pierce."

"I'm Charlie Arthur, and I'm from nearby in Watertown." The two shook hands.

"Did you come on account of the posting in the paper?"

"Seemed like a good idea at the time. I'm beginning to wonder after waiting for so long. But I guess they're doing the best they can."

After talking with some of the other men, Robby found out everyone in the group were devout Christians and hated the British. "This is a smaller group than this morning," said Robby. "Did some of boys get sent away?"

"Quite a few, actually," said Charlie, and some of them were pretty upset about it."

Willis came out the tent about an hour later, and came over to Robby, "Looks like not being able to read and write very good mattered very much. I sure did give that sergeant a shilling's worth on my feelings about the British. I sure hope he was telling the truth about not being a British sympathizer."

It was late in the day when the last person was interviewed. Sergeant Seacrest came out of the tent and stood in front of the men. "I apologize for the long wait most of you have had today. You 47 men represent those who've passed the first test in our selection process. As you can see, we have three wagons. I think we can fit you all in, so get aboard."

"Where are we going," asked one of the men?

"Someplace a little more private," said Seacrest. "It's a place we've already chosen and set up.

There was just enough room to fit all the men into the wagons, and they rolled away. Seacrest led the wagons out of Boston and pulled into a wide meadow far away from any houses, with woods lining the meadow. They put the wagons into a sort of circle, and Seacrest hopped down. "We need a fire. Some of you boys head over to the forest and gather enough wood to last the night. Half the group jumped out of the wagons immediately and headed for the forest.

Seacrest nodded his head to his own men, and they went to the wagons bringing back several large cardboard boxes and three big coolers. They quickly set up the tent again and put the three tables together, with the boxes and coolers sitting on them.

The men began coming back with bundles of wood. One of

Seacrest's sergeants gathered up a hand full of dry grass, pulled a small tube like thing out of his pocket and flicked the top of it. There was an instant flame, and in no time a fire was lighting and warming the encampment. There were also several lanterns set out, but they were unlike anything the colonists had ever seen. They seemed to light without anything more than flipping a switch.

"Ever seen anything like those lanterns or fire starter?" asked Robby to Willis, who just shook his head.

Sergeant Seacrest turned to the group and asked, "Anybody hungry?"

There was a rumble of agreement among the young men.

"All right then," said Seacrest, "we have a meal for you right here, just line up and pick up a box, there are cups for your drinks. By the way, the drink is not water, but a special mixture of ingredients very healthy for you. Before we do eat, I would like to offer thanks for our meal."

Everyone bowed their head and a few of the men kneeled as Seacrest prayed, "Dear Lord, we offer our praise and gratitude for this day, and bringing together these young men. May they all be successful in our efforts tomorrow. Bless these men Lord, and watch over them and protect them. Now we offer thanks for our meal, you have provided. We pray in the name of our savior, Jesus Christ, Amen."

Robby and Willis got in line and received a large brown box, and a big glass that wasn't glass, but made of strange material, which bent easily if you squeezed it. They pushed a button on the cooler and an amber fluid came pouring out.

The two sat down on the grass and opened their boxes. They were crammed full of packages Robby read, "It says to push the top of this package and mix the ingredients with the water at the top." He did that on the biggest package, breaking the seal of water and massaging the package. As he was doing this, the package got hot in his hand. There was a line down the middle of the package, the instructions said to puncture with the enclosed knife. The knife was hard but clearly not metal, but it cut open the package and the delicious smell of beef stew came out. Both men took the provided spoon and fork and dug in. The food was quite good, and very filing. They opened other packages containing bread and finished with a hot pudding for dessert. At the bottom of the box was a large package saying "chocolate" on it. Neither, Robby or Willis had ever eaten chocolate, but they had heard about it. They wolfed it down, wondering how they had missed such luscious stuff all their lives. The drink was cold, and was quite sweet with a hint of tartness It was delicious.

It was fully dark when they finished. The Sergeants came around and gathered all their trash in bags, which they threw on the fire. When everything was burned, there was no trace anything had been there.

Sergeant Seacrest stepped forward and said, "Men, I hope you got enough to eat." There was an outburst of applause and cheers of agreement. "When we're in the field like this, we have to make do as best we can."

Robby and Willis laughed at this, they hardly ate better when they were in their own homes.

Seacrest continued, "Tomorrow we'll get up early, have breakfast, and then begin the physical portion of our testing. We'll be seeing how fast you can run, how much weight you can lift, and we have agility tests. Men, we are looking for a particular kind of person, with certain skills. We need special people to do very specialized tasks. Not all of you have them. If you don't meet our standards, we don't want you to feel slighted or disgraced in any way. Remember the ad only promised you an opportunity."

While he was talking, the other four sergeants spread out a huge canvas not far from the fire. "I'm sorry we can't provide you with better sleeping arrangements," said Seacrest. "For those of you who did not bring a blanket, we have enough to go around. Our field cover will keep the chill from reaching you. We can't do much about the bumps in the ground,. Remove your shoes and boots before walking onto the field cover. We have dug slit trench latrines just beyond the far wagon. Please use them."

"That's all I have for you tonight. Get as good a rest as you can and we will see you for breakfast. May God bless you all."

Robby didn't realize how tired he was. He went to the edge of the field cover and slipped off his boots. He was very surprised to find his stocking feet where stepping onto warmth as he walked onto the field cover. He lay down, and the whole field cover was radiating a cozy heat from it. He pulled his blanket over him and looked at Willis settling down next to him.

"All of this is getting stranger and stranger," he said, "Food you don't have to cook and comes out hot all by itself, now this big cover that radiates its own heat."

"It's strange all right," said Willis, "but it's all been good. I can't wait to see what tomorrow brings. Night, Robby, sleep well." Willis turned over and seemed to be asleep in a minute. Robby was not far behind him. The rest of the men went to sleep quickly as well."

Chapter 18
The True Story
Outside Boston, Massachusetts

The following morning Robby woke feeling quite refreshed. He was warm all night from the heated field cover. He was one of only a few men awake and stirring. He gave Willis a shove, and the big fellow rolled over coming awake and wiping the sleep from his eyes. The two of them stepped over other sleeping men and found their boots. Then they went to the tent where they got another box of rations. There was a big pot of coffee hanging from a frame over the fire. They poured themselves a cup in a different kind of glass then they had used the night before. This one did not let the heat of the coffee burn their hands. Robby tasted the coffee and found it was excellent, the best he'd ever drunk.

They opened their boxes and found the big bag contained sausage and gravy. There were biscuits in another bag and a plate spreading out like a fan to make a circular plate. They opened the warm biscuits and poured the hot sausage gravy on them. At the bottom of the box was another big chocolate bar. It was a very satisfying breakfast. Robby had two cups of the coffee.

When the entire party had eaten, three of the sergeants hitched up the wagons and headed back into Boston. Their job was to bring in another group of recruits.

Sergeant Seacrest stood in front of the men and said, "We've set up a course for you to run today. It begins with a test of agility. As you can see, we have set up a series of posts in the meadow, they're spread out in two rows, and there is a small dummy on the top of each post. We want you all to line up and run this course. I'll demonstrate how I want it done. Then he took off from the starting line toward the first post, slapping the dummy going by. It let out loud click. Seacrest was racing for the second post on the other side of the line and further along, he hit another dummy and got another loud click. He continued through the course, producing ten loud clicks. Then he sprinted across the finish line. Everyone was amazed how fast and agile the Sergeant was.

"I ran the course in just under 30 seconds," said Seacrest, the maximum time for you is 45 seconds. The men lined up at the starting line and Seacrest went to the finish line with a flag he dropped to start each man on his run. Robby watched the men run the course. None of them was as quick as Seacrest. He recorded the results for each man.

When Robby's turn came, he dashed with all his might, making the sharp changes in direction and slapping all ten of the dummies.

"Good" said Seacrest, "you did the agility course in 33 seconds."

The next test was a run of 40 yards. The course was marked off with a start and finish line. Seacrest demonstrated again. He crouched down in a stance and then shot away at great speed, crossing the finish line, and causing most of the men to look at each other in surprise at how fast the big man was.

"Now each of you try it. The standard is eight seconds. I did it in a little over five."

Once again, when Robby's turn came, he crouched down as Seacrest had and ran as fast as he could. "5 point 5," said Seacrest, "Not bad."

The tests went on. Robby was required to lie on his back on a bench and lift a bar with weights on each end. He did it five times. There was a vertical jump pole with dowels sticking out horizontally from the pole. The idea was to jump as high as you could and hit the highest dowel you could reach. Seacrest wrote down all the results.

Finally, Seacrest called all of them together and showed them an oval marked with short poles and string between them. "This is our long distance run. You must run around the oval, staying outside the poles and strings, four times. The distance you are running is one mile. You will run in groups of four and I will record your time as you finish. The standard for this distance is eight minutes. That's not very fast, and you're not wearing proper equipment. Do the best you can. I'll shout out your times as your group passes the start/finish line with each lap."

Robby was happy for this test, he ran long distances every day on the farm and was sure he could do the distance in eight minutes, although he'd never timed himself.

`As it turned out, he ran the fastest of anyone that day. He was happy Willis ended up in the top five.

Seacrest went to the tent and sat down to count up the results. When he was finished, he came out and called 11 names. He took all them aside and Robby could see they were very disappointed. They had not passed the tests with high enough scores to qualify. When the wagons came back from Boston, loaded with another group of 50 eager men, the 11 were loaded on one of the wagons and driven back into to Boston.

While the new arrivals were gathering wood, and being fed, Seacrest took his group of 36 qualifiers away from the main group, toward the tree line. He carried a lantern and had five more brought by people in the group. All of them had their personal bags with them.

"Men, you are the 36 who have passed our screening and physical tests to move to the next level. Since we started out with more than 60, I think you can congratulate yourselves on making the cut. Now we come to the really sensitive matters."

"How are you at keeping secrets," asked the Sergeant, "a solemn oath taken before God with your hand on a Bible? If there is one of you who is unwilling to do that, please drop out now, because after this there is no turning back"

"I can do that," said Robby, looking straight into the Sergeant's eyes.

"Very well," said Seacrest, "sit down and let me tell you a story. All the men sat down by the light of the lanterns. "Our ad was run in every paper in all the colonies. There are teams out now doing exactly what we are doing here. However, we could not very well put our real purpose in the ad. The British would take a dim view of that. So, the ad was written to attract the best men in the colonies. It's true you will experience the adventure of a lifetime, and be well paid for your service. It is also true you are making a career commitment lasting at least fifteen years. You will have opportunities to visit your families, but they will be few and far between and you're not permitted to tell them the entire story of our total mission."

Seacrest looked over the group, "Is there anyone who is not willing to make this pledge?" Nobody spoke up.

"Good, you will not be explorers as the ad said, at least not in the beginning. What we are doing is recruiting a professional army carefully trained and equipped with special weapons to defeat the entire British Army and allow us to form an American nation."

There was a buzz of talk over this announcement and Seacrest let it go on for several minutes.

"When you complete your training, you will be the best fighting army in the world. You remember our ad said we were looking for the brave, the proud, and the few. With what you learn, and the weapons we will provide, we can defeat any army in any country with a single reinforced Brigade of 3,000 men.

"After we finish with the British in the colonies, we intend to conquer Canada, Mexico, Central America, and all the islands of the Caribbean. The new United States will be the largest and most powerful nation on earth."

"Obviously, we must build and train this secret army without the British, or any country finding out. We must also defeat the French, and the Spanish. When all of this is completed, we will be a free country, where every man and woman will have the liberty to go where they wish, say what they want, worship God in any fashion they like. It will be a country, unlike any other. The power to govern will come from the people, not from a King, or any legislative body. The government will function only with the consent of governed."

Willis put up his hand, "Your ad said you would educate us to read, write, and do numbers, is that still true."

"When we are finished educating you, expect an advanced degree from Harvard. You will be that advanced."

"How long will this training take," asked another man.

"We have less than five years to turn you into the fighting force we need. During that time, you will live at a place called Fort Independence. You will be paid 8 dollars a month in silver coins throughout your service, including training. You will receive comfortable quarters in which to live, three meals a day, and we will provide you with all your uniforms and equipment. However, make no mistake about it, your education and your training will be very challenging."

"This is even better than I thought it would be," said Charlie Arthur.

"I'm glad you feel that way Private Arthur," said Seacrest. He picked up his shoulder bag and pulled out a stack of papers and a Bible. "For all of you who are still willing to volunteer for this career, step forward and sign or make your mark on your enlistment papers and swear on this Bible you will keep our secrets and willingly face the tough job ahead of you."

The men surged forward, signed their papers, and made their oaths on the Bible.

When it became Robby's turn, he signed the paper, put his hand on the Bible and said, "I so swear."

All 36 men did the same. Seacrest had not expected anything less. He didn't have a doctorate in Psychology and Human Behavior for nothing.

Seacrest pulled a small black case off his belt and spoke into it, "Ready for pickup."

He then turned back to the group and said, "Follow me men, your transportation to Fort Independence is on its way." He walked through the forest of trees until he came to another meadow. It was not very big, perhaps a hundred feet across. "You might just as well get your first lesson in how advanced this army is going to be. Wait for it."

Robby stood next to Willis while Seacrest took his lantern out to the middle of the meadow and turned it up. It was a very bright light.

In the background, Robby could hear the faint sound of a thumping growing louder in the next couple of minutes. He looked up and saw a huge machine descending onto the meadow. Later Robby would learn the machine was a C-48, "Chinook" transport helicopter coming in on whisper mode. At the moment, he just watched in wonder as the big chopper came to rest light as a feather on the meadow. The rear ramp augured down and the men climbed aboard. Men on the craft guided them to seats and showed them how to fasten their seat belts. Then the helicopter took off and Robby caught his breath as the ground fell away and the adventure began.

Chapter 19
The Farm Boy Vanishes
Fort Independence, Virginia

The flight to Fort Independence took almost two hours. As much as Robby wanted to look out and see the countryside from the air, it was night and there was very little to see. He finally dozed off.

He was roused when men in fatigues came walking along the rows waking people up in preparation for landing. Robby looked out the window and could see a blaze of lights coming from a large, busy place below. There were row after row of long buildings surrounding a central complex of bigger buildings and a big parade ground at one end. He could see other helicopters like his were also landing and taking off.

As they landed, the rear doors opened again. Men in fatigues rushed aboard wearing masks on their faces, but yelling loudly through them. "You men line up six wide, and line up behind the man in front of you. The troopers did the best they could to accomplish this simple formation, and were shoved around by the men in fatigues. When they were grouped in a square of men six wide and six deep, one of the men, with three stripes of his shirt yelled out, "Come to attention, stand up straight. Now we're gonna march to the infirmary. Start walking with your left foot when I say 'March' and stay in step. Ready, forward, march!"

The formation lurched forward and didn't get the step right until they'd walked 200 yards, then they marched in somewhat good order, until the sergeant bellowed, "Prepare to Halt, ready Halt!"

Of course, some of the men didn't halt and the formation became a logjam again. "First row, go through the door on the left, then each row follow." Robby and Willis, who were standing next to each other near the center of the formation made their way through the door and into a brightly lit room where a number of men and women wearing white coats and all wearing masks directed them to lines in front of several large stations containing all sorts of strange equipment.

A women wearing a mask came up to Robby and Willis sitting next to each other and said, "Relax, boys, you're in the infirmary at Fort Independence. The reason why this is your first stop is to make sure you stay healthy. The first thing we do is to draw a small amount of blood from your arm to be tested for any diseases. Then we give you a dosage of a wide number of vaccinations for things like measles, mumps, chicken pox, tuberculosis, influenza, yellow and scarlet fever, polio. After you have this vaccination, you will immune from all those diseases for the rest of your life. We also do a full body scan to make sure you don't have any tumors or a large number of other things."

She drew the blood, placed a flat gun-like instrument on their arms, and pulled the trigger. The shots only hurt a little. Then she vaccinated them for TB, and had them lay flat on a table that moved them into a large tube and vibrated. As they came out, the nurse pulled a sheet of paper out of a machine and read the results of the blood test. "Healthy as a horse, both of you, any problems with your teeth? Both men said they did, and were directed to another room where they sat in a chair and a masked man checked their teeth. He called off numbers to a nurse who wrote them down. "Both of you are going to need some work, but nothing that can't wait. Give them an appointment." The nurse looked at a calendar on a screen, and wrote a day and time for their next appointment. They added the paper to the large envelope they had gotten back at the meadow with their enlistment. Now the envelope was filling with medical records.

The next stop was a room with more chairs and barbers cutting hair. The process of removing all the hair on their heads took about a minute and both Robby and Willis ran their hands across their heads in wonder. Next, was a large room with a lot of semi-naked people in it. A man came up, also masked, and said, "Remove all your clothing then go through there to the showers. A little sheepishly, they took off their clothes, which were taken away in a rolling basket. They got towels and went into the showers, where they were told to hang up their towels and step up to the showers. A man showed them how to adjust the temperature and handed them a scrunchy blob. He showed them the button to push for shampoo and the other for soap to put on the scrunchy. "Make sure you wash thoroughly," said the man, "then dry off, wrap the towel around your waste and go through that door."

Neither of the men had ever had a shower before, so the experience was unique. They were careful to follow the instructions to wash thoroughly, although Willis said using shampoo on a nearly baldhead seemed like a waste of time.

The next hall was noisy and filled with people, both recruits and men. None of them had masks. The man at the desk looked them over and directed each of them into two different lines. They went through the lines and got a big bag that began to fill with boxer shorts, socks, t-shirts, a bar of soap, a toothbrush, and toothpaste and finally to a man who did quick measurements with a tape. He then rummaged through racks of green fatigues and pulled out two pairs of uniforms for each man. He had them try on the shirt and pants, and Robby was surprised how well they fit him, maybe a little big. The other uniform went in their bag and they moved to the next station. Here they stood on a foot measure and were given brown boots. They sat down, pulled out a pair of green socks, put them on, and then slipped their feet into the boots. The boots were stiff, because they were brand new, but they were the right size. The men laced them up and the man handed them a couple pairs of blousing rubbers. He had them put on a pair and then roll the bottom of their pants under the stretchable bands, just above the boots.

The final station provided them with a wide, webbed belt, with lots of metal clasps on them, and a green beret with an emblem of a flag on the front. They were asked their last names and a machine printed a cloth tab that said Pierce and Grant on them. Some kind of strange material attached them firmly above their right pockets and they got another tab saying U.S. Army on it. It attached to the funny strip above their left pocket.

The door opened to the outside and the fresh recruits followed a real soldier whose fatigues looked ten times better than theirs to a big mess hall, where they got trays and utensils, and walked through a cafeteria line choosing from a wide selection of food. They got large cups, real ones this time, of coffee, and cold water with ice cubes in the glass. The novelty amazed them both. Robby spotted Charlie

Arthur sitting along a table with several other men. He and Willis made their way over. The men at the table made room for them. Everybody introduced themselves. Robby learned a lot of last names, because they were on the uniforms, but forgot most of the first names.

The food was hot, tasty, and plentiful. The men had not eaten since lunch so they were famished and ate with gusto. They all talked about their experiences and especially the wonderful machine that flew them to the Fort. Robby rubbed is arm where he'd gotten the jet spray of vaccines. It was a little sore.

Presently a soldier with two stripes came up to the table. "You guys came in from Boston?" They said they had. "OK, if you're finished eating, I'll take you to your quarters. Pair up, these are two man rooms." Again, they went outside and across the street to a long row of two story barracks buildings. The corporal stopped at the third one and went in. "Since you guys, are among the first to arrive, you get barracks close to the mess hall, and the ground floor. Move in and pick a room. Doesn't matter which, they're all the same."

Robby and Willis turned into the first room on the right side of the long hallway. They opened the door and stepped inside. The room was dark. The corporal reached around a corner flipped a switch and a light came on. There were two bigger than single beds with a wide cabinet between them and lights with two flexible arms pointing at the beds. There was a desk and chair on both sides of the room with lights on top of the desks. At the back of the room was a closet to hang clothes and a chest of drawers in the middle, with six drawers. The walls were painted a light blue and there was an attractive rug on the floor between the beds. The rest of the floor were tiles. Attached to the walls next to both desks was a bookshelf.

There was a bathroom with a shower and two sinks, plus a strange looking appliance with a seat and water in the bowl under the seat. Towels hung on racks on the wall, and there was a mirror across the whole front over the sinks. On the wall was a cabinet, which opened to hold toiletries.

The Corporal finished getting everyone in their rooms and came back to Robby and Willis. He pointed at the door with two plastic sleeves on it. "You put your last names in these sleeves so people can find you. That's all for tonight. Reveille is at 5:50. You will hear the bugle on the speakers outside. When you hear it, you have ten minutes to get up, make your bunks, get dressed in the uniform of the day, which is what you have on now, and fall out for the morning meal formation. Don't be late for the 6 AM bugle. It's not going to be pleasant if you are.

When he left, Robby and Willis realized how big a day they had experienced.

"Does it seem cold in here to you?"

"Yeah, it does," said Willis.

"Wait a minute, I saw, an instruction manual over there on the table between the beds. Robby read the pages, and found there was a small box on the wall showing the temperature in the room in a lighted display and a button to set the temperature. The room was 55 degrees. Robby pushed the button and moved the number up to 70. Almost immediately, the sound of air came through vents on both sides of the room in the ceiling. Willis reached up and said, "There's warm air coming out of these vents."

"Guess we won't be cold at night," said Robby.

"What's the book say about that thing in the bathroom?"

Robby checked the index and read the part about the "thing."

"It says here it's called a toilet and you use it to go to the bathroom."

"I'm gonna try it," said Willis, "I got to pee."

He stepped into the room and lifted the lid. He peed, and said, "Now what?"

"Turn the handle," said Robby .

Both men watched in amazement as the toilet cycled.

"I wonder what time it is," asked Willis, "I'm plumb tuckered out."

"Me too, Guess we can sleep in our boxers and a t-shirt."

The men pulled down the covers and got into bed.

"What a comfortable bed," said Robby .

"Yeah it is, you gonna go shut off the light?

Robby looked at the lights on the cabinet. "They have switches too" He pushed the one on his side and the light went out. Willis pushed his button and the room was dark. Both men were asleep in minutes.

Chapter 20
Very Basic Training

Fort Independence, Virginia

It seemed like Robby had just closed his eyes when he heard the blare of a trumpet cascading through the Fort from speakers everywhere. He shook his head to clear the cobwebs and jumped out of bed, shoving Willis in the process.

Both men made up their bunks, trying to make them look as neat as they had found them the night before. Then they quickly dressed and left their room. Several other men were running down the hall toward the front door.

They went outside to the street in front of the barracks and found two soldiers standing there with strange hats on their heads. They were round and creased in the middle. Their uniforms were perfectly tailored. One had three stripes down and two stripes up on his sleeves, the other three stripes. The Sergeant was not a huge man, about Robby's size. Many of the recruits were bigger and broader than he was. He had broad shoulders, a narrow waist, and his face was lean with a long nose. He had sharp, dark eyes. The Sergeant was muscular and had a pleasant face.

He walked back and forth in front of the 50 recruits. "I am Sergeant First-Class Boswell. This is Sergeant Carson. We will be your drill instructors for basic training. I want you to organize yourselves with the shortest man here in the front right corner and the tallest man back there in the left corner. Ten men in each line in front of me. Do it now! If the man in front of you is taller move up. If the man to your side is taller, move down," he said as the men struggled to find the right spots. When the unit had formed up properly, Boswell said, "Now, I want you to stretch out your right arm and make space so

your fingers are just touching the shoulders of the man next to you."
The 50 men shuffled around. "Straighten up these ranks, when I stand
in front of the man in the front row, I don't want to see nothing but
him." More shuffling.

"During the next six months, we will train you in the
fundamentals of military service. You are the First Platoon of
Company A, of the First Regiment of the Ranger Brigade of the
American Army "Right now it's time for you to eat breakfast, and I
want you back here, in exactly this formation in 45 minutes. Fall out."

The men made a wide arc around the sergeant and ran for the
mess hall. They were the only recruits in the huge mess hall at the
moment, but within minutes, another platoon of 50 men came rushing
in, and on top of them another 50 men arrived.

The food was excellent. They had scrambled eggs, bacon,
sausage, biscuits and gravy, pancakes, toast, orange juice, wonderful
butter, a superb collection of jams and jellies and rich maple syrup.
They also had more of the fabulous coffee. If anything, it tasted better
than the night before.

The time went very quickly. Robby paid special attention to the
big clock on the wall to make sure they got back in the correct time. It
was exactly 45 minutes and the entire unit was back in the formation
they had when they fell out from reveille. Sergeant Boswell nodded
with satisfaction.

"Our training cannot proceed in the manner of most armies," he
announced. "In many ways it will be run on an almost individual basis,
since you all come from such different backgrounds and social
situations. So, your training will begin in a classroom. However, when
you're formed as a platoon, as you are now, we move in unison from
place to place. We call this short order drill. The sooner you learn
these simple skills, the sooner you will be able to function as a team."

For the next two hours, Boswell conducted instruction in coming
to attention, turning in place, and fundamental marching. Robby and
Willis learned very quickly, there were consequences for failing to
follow the orders. Almost everyone in the platoon found themselves
called out and required to do push-ups, when they forgot.

Eventually, the platoon marched in semi-order down the street,
past the mess hall and the Administration Building, to a two-story

structure. As they went inside, they found the building divided into classrooms holding 50 students. There were desks in lines, a podium at the front, and a large LED screen hung on the front wall. Of course, the colonists had never seen such a thing before, and since it was black, they assumed it was some kind of a blackboard.

When everyone was settled, Sergeant Boswell said, "We are going to begin with some basic orientation." He pushed a button on a pad and the big screen came to life in full high definition color.

The video began a tour of the lands of North America. There were great forests, big rivers, spectacular snow-capped mountains, breath-taking canyons, and wide savannahs with huge herds of black beasts. There was music with the video and it was an inspiring look at the entire North American continent. Robby looked over at Willis. Both of them were deeply impressed with what they saw.

As the video came to a close, a half hour later, there was a lot of conversation among the men, and general applause. The picture changed to a man standing in an open field. He was wearing the same green fatigues as everyone else. He smiled into the camera and said, "Hello, Americans, I am General Compton, the Deputy Commander of the Brigade of which you are all a part. We shall be known as the Rangers. When we are finished with you, in about five years, you will be the best educated, best trained, most effective, strongest and most lethal fighting force in the world. Believe it men. When other armies, no matter how many men they have, hear 'The Rangers Are Coming,' they will shake in their boots with terror.

"In order to accomplish this, we will proceed along several lines. First, we'll be conducting a program in general education. Not only will all of you read, write, and do arithmetic, you will learn new things none of you knows, and your education will be more advanced than any university anywhere in the world.

"Our second objective is to improve your physical conditioning to an extremely high level. You will be amazed at what you can actually do, given the proper motivation.

"Next, we will be training you to work as one team, with a common purpose. This will require rigorous training in a military environment. You will walk, talk, shoot, shave, shower, and function as a single effective force. Each of you will learn to watch each other and to protect each other, as if they were yourselves.

"Next, in the final three years of your training, we will teach you to use the very special weapons we have available to us. I can assure you, no other army will have the kind of equipment and weapons you will possess. This is why a single Brigade of 3,000 Rangers will be able to defeat any enemy force we face. I know this sounds like so much nonsense, however, I can assure you it is true.

"The following is very important. The greatest cause of death on the battlefield is not being killed in combat. It's caused by infection from wounds, and from disease. The first one is battle injuries. The Rangers have the most effective medical treatment and the best corps of doctors and medics to be found anywhere in the world. If you are wounded in battle, the chances of your survival with all your limbs intact is 90%. As opposed to the current levels in the British Army where their best efforts are less than 25%. The second part is disease.

"All of you have received vaccinations against all the common ailments. However, in order for us to insure your medical safety, we must rely on one very important policy, which is not to allow disease to creep into our ranks because of poor personal hygiene. You will shave and shower every day. Your personal quarters will be kept spotlessly clean and in perfect order at all times. Your drill instructors will inspect your quarters on a regular basis and anyone who doesn't meet our high standards will find there are consequences. We will not beat you, but additional physical exercise will be the penalty for not keeping these standards. Some of you have come from clean homes some of you have not. The most privileged of you, have not lived in a home with anything like the standards of cleanliness we maintain here. It's for your protection, and you will learn to appreciate it.

"Finally, you are all volunteers. Nobody made you come here. You have already had three chances to back out. Over 25% have done so. This means you are already the best of the best. However, if you find our standards, rules, training and discipline is too much for you, then quit. Ring the bell in front of the mess hall and vacate the Fort. By the way, we are a secret army being built by the American colonies without the knowledge of the British. If you quit, at least until we open our offensive operations to conquer North America, Canada, Mexico, Central America, and the Caribbean, you will not be permitted to go home. You will be held in segregated facilities to insure our secret stays a secret. We are sorry it has to be this way, and following the open establishment of the Rangers to the public, anyone who quits will be permitted to return to whatever life you had.

"Now, I want you to know we are a Christian organization. We will have church services every Sunday. We believe, in our hearts, we are doing God's work here and are warriors in the service of our savior and redeemer, Christ Jesus. You will soon learn how serious we are about this part of our lives.

"So let us begin. Your drill sergeants have their orders for how we proceed from now on. Good luck, Rangers, and May God Bless you all."

"Men," said Sergeant Boswell, "lack of education is not a disability or anything to be ashamed of, nobody will discriminate against you for needing to learn, and especially to those of you who do have education. We expect you to provide aid, encouragement, and personal tutoring for all who are struggling to learn. Is that understood?

"Yes, drill sergeant," cried the men in unison.

"I can't hear you," hollered Boswell.

"YES, DRILL SERGEANT!"

"That's better. Now stand up as I describe your current educational level. All men who have had formal schooling, can read, write, and do numbers, stand up."

About 15 men stood up. "You men, go upstairs to room 201."

"All men who are able to read and write and do some numbers, but have not had formal education in a school, stand up."

Robby was one of about 30 men to stand. "Your classroom upstairs is room 203. Go now."

There were now five men left in the room. "Is there anyone here who cannot read at all?" None spoke up. Finally, Willis raised his hand, "Yes Grant," said Boswell.

"It's not I don't read, drill sergeant. I don't read very well, and it's hard for me to write a proper sentence. As far as numbers are concerned, I'm dumb as a post."

"Are the rest of you in about the same place," asked Boswell?

All nodded this was about where they were.

"Fine, your place is upstairs in room 205. Get moving."

At lunch Willis and Robby traded stories. Robby said, "It was the strangest thing, the teacher had us all sit in front of machines with a lighted window like the one we saw when we were together. It had a keyboard for putting the letters on the screen. The first thing I did was to put a thing over my head that covered my ears. Then a strange woman spoke to me and told me what buttons to push to turn on the machine, it's called…

"A computer," interrupted Willis. I got the same thing. I spent four hours learning simple reading. We got one break for 15 minutes in the middle and I went down the hall and used the toilet. Do you know they have soft paper to wipe yourself off? Then you just push the handle and it all goes away. There was a sign saying, "Everything gone? If not use the brush to clean the toilet. Make sure you wash your hands with soap and hot water before you leave." I guess that's part of the being clean speech we got this morning."

After lunch, Sergeant Boswell and Corporal Carson led them at a trot down the street to the huge parade ground. For the remainder of the afternoon they alternated between running through a very difficult obstacle course, and more close order drill. like coming to attention and making turns in unison.

Boswell explained the protocol for saluting, "You will salute me as if I were an officer at every appropriate time, but when training is over you will stop. I am an enlisted man, like you, and do not rate a salute."

The next morning, following breakfast, the drill instructors went into the rooms of the recruits and demonstrated the proper way to make a bed, and how to keep the rest of the room clean. They were introduced to mops and strong cleaners with pungent smells to scrub the floors. Rags with another kind of cleaner were for the furniture and fixtures in the bedroom and bathroom. The standards were very exacting and over the next week, many beds were torn apart, by the drill sergeants, and many floors and fixtures were done over. Always, the penalty for not passing the inspection was to run the half mile round trip from the barracks and across the Parade Ground, around the flagpole and back. There was a time limit, and the penalty for not coming back within that limit was to run the course again.

Every morning, the men exercised, ran the obstacle course, and gradually learned to march in unison. Every afternoon was spent in the classroom, learning more and more advanced reading, writing, and mathematics. The students had long since learned how to operate the computers and type their papers on the assigned subject. They learned a complete encyclopedia was contained in the computer and all they had to do to research a topic was to type in keywords about it. Robby was amazed at how much he was learning and astonished at how fast Willis progressed. He was now almost as good at reading and writing as Robby .

The social structure of the Brigade changed as well. By Christmas of 1770, the ranks were nearly filled with men recruited in the same way as Robby and Willis. There were more than 3000 men at Fort Independence. There were also 50 women, 200 blacks, and 100 Native Americans.

For months, the educational system was not only teaching men to be literate, but also educating them in the concept all men…including women were to be treated equally under God in the new nation. Racial and sex discrimination was absolutely not tolerated and the first of a handful of men not accepting this rang the bell and were escorted away from Fort Independence.

As Sergeant Boswell told them, "Only the best from the past."

Six men left the platoon, four quit, and two others were found to have medical issues allowing them to stay in the Brigade in various non-combat positions. The six replacements were four black men and two Cherokee Indians.

After a few weeks, it was amazing to see the newcomers no longer were seen as different, just fellow sufferers under the relentless barking of orders and endless physical exercise. The women in the ranks proved to be every bit as tough as the men.

The modern computer system being used by the students brought the illiterate blacks and Indians up to speed in short order. In fact, one of the black men proved to be so good at numbers he received training in advanced mathematics and was soon tutoring his fellow recruits who were struggling at the lower levels.

Sundays were always special. It was a day off in which all sorts of sporting events were held with teams who represented their platoons competing for week long bragging rights in soccer, basketball, track and field, and martial arts. This last competition was an extension of basic martial arts all recruits were learning.

But, Sunday was also a time for Church and was conducted in a non-denominational manner. Actually, it was a mixture of Evangelical and Pentecostal with a weekly communion thrown in. This was not the reason why the Brigade, who crowded into the big assembly hall serving as a church on Sunday, liked it. It was the Pastor of the church who held them spellbound each week with tremendous sermons on a variety of subjects, especially stories of Jesus and why he did the things he did and how those teachings were just as true today as they were 1800 years before.

Secretly, every man in the Brigade was in love with their Pastor. She was a tall, beautiful woman, about their age, with long flowing blond hair and the most amazing blue eyes. Her name was never far from the lips of the Brigade…Arcadia. She always wore a long, flowing white dress that looked almost like a robe with a silver belt. She was clad in this shining, shimmering dress from her neck to the floor and had long sleeves.

She was often seen walking through the Fort, watching the training, and was always on hand for the sporting events where she passed out the traveling trophies to each winning platoon. The men always bowed when they passed her, but spoke to her only when she spoke to them. In many ways, Arcadia became the symbol of the new America they were all training to achieve.

Chapter 21
The Net Is Thrown

<u>Mount Vernon, Virginia</u>

In the summer of 1772, Arcadia determined the time was right to begin turning Virginia into a non-slave state. Her first experiment with Jefferson at Monticello and with Washington at Mount Vernon proved to be unqualified successes. Both Jefferson and Washington believed the plan was, not only sound philosophically, but a very practical method for reorganizing labor.

Washington organized a lavish party and invited every large landowner in the colony. Since Washington was held in highest esteem by all of Virginia, everyone came early and stayed late. Since it was Washington's party, he was expected to establish the agenda of events and topics. He crafted the discussion with care. In the morning, the men discussed the current state of affairs with England and what should be done about it. Washington suggested it might be possible for the 13 colonies, acting in unison to establish an American nation. Since this was a popular belief among many of the wealthy landlords, it was fairly easy for Washington to move the conversation to the character of such a country, the concepts of government by the consent of governed, equality for all, the principle of every man being created equally, were all equally popular.

Then Washington, joined by Jefferson revealed what they had done to both carry out the principle of equality among men and remain profitable at the same time. They told about selling all their salves to a company called the Foundation, who emancipated them, and then offered all jobs as employees at the plantations. They talked about their successes in educating their former slaves, how much money they were making with the new system, the Emporiums for the purchase of a wide variety of products and food, and how much more productive the workers were when they were free and had a solid future for their families.

The landowners were fascinated with the revolutionary new idea and were especially intrigued with the idea of making more money while shedding the veneer of guilt caused by slavery in principle and treating people as property. They asked if it would be possible to speak to the head of this company, the Foundation and get further details.

Washington smiled, his new teeth glistening in the sun, "As a matter of fact, the President and the owner of The Foundation is present at the party. The reason you have not met this remarkable person, whose insight and intelligence I admire greatly, is because she is a woman."

"A women, in a position of such authority?" said one of the members of the numerous Lee families, "That seems rather unlikely."

"Elizabeth ruled England for over 50 years and turned it into the greatest power on Earth. Nobody thought it was strange or unlikely," answered Washington.

"Would it be possible for us to meet this remarkable woman, "said Henry Lee?

"Absolutely," said Washington. He sent one of the servants, to fetch Arcadia. Jefferson winked at Washington, knowing the trap slammed shut. It was unlikely many would be able to escape Arcadia's charm, and brilliant logic.

A few moments later, the servant returned with Arcadia on his arm. As she approached the group of men, they all stood. Many of them had seen Arcadia at the party, wondered who she was and secretly believed this was, by far, the most beautiful woman at the Mount Vernon Mansion.

Arcadia glided up in her white gown, with her long blond hair and crystal blue eyes. Her smile sparkled through the group of grinning men. "I gather," she said, "Mr. Washington and Mr. Jefferson have gloated to you about their fat purses and the relief of their consciences?"

That got a loud laugh from all the men. Someone set a chair for Arcadia and she began the process of altering the lives of all who lived in Virginia. She spoke for nearly an hour, answering questions and overcoming objections. When the debate was over, Arcadia spent over three million dollars, and purchased the lives of 200,000 human beings.

❖

This was a formula she would use for the next several years. Arcadia corresponded with many large slaveholders regarding the possibility of them doing what was done in Virginia. The movement began to catch on in other southern states With a fine sense of timing, Arcadia had her agents, find a man named Eli Whitney, and found out he was only six years old. She decided they couldn't wait until he grew up and invented the cotton gin. She knew the introduction of the cotton gin caused a huge increase in cotton production and the resulting importation of 600,000 more slaves from Africa. The work force needed to come from elsewhere, there were plenty of people in Mexico to fill the jobs, and the new technology would only help her in her providing labor from the Foundation. This new tool gave Arcadia a powerful weapon to use to convince southern slaveholders to switch to the better work system.

Between 1770 and 1775, Arcadia would emancipate over half the slaves in America. The alternative method of using labor in this fashion would ultimately take the heat out of the debate on slavery when the Second Continental Congress introduced the revised constitution in 1776.

Her Emporium empire blossomed with the increase in the number of stores. Arcadia had been right. Using the Wal-Mart concept of buying in large bulk, she reduced the costs in all the stores, sold her products to "employees" cheaper and still made money.

Since all of the original Colonial leaders attended the party and because they had not met for a while, Washington had them stay at Mt. Vernon and the next day they gathered in the dining room at Mount Vernon.

"We've all been busy with our projects," said Arcadia, "I know some of you have a lot of news to tell, so let's go around the table and get caught up."

Franklin seemed the most eager, so he went first. "Using the example of the small steel mill at the Fort, and with Arcadia's money, we are building a much bigger plant in Philadelphia. It will be powered by building a bigger generator driven by a bypass we dug off the river and run through pipes to dynamos. Using the plans of the steam locomotive we have, the plant is turning out the main parts of the machine. They're shipping the parts to Philadelphia. It is now nearly complete. Within a year, we will have both our steel plant and the means to build a rail line out of Philadelphia toward New York and on to Boston. We have managed to do all this right under the British noses. They have no idea what we are doing."

Jefferson spoke next, "Yesterday, Arcadia convinced all the slave holders in Virginia to use her plan for emancipating slaves. The system at both Monticello and here have proven it's a way of increasing profits and freeing slaves. I'm going to introduce a bill in the House of Burgesses to forbid any slave ships to enter any Virginia ports. It will reduce the importation of slaves considerably.

John Adams and James Madison reported they were working with the delegates they knew would be coming to the Second Continental Congress. "We have decided the First Congress should go ahead despite their ineffectiveness. They do solve some problems regarding western territories and the establishment of new states.

"However, the Second Congress in 1776 needs to pass the Declaration of Independence as well as pass the real constitution. We are lobbying these delegates to have a positive view of our plan," finished Madison.

Hamilton was next. "I've read modern economic theory and banking practices, and with the use of Arcadia's rather wonderful computers, I've been able to formulate budgets for the country over the next 50 years. I'm certain the institution of the income tax was and is a mistake. A flat tax on all income regardless of the entity, be it individual or company with no exceptions is the most fair and profitable system."

"Where do you intend to set the tax rate," asked Arcadia?

"I believe we can get along very nicely for the foreseeable future at 10 percent, the same as a church tithe. I estimate this rate will produce surpluses every year."

"And now, Mr. Washington," smiled Arcadia, "everyone is eager to hear about the remarkable progress you have achieved in building a brigade of Rangers."

"Arcadia is giving me entirely too much credit for the work at Fort Independence. However, we achieved a full complement of soldiers last year, which topped out at 3,879. Of those 337 are black,

146 are Native Americans and we have 63 women. After nearly a year of conditioning and education, we had 116 recruits quit, 37 of which were medicals and were reassigned to other duties. The rest are being held in our holding facility. They are reasonably happy. We treat them well, and even though they all say they would never tell anyone our secrets, they understand our hesitancy to take a chance."

"We have 100% literacy in both reading and writing. Most of our recruits are at levels near the same as ours. They are now studying history, science, and government. I have to say they are the best soldiers I've ever seen. They've done so well, we are planning to give them all a three-week furlough for the Christmas season at the end of next year. We don't see any problems with that. They've all been writing home with various cover stories about how they've been spending their time. I doubt we have a security problem. The men are paid so well, they have all been able to substantially help most of their families since all their basic needs are provided."

"Next year we are going to begin concentrating on martial arts training. This is basic hand-to-hand fighting, but it's nothing like you have ever seen before. The human being is a lethal weapon simply by existing."

Arcadia rose to her feet. "Gentlemen, we have only four years before the Revolution begins. It's important we let matters take their course as much as possible. The support of the people is critical to our success, and we won't have that until England starts to truly abuse the colonies. As difficult as it will be, both in hardships, and loss of life, we cannot release the Rangers until after July 4, 1776."

Afterwards, a lot is going to change. We have successfully integrated the force. Our blacks and Indians are treated no differently than anyone else. We want the entire country to be like that. We are already using our Indian soldiers to begin the process of successfully and peacefully integrating all the Native American population into our nation. We have already done a tremendous amount of damage to the tribes who lived along the east coast. We must not repeat that mistake as we move west."

"In a year or so we will start breaking the Brigade into its special units. One of those units will work its way west, north, and south. We need active agents in Canada and especially Mexico. They hate the Spanish, but we need some cohesion in the coup to throw them out and have the Mexican population want to join the United States. The same is true for Central America all the way to the Isthmus of Panama. We have some of our students learning Spanish and French."

Chapter 22
We Are So Different
Fort Independence, Virginia, Fall, 1772

Robby Pierce was in a reflective mood. He closed his laptop and looked over at his roommate Willis Grant.

"Willis, how long have we been here?"

"Sometimes it seems like I've never lived anywhere else."

"Exactly," said Robby. "We came to Fort Independence in September of 1770, two years ago. Does it seem like two years to you?"

Willis put down the book he was reading and stared away for a moment, thinking about it. "Come to think of it, I didn't realize it had been so long. We haven't really had much time to think about it. It's been a mad rush to finish the work every day"

"Sure, we've been busy, but that's not it. The cadre of permanent party here have transformed us into something entirely different. We aren't the same people who came here. We were just country boys who had no real idea of the world outside, I thought I was lucky to be able to read and write. You were barely literate. Now look at you, what book are you reading?

"Robinson Crusoe" said Willis.

"And what book before that?"

"I don't know, Paradise Lost, or one of the Shakespeare plays."

"What's the square root of 49?"

"It's 7, are you giving me a quiz?

"Not at all," said Robby, "but doesn't it seem amazing you can do these things."

"I guess it does. We sure do know more about just about everything, especially politics. I was reading one of Thomas

Jefferson's papers the other day and he makes a powerful argument for why the colonies should band together and form a new country. Before, I was just resentful of the British for the arrogant ways they treated us, now I know why they do what they do, and it's going to cost them everything they own in North America, the same is true for the French and the Spanish."

"And yet, even though we've seen some amazing technology, they still haven't shown us a single modern weapon."

"Speak for yourself," said Willis, "I think of myself as a weapon. The advanced martial arts, Judo, Karate, and the rest of it, we've been taught this last year makes me feel I could defeat any man, armed or not."

"You are better at it than most," said Robby, "Almost better than me, but we still never been able to take down the Black Ninja."

"Nobody has," that guy comes up with moves beyond belief."

"But then he helps you up and shows you what he did."

"It's the way I get better."

"You remember when we were tested and had to run a mile? I was giving it everything I had to make it in less than eight minutes."

"Since you are smaller than me," said Willis, you could always run faster. What was your time on the ten mile run the other day?

"Just under 55 minutes."

"See, I haven't been able to break the 60 minute barrier."

"And yet we both weigh a lot more than we did when we came here."

"Well, what's the point of all this," asked Willis?

"We are better men than we could ever have been in Concord. It's like Arcadia tells us, God has transformed our bodies, and our minds. I trust and honor every person at the Fort. My heart is filled with love for God, you, and all our comrades, and I believe our surrender to His will has made us what we are."

"I would accept that as axiomatic truth."

"See, two years ago you didn't have a particle of an idea of what an axiom is."

"All I know is it's going to take another four years to complete our training and turn us into the super army they say we're going to be. I can't imagine what that's going to mean, but I'll say one thing. Even though we have a wonderful life here, I would still like to go home for just a little while."

"We both write all the time. Your father says your training must be pretty good, because your letters are getting so much better and interesting."

"I don't like not being able to tell them what we're really training for here."

"None of us do, but all of us recognize the need for secrecy. Also, we are making life a lot better for our families because of all the money we send home."

"Amazing isn't it, we write a draft for our pay and send it home and our folks make the trip to Boston once a month to pick up the money in real silver."

The conversation the men had that night seemed like someone was reading their mind. The following morning, an announcement came over the speaker there would be a general assembly of the Brigade in the theatre after breakfast. All 3600 men and women crowded into the big assembly hall normally used for church every week.

General Washington walked out onto the stage, and the entire brigade immediately came to attention. "At ease, men," said Washington, "Please take your seats."

"All of you, have been training here at Fort Independence for two years. I want you to know my staff and I are very proud of the progress you have made. We have made scholars of you all. You now have the equivalent of a college education. This was necessary because of the rather advanced training commencing at the beginning of next year. At that time, we are going to break up the training platoons and start assigning you to the jobs you will have when the brigade takes the field in about 42 months. We will begin the year by supplying each of you with your personal weapons. After you have become thoroughly proficient with these, we intend to begin training you with some of the more complicated equipment, such as the artillery pieces, and the big motorized vehicles locked up in storage for the past two years. During the next year, many of you will be leaving Fort Independence for advanced field exercises and other missions we will explain when the time comes. A few of you will also learn to fly the helicopters you already have seen. There are a number of other specialized jobs we will assign, based on your skill levels in the training you have already had."

"As of now you are already the best educated, most physically fit army in the world. When we add the new equipment and skills, you will be invincible."

Because of the many hours of hard work and dedication all of you have shown, we believe you deserve a break. Beginning the first week in December and continuing through the New Year, all of you will be given a furlough, so you can go home and see your families."

There was a stunned silence in the hall for a few seconds and then a huge outburst of cheering and applause. Washington let the men enjoy the moment and then held up his hands again for attention.

"I don't need to tell you our mission to remove all European powers from North America remains the greatest secret in history. You have all established cover stories concealing your activities over the past two years. Make sure you stick to them and don't take the chance of exposing your families to danger by telling them information the enemy could use.

For the men whose homes are nearby, we will provide horses for you to get home. For the men who have come from long distances, such as Massachusetts and other New England colonies, we will use our Chinooks to transport you to central locations from which you can make it home. These flights will all be at night and use the whisper mode of the choppers to avoid attention. We have men on the ground at these locations to insure you get in and out unnoticed."

"I'm afraid you will have to wear civilian clothes. Our uniforms are unusual and the British have been growing more and more suspicious of anyone who seems out of place. We will provide you with suitable clothing to match the kind of dress you came to us in. Happily this clothing is specially made and you will be far more comfortable than the heavy, clothing you wore before."

"You must avoid any confrontations with British soldiers. Only if you or a comrade is in danger of being captured or killed, may you use lethal force, and it must be covered up completely."

"We'll provide you all with an extra two month's pay for your furlough. I'm sure you'll find many reasons to spend it on your families for Christmas."

"You are all to report back here, ready for hard work, on January 3rd. This furlough will likely be the last time off you will have until after our mission is accomplished. I don't recommend any of you take a wife or a husband during the holidays."

"We still have three weeks before your furloughs begin. We'll spend the time with some new education and a great deal of personal combat, so don't start letting up until you actually leave the Fort. We are giving you this advance notice so you can write your families to expect you."

"That's all men, I believe you have loafed around long enough for one day. A whistle blew and the Brigade snapped to attention. "Dismissed," said Washington.

After the men left the auditorium, Robby and Willis found Charlie Arthur walking slowly along with his head down. "Hey Charlie, aren't you excited about our furlough," asked Robby.

"Not much. You see, I'm an orphan, I don't have a family to go home too, and the friends I had are not the most reputable people in Boston."

"Guess we're going to have to adopt you," said Willis. "You can come home with us and we'll be your family."

"Really!" said Charlie, "That would be wonderful. Thank you so much."

"It's the least we can do for a fellow Ranger," said Robby.

Chapter 23
Home For Christmas

Concord, Massachusetts, December 1772

The Chinook was jammed full. It let down in the same little meadow the men left from two years before. Robby, Willis and Charlie, jumped off the rear ramp of the hovering Chinook and so did everyone else. The helicopter was gone in the wink of an eye. It made very little noise to wake anyone up in the middle of the night.

Robby hitched up his pants and tucked in his shirt. He couldn't believe he used to wear such clothing. At least he was wearing his boots. It was very cold. After all, this was winter in New England. All three buttoned up their heavy coats and wrapped the scarfs around their necks. They wore warm cotton stocking caps that could be covered with the hood of the coats, and they wore insulated gloves with chemical heat liners sewn into fabric. They all had shoulder bags filled with spare clothing and personal items. All the men were permitted to wear their long knives and each had a canister of mace. Willis had snuck in his garrote.

They made their way through the short forest and out to the frozen road taking them to Concord. "It's about 20 miles," said Robby. "If we walk and jog, we can be home before sundown tonight."

They walked briskly and jogged, making good time as the sun came up. It was still cold, but the sun was warm on their faces. As they walked along in high spirits, a couple of horsemen came into view ahead. As they grew closer, Robby could see they were British soldiers by their red coats. "I wonder what those soldiers are doing out here so early," said Robby.

"Can't be anything but trouble," said Willis.

The horsemen grew closer and Robby thought they were going to just keep going when one of them pulled his horse to a stop and said,

"What are you men doing out so early in the morning."

"We had business in Boston and left early so we could be home before tonight," said Robby.

"And what business was that," snarled one of the British soldiers. Sneaking around for some secret meeting."

Robby smiled, "Nothing of the sort. We only went to Boston on some family business."

"Nobody travels in a gang like yours in the middle of the winter, unless they're up to no good," said the soldier.

"We aren't a gang," said Willis, "we are friends keeping each other company and minding our own business."

"Don't get uppity with me, kid," growled the soldier. He turned to the other and said, "Maybe we should take these boys along to quarters and find out what they know."

The three spread out to have one on each side of the soldiers and one in the middle.

"Sorry, we can't go anywhere with you," said Robby, "Our families are expecting us."

One of the soldiers reached down for the flintlock pistol in his belt. The three Rangers acted instinctively. Charlie smacked both horses hard across their muzzles and both reared up of their front feet. Robby and Willis snatched the men from their horses and threw them to the ground, minus their hand weapons. Both soldiers started to struggle to their feet, grabbing at their swords. They never got them out of their scabbards. The Rangers countered with several hand chops, foot kicks and twisting tosses throwing the soldiers over their shoulders and on their knees. With quick dispatch, Robby and Willis snapped the two Red Coat's necks. The entire encounter took less than ten seconds.

Quickly the three Rangers pulled the dead British into a low swale off the road and used their knives to cut limbs from trees, adding piles of rocks and leaves to conceal the bodies.

"What do we do with the horses," asked Willis?

"We can't take them home. Someone might recognize them," said Robby.

Charlie picked up some stones and threw them at the rear of the horses and they both went galloping away, back toward Boston.

"Let's get out of here, before someone else comes along," said

Robby, and began a loping trot down the road. The other two followed and they ran at least three miles before, Robby called a halt. "Now we can go back to being common farmers on our way home to Concord. We're close enough now we shouldn't attract any more attention, and we might see some people we know."

"Nothing of this can be told our families," said Willis, "They can't confess something they don't know no matter who questions them."

"Agreed," said Robby.

"Training sure comes in handy," said Charlie, "It works just like we practice it, except for the broken neck part."

It was early afternoon when the three, arrived in Concord. They crossed the square to the home and shop of Robby's father, who was a wagon maker. He called out loudly, "Anybody Home?" The whole family came running out the front door. They descended on their son and hugged and kissed him to pieces. Willis got much the same treatment, and Charlie was greeted equally as warmly when he was introduced as a comrade in arms, with no family.

Robby's father held his son by the shoulders and looked at his squarely. "Why you've come back a man. You must weigh 30 pounds more and it all looks like muscle. Have you actually grown an inch or two? Anyway, son, you look wonderfully fit and in good health."

His mother just clung to her son and cried tears of joy, while Robby's two other brothers, one older and one younger, and three sisters, all-younger, hugged him as best they could.

"We have more room than the Grant's," said Robby, "could Charlie stay with us?"

"Of course," said Mother Grant, you are more than welcome, Charlie."

"I'm most grateful, Mrs. Grant, "Thank you for your hospitality."

"If you don't mind," said Willis, "I'm kind of anxious so see my family, so I'll run along as see you later."

Everybody said welcome home, best wishes to Willis' family and they would all get together soon. Willis smiled and headed out, trotting for his home a mile away.

Robby found himself sitting at the family table with everyone firing questions at him. He held up his hands and laughed. "I'll be here for three weeks, we have plenty of time for all your questions. I'm just so glad to see you all. Haven't you been getting my letters, they tell pretty much everything we're doing.

"Of course, we get your letters," said his mother. "I have to say they've changed a great deal over the last two years. The education you talk about receiving must be doing some good. I find myself going to the dictionary to look up some of the words you use."

"I'm receiving a first class education, Mother. Our commanders say when we are finished, we'll know more than a Harvard graduate.

Robby's older brother chimed in, "When you left you were sort of a beanpole, a little skinny and scrawny. Now I find myself a little afraid to say that to you, because you have filled out so much and seem so fit."

That got a general laugh, and Robby said, "There is nothing in my heart for you, brother, or any of you, but love, respect and honor. I'm proud to be part of our family."

"He's gotten polite too," said his father.

"General Washington would be very upset with me if I weren't."

"You mean George Washington, asked his father? You actually know Mr. Washington?"

"He's our commanding officer."

As soon as he said it, Robby regretted it. In his excitement, he let slip a piece of his story that should have remained unspoken. He recovered and asked, "Tell me all the news of Concord."

"It's a grim story, son, the British continue to abuse and insult us, as if they were the masters and we the servants. Just yesterday, two Red Coats came to town and summarily ordered us all to meet in the church. There they told us King George is not at all pleased with the behavior of his subjects in the colonies and Parliament is considering a number of new measures to insure our compliance with their directives. I spoke directly to the officer and asked him why we should comply with laws over which we had no part in formulating."

"What did he say to that," asked Robby?

"He said it was that kind of impertinence which had caused the King to send 5,000 more troops to Boston, to insure we understand the King's mind. Then he ordered me to build a new wagon without a mention of being paid for my work."

"When does he expect this wagon to be done?

"He said before the first of the year."

Robby thought furiously. The Red Coats his father had mentioned could not be any other than the very ones he'd killed hours before. They had stripped the bodies, taken the weapons, and what money the men were carrying to make it look like the men were attacked by a larger group of men, or even Indians, in a robbery. When they did not report back or the horses returned, a search party would go looking for them. It might take days to find the bodies. Still there were many people present and the appearance of the Red Coats in Concord would be known, along with the order to build the wagon, so they could not say the men had never come to town.

Undoubtedly, more soldiers would come to Concord to make inquiries. They had no reason to suspect anyone in Concord had done the killing. Robby could not say anything about the incident. However, he could help his father build the wagon. Taking care of the equipment at the Fort was a part of a Ranger's duty and he'd worked on their wagons fairly often.

"I can help you build the wagon, Father. Repairing wagons is one of my regular duties at the Fort."

Eventually, Robby told his entire story of life at the Fort and their preparations for taking a force of men into the wilderness to explore the lands to the west and to make contact with the native tribes to learn if trade could be established. He said map-making, recording their findings and being able to put it all down on paper was an important part of the process, so that was why the education was so thorough. He also pointed out pioneering was extremely labor- intensive work, so the entire command had to be hardened and made as fit as possible before they set out. He bragged about the careful preparations and how they would certainly spell success for the enterprise. It was a completely plausible cover story and no one in the family doubted it.

When they were alone, Robby's father remarked, "Your expedition organizers must be very wealthy men, to gather over 200 men, educate them, feed and house them and still pay them so much money. I must say, son, it's a very large benefit to this family to be able to take your draft to Boston every month and receive 2 pounds, 2 shillings in Sterling. I'm most grateful."

"I'm glad it eases the life of the family and makes your cares less, father."

"It does that. Your mother has things other families in Concord don't because of the extra income you provide. We are careful not to let it show."

The first Sunday Robby was home, the entire family went to church and he was warmly welcomed by the entire community. Charlie was generally adopted as well. Robby had never seen Charlie so happy. At the service, the pastor of the Congregationalist church asked Robby if he would come to the pulpit and tell some of the religious principles taught at the Fort. Robby had not expected anything of the kind, so he repeated one of his favorite passages from one of Arcadia's sermons.

"Jesus Christ is Lord," said Robby, "to me Jesus is saying, make me your focal point as you move through this day. Just as a spinning ballerina must keep returning her eyes to a given point to maintain her balance, so you must keep returning your focus to Me. Circumstances are in flux, and the world seems to be whirling around you. The only way to keep your balance is to fix your eyes on Me, the one who never changes. If you gaze too long at your circumstances, you will become dizzy and confused. Look to Me, refreshing yourself in My presence, and your steps will be steady and sure."

This seemed to make sense to the congregation, even though they had never heard it quite that way. In general, Robby's remarks were seen as refreshing and certainly devout. His family smiled proudly at him.

Charlie joined with Robby to build the wagon. They incorporated a number of improvements to the overall design, particularly with the wheels. Robby packed in a thick layer of grease filled with ball bearings he had constructed in his father's forge, using shotgun buckshot molds to make the ball bearings. He also put an extra layer of springs under the axels to make the wagon ride easier, and made the seats more like bucket seats for comfort. The two of them built the entire wagon in two days and nights while Robby's father was helping a neighbor with his harvest.

When his father returned and found a new wagon sitting in the yard, he was amazed. He was even more astonished at how much more comfortable the wagon was and how smoothly the wheels turned, making the job of pulling the wagon easier for the horses and increasing the effective daily range of the wagon.

"They certainly have taught you some practical improvements in wagon making, said Robby's father. " I hate to hand this beauty over to the British."

"Don't worry father, most of the improvements they could not do on their own and they would never take the wheels apart to find the ball bearings. However, others will come to know of your better wagon and you can make more and charge more. Let me run through the improvements with you, so you can make them on your own."

On Christmas day, Robby pulled out all the things he brought for his family. For his mother he gave a large plastic bottle of dishwashing soap, and a very concentrated box of laundry detergent. For each member of the family he gave a large bar of sweet-smelling, long-lasting hand soap. For his father Robby gave the proceeds of the dollar each month he had held back for 24 months. It amounted to almost 10 pounds sterling, a huge amount for that time. Before anyone had gotten up Robby and Charlie hid silver shillings in places all over the house, and when the family rose, he sent them all on a big treasure hunt. It was a wonderful highlight for the day.

Robby knew Willis had done much the same for his family, and for them it was an even bigger benefit, for the Grant family who did not enjoy all the luxuries of the Pierce household.

In the final days of his visit, it was Robby's mother who almost blew his cover. On afternoon when the two of them were alone in the kitchen, chatting, Robby's mother, whose sharp mind he'd always admired, said to him, "Robby, my guess is there are a great many things you have withheld from us. You must know the circumstances under which you are living, the wondrous things you've brought, which do not exist in any other place I know of, and must be part of something much bigger and more important than you have told. It's almost as if rich, incredibly advanced foreigners had come to these colonies for the purpose of helping you throw off the mantle of the British.

"I do not ask you to break trust and explain any of these wonders to me, just know I know they exist, and believe they are for good and not evil. I also know your duties will eventually put you in harm's way. In those moments, may the Lord be with you, and return you to me."

"You must not speak your suspicions to anyone, mother. I beg you and ask your word what has been said will not be repeated."

"I promise, Robert."

"In that case, I will tell you one thing. You are much closer to the truth than you know. However, in due course, everyone will know, and on that day you will rejoice."

For the young Rangers, the goodbyes were tearful and also joyful. The three companions left on a cold January morning and walked back to their rendezvous point.

Late that night, they were home again in their warm rooms and comfortable beds at Fort Independence.

Chapter 24
Arming The Rangers
Fort Independence, Virginia

Just as promised, the training intensified after the Christmas furlough of 1772. For the first time, the soldiers were issued their basic weapons. Robby expected something different, but could not have imagined what he got.

The first thing issued were helmets fitting snugly on their heads because of the liner, and were shaped to cover down to the ears. The next thing the soldiers got was body armor. It took some time to get used to wearing it, since it covered their entire upper torsos and had flaps extending to their necks.

Now fully equipped in battle dress, the soldiers were run through relentless drills and obstacle courses until they were as fast as they had been without the armor and helmets and the equipment felt as if they had worn it forever.

"I guarantee this equipment will save your life," said Sergeant Boswell. "Let me demonstrate." Another sergeant came forward with a standard British musket. Boswell walked over to Robby and handed him the musket. "You're the best shot in the brigade, so I'm counting on you to hit where I say," said Boswell. The sergeant walked about 100 feet away and turned around. "OK, Pierce," he said, "put one right in my heart."

"You must be joking," said Robby.

"Not at all," said Boswell, "just don't miss."

Robby raised the musket, cocked it and aimed at Boswell's heart. He fired. There was the usual amount of smoke from the musket, and when it cleared, Robby saw Boswell, climbing up off the ground.

"Gather around," he said. The musket ball hit dead center in the heart of Boswell's armor. He peeled off the armor and showed the musket ball stuck in the Kevlar. "It stings a little," said Boswell, but I could stand here all day and nothing the British fired would kill me, as long as if it weren't a cannon ball from the same distance," he grinned. "This equipment makes you guys awfully hard to kill."

Next was the issue of the weapons for the Rangers.

"Men," said Sergeant Boswell, "This is the M-16A1 Assault Rifle, with the M-203 grenade launcher. It is a shoulder mounted, gas operated, selective fire, magazine fed weapon with a 30 round magazine. It fires a 5.56 mm round with a range of 600 yards. The rate of fire for this weapon is 600 rounds per minute. The M203 grenade launcher fires a 40 mm explosive of various types and is used instead of a standard grenade. Its effective range is 200 yards. The weight of this weapon is 8 pounds.

For the next week, the men were trained to take the weapon apart and reassemble it blindfolded. This was to maintain effectiveness of the weapon by keeping it clean. The practice of sighting and clicking the rifle went on for hours. To Robby, the weapon seemed like a toy. It was so much shorter and lighter than the long muskets he had grown up using.

Finally, the men were marched to the rifle range and set up in long lines in front of targets placed 50, 100, and 200 yards apart. Sergeant Boswell explained, "The M-16 has two firing settings. The first one will fire a round every time you pull the trigger, which is what we will use here. The second is fully automatic. What this means is before your first spend cartridge-casing hits the ground, your 30th round is already headed downrange.

When it came, Robby's turn to shoot, the instructor laid down next to him on the ground and said, "Just relax, sight the target down the barrel and centered between the aiming notches at the end of the barrel. Don't jerk the trigger just squeeze it, like you were milking a cow. I want you to fire five rounds at each of targets, starting with the nearest one. I am going to help you get your rifle sighted in with the use of these binoculars. After we do that, you will fire again to make sure we have set up the rifle properly.

Robby aimed down the barrel at the near target, remembering his father's advice from the time he was a boy, "Aim small, miss small."

He squeezed off the first five rounds. The weapon did not kick as much as a musket, nor was it as loud and there was no smoke at all. The instructor looked through his scope, and shook his head, "Very nice shooting, son. Your shot pattern is not more than two inches wide. Try again with the middle target." Robby switched to the target 100 yards away, and pulled the trigger five times. One again, the instructor looked at the pattern through his scope. "You're shooting straight, try the far target." Robby looked at the target 200 yards away. He had killed dear from this range, so he relaxed and shot his five rounds in rapid succession. The Instructor looked through the scope and whistled, "Your shot pattern is still only about two inches apart. It looks like you're a natural."

The instructor took the rifle and showed Robby how to click the dials on the front of the rifle to correct for the tendency of the rifle to shoot off the bull's-eye. Then he had Robby replace this magazine and shoot at the targets again. When he was finished, instructor looked through his scope. "Wonderful shooting, son, every round at all distances are inside the bulls-eye circle. I guess you grew up handling a rifle.

"Yes sir," said Robby, "I had to go out and shoot dinner for the family when I was younger. My father only gave me two musket balls, since that was all we could afford. If I missed, both shots, the family had no meat that day."

"Well, you're a sure-enough dead eye shooter. Looks like you will have a special assignment in your rifle platoon."

"What's that," asked Robby?

"Sniper," said the instructor.

Willis shot almost as well in his test and the two found themselves assigned to headquarters platoon of company A of the 2nd Battalion of the Ranger brigade. They would go where the company commander ordered them to go to do their jobs. Both men were issued new weapons. They were called the M-4 Sniper rifle, and you had to turn the bolt for each round. It was twice the size of the assault rifles. The barrels were considerably longer and the weapon was a little heavier.

They were taken out to a special firing range and practiced for days shooting targets as far as 1000 yards away. Robby was even able to hit a target dead on at a mile. Their weapons were brown and wrapped with camouflage fabric to keep them from shining in the light. The men also received special coverings to wear over their uniforms, called ghillie suits. When they wore them, they were all but invisible, lying in the grass or in a forest.

Now, as planned, the training platoons were broken up. Robby and Willis went with the majority of the troops to the ground assault platoons and their new positions as snipers in headquarters platoon of Company A. They moved to a new barracks building for Company A. The rooms were the same, and so the adjustment was minimal.

Charlie Arthur was assigned to the Artillery battery. The artillery battery began training in firing the 105 mm Howitzers. Each had a crew of eight, plus a fire direction center, which trained, both by computer, and manually how to find targets, read the maps, and direct accurate fire. The entire Brigade got a demonstration of what the Howitzers could do. They stood on a hill overlooking a valley outside the Fort and watched as the 105's shot rounds from 7 miles away, hit their targets of old wagons and even small barrels with perfect accuracy. The destruction the Howitzers could inflict was a sobering experience for all.

Now the big garages were unlocked and the Rangers saw, for the first time the "horses" that would carry them into battle. The Humvees and the Bradleys' were rolled out and instructors carefully trained the operators of the vehicles. The Humvees were the easiest to learn. They were just big trucks, but it took two months to train the crew of three to effectively operate and accurately fire the weapons on the Bradleys.

The men of the Ranger Brigade were learning everything their leaders had told them about being the most lethal fighting force in the world was completely true. As the machine guns, the flamethrowers, the grenades, both hand held and rocket propelled, and the rest of the weapons came rolling out, the men believed nothing could make them better. They were wrong.

At companies all over the brigade, the sergeants were bringing out one final piece of equipment. It was small, merely a headset fitting into the helmets, and had a small microphone attached to it. The men put them on and clicked a button on the side. Instantly they heard Sergeant Bowell speaking to them in their headsets. "If you need to transmit a message of your own, you reach up and push the button at the front of the radio. Everyone did that, and the din of overlapping voices was unrecognizable. "As you can see, gentlemen," said Sergeant Boswell, "the radios should only be used when you have something to say. These radios are set on a frequency to talk to everyone in the company. Further, up the chain of command, the radios are more complicated. They can talk to all of the companies and all you men at the same time. It makes it so much easier to move you from one place to another without trumpets, flags or smoke signals. In fact, the General can speak to just one of you, individually, if he wants too."

Sergeant Boswell had the whole company together, 200 men. "Now we come to the battle tactics we will employ. He took his pointer and pointed it at a screen of a British Army and the way they were organized. "As you can see, the cannons are at the rear or sides, the command center, the officers running the battle are in the rear, in a high place where they can see their army in front of them. The soldiers march in long ranks with their artillery shooting in front of them. The opposing army is organized the same. Each has a cavalry of horses to sweep down from the flanks and break up the lines.

"The armies march toward each other until they are within musket range, then they stand there shooting at each other until one of the armies breaks and retreats. This is the way all armies fight.

"Now watch what we're going to do. The simulation changed to show the Bradley's alone in the center and advancing. "Artillery, from a much further distance, than British cannons fire into the enemy ranks. At the same time, the Humvees and our troops emerge onto the battlefield from all sides, including the rear. They simply advance, making the circle smaller and smaller until all the Red Coats are dead or have surrendered. Our snipers will have worked into a position before the engagement, and when the shooting starts they kill the commanding officer and all his staff, one by one."

"Scratch one British Army. If we do this, two or three times, there will no longer by any more Red Coats to fight. The war is over, and we are free to move on to our other objectives, Quebec and Canada will be first, than we move into Mexico and Central America and conquer the Spanish. We estimate in about three years we will have subdued the entire North American continent, including the islands of the Caribbean and established the United States of America. Then we announce to the world the United States is open for business to anyone who wants to trade with us, and to anyone who wants to emigrate here, and declare our strict neutrality to any foreign conflicts."

The Rangers trained in tactics, deployment and the coordination of their forces for the entire year of 1773. It was not all field training. Large blocks of time were devoted to learning a detailed geography of North America, the location of principal foreign strongholds throughout the continent and in the islands of the Caribbean. They also were given detailed instruction on the indigenous Native American tribes scattered throughout the continent. Plans were drawn up to send small units of soldiers into these areas and establish peaceful relations with all the tribes and designate places where they would be able to establish their own singularity after giving them the full resources of the U.S. government to allow them to adapt to new ways of living by cooperation, rather than confrontation.

One of the new skills, Robby and Willis learned was fluency in Spanish as well as a complicated sign language system that could be used to communicate with Indian tribes. Their training in Martial Arts intensified. Not a single day, except Sunday had less than a twelve-hour work schedule.

There came a day in the spring of 1774, when a competition was held to determine the most proficient marital arts champion in the brigade. Excitement was high for each platoons champion. A field of 64 men were selected and put in brackets matching the best with the least and so forth, to insure some fluke of competition did not knock out the top seeds. Robby was one of the four top seeds, and began working his way through the brackets.

There were some significant surprises as some of the lower seeds knocked off men who were supposedly better, but weren't on that day, either through great heart or pure guts on the part of their opponent. It even happened to one of the top seeds who were upset by a ninth seed in the third round. The field grew smaller and smaller and Robby found himself in the final four. He won the match and advanced to the finals where he actually won easily.

As he was holding his trophy aloft and being mobbed by his platoon, the ranks parted and into the circle strode the dreaded black ninja. Nobody knew who this was. His face was covered by a black scarf that fit closely and had only small holes for eyes and mouth. The Black Ninja was the supreme teacher of all the men of the brigade. None had ever been hurt, at least not badly, but there was no question this fighter was the best by far.

The Black Ninja stepped into the competition circle, bowed low to Robby and then rushed across the ring in full attack. The battle went on for a long time. Robby's technique against the speed and guile of the Black Ninja. Finally, in one furious exchange, both combatants found themselves on the ground with a fatal lock on each other. Amazing as it seemed, the contest was a tie.

The two carefully disengaged and rose to their feet. Robby bowed as did the Black Ninja. Then the dark warrior did something completely unexpected. He removed his black scarf to reveal his actual identity. There was a gasp through the crowd and cries of surprise. The "He," was a "She." Standing in front of Robby was none other than the spiritual leader of them all. Her long blond hair untangled from the bun enclosing it and cascaded down her shoulders.

Arcadia turned and looked at the astonished faces, "It has been my honor to serve you all these years. Now the time is coming when we will change history. Since this is the case, if we must fight, we fight. Congratulations, Robby, you are the best of us all."

The men listened to Arcadia speak from the pulpit every Sunday for years. She was always dressed in her shimmering white gown/dress. She glided through the camp and could be seen often at many of the events and exercises. She was held in the highest possible respect and honor by every person at the Fort. They spoke to her only when she spoke to them. She was their angel. Now they realized she was also their greatest warrior and hundreds of them had battled with her as if she were nothing but another opponent. Robby was the first to bow deeply again, and then to applaud. He was soon joined by the entire brigade and the true bond, which was Arcadia's purpose in the first place was now complete.

Chapter 25
The Sioux Nation
The Black Hills, South Dakota, Summer, 1774

The Great Plains were giving way to the lovely forest and steep escarpments of the Black Hills. This was heart of the Sioux nation and its many allied tribes throughout the center of the country from the Missouri to the Rocky Mountains.

Robby and Willis were filled with wonder and fascination as the big Chinook hopscotched across the country. Not only were they caught up by the dark forests giving way to endless plains after they crossed the big Missouri River, but they were completely in awe of the millions and millions of huge buffalo thundering in clouds of dust for miles and miles.

The whole trip was a dream-like adventure. Following the martial arts competition, Arcadia sent for Robby. He went to the administration building and was escorted deep into it, to places he didn't realize existed. At last, the escort came to a stop in front of a door and gently knocked, "Come!" was the response, and Robby entered the holy of holies, the office of Arcadia. She was standing in front of a row of monitors covering half the room. She was not wearing her familiar dress, but a pair of tight pants and a floppy sweater.

"Welcome to information central," she said brightly. "Have a seat." Robby said down almost on the edge of the chair. "Just relax Robby," said Arcadia, "you would think I was mad at you or something for fighting so well yesterday. To tell you the truth, I'm proud of you. That was some quick thinking last year when you took out those Red Coats. You covered your tracks very well, and the people of Concord were never suspected in the incident. It was written off as an assault and robbery by persons of ill-repute."

Robby wasn't sure how Arcadia knew so much about the incident. They had reported it, of course, when they returned, but nobody had mentioned it since.

"I see from your records," said Arcadia consulting a computer screen you made a shot from almost a mile. That's good shooting."

"Thank you, ma'am" said Robby.

"Please call me Arcadia. I have a special mission I've been planning for a while, and I wonder if you might like to help me do it."

"Anything, I can do to help, Arcadia," said Robby.

"Do you believe all men are created equal and are endowed by their creator with rights from God including life, liberty and the pursuit of happiness?"

"I do believe that."

"Would you say this applies to all people, no matter their race or social situation?"

"I'm opposed to slavery, if that's what you mean," said Robby firmly.

"Yes, of course, but did you know there are almost as many Native Americans living on this continent as there are colonists?"

"No," said Robby in surprise.

"There are millions of people and God will not honor us for having this opportunity to change history for the better, if we did not include these people. If we do nothing, all but about 100,000 of them are going to be killed, driven from their ancestral lands, and reduced to poverty and misery in the future."

"That's tragic," said Robby.

"It's something we're going to keep from happening. You know we recruited several hundred Native Americans into the Rangers. We attempted to get representatives from as many different tribes as possible. On their holiday furlough, we sent these men home and had them assume personalities inspired by the deities they worship who told their people the truth of their fates if they do not alter their lifestyles. We sent some pretty convincing technology with them. When they reported back, we found they were successful in changing the key elements of their societies to allow them to co-exist with the white majority headed their way, or who has already clashed disastrously with the white settlers who have moved in. Right now, our

Cherokee Rangers are talking to the big Cherokee nation in the south to attempt to do the same. Which brings me to our mission, there are about a million people living out in the plains. The largest and most influential groups of these are the great Sioux nation, principally the Lakota Sioux. I'm going out there and make contact with them in an effort to ease their society onto a new path. In addition to being a little dangerous, I'm going to need some men who have already proved to be cool under fire, and possess skills I may need. So the question is, would you and Willis like to come with me to visit these people?"

Robby's head was spinning. Over the years, he'd become accustomed to absorbing new and strange concepts and equipment, but this expedition was simply beyond anything he had ever imagined. He was excited by the prospect and honored Arcadia had chosen him. "I would be very happy to help you," he said.

"Wonderful," said Arcadia. "Get with Willis and brief him on what we've discussed. We'll be leaving the day after tomorrow. I've made arrangements for the special equipment you need to bring along. You already have your rifle, Report to the quartermaster, and pick up 200 more rounds of ammunition. He's working on your packs."

Robby ran to find Willis and tell him the exciting news. Then they both went to the big supply building and reported to the quartermaster. He seemed ready for them.

"Heading out with Arcadia, I see. Well, here are your packs. We tried to keep them manageable but they're still a load."

Robby estimated the pack weighed at least 40 pounds. He shouldered it with an effort.

They spent the next two days studying the geography of the plains and the customs of the Lakota Sioux.

Early in the morning, they reported to the airstrip where a big Chinook helicopter was waiting for them. When they looked inside, they found a Humvee, and one of the four-wheel ATV's the brigade used for scouting the terrain in rough country. There were also two other men, in the Chinook, obviously Indians. Robby and Willis knew them both as trained medics. They slapped hands with Magua and Chistauk and were glad to see them along on the trip. They were good men, reliable and smart.

The trip across half the continent took three days. Robby learned from the crew the helicopter would cruise at about 150 miles per hour and had a range of about 300 miles. This meant the helicopter had to stop for refueling about every two hours. He asked Arcadia how the fuel got there.

"You have our friend Ben Franklin to thank for that. He's been working on a number of big projects since we arrived. One of them was to take a crew out to western Pennsylvania and drill an oil well. Using our design he built a refinery and started turning out fuel to run all of our vehicles."

"In advance of this mission, and others like it, he's constructed a number of steel fuel tanks and placed them at strategic locations along our flight route. They are filled with diesel and aviation gas for us to refuel. It was a very big job and took years to finish. It's why our mission could not start until now. Don't worry, we have a healthy reserve."

Arcadia was looking at some very detailed pictures of the land. They were obviously taken from the air. "Did you take these pictures on a previous scouting mission," asked Robby.

"No, we've never been here before," said Arcadia.

"Then where did these pictures come from," asked Robby?

Arcadia looked squarely at Robby, "In the time you have been training as a Ranger, you have come into contact with many new, wondrous things. You know what a computer is, you know what a video is, you know we fly in great machines, and make war with weapons beyond anything you could have even imagined. Where do suppose all this came from?"

"A gift of God," ventured Robby?

"That's a good answer. It's true none of what we're doing could be anything except by authority of our God. I will tell you the truth Robby, but it is for your ears only. None of the colonial Rangers knows the 'why and how' of how we are doing all this. Do I have your sworn oath you will not repeat what I am about to tell you to any other living person?"

"I swear," said Robby.

"Don't be so fast, Robert, said Arcadia seriously. She handed him a small packet. "Inside this plastic covering is a pill of poison. It will kill you in about a minute. The information you are asking for is secret and must not be known by anyone outside the brigade. I carry such a pill, as does all the permanent party at the Fort. Even George

Washington has one. If you are captured by any of our enemies, they will torture you to tell them what you know. Every person has a breaking point, and we cannot permit our secrets from falling into any other hands. In such event, you are expected to take your own life to protect the information. Now do you still want to know, or are you just going to continue to be a good soldier and watch the events play themselves out."

Arcadia was quiet as she held out the pill packet to Robby. She was looking him straight in the eyes.

"I choose to remain loyal to you and to continue to do my duty as you order it to the best of my ability."

"I knew I'd chosen the right man for this mission, Sergeant," laughed Arcadia putting the pill back in her pocket. Six other men have figured out at least as much as you have and I made them all the same offer. None of them accepted."

"Did you say Sergeant?" asked Robby.

"We promote our best as soon as we can. Your many skills and your good sense means you deserve promotion as well."

"Thank you very much, Arcadia," said Robby, "I will try to deserve the honor you have shown me." He paused and then said, "All right, what do we see here?" pointing to the pictures.

"These are the Great Plains west of the Missouri river. The most holy spot for the Sioux are in the Black Hills."

"We're getting close to the Sioux encampment. In the early summer, many of the tribes come together to celebrate and to join together for their big buffalo hunt. I am going to drop in on their evening rituals tonight."

The plan was the Chinook to touch down a few miles from the big camp, unload the Humvee and the ATV, and leave Robby, Willis and the two medics to work their way to locations around the camp. Robby and Willis would go first and the medics would follow at some distance in the Humvee. Arcadia would direct the operations by radio using pre-arranged code words.

Then the Chinook would fly directly over the camp, masking the engine noise with thunder from speakers and simulate lightning with static discharges along the fuselage. Arcadia, dressed in her shimmering white dress would be lowered to the ground in a sling and step into the campfire of the several thousand Indians.

Arcadia spent weeks learning the Lakota language and hoped her arrival would signal to the Lakota they were being paid a visit by the Spirit Mother. Robby's job was to get close enough to kill anyone who threatened Arcadia. He set up about 500 hundred yards away on a bluff overlooking the camp and downwind from the horses and dogs. In his Ghillie suit, he was invisible. His night scope gave him a clear view of the camp.

The Sioux were dancing ceremoniously and the drums were beating as the huge crowd sat in a wide circle around the blazing fire. Suddenly there was the sound of thunder and all looked up to see lightning flashing in the sky. A figure was slowly descending. The drums stopped and all gasped to see a tall woman with golden hair and wearing a pure white and shimmering robe with a silver belt, coming toward the ground.

Arcadia landed between the fire and the crowd. The dancers scattered. Arcadia was happy to see fear on most of their faces and not anger. She quickly stepped out of the sling and it ascended rapidly back to the Chinook that flew quickly away.

She raised her arms and spoke, "I bring the love of the Sprit world of which I am a part to the great people of the Sioux nation," she said in flawless Sioux. "I welcome the Lakota, the Brule, the Ogallala, the Arapahoe, the Cheyenne and all the clans of the Sioux at this celebration to give thanks to your Spirit Mother and prayers for a successful hunt this season. I will bless you with the greatest hunt you have ever known."

One of the fiery warriors jumped to his feet and screamed, "You are not the Sprit Mother, but a demon from under the earth!" He raised his tomahawk and moved toward Arcadia. "Take him," said Arcadia into the nearly invisible wire microphone across her cheek.

Robby was watching the scene and had a round in the chamber. As the painted warrior came toward her, he aimed and fired. Just before the warrior reached a calm and quiet Arcadia, the warrior's head blew into a hundred bloody pieces.

"Are there others who doubt?" asked Arcadia. " Do you not know I have come to offer great counsel to the chiefs of the Sioux? The entire people are in mortal danger. I have come to save you from death. Why else would I have come at this time when you are all together to hear my words?"

One of the older men, with a full headdress of eagle feathers, held up his arms and cried, "The Spirit Mother has come! We shall take her counsel with gratitude and learn what we must know to spare the lives of all."

"Wisely spoken," said Arcadia. "The ATV will pick you up, outside the camp," she said into her mike to Robby and Willis. Then she looked at her dress stained with blood. "I shall not speak to you with the blood of ignorance upon me. I shall return after the sun has risen. I ask the two principal leaders of each tribe be present. I have much to tell you." Without another word, the Chinook returned, lightning and thunder booming. The sling was lowered and Arcadia was lifted magically away.

Robby and Willis jumped into the passing ATV and drove back to the Humvee.

"Nice shot," Arcadia said to Robby, "Very effective. I didn't know if I might be challenged. I'm glad there was just one. It was so bloody and graphic, I'm sure it prevented anyone else from objecting to my identity."

Arcadia slept in a cot inside the Humvee. The men pitched a tent and rolled into sleeping bags. They kept a watch through the night, but nobody came close.

The next morning, Arcadia was up and moving at sun up. She pulled a clean dress out of her bag and put it on. Then she came out and had breakfast with the men.

"Today, I am going in on the ATV. Willis, you drive. You will seem like a giant to these people. Robby you take your place again in case things get ugly, and they might. I am about to scuttle the entire lifestyle of these people and it won't be easy."

"Have the Humvee ready to come in when I call. We need to get these people vaccinated as soon as possible."

Willis dropped Robby off at his spot and he and Arcadia went driving boldly into the camp. The sight and noise of the vehicle caused a lot of people to scatter. To their credit, none of the leaders sitting in a large circle did more than rise to their feet. They remained standing as Arcadia, wearing a fresh gown stepped into the circle. Willis took a canvas-folding chair out of the ATV and placed it in the center of the circle. Then he stepped back several steps and stood quietly. He was armed with long knives and a combat ax. They stuck out of his wide belt, along with a big pistol. His camouflage fatigues seemed to make him blend in against the distant trees.

Arcadia spoke, "Your great grandfathers walked the wide grasses on foot, until I gave you the gift of the horse and set you free to follow the Buffalo, is that not so?"

The chiefs nodded in agreement.

"It was a time of great change, and you changed to make a better life for yourselves. Now a new change is coming, and unless you prepare for it, your entire way of life, indeed your lives themselves, and those of your wives and children will be gone as water poured on a fire.

"Far to the east, a new people have come to live in this land. Already they have built large cities, and their numbers are many times greater than the entire Sioux nation combined. Arcadia took a large picture out of the portfolio and held it up. It showed Philadelphia, the largest in the colonies, with thousands of people, wagons, and buildings. They look like this man behind me. All the chiefs had already noted the size of Willis and his commanding presence. They will come in vehicles such as I have arrived today.

Arcadia, whispered into the mike to Robby, "Get ready to shoot this when I signal." Then she took a large balloon out her pocket and blew it up. It had the face of an Indian in full headdress on it. She tied it off and walked over and picked up the long spear of one of the chiefs. She stuck it in the ground, and tied the balloon to the top of the spear. Then she raised her hand and dropped it. Almost instantly, the balloon exploded and the confetti inside flew all over the men in the counsel.

"These people possess weapons such as these, said Arcadia. " Did you hear the noise? Can you see where it came from? She pointed directly at Robby and said, "Look, can you not see your attacker?"

All the chiefs got up and looked in the direction Arcadia was pointing and one finally said, "We cannot see him."

"Stand up Robby," said Arcadia. Almost 600 yards away a figure stood up, much farther away than any chief had looked. They spoke to each other urgently for several minutes. Arcadia let them babble.

When they had quieted down again, she said, "What do you believe?"

The same older chief who spoke the night before said, "We

believe we live under your sky, Spirit Mother and if we are kind, true and have honor you will allow us to live in peace, and to be free people in the land."

"So we can say the Great Spirit who guides even me, has spoken and said all men are created equally, and have the right to life, liberty and the pursuit of happiness."

"We have not heard words spoken in such a way before, but they are true and we believe them."

"I have good news," said Arcadia, "the white men who are coming to your land believe exactly the same thing."

"Then why are we in such danger from them," asked the chief.

"There are three reasons," said Arcadia. "First, the white men are a completely different race and they carry diseases with them which do not kill them, but will certainly kill you. This I can prevent. Second, the white men drink a substance, which contains a poison deadly for our people. You are forbidden to drink it. Third, the white men come from a heritage very, very old. In this heritage, they have developed a group of laws governing their behavior. You must adopt these laws before they come into your country."

"What are these laws," asked the chief?

"For you and your many tribes, the most important laws are about land. You have always believed you do not own the land, but are a part of it. The whites do claim land as their own. In order to protect your people, you must do the same."

"How can we do this when we must travel great distances to hunt the buffalo, which is the way we exist?"

"The whites live inside great expanses of land called States. Each state is free to make its own laws as long as they do not interfere with the great laws governing all the states. This greater government rules only by the consent of the governed. It holds elections and sends representatives to the capital, where the good of the people is decided by a grand council, such as the one we have here today."

"In order to have your rights protected, the Indian nation must create its own state. Inside the boundaries of your state, you can hold millions of buffalo. You need not travel great distances to find them, they will be as your horses and kept for your use within the boundaries of your state."

"And if we defy this principal," asked the old man?

"Then the white man will come, see you have no government, claim your land and take it from you. They will kill all the buffalo, kill you and your lives as a free people will be over."

"And if we do as you command," asked the chief?

"Then you will be saved, free to live your own lives. The white man will respect your boundaries, trade with you, and help you to have better lives. You will be citizens of the Republic and have all the rights and privileges of citizenship."

"Your words are hard," said the chief.

"Let me show you the world as it exists today," said Arcadia. She pulled a laptop out of her portfolio and displayed the earth. She showed the huge population centers in Europe, China, Asia and Africa and along the East coast of America. Then she zoomed in on North America and showed how, in terms of total population, how empty the western plains were. "Unless this land is claimed by someone, it will be an open land grab by immigrants who are coming to America with the sole goal of owning their own land. If you do nothing, this is what you will get." She punched a button, which displayed the actual reservation system in the modern United States. There were pitiful little pockets of land sprinkled around the country.

Arcadia drew a line on the computer from the Red River in North Dakota in the north to the Platte River on the south, and from the Missouri River on the east to the Big Cat hills on the west, along the existing boundary of Colorado and Nebraska. "Or you can claim all this land, enclose millions of buffalo inside this space, built permanent homes and cease your lives of endless wandering. Surely this is better than the nomadic lives you are forced to live now."

Arcadia paused, and then said, "You must meet in council now and decide what you will do. This is the biggest decision you will ever make, and will require all the tribes of Sioux move into this land. There are other decisions that must be made in the future, also important, but until you make this one, nothing can happen."

"I can tell you the Great Spirit, whose name is God, will honor you in this difficult time and will bless you."

Arcadia bowed, and said, "I will be nearby and will return when you have searched your hearts and come to a decision." She turned and walked out of the camp with Willis following. They jumped into the ATV and roared off, picking Robby up as they went by. The three of them drove back to the Humvee.

It took four days for the council to come to an agreement. Robby kept a watch in his place on the hill overlooking the big camp. It was not a peaceful council. Several times, there was violence and several men were killed. Finally, the old chief came forth from a Teepee and held his arms up to signal the Spirit Mother should return.

Arcadia went back alone and met with the council. Robby and Willis guarded her from the hill. As the evening approached, Arcadia called Robby and said the council had chosen the statehood pathway and for them to bring up the Humvee with the medics, so vaccinations could begin.

It took many days to do vaccinations of the several thousand Sioux in the camp and the hundreds of others who came in from outlying areas after the chiefs sent runners.

Arcadia met privately with the chief and asked him to select a dozen young men, sixteen to eighteen years old, who were regarded as the most intelligent of all, and were willing to return to Fort Independence for several years of training. In the end, the choices were made and the young men were packed away in the Humvee.

For Arcadia herself, she waited until her men and equipment drove off before calling the Chinook to retrieve her in the same manner in which she had arrived. It was at night, with a great fire burning and all the people gathered to watch. She waved and blew kisses at all as she disappeared in the thunder and lightning.

The Chinook bounced the few miles and picked up the Humvee, the ATV, the Rangers, and twelve wide-eyed Sioux for the return to the Fort.

Chapter 26
The Rangers Strike

Fort Independence, Virginia

1774 was winding down. Momentous events were occurring and not occurring in Colonial America. Arcadia had already significantly altered the timeline of American history.

The British Parliament passed the Tea Act the year before, and the Sons of Liberty became active in Boston, resulting in the Boston Tea Party on December 16, 1773.

Benjamin Franklin was supposed to go to London in 1774 to argue against the Tea Act, but he was so busy with his plans for a rail line, finishing the big steel making plant, and refining oil in Pennsylvania Arcadia sent James Madison instead.

Then in 1774, the British passed what was known as the Intolerable Acts. These included the Boston Port Act, which basically blockaded Boston Harbor. The Administration of Justice Act, made it nearly impossible for Colonial Courts to try British citizens for crimes. The Massachusetts Government Act, revoked the charter of Massachusetts to operate as a colony, and put it under the direct control of England. Perhaps the most intrusive stroke was the Quartering Act, which required Colonial homeowners to house British Soldiers.

These actions worked to Arcadia's advantage since it fired the patriotism of all the colonies toward a break with England. The First Continental Congress met that year and she let it run its course.

In a meeting with George Washington at the end of the year, Arcadia and Washington agreed the tipping point for the Ranger campaign should occur as soon after Washington was appointed

Commander in Chief in June 1775. This put the major timeline change between the battles at Lexington and Concord and the Siege of Boston.

The Ranger brigade was at a razor's edge. Intensive training over the years made them the formidable force Arcadia intended. The winter at Fort Independence was mild and the brigade ran a dozen full-scale drills of the engagement set for the following year.

On April 19, 1775, the British marched out to Lexington and Concord and the "shot heard round the world" was fired. The British withdrew to Boston taking a lot of casualties to guerilla action along their route of march.

The British reinforced their troops in Boston with 6,000 redcoats, under the command of General Howe. George Washington was summoned to Philadelphia in April and was given the command he needed.

Washington was now as good a tactician in modern warfare as anyone in history, and he took charge. During the month of May 1775, he began moving the brigade into a position with all the appearances of a foolish choice of ground at the bottom of a valley 20 miles from Boston. In 1775, it was a poor choice; for forces from 2030, it was perfect.

The Humvees, Bradley's and Artillery were slipped north on back roads and open fields. The vehicles were filled with Rangers. The rest of the Rangers were moved by the Chinooks in night flights to the rally points surrounding the valley. In a few days, the brigade was in position.

Arcadia was with Washington the first day of June. The general sent a pair of marked riders into Boston to deliver a message to General Howe. The men, actually Rangers wearing colonial uniforms said their orders were to wait for a response.

General Howe was typical of British field commanders and had a very low opinion of the sustained fighting power of the colonial militia. So, he was surprised to read the contents of the dispatch.

To General Howe, Commander of British Forces in Boston
From: General George Washington, Commander in Chief, Colonial Forces of the United Colonies of America.
Sir,
Your assault on the Massachusetts towns of Concord and

Lexington last month signals to the combined wills of each of the 13 American Colonies a breach of relations has occurred between these Colonies and the British Empire.

Therefore, we are resolved to meet the troops under your command in battle, outside of Boston. It is our intention to inflict such severe damage to your forces the British Government shall have no choice but to sue for peace and surrender control of the colonies so they may form an American nation.

I should caution the Honorable General, we possess sufficient forces to defeat any army you should choose to put into the field. We therefore offer you a single instance amnesty, in which the British evacuate the Americas in all respects without incurring injury or death.

Should you elect to ignore this act of mercy, then you must be prepared to suffer the consequences of your poor judgment.

Sincerely,

G. Washington. Commander Colonial Rangers

Howe read the dispatch twice and then called for his adjutant to read it as well.

"This fellow Washington has a rather inflated view of the quality of his troops," said Howe.

"If I may, sir, Washington is obviously staking his entire army on this single engagement. When you defeat him, it will set the talk of treason in the colonies back 20 years. The King would certainly applaud the destruction of the entire rebel forces in a single blow. I would suggest you take your entire command to the field and thrash this rascal."

"It is very seductive," said Howe, "What is our total force available for service?"

"Over 6,000 regulars, sir."

"Give the order to march in 48 hours."

"Yes, Sir!"

"Get those marked riders back in here."

When the Rangers came into the office of General Howe, he pulled himself up to his greatest height, since the men facing him were unusually tall and broad.

"You may tell your General Washington His Majesties' Regular

Army will march out of Boston in 2 days. We accept his offer of battle."

"Since that is the case, General," said one of the Sergeants. "General Washington says he will be encamped 20 miles west of Boston. He also instructs us to convey one other statement."

"Which is what," asked Howe?

"The Rangers Are Coming." The soldiers saluted smartly and left the office.

The two men high-fived each other as they went out the front door of the building.

Four days later, General Howe positioned his force in a bivouac on a large, long meadow, surrounded by forest leading up to the brow of a wide hill. He looked down into the valley and saw six large tents. He was confused. He had expected to see long rows of tents and men scurrying here and there.

He formed up his companies in wide lines, several deep. He deployed his six-pound cannons behind his main line. The entire 6,000-man regiment was at the ready. He waited for the colonials to take the field.

What did happen, were 200 men in garish green uniforms came oozing out onto the field surrounding the tents. They all screamed in unison, "Rangers," followed by a string of obscenities of the most personal nature, especially toward General Howe, who sat on his horse at the top of the hill with his other officers.

"Order the advance," growled Howe, "Open fire with the artillery."

The artillery was clearly out of range for the troops or the tents, and the men hooted in laughter. The British lines marched down the hill. Just about the time when the British were within musket fire of the Rangers, they wheeled to the left and right and the tents were pulled off the six Bradleys. The cannons began firing, and the British started dying.

At the same time, the Ranger artillery began shooting, taking out all of the British Artillery in two barrages. To the shock of the British, the forest next to the meadow on both sides was suddenly alive with machines and men.

Howe ordered his cavalry to attack the right flank and the 600 horsemen were mowed down with 50 caliber machine guns on the

Humvees. Now accosted on three sides, the British lines broke and the retreat began. Artillery fire exploded again along the tent lines of the British. Howe realized he was trapped. He knew things were getting very bad when, one after another, his senior officers were suddenly just bloody gore as their heads disappeared from their bodies.

The British fired point blank into the ranks of the onrushing Rangers, but not a single one went down. Now struggling to reload, the redcoats were slammed by the Rangers with short bursts of gunfire from their assault rifles. The circle grew smaller and smaller until less than 500 British soldiers remained on their feet. A smaller number of Rangers dropped their rifles, pulled their knives and waded into the redcoats.

General Howe watched in horror as his soldiers were overwhelmed by essentially unarmed, green clad soldiers. The ways the men moved were amazing to see, as they bobbed and weaved, and struck out with their legs in whips cutting down the redcoats.

Washington spoke into his command circuit to his troops. "I want 20 left alive."

The Rangers quickly separated 20 men from the clot of soldiers in the middle of the meadow, and efficiently dispatched all the rest.

The entire battle lasted 22 minutes.

General Howe sat alone on his horse, wide-eyed and alone on the hill. From the forest to his left, a single ATV came roaring out of the bush. It pulled up to General Howe, and George Washington, wearing his fatigues, helmet and full battle armor stepped out of the ATV and walked slowly toward Howe. When he got closer he said, "Get off your horse, General Howe."

Howe dismounted and looked into the grim faced figure of George Washington. Washington took off his green gloves and said, "This is the army of the United States. You should have surrendered when I gave you the chance. The British are finished in North America. There will be no reinforcements. As you can see, we possess weapons and firepower superior to any other army in the world. The same is true at sea, any troop ships attempting to land in America will be sunk. This war for the colonies is over. We will declare our independence shortly. I have dispatches for your King, which includes an unconditional release of the colonies by formal treaty. You will also surrender all your holdings anywhere in North America, as well as all your holdings in the Caribbean. You needn't feel lonely, we are making the same demands to the French and Spanish.

"This is outrageous," said Howe, "the British Empire is the greatest in the world. You don't seriously expect us to accede to these demands."

"I do, indeed, General, 30 minutes ago, you had 6,000 soldiers, now you have 20. But I can see additional examples have to be made."

Washington spoke into his clear mike, Ranger Pierce, report to me."

A few minutes later, a strange looking man came out of the forest. Howe could barely recognize him. He wore the same uniform as Washington with an outer layer of strips and long straps. "This is the sniper who killed all your officers. Robby, how far is it to the flagpole with the British flag at the end of the camp?" Robby held up an instrument, "456 yards, General."

"Shoot it down."

Robby dropped to his knees and held up a lethal looking rifle with a long barrel. He sighted through the scope, made an adjustment on the back of the rifle and took aim. He fired. A second or so later, the flagpole just below the flag shattered and the Union Jack crashed to the ground.

"I can assure you, he is equally as accurate from three times that distance," said Washington. He spoke again into his mike, "Alpha battery, target the center of the British encampment, standard HE."

A moment or two later, Howe heard six thumps from some distance away.

"This artillery is seven miles away," said Washington.

The explosions in the direct center of the British camp were tremendous and flattened an area 200 yards across.

"First platoon, Company A, front and center."

A group of soldiers came running up from the scene of the final stand of the redcoats. They came smartly to attention in perfect order in front of their general.

"There's still a row of tents standing at the front of the encampment, take them down."

The soldiers spread out into a line and raised their weapons. The air was full of a tremendous burst of gunfire from the assault rifles. The tents, 200 yards away were shredded.

"These Rangers just fired 500 rounds of ammunition in 10 seconds," said Washington placidly. "Tell me General Howe, is your pistol still loaded?"

"Yes it is," said Howe.

"Then be so good to shoot me. Aim right for the heart."

Howe turned finally with a chance to do something. He aimed his flintlock at Washington and fired. When the smoke cleared, Washington was still on his feet and grinning at him.

"Our combat battle armor will stop any musket ball you can fire."

"One final demonstration," said Washington. He spoke into his mike, "Blackhawk, fire mission, mini-guns."

Moments later, a black helicopter came zooming over the battlefield. It began firing thousands of rounds of ammo across the remnants of the encampment. "The rate of fire of this machine is 3,000 rounds per minute."

Just then, the Humvees and the Bradley's pulled up to encircle the two generals.

"This is more of our firepower and capabilities, General Howe. I won't waste the ammunition having them put on further demonstrations. Take your soldiers and march back to Boston. Take the first ship available for England. Take these documents and this instrument. It will show you the entire battle just as it occurred. Just push this button here and press start. They wouldn't believe you anyway. Our ambassador in London will contact your prime minister to complete the details. That is all, General Howe. You are excused."

Howe mounted his horse, had his men gather up twenty horses that were still alive and they rode off at full gallop.

Washington's radio chirped. It was Arcadia. "Congratulations, George. For your information, two more troop ships were approaching New York harbor. We sunk them."

Chapter 27
A New Nation

Philadelphia, Pennsylvania

The news about the spectacular defeat of the entire British Army outside of Boston spread through the colonies like a summer storm. The appearance of a previously unknown Continental Army with lethal capabilities came as a surprise to everyone in America. George Washington was hailed as the greatest military leader in history.

Thomas Paine, already writing his little book Common Sense, was moved to publish his book six months in advance of its original publication in January 1776. As before, the book galvanized public opinion on the prospect of a free and independent American nation.

Arcadia met with the Colonial leaders at a previously arranged meeting in Philadelphia. All of them were there, except James Madison, who was delivering the terms of the new state of affairs to the British in London, and George Washington, who was already transporting his army to Canada to attack Quebec. However, Jefferson with a completed copy of his Declaration of Independence and John Adams with the revised Constitution were there, along with Ben Franklin and Alexander Hamilton.

Messages went out for the colonies to send their delegates to the Second Continental Congress to convene at the end of May in Liberty Hall, and they were on the way.

Arcadia called a meeting of the original conspirators and began by saying, "A second time window opened last month and elements of the new American Navy came through. It comprises four destroyers, one submarine, and a large cargo ship. They've been working their way north to engage British ships carrying troop reinforcements. They caught two of them near New York and sunk them. One of the ships will stay on station along the east coast to keep the British from sending anymore troop ships. Commercial traffic is not being affected at all."

"We are now ready to convene the new Congress, but the circumstances of that meeting will be dramatically different from the way it originally happened. As we have long planned, this Congress will be given circumstances much different than they originally had. No longer are the British a force in the Colonies. Our estimates are fully 70% of the population now favors complete independence and is waiting for Congress to act. The Congress is free to make whatever decisions it wishes, and the delegates are brimming with enthusiasm to proceed without delay."

"Our plan is for Thomas to introduce his Declaration of Independence document and have it adopted by the Congress. Next, John and Ben will present the new and revised constitution. We don't see any significant difficulties in getting it adopted. As you know we have transformed the biggest plantations in the south to adopting the Foundation plan, so the new constitution says all slavery will be abolished in the United States in 20 years."

"About the time Congress is considering the new Constitution, they are going to receive word Washington's Rangers have taken Quebec and broken the back of British Control in Canada. You leaders can then propose Canada be included in the new United States, and to suggest in order for the United States be permanently secure it also should annex Mexico, and Central America.

"Our navy is already moving ships and our soldiers into the Caribbean to seize Cuba, Jamaica, and Puerto Rico from the Spanish. We are certain by the time we get to actually occupying these islands, the people, the enemy soldiers and the governments will be terrified when they hear the words, 'The Rangers are Coming'."

"My belief is when Congress gets it into their head the United States is going to suddenly become the largest country in the world, they will jump at the opportunity. We bring Washington back from wherever he is at the time and conduct a national election this fall with him as the first President."

"This will substantially complete Phase 1 of our overhaul of

American history and set the country on the road to saving the 150 million people in 2030, as the angel told me."

"I gather," said Ben Franklin we are not out of the woods yet for the far future. I need to ask you Arcadia, how long are we going to be blessed with your leadership?"

"Only God knows the answer to that question. He can jerk me back to my own time whenever he likes. However, I know there are a bunch of major issues needing to be faced over the next hundred or so years. I think he will keep me here for some time. One thing I know for sure. He doesn't intend for me to take a public part in this process."

The Second Congressional Congress convened on May 10, 1776. All of the original delegates were there. They came in high spirits and full of confidence. These were not nervous leaders scared to death of the British Army. In many of their colonies, British officials had simply been rounded up and sent to holding camps to await shipment back to England. All of them knew Washington had unleashed a modern and highly effective army. They were very curious about how it was accomplished without the knowledge of any of them.

Jefferson, Adams, Franklin, and Hamilton pulled out the first ad, published in 1770, calling for brave men for a dangerous mission to explore the lands to the west. As Adams said, "We all knew it was inevitable the colonies would eventually turn on the British and declare for independence. Therefore, we recruited an elite force of men, called the Rangers, and spent five years training them. We also developed somewhat better weapons. All of you can see the results of that training. The British are finished in America. It's time for us to declare our independence. Mr. Jefferson and Mr. Franklin have prepared such a document. Copies are on your desk before you, and I now ask the Chairman of the Congress to permit Mr. Jefferson to read this Declaration of Independence to the delegates."

"Without objection," said John Hancock, "Mr. Jefferson can proceed."

The document clearly stated the grievances of the colonies, which were not in question, and since the colonies had already done something radical about it, the delegates sent back word to their colonial assemblies for approval. Arcadia was not particularly surprised to find the document approved on July 4, 1776.

In the middle of this debate came the startling news Washington's

Rangers had conquered Quebec and defeated all the British forces stationed in Canada. Washington sent his recommendation Canada be included in the new United States.

It now became very obvious the new country needed a new governing document, given the new realities, and it vast expansion. Adams and Jefferson led Congress through the logic of what such a document should include and day by day, introduced portions of the constitution to the delegates.

Everyone held their breath for the debate from the southern states over their slaves, but Henry Lee, one of the leading plantation owners in Virginia, surprised the Congress saying the new Foundation system was a great success and the House of Burgesses of Virginia had voted to abolish slavery. Virginia ports were already closed to the importation of more slaves. One by one, many of the leading plantation owners in Georgia, North and South Carolina said they had been contacted by a very persuasive young woman who had proven to them the new system was clearly an improvement. That part of the constitution sailed through with very little debate.

A new dispatch arrived, saying the American Navy had captured New Orleans, and sunk over 100 French and Spanish warships. The word spread throughout the Caribbean the invincible Rangers could invade at any time. So, without firing a shot, the French, British and Spanish evacuated all their citizens and business interests from everywhere in the Caribbean.

The Mexican people, long oppressed by the Spanish began a revolution of their own, and were getting a great deal of help from elements of the Ranger brigade who dumbstruck both the Spanish and the Mexicans by employing a large variety of very lethal weapons. Ranger units were marching onto Mexico and slaughtering the remaining Spanish army and their entire government infrastructure. The Mexicans were clearly frightened of the powerful Rangers, but hailed them as their deliverers.

The Constitution, which was already popular with the majority of delegates, began to take a back seat to the reality of what kind of United States Washington's army was carving out.

Arcadia and the other leaders waited for this moment to arrive and unveiled a new and very accurate map of what this huge new country would look like. It had all the states in mostly their same familiar places with a very large state in place of North and South Dakota, and half of Nebraska. In fact, Nebraska didn't exist at all. Its southern half was now all Kansas. The states of Canada were the same, and the large districts of Mexico given state names. No new names were selected for the other central American countries and they were designated as states on their own.

The Continental Congress looked in wonder at the new country. Jefferson made it clear the native American tribes would have full citizenship and the state 'Sioux', would enclose all of the plains Indian tribes. Other, smaller tribes were given sovereignty over large counties within states. He said simply, "We said in our documents all men are created equally and are endowed by God with rights. If we are to be true to this creed, than we must include all people currently in the United States we are creating, whether they are black, brown or oriental."

The Second Continental Congress adopted the entire new Constitution and the colonial assemblies ratified the new law of the land.

The new states might be almost devoid of population, but they existed. The next step was to start filling them up. Arcadia began her plan of dealing with the rest of the world on what would be the new order of life on earth.

Chapter 28
Mission To Mexico

Montreal, Canada

Staff Sergeant Robby Pierce dozed as he rode in one of the Chinooks on the long ride to Mexico, and reflected on the recent Canadian campaign. He'd distinguished himself in the battle for Quebec city.

The Rangers had finally faced an enemy where they were not supported by the majority of the local population. The French Canadians were very independent and didn't like anybody except their own kind. General Washington attempted to negotiate with the city of Montreal itself. He sent in some emissaries to the city walls. Robby was standing guard from cover. As the emissaries approach under a white flag, Robby spotted a man with a musket aiming at the leader.

He quickly took aim and shot the man. Washington withdrew the peace party and ordered in the Bradley's and the Humvees with ground support from the Rangers. The battle was soon over as the Canadians surrendered and signaled they wanted to talk. This time they came to Washington.

"Your people tried to kill my negotiator under a flag of truce," said Washington. Your city has paid the price. I will now tell you what my emissary was going to say and then you decide what you want to do."

"As you no doubt know, the British army in the colonies is defeated. We will establish our own nation and we would like for that nation to include Canada. We are kindred spirits with much in common and a large trade business. You can choose to disengage from the British and join us. You'll have your own states in which you will have religious freedom, freedom of speech, freedom to petition the government for grievances, the right to trial by a jury of your peers, and the freedom to hold and keep arms. You have much to gain by being a part of the United States. We offer you protection from enemies, peace with the Indians and free trade."

"Who protects us from you," said the Canadian with a heavy French accent?

"Our new government is based on the principle it governs by the consent of the governed…the people. All power is derived from that principle. You will elect representatives to come to the Capitol, where you will have the same say as the other states. All of this is contained in our new Constitution. I have a copy of it here. Perhaps you can take it, study and share it with your officials and make a decision."

The Canadian took the papers and said, "We will consider your offer and give your our answer in due time."

"Thank you for coming. We regret the loss of life and property you have experienced. The Rangers are a formidable fighting force"

"Like nothing anyone has ever seen."

"It was built to defeat the British, the French and the Spanish, not our friends in Canada. If you have 30 strong men 18-22 years old, we would be happy to recruit them and possibly make them Rangers. I need to tell you our standards are quite high and not all who volunteer are able to qualify."

"That is the most generous offer you've made so far," said the Canadian. "We will consider all you have said." He walked out of the tent.

Robby was summoned by Washington and was waiting while the General gave his speech. "You wanted to see me, General. Are we going to do that…recruit more Rangers?"

"We're going to form a second brigade. We believe the European powers may try to form an alliance and mount some kind of attack."

"They would be foolish to attempt such a thing."

"We're spread pretty thin. We have no Rangers at all on the west coast and the British have a fortress in Vancouver. They could cause a lot of trouble before we got them stopped."

"Hasn't our reputation gone ahead of us," said Robby.

"Oh yes," said Washington, "the Spanish army ran away across the Rio Grande as soon as they heard the Rangers were coming. Just the mention of our name causes people to quake in their boots. Of course we had just sunk their entire grand fleet."

"I wanted to thank you for saving my officer on that parley," said Washington, "How did you spot him?"

"His was the only rifle over the wall. It wasn't very hard."

"We are pushing into Mexico. The Spanish are withdrawing to a strong fort in Veracruz. I want you to take two squads of men, and a Humvee and take them out. The best outcome would be to negotiate as I have just done with the Canadians. Of course you are going to have to deal with the Spanish first."

"Twenty men and one Humvee, against a whole fortified city," said Robby with a raise in his brows.

"Most of their firepower is pointed out to sea. I think you can sneak into the city and eliminate their commander and his command point. Cut off the head of the snake and the troops will not be very effective."

"We'll give it a go, General."

"Thank you, Robby," said Washington. "Pick good men."

"There's none better than Willis' soldiers. I'll have him pick me 20 mighty warriors. Of course, he'll insist on going with me."

"Start your Chinook hops as soon as you're ready. I'll make the arrangements." Washington picked up a radio off the desk and handed it to him. "Stay in touch by radio. This one has an extra circuit allowing you to contact central headquarters and me."

"Guess I'll be able to use the Spanish I've learned," said Robby.

"Good luck, Lieutenant," said Washington shaking Robby's hand.

When Robby found Willis, camped at the edge of Quebec city. He was sitting in a chair under the tent flag of his Humvee. The rest of his men were scattered around some tents they'd erected and there were several fires burning.

"Ah, the great and terrible "Hawkeye," said Willis, using Robby's code and nick name as he walked up."

"Greetings, my friend," said Robby, "Just been talking with General Washington. He wants me to take 20 mean men and capture a whole city in Mexico."

"I know we're getting quite a reputation," said Willis, "but don't you think the General might be reaching a little on this one."

"It's a smash and dash. We sneak into a town called Veracruz. It's a Spanish strongpoint, but most of the defenses point out to sea. Our job is to break into the Command Center, or whatever it is and take out

- 162 -

the senior Spanish Officers. The General thinks without someone to give them orders the soldiers will surrender."

"How do we get to the Command Center?"

"Guess we will have to find our way. I've got an overhead picture with the center marked."

"Opposition?"

"Bound to be some, we can't use the Humvee. They'd know we were coming."

"We'll leave it outside of town in case we have to make a fast exit."

"Are we gonna hop all the way down there in a Chinook?"

"Right you are. We'll go at the end of the week. Hope the pilot can find the fuel dumps."

"OK, then, I'll get the men ready."

"Willis, this is not going to be the easiest thing we ever did. Have your men take plenty of ammo and firepower."

"Right, I'll get in some training and brief the men thoroughly on the mission."

❖

It took two days for the Chinook to make the long journey from Montreal, Canada to Veracruz, Mexico. They overnighted someplace in the south where the new map of the United States said was Texas.
The next day they flew to within 20 miles of Veracruz and grounded in a small meadow in the middle of a tropical forest. It was hot and humid. They found a small pathway going toward the city getting better the closer they got. Willis and Robby set up the range finder and studied the city map to find the shortest route to the Army headquarters. The Humvee went back for the rest of the men. It was nightfall before the unit was together. Willis called them into a huddle.

"Alright, Robby is going to go to the top of that church tower over there and provide cover while we work toward the Spanish headquarters. He showed them the overhead photo and the marked route. We'll advance in standard two by two overlaps. Attach your silencers we don't want to wake up the whole town. Kill if you must, but keep moving. This is a straight search and kill mission. The idea is to take out their leadership and then hang around and harass the soldiers before we send them packing. Any questions?"

There were none. Silently the Rangers slipped into the city. Robby flipped down his night scope over his eyes as he entered the church and found the stairs to the steeple. When he got to the top, he looked out and saw the squad moving quietly in the dark. The ultraviolet stripes on their helmets made them easy to spot.

As the team got closer to the headquarters there were soldiers all around the building. Robby screwed on his silencer and began to pick out targets. He started at the farthest edge and tried to pick men who were alone or in two's. He shot half a dozen men before his shots were seen by other soldiers. They were quickly on their feet and on guard. Willis team was close enough now to engage and they swept up the stairs of the building in a fan formation. The sound of their gunfire muffled through the streets.

A man stuck his head out of a second story window and Robby neatly picked him off. Now the entire team was inside the building and Robby could only wait. He shot several other soldiers running toward the building He saw the team reach the second floor, the sound of a grenade was followed by two more blasts, one of them from a shoulder rocket.

It seemed like a long time but it was only a few minutes before the team came running out. They were helping one man along hanging between two of the Rangers. They raced toward the city walls and into the dark toward the Humvee.

Robby quickly exited his hiding spot and caught up with the rear guard as he ran through the entrance in the wall. A lot of soldiers were now awake and trying to spot the camouflaged soldiers as they ran toward the trees.

Just then, the 50 caliber of the Humvee opened up and swept the top of the walls. Men came flooding through the gate and the Rangers turned to shoot them down, while the 50 caliber rained death everywhere.

Robby was the last person into the Humvee, moving back toward the Chinook, while most of the men trotted along to hold cover. "Did we take a casualty," he asked?

One of them looked up with great sadness in his face, "It's Sergeant Grant. He took a headshot. We wouldn't leave him behind, but he's dead."

Robby's heart thumped loudly. Could it be true his lifelong friend was gone? He couldn't believe it. Casualties among the Rangers were not common, but each one was a major blow to his platoon specifically and to the Brigade in general. Now his closest friend lay dead at the front of the Humvee. Grief stricken, Robby cried hot tears.

Suddenly, there was the sound of more gunfire. A mounted cavalry unit was closing on their position. There were at least a hundred of them. Robby knew he now commanded the platoon. He surveyed the situation. It was still night and the Spanish were riding with torches.

"We need to make a statement here," said Robby to the sergeant who was talking on his radio to his men to keep them moving in the right direction. Robby clicked open the platoon circuit, "Sergeant Grant is dead," he said. This bunch needs to know what it actually means to engage the Rangers. Spread out to encircle them. When we've cut off their retreat let me know.

The Rangers wheeled and streamed along the ranks of the mounted horsemen, letting them ride forward before closing the loop at the rear. "We need to leave enough of them alive to be able to report what they see. I'll do some shooting to see if I can confuse them. The rest of you pick selected targets until we get them to surrender."

Robby raised his M-4 and began making very messy head shots at several places in the formation. Meanwhile, the Rangers were killing a few and forcing the Spanish into a smaller and smaller area.

Then Robby jumped to the front of the Spanish, in full view, and screamed in Spanish, "If you value your lives, stop firing and throw down your weapons. One of the Spanish soldiers cocked his flintlock and fired at Robby. The musket ball jarred him, but his body armor stopped it. The man who fired the flintlock was immediately cut into pieces by at least 200 rounds.

"I said if you wish to live, throw down your weapons and get down off those horses."

This time the Spanish obeyed. There were about sixty of them, some were hurt, but most stood uncertainly as the Rangers stepped out of the bushes. To the Spanish, they were terrifying. The Rangers were very large men, wearing uniforms making them hard to distinguish from the terrain, even in the open. They were wearing helmets of the kind the Spanish had never seen, and their eyes were covered by the night scopes. They were also wearing black camouflage paint in wide strips across their faces. Their weapons looked very deadly.

"Who's the ranking officer here?" shouted Robby in perfect Spanish. "Step forward immediately."

A man wearing epaulets, signifying him as an officer came forward slowly. He was sweating and his eyes darted around the scene at other Rangers.

"Do you know who we are," asked Robby?

"There are stories of an army of giants with deadly weapons, who move with no sound, striking without warning and killing every person on a battlefield. They are beasts of the Devil," said the shaking officer.

"We are not demons of Satan," said Robby, "Every man here faithfully worships God. We are Rangers. Our mission in Mexico and Central America is to drive out you foreign Spanish Europeans, just as we have the British in the American colonies, and Canada. Your time of occupation is over. From now on North America is only for those who were born here and see it as our native land."

Robby paused, "We've just attacked the city of Veracruz and killed all of your senior commanders in the headquarters. We did this with just 20 Rangers. You must know other Rangers are in Mexico and are liberating the people from you Spanish.

"We are going to release you all, alive. You are to report to the Spanish leaders in Mexico City they must all leave this new part of the United States in 30 days, or we will be back. Tell your commanders what happened here and say, 'The Rangers Are Coming.'"

Robby looked over the group, the sun was just coming over the horizon, and his men flipped up their night vision scopes, not that it made them look any less menacing. Within the Spanish, there was mostly awe and fear. However, at least two men stood tall, undefeated and angry.

"I can see not all of your men are convinced," said Robby. He pushed his way through the crowd and up to three men with hatred burning in their eyes. Robby smiled, "I know what you are thinking. We're not so tough. If we didn't have our weapons, you could tear us to pieces." One of the men spat on the ground.

Robby shrugged, "Very well, let us see if you are right. Take off your belts. The rest of you make a circle around these men, so you can see." Robby whispered into his mike, "Make sure you send your best two fighters in here."

Two Rangers came forward through the crowd. Robby was already stripping off his body armor and dropping his belt. The other two Rangers did the same.

"Now we are all just men," said Robby. "Kill us, if your can."

The three burly Spaniards rushed toward Ranger. The man who spit squared off against Robby. He lowered his head and tried to tackle Robby. He found himself flying through the air onto his back. He jumped up and threw punches at Robby, who calmly fended off the blows and sent the man crashing on the ground again.

Robby made sure the demonstration went on for a while, until the Spaniard's mouth and nose were bleeding. It looked like he had several broken ribs and a dislocated shoulder. The other Spaniards looked no better.

Robby walked back up to the officer, barely breathing hard. He grabbed the officer by his tunic and pulled him close. "We are the best trained, most deadly, army in the world. We can defeat your best with or without weapons. My patience grows thin. Leave for Mexico City right now and tell your commanders, 'The Rangers Are Coming'. You have 30 days."

The Spanish rushed to their horses and rode away, nursing those who had been injured in the skirmish.

As soon as they were gone, Robby called the Chinook to pick them up. "Make sure everyone in Veracruz sees you, and put a rocket into their headquarters. Then come get us."

He flipped the command switch on his radio and said, "Crystal Palace, this is Hawkeye." Almost immediately the answer came back, "Roger, Hawkeye, this is Crystal Palace, stand by for Papa Grizzly." Papa Grizzly was Washington's code name and in just a moment he was saying into Robby's ear, "Roger, Hawkeye, this is Papa Grizzly, report mission status."

"Papa Grizzly, this is Hawkeye, main target engaged and neutralized, estimate body count of 200, including all senior command. Have further engaged mounted force on horseback and sent them to Mexico City with warning all foreigners evacuate Mexico in 30 days. Must sadly report one casualty, Raking Punch is dead. We're bringing him home."

"Sorry for your loss, Hawkeye," said Washington. "Congratulations on successful mission. Return to Home Plate

Chapter 29
Returning Home
Fort Independence, Virginia

Robby hadn't been back to Fort Independence for six months. The Fort was not very crowded with the majority of the Brigade still scattered across the continent and engaging in skirmishes. The majority of the operations were headed into Mexico. Robby's raid had the expected results. The main port of Veracruz was neutralized, and the whole city saw the Chinook take out the main headquarters building. The men Robby released went immediately to Mexico City and did not have to embellish the story of their encounter. The term, "The Rangers Are Coming" brought terror to the Spanish and happy tidings to the Mexican nationals and native tribes.

Robby learned this in his after action briefings as he got caught up on the news. There was a lot of it. In addition to what he already knew about the publication of the Declaration of Independence, he learned of the subsequent ratification of the new Constitution by the Continental Congress. There was the movement on the part of the colonies to ratify it as well. Six had already done so, and approval was expected from the others, even the southern ones of Georgia and North and South Carolina.

The most interesting news was from abroad. The English Parliament had no choice but to accept the existence of the United States and agreed to abandon all their claims in the western hemisphere. The French and the Spanish were outraged by being summarily kicked out of the same territory. However, all three of the great European powers were astonished to find America apparently bore no ill will to anyone. They offered full trade with Europe and offered a tempting list of consumer products in addition to the cotton and tobacco they were already exporting. They also offered open borders inviting anyone who wished to immigrate to the new and vastly expanded, United States.

The entire experience was bittersweet. Robby would have to find some way to tell the Grant family their son and his oldest friend had died 2,000 miles away. He moped around the room they shared following the briefing and couldn't seem to concentrate on anything.

The morning following his return there was a gentle knock on his door. He opened it wearing nothing but his fatigue pants and a t-shirt. Standing there was both General Washington and Arcadia.

"Good morning, Robby," said Arcadia. "Can we come in for a minute?

"Of course," said Robby. "Sorry about the mess."

"That's quite all right," said the General, "you've only returned from a six month deployment, and we know you have a heavy heart."

"When you talk about suffering 5 or 10 percent casualties, you always think it's going to be someone else, but when the casualty is you or someone you know, the rate is 100 percent. Part of me died when I lost Willis."

"We would like you to lead an honor guard to take him home for burial," said Washington.

"That would be very much appreciated, General," said Robby, "I know his folks would be happy to know he didn't die without cause. What do we do?"

"Arcadia has shown me the burial ceremony used in her times. I think it's a very moving and respectful last rite," said Washington.

"I would be honored if you will allow me to do the ceremony and speak at the funeral," said Arcadia.

"Thank you, Arcadia," said Robby, "You being there would be a great tribute."

The honor guard turned out to be 20 of Willis' platoon. They were all, along with Robby, fitted for new uniforms. General Washington said they were dress blues for special occasions. "We're not in combat here, so our fighting uniforms will be replaced by these.

Robby had to admit he'd never seen such beautiful uniforms. They were made up of blue coats and pants, with mirror bright black shoes, headgear that was sharp, round hats with a shining visor in the front. The ranks of the soldiers were sewed on the shoulders in gold.

The nametags were outlined in white, and there were gold buttons on the collars that said "US Army." The decorations and awards of the soldiers were a blaze of color in rows above their left shirt pockets. Starting at the right shoulder was a white length of braided cloth looping down under the arm. This, Robby was told, was to symbolize the men were all Rangers.

With need for secrecy no longer necessary, Robby flew up to Concord in one of the Huey helicopters. It was his sad duty to inform the Grant family of the death of their son, and to make arrangements for the funeral. For this mission, he wore his combat fatigues, helmet, radio and he was armed with his M-4 sniper rifle and accompanying side arm of a Glock 22 automatic pistol. For Robby, there was nothing new about this; except for the shiny new officers bar he now wore, signifying he was a Second Lieutenant.

The helicopter landed in the town square of Concord, and instantly drew a crowd. The marvel of a flying vehicle only added to the legend and fame of the mysterious Rangers who had so soundly defeated the British and gave the colonies their independence. The papers were full of news about their exploits in expanding the country to include Canada and Central America. Almost everyone had read the Declaration of Independence and the New Constitution, considering them to be among the most important documents ever written.

Robby stepped out of the helicopter, and the crowd instantly stepped back. The lethal reputation of the Rangers was well known. He smiled at this and looked through the crowd for his own family. He saw his mother first. He took off his helmet and said, Mother, is this the best greeting you can muster for your son?"

"Robby!" she cried and ran forward to embrace him. The rest of the people of Concord now were able to look beyond the uniform and see it was filled with one of their own. Robby hugged his mother, and then his father, brothers and sisters. He shook hands with the dozens of others who crushed in to greet him.

"I'm sorry," he said, I'm on official business. He broke away from the crowd and separated the Grant family taking them off a distance to speak to them privately. He sadly delivered the news of the death of their son.

Willis' mother leaned against Robby and cried. Robby did too. He reached out to take the Grant family in his arms to console them.

"How did he die, asked Willis' father?

"Very bravely, in combat, he led our the unit in the attack of a very large installation. You can be proud of Willis, Mr. Grant he was a credit to the Rangers and to the United States of America."

"Where is he," asked his mother?"

"At present he is being prepared for burial at Fort Independence in Virginia. Tomorrow we'll bring him home and formally lay him to rest in the village cemetery."

Robby turned to the crowd, now comprising the entire population of Concord. "My friends, I am here with sad news. Sergeant Willis Grant was killed in an operation of the Rangers, three days ago. It is a terrible thing when a Ranger falls. I would like to ask your permission to return Willis to Concord tomorrow for a formal burial, and I ask all, who can, come to the ceremony."

There were general outbursts of grief among the villagers. "As you all know, Willis was my oldest friend. He and I fought together for the independence of America, and his loss is greater than I can bear."

One of the soldiers on the helicopter jumped out with a long bag with Robby's uniform, his pack, and his rifle, and brought it over to him. "With your permission, sir, we are ready to depart."

"Permission granted," said Robby, "Thanks for the ride."

"It's the least we can do for the man who saved so many lives and is a hero of the Rangers," said the Corporal. He saluted sharply then jumped back aboard the helicopter and soon it lifted and was gone over the trees.

Robby turned back to the villagers of Concord. "I know you have many, many questions. Some of them I can answer, some I cannot. However, I am willing to tell you what I know, if you are interested in listening to me for a few minutes.

The fact the entire village sat down on the village green made it clear they were willing to listen to Robby for as long as he wanted to talk.

"Five years ago, a secret group of American patriots, who anticipated the coming war with the British over the question of Independence of the Colonies, ran an ad in papers everywhere, saying they were organizing a grand exploration of the lands to the west and were recruiting young men for the adventure. This was a deception, to prevent the British from becoming suspicious of our true intentions.

Willis and I were accepted as recruits and went to a special installation in Virginia, called Fort Independence. There we were intensely trained. We received a very comprehensive education and now all of us have graduate degrees recognized at Harvard, so, along with my rank, I am also Doctor Pierce with a degree in politics, history, and sociology.

"But education was only the beginning of our training. We were part of what has become the Ranger Brigade, which as you already know, is the best army in the world. I am not at liberty to disclose our exact numbers, but you would be very surprised how few of us there really are.

"Our modern battle tactics and superior weapons made us more than a match for the British." He held up his M-4 Sniper rifle, "This is my weapon. I won't demonstrate its use now, but let me just say I can hit a target from more than a mile away.

"As you have read in the papers, the new United States has a constitution based on the belief government exists by the consent of the people. This is a concept, which is unique in the entire world. Basic rights are given to you by our new constitution. We believe these rights are those of all men and are given to us by God, who is our ultimate authority.

"I know you have also read, mostly garbled and confused reports in the papers about the use of the Rangers to expand the actual size of America and the creation of states now under the new national government. The papers simply do not understand the scope of Ranger operations. How could they? The truth is such a stretch of the mind it's incomprehensible to most people.

"Here is the actual truth. At the present time, the United States of America comprises the entire North American continent, from the Atlantic to the Pacific oceans. We have absorbed Canada into our union. We are currently doing the same in Mexico, Central America, and all of the islands of the Caribbean. We have defeated not only the British, but also the combined strength of the French and Spanish fleets and forces stationed in North America. We are now the largest country in the world. Very soon, we will invite immigrants from all countries to fill the empty lands by giving them land of their own. We'll also begin to produce a long list of goods and products to sell to any nation wishing to buy them, or trade things we need for our own purposes.

"Here is the most important thing I'm going to say today. We are a Christian nation. We believe in the power of God and life, resurrection, and forgiveness of sins by His only son, Jesus Christ. We live our lives in this manner, with the Holy Spirit in each man and each woman, regardless of race or sex, or national origin, guiding us to eternity through faith, not works. The United States will remain the most powerful nation on Earth; however, we seek no further conquests of land or people beyond what we now have. We are neutral in the affairs of all other countries. We offer fair trade with all nations. However will not interfere with their governments or how they govern their own people in any way.

"Tomorrow, we will lay our brother Willis Grant to rest. An honor guard of Rangers will conduct the ceremony at the gravesite. There will also be speeches, not from me; I have already told you all you need to know. You will hear from none other than our Commander in Chief himself, General George Washington, and you will hear from one other person, whom none of you know, but is considered by every Ranger to be the heart and soul of our consciences and who has led us spiritually all these years. I wish I could tell you what a singular honor you're receiving by her presence, just believe me when I tell you it is so. Her name is Arcadia, and her name is on the lips of every Ranger each time he steps into harm's way. If George Washington is the Father of our Country, she is the Mother."

Robby glanced at his watch. "I think I have spoken long enough and given you plenty to think about. Our burial ceremony begins at two pm tomorrow. I'll see you all then."

He walked over to his family and they all walked off toward the Pierce home. His younger brothers and sisters fought over who would carry Robby's bag and uniform cover. Robby's father put his arm around his son's shoulder. "There have been some changes since you were last here. That marvelous improvement you gave us for wagons has made our wagons the most popular in all of New England. We have bought more land and put up a building to make wagons to keep up with the demand. I have over a dozen men working for me. They're very happy. They make a good wage and support their own families very well."

"Keep it that way, father, and you'll never have any labor problems."

Just then, Robby's radio came to life, "Crystal Palace to Hawkeye, do you read?"

Robby paused while his family looked on and spoke into the radio, "Hawkeye to Crystal Palace, Go."

"Papa Grizzly here, Hawkeye, are you prepared for the ceremony tomorrow?"

"Roger, Papa Grizzly, I gave the village the approved information, and set the ceremony for 14:00. You can adjust your schedule to that."

"Well done, Hawkeye. See you tomorrow, Papa Grizzly, out."

"What in the world was that," asked Robby's father.

"See this little clear strip," said Robby? He took off his helmet and showed his family the compact radio built into it. "With this, I can speak to anyone in the brigade, including the headquarters, which that was, or anyplace in the country. If you want to know how it works, I can't tell you. I understand the principal, but how the message is transmitted, I don't know."

"You used strange language," said Jonathan Pierce. What was it all about?"

"Nobody in the world has this kind of communications equipment, so we could just talk to each other in plain language. However, there will come a day when this kind of equipment is common, so we've adopted the use of code from the beginning."

"So what were you saying?"

"Just that I arrived, spoke to the people and confirmed the time for the ceremony for tomorrow. I'm afraid I can't tell you anymore."

"I don't believe you can shoot that musket of yours accurately over a mile," said Robby's older brother.

"Do you have a small bag of gunpowder?"

"I'm sure I do," said his brother.

"Do you see the post across the village green, which marks the entrance to the village how far away would you say it was?"

"Almost a mile," said his brother.

"Since you want the demonstration, take the bag of gunpowder and go set in on top of the post. Then back off at least 20 feet, I wouldn't want you to get scorched," smiled Robby.

The whole family watched as Robby's brother grabbed a rather large bag of gunpowder and went sprinting off to the city limit's post.

While he was doing this, Robby pulled the M-4 out of its case, got himself a block of wood, and tossed a handful of dirt into the air. Then he turned some nobs on his weapon and lay down on the ground with the rifle on the block of wood.

By this time, Robby's brother had reached the post and set the bag of gunpowder on top of it. He backed away a few feet. "He's going to be sorry he didn't get further away," said Robby as he sighted through the scope at the target. He pulled a large cartridge with a red tip on it from his belt, opened the breach of the weapon, and inserted the round.

He lay still for a moment and then fired. It made a big noise making everyone jump. However, nobody jumped faster than Robby's brother who scampered away, pounding his pants when the bag of gunpowder blew up in a flash of light and fire. The noise of the explosion reached them a second or so later.

"Good Lord," said Jonathan Pierce, "if I hadn't seen it with my own eyes, I would never have believed such a shot was possible."

"It's for that reason and many more when an opposing force hears, 'The Rangers Are Coming' they often surrender without a fight. I hope Ben didn't get burned to badly."

Ben eventually returned to the family's open space in front of the house. He was grinning and grimacing at the same time. "The next time I hear 'The Rangers Are Coming', I'm going to run in the other direction as fast as I can."

"That's exactly what Robby just said," said Jonathan.

"Are you hurt Ben, I told you to stand further away."

"The gunpowder set my shirt on fire. I burned my hand stamping it out."

"Let me see," said Robby. Ben's hand was red from second-degree burns. Robby reached into his pack and pulled out a tube, which he opened and squeezed a white cream into his hand. Then he rubbed the cream onto Ben's hand. Almost immediately, Ben shook his head and said, "The pain is all gone."

"This will also heal the burns. I'll put some more on you later."

"You must be the best shot in the world," said Ben.

"Likely, the truth," said Robby sadly. "The trouble is I'm seldom shooting at bags of gunpowder."

The remainder of the day and evening Robby told stories about life at Fort Independence. He spoke with authority about subjects his family knew almost nothing about. He pulled a map out of his bag and showed them what the United States would look like with all the states in their places. It was an eye-popping experience. None of the family had ever been further than Boston. Robby was showing them places he had seen thousands and thousands of miles away. He talked about his experience with the Indians of the Sioux nation and showed them their state on the map. He also showed them Veracruz in Mexico where Willis was killed.

"Normally our battle armor will protect us from anything shot at us. About the only way to take one of us down is to shoot us right in the face, which is what happened to Willis, and why we'll conduct a closed casket ceremony tomorrow."

Later, when Robby was alone in the kitchen with his mother, she looked at him and said, "Do you remember me telling you I knew what you were doing was a good deal more than you were saying?"

"I remember, mother, I was never so close to blurting out the entire story to you, than I was at that moment.

Chapter 30
Laid To Rest

Concord, Massachusetts

The first Chinook set down at 9am. Fall had returned to New England in 1776 but the weather was clear and unseasonably warm. The Chinook was filled with Rangers in standard fatigues with berets and no body armor. Robby met them and directed them to the place the Grant family had designated as the burial site for their son. The soldiers began digging and had the grave finished in two hours. Then they erected a large tent over the site and hid the grave with a gold frame of round poles draped in blue velvet. A set of heavy straps were fixed over the frame to hold the casket and a winch installed to lower it. All the dirt and the area around the burial site was covered with a green turf-like material looking like grass but actually synthetic. Chairs for the family were placed near the gravesite. In all, it was a truly lovely setting.

Robby spent the morning with the Grant family, telling them all about their son's bravery in battle and his leadership of a platoon of 50 men who had loved and followed their leader, and was considered the best soldier among them. "He was always the first to step onto the battlefield, and the last to leave it. He never left a man behind, living or dead." He described in as much detail possible, the engagement in Veracruz that took his life and said it was just a chance shot in the wrong place. Robby joined the Grant family in weeping for his loss.

At 1:30 pm, a second Chinook set down on the edge of the village green. Robby, now dressed in his perfectly groomed dress blues was there to greet them. When Robby came out of his room wearing the very smart and elegant uniform, his family whistled in admiration. They had never seen such a splendid uniform, even among the most distinguished of the British officers. They fingered his three rows of colored strips of medals on his uniform, demonstrating he had been decorated for bravery many times. His elegant braided ring in pure white around his right shoulder was the badge of honor of a Ranger. He wore a hat raised at the sides, flat on top and rose to a peak going down to a shining visor. In the center of the flat space in the front of the cap was an emblem, like a coat of arms, the symbol of the Rangers. His shoes were so shiny, you could see your face in them.

The entire population of Concord watched as the honor guard, all wearing the same dress blue uniforms marched off the back of the Chinook and formed a perfect square formation in front of Lieutenant Pierce. All of them had rifles, much shorter than muskets, but deadly looking. Actually, they were carbines, broken out especially for this ceremony and drilled by the soldiers.

The detail came to attention with their rifles at their sides. Robby barked, "Detail, right shoulder arms. The soldiers moved in exact precision in shouldering their rifles. "Display formation, Move!" ordered Robby. The soldiers spread out by turning a left face and marching forward. The back rank stayed put and the three succeeding rows moved forward, stopping by rank until the first rank came to a halt. This put the formation into a bigger square with about three feet between each man.

"Drill exercise, march," cried Robby.

The men began marching. Without any further orders from Robby, the detail went to port arms and began spinning the rifles in unison. They moved in complicated patterns, spinning the rifles and once turning to face the crowd throwing the rifles in the air and catching them in mid-air in a perfect Queen Anne salute. Once while marching in three rows, the lead man threw his rifle in the air spinning and was caught by the last man in the rank who then passed his rifle up to man in front of him. Since all three rows of men did this maneuver at exactly the same time, the crowd whistled and cheered.

When the demonstration was over, the men returned to their tight formation. Robby had them place their weapons at their sides and ordered at ease. The audience gave a long round of applause.

Just as they came to a stop, another, smaller helicopter came down just in front of the formation and out stepped General George Washington, dressed in the same dress blues with gold braid on the visor of his cap, and two silver stars in the epaulets of his shoulders. He was wearing white gloves, as were all the soldiers, including Robby.

"Detail, attention," ordered Robby. You could hear the shoes snapping together in unison as the order was given. Robby turned and faced the General and rendered a very crisp salute. "Sir," he said, "the detail is formed."

"Carry on with the ceremony, Lieutenant," said Washington, returning the salute as smartly.

Robby marched to the back of the Chinook, "Honor Guard march!" he barked.

Six men came marching in slow time out of the Chinook. They were carrying the gleaming wooden casket containing Sergeant Willis Grant, covered by a flag. They were flanked by the honor guard, which had unveiled two flags, one of the United States, the same as on the casket, and the other the colors of the Ranger brigade. In perfect slow time, the formation marched to the gravesite, followed by all the people of Concord with the Grant family dressed in black, leading the way.

The Rangers set the casket on its frame and stepped back at attention. The rest of the detail formed up at the front of the casket in two rows on each side. General Washington reached his hand into the helicopter and out stepped Arcadia. She was stunning as usual. Her long blond hair hung down gracefully past the shoulders of her shimmering white gown that went all the way to the ground. Robby always got goose bumps when he saw her in the elegant gown, with the silver belt around her slim waist.

She nodded her head gracefully as she walked slowly with her arm wrapped around Washington. The people of Concord took a collective gasp as Arcadia came past them, through the ranks of the Rangers. They were as struck by her as everyone else. Her crystal blue eyes emanated wisdom, compassion and love.

All were surprised to see her knell on a cushioned stool as she came to the casket, and bowed her head in prayer with her hands folded together.

General Washington addressed all in clear voice. "It's never easy to bring to rest one of your own, especially Sergeant Willis Grant. He was among the very first to volunteer for a life as a Ranger. His service to the Brigade reflects great honor on our country, and our band of brothers who take him to his final rest today. As his commanding officer, I will say I never saw a more brave and capable soldier. As his friend, I will say I will miss him, his quick smile and his happy disposition.

He was so important to the Rangers our spiritual leader, the one who has kept our faith all these years, who has given us the word of God in such clarity and insight, has asked permission to attend this ceremony and speak to you. Ladies and Gentlemen, it is my distinct honor and privilege to present to you the lady Arcadia.

Arcadia rose and stepped forward, as always to Robby her voice was like a harmony of lovely sounds speaking truth, love of God and His love for us.

"Willis was my friend. I grieve I will not be able to speak to him in this life, anymore. Of course, this does not mean Willis no longer exists. He exists today more gloriously than ever before, because he has taken his place in the presence of the living God of the Universe who is nothing less than pure love.

"God is like the ocean. The ocean does not have wet – it is wet. You jump in, you get wet. God does not have love – He is love. His love is not a possession. He can't give it away as a reward for those who are good enough to earn it. Love is simply who He is. He loves each of you because of who you are. You were created to be the object of His love. Nothing you do can change that. It is His nature. Loving you is as natural to Him as breathing is to you.

"God became man in the person of Jesus Christ. Jesus had to live as a man in order to experience all the things crushing us on a daily basis. He had to suffer as a man, die like a man, in order for God to resurrect His soul and count him as the price for all our sins, and then to give us all the Holy Spirit so the Jesus who lives within us all can join in fellowship with Him and with God.

"Through Jesus, God is asking us to surrender our wills to Him. He is asking you to let Him control your mind. The mind is the most restless, unruly part of mankind. Long after you have learned the discipline of holding your tongue, your thoughts defy your will and set themselves up against Him. Man is the pinnacle of His creation and the human mind is wondrously complex. God risked everything by granting us Free Will, and the freedom to think for yourself. This is a

Godlike privilege, forever setting you apart from animals. He made you in His image, precariously close to deity.

"Though the blood of Christ has fully redeemed you, your mind is the last bastion of rebellion. Open yourself to His glorious presence, letting His light permeate your thinking. When the spirit of Jesus is controlling your mind, you are filled with life and peace.

"Why have I spoken to you in this manner today, in the presence of the body of our fallen comrade? It's because the words I've spoken were his words. Yes, your Willis had grown far in the mind of God. So well, he was able to speak with such clarity I will never forget how perfectly he understood. And, all of this in the middle of a war of rebellion, in which he had to believe in victory as an act of faith. Every man you see before you today has made the same choices and that is why, if it were them in the casket now instead of Willis, it would not matter. It would be they who would be sitting face to face with Jesus in Heaven at this moment. Grief is human, but never forget eternity is still eternal. May God be with you all, and may the light of Jesus burn brightly in your hearts."

The stunned crowd of traditional Congregationalists had never heard the Gospel spoken in such a manner. Arcadia's words burned down to the core of their souls and all would say afterwards they were never so moved.

The honor guard stepped forward, fired three rounds in unison from their carbines, and conducted the precise ceremony of the folding of the flag. Washington took the folded flag and laid it in the lap of Willis' mother saying, "A grateful nation thanks you for the service of your son." Then he slowly saluted, bowed and stepped away. Arcadia went with him. The special unit marched to the Chinook and both choppers took off. The remaining chopper of men who had set the site, would wait until the casket was lowered and the crowd disbursed before cleaning the sight and placing a rectangular stone with a carved inscription of the name, rank and dates of birth and death on it, with the added words, "Died bravely in battle." Then as night fell, they too took off and only Robby was left.

The hubbub over the events surrounding the funeral did not die out in a day or so. It was the main topic of conversation for all the time Robby remained on furlough in Concord. A lot of the talk was about Arcadia.

"How is it we have never heard of this great leader in the war for freedom," Robby was asked? "Are there times when her counsel is sought in meetings of importance"?

"I've been to meetings in which hers was the only voice, and when she was finished speaking, everybody got up to do what she said."

Ben was more direct, "That was, without a doubt, the most beautiful woman I've ever seen in my life. She is like an angel, and her voice was like poured honey."

"I will tell you something, brother," said Robby, "there are a great many things about Arcadia that are special. You will, no doubt, be surprised to learn I had to beat over a dozen men in the combat martial arts tournament, just to get the privilege of meeting her in the ring, and the best I could do was a tie."

Before Ben could answer that remarkable bit of information, one of Robby's sisters came running out of the house, "Robby you talking machine is making a noise."

Robby ran inside and picked up his radio, which was chirping an incoming caller was on the line. He answered, "This is Hawkeye, go."

"Hawkeye, this is Papa Grizzly, I hope you've enjoyed your leave, you earned it but it's time to go back to work. I will come right to the point. We are forming a second brigade of Rangers. We need to fill the ranks of the first brigade. Willis Grant was not our only casualty, and we need to expand our forces to cover and protect the rather huge country we have established."

"We are running a new ad in all the papers. No subterfuge this time, we are actively recruiting new Rangers. The ad will appear in the papers during the next several days and you'll stay to meet potential recruits in Boston Commons October 1 through October 5. I am sending you a detail of Rangers to help you manage a big crowd, I imagine. Don't recruit anyone you would not be willing to serve next to you. I suspect you will be turning away a lot of eager lads."

"I am also sending a special detail looking for men and women to serve the country in a different way. The men I'm sending are some of the original permanent party who are specially trained to screen for such individuals. Any questions, Lieutenant," asked the General?

"No sir, I understand perfectly."

Chapter 31
New Recruits

Boston, Massachusetts

Robby took the ATV the Rangers left behind to Boston on the day before the open enrollment was scheduled. His arrival in Boston created a great stir. Many of the people had never seen a live Ranger before, although they had certainly read every word about them they could get their hands on. Most of the people were in awe of the young man in the green fatigues, and jaunty beret. They were especially impressed with the strange machine he drove, running all by itself without a horse in sight.

A full-sized Chinook flew over Boston and landed on the margin of the Boston Commons. It drew a huge crowd of awe-struck Bostonians. The helicopter was loaded with no less than 20 men. They unloaded two large tents and set them up with signs saying, 'Ranger Recruits' and 'Special Education'. Robby had read the ad.

Do You Have What It Takes?

A second Brigade of Rangers is being formed to serve in locations throughout the United States of America. The requirements for selection are the same as the current Rangers on duty today. You must be able to undergo training of the most extreme nature and only those of superior mental toughness and character will succeed. We will provide advanced education for those who need it. We offer a good wage and full provisions during your service, which will be for a period of not less than fifteen years. We offer high adventure, dangerous assignments, and an opportunity to be a part of the best-trained, best-equipped army in the world.

The selection process will occur in the capital city of each state formally established at this time on Oct 1-5.

Additionally a Special Education unit is being formed with duties that may not be directly connected to Ranger operations. The requirements of this unit are we more mental than physical . An advanced curriculum of science, mathematics, engineering, and industrial design will be offered. Benefits are the same as Ranger duty, and the term of enlistment will be not less than fifteen years. For those individuals regardless of sex, race, or national origin, who believes they possess these qualities, interviews, will be conducted at the same time and place as Ranger enlistments.

Robby was certain they would be very busy. He was not briefed on the "Special Education" element of the personnel search, but he suspected Arcadia was engaged in a program to give the United States the edge in fields other than warfare.

The next morning the Rangers who were assigned to recruit more Rangers met with Lieutenant Pierce. He was the senior officer of the detail. He pulled out the questionnaire to be used for questioning candidates. It was much the same as the one he had at his enlistment interview.

"Remember men we are looking as much for character as we are physical qualities. Each one of us has paid a big price for the right to wear the Ranger patch. Think about that as you interview the candidates. Ask yourself the question, 'would I feel comfortable with this man next to me when the going gets tough'."

Robby also met with the leader of the special education detail. He was a full Captain. "I read the ad. I assume you are looking for people who can stand advanced training to develop technology to give the United States a trading edge over other countries. Excuse me for making assumptions, but based on my own education, the weapons we employ, and the advanced equipment we possess, I believe there can be no other explanation than you, the rest of the permanent party, and especially Arcadia have come to us from some time in the future. It seems reasonable to assume you will not just hand over this body of technology in whole to these students, but also rather give them the tiny hints they would need to push our existing technology to the next

- 184 -

higher level. My question, if you are able to answer at all, Captain, is how far into our future do you intend to push our technology?"

"About a hundred years," said the Captain. "Congratulations Lieutenant, you're only the second person to have reasoned out the reason for the existence of all this advanced technology. Of course, there is a good deal more to the whole story, which I can't tell you, however, now you've gotten this far, we'll enroll you in the same special education program. It will be very hard on you General Compton has you pegged as the commanding officer of a platoon of new recruits."

"General Compton," said Robby a little surprised, "What about General Washington?"

"General Washington is busy lining up his candidacy to become the first President of the United States at the election in November. There's no question he will win, and he might have something special in mind for you. He likes you a lot, and will be thrilled when I tell him you've figured out the masquerade."

Almost 1000 men and women showed up for the interviews. Rangers went down the long line and determined which were there for Ranger interviews and which had come for special education. When the split was known, Robby and the Captain got together and determined how many people could be interviewed in a day. For the Captain, the interview time was 45 minutes, for Robby it was 30. They divided the groups by the number of interviewers they had, and made appointments for each of the people in the line. They passed out cards with the interview time and date written on it, and sent everyone on their way, to return at their appointed time.

Then they started the interviews.

The first man who came into the tent cubicle for Robby was cocky, certain he could beat any Ranger and was ready to get started. Robby thanked him for coming and said if the Rangers had any further questions they would be in touch. The young man exited the tent.

Robby was surprised to find how few real candidates there actually were. After a full day of interviews by him and the rest of the team, they had a group of less than 40 men. When he checked with the Captain, he found they had qualified even fewer, 14 men, one who was black, and 6 women.

At the end of the six-day interview process, a repeat of what

Robby had experienced, the Rangers had 267 recruits and the Special Education group had 89. Arrangements were made to transport all of them by Chinook the following month. The recruit detail went back to Fort Independence.

Robby was astonished to find there were now two Forts. Both of them identical in size and configuration and ten miles apart. The new camp was called Fort Freedom. He had no idea how such a fort was constructed and equipped in the month he'd been away. He suspected it was part of the time travel concept he had discussed with the Captain.

Immediately on arrival, Robby was ordered to the office of General Washington. He reported and was ushered into his office. "Have a seat, Robby," said Washington smiling as he shook his hand after they had exchanged salutes. "I understand you've figured out our mystery. I was hoping you would be one of the few. I've always been impressed with your ability to solve puzzles and your intelligence. Actually, it's something of a relief. How did you figure it out?"

"That speech you gave me for the people of Concord," said Robby, "It had such a depth of planning to it. I figure someone had already seen this time in the future and had devised some way of coming to this time to change the future for an unknown reason."

As he was speaking, Arcadia came into the room. "Everything you suspect is true, Robby. Let me tell you a story. Arcadia told of the attack on the United States in her time of 2030, and the death of 150 million Americans. She said her family had always had a special relationship with God, and an angel appeared to her in the flesh and told her where the alteration in history would have to be made, and gave her the means to do it.

"We built Camp Independence first in my time, and it was transported to this time. We also pushed four modern Navy warships into the past. They are three ships called Destroyers, and one submersible ship called a submarine. These are the ships that attacked and sunk the troop ships with British reinforcements. We then left one destroyer on patrol in the Atlantic and moved the other two and the submarine to the Caribbean to take on the French, the Dutch, and the Spanish warships. We sank a hundred of them. We didn't sink any commercial trade ships. They were all permitted to land normally. We bombarded and destroyed all the important forts in the Caribbean and the Rangers moped up in Mexico and Central America."

"Everything we've done up to this point is to establish the United States as the largest country in the world. In the process, we interfered with the slave issue with our Foundation Company and the establishment of Emporiums as stores for the former slaves. It was a fundamentally better plan and more profitable for the plantation owners. This made it possible for us to ratify the new Constitution for the country. It's not completely the original. In the next 250 years, there were 30 amendments to the first one. We rewrote the constitution to correct the problems the founding fathers had no way of anticipating, such as the question of slavery. In the past, we know in 2030, the country was divided by a terrible civil war with the death of over 600,000 Americans in a four-year war. Now that's not going to happen."

"In fact we've already changed your current history. General Washington here had to fight the British for over seven years before he was able to defeat them. The country had a different set of laws to govern for several years after the Revolutionary War. We've erased all of that. Phase 1 of our plan is now complete."

Robby had spent the last five years listening to powerful, thought provoking and very deeply religious sermons. Hearing her speak in this fashion was a true shock. All he had done and learned in his time with the Rangers now came into crystal clarity. "What is Phase 2," he asked?

"What do you think," asked Arcadia.

"If it's important we maintain neutrality, we must be secure from attack and superior in technology."

"Correct," said Arcadia, "Why don't we just hand over the technology to the people of America."

"America must make these improvements on their own," said Robby, "Otherwise we would handicap our people in a way in which the general population would not have assimilated the information independently. Any breakthrough by any other country would make us weaker and vulnerable."

"I could not have said it better," said Arcadia.

"Therefore, the special education schools," said Robby. "My guess is you are recruiting only the very best in each of the fields you think are important. In their studies, the introduction of even the slimmest clue to a major improvement would appear to come from the American inventor."

"Also right on the mark," said Arcadia. "How could you improve the entire system?"

"You have already begun the process by educating the former slaves. You need an educational system that is universal and provides a first class education, with the best students fed into your special education program. If you do that, some of your students are going to come up with technology even you don't know about."

"What are the dangers to this system," asked Arcadia.

"Technology will become like a religion in its own right. We run the real danger of losing our faith in God and the truth of Christ on the resurrection of sins by accepting him."

"Right again," said Arcadia. "How would you approach that problem?"

"I suppose I would begin by demonstrating to your special students science does not kill God, but authenticates God."

"Exactly our intentions," said Arcadia, "but there are risks to revealing the Genesis Code to our students. It's rather advanced science."

"Assuming you can overcome that issue and keep America on track as a Christian country, what are your plans for building a trading empire of the United States?"

"Excellent question, Robby," said Arcadia. "We already know the British are on the verge of an industrial revolution that will bring forth an avalanche of new technology. Our plan is beat them at their own game. If we can provide products, which are the result of the Industrial Revolution, cheaper than they can produce them, we'll have a trading advantage. They will get all the results of our technology without us having to show them how we did it."

"The British are already having trouble feeding their population. How about exporting food products to them?"

"That's one good idea," said Arcadia. "We also think there's a market for steel goods, textiles, and transportation."

"You aren't thinking of giving them a bunch of ATVs"

"No," said Arcadia seriously, "we think we can sell all the European powers new ships."

"They already have plenty of ships," said Robby.

"Not for long," said Washington speaking up for the first time. The major European powers are very upset about losing all their holdings in North America and the Caribbean. Our ambassadors, report there are secret meetings going on with the British, Dutch, French, and Spanish, to combine into a huge armada aimed right at us."

"If they send a thousand ships, can our Navy stop them?"

"Unfortunately not," said Arcadia. Some of the troop ships will get through and be able to land on our shores. That's why we need another Brigade of Rangers."

"We will still win," said Arcadia, "despite the loss of lives. It will leave the Europeans short of money, ships, and the ability to feed their people. We'll demonstrate a Christian nation does not hold grudges and start doing all the things the Europeans can't do for themselves. Of course, they won't be able to pay for all this, so we will extend them credit. In the end, we'll initiate a great trading relationship and with the Europeans owing us so much money, they will think twice before offending us again. Our neutrality will be secure."

"Does this solve all our problems for the future," asked Robby?

"Not by any means, there will be new issues and new problems beyond your lifetime, and these may not be in our history books. We might have to find new answers to new threats."

Chapter 32
A New Brigade

Fort Freedom, Virginia

The new recruits were pouring in. Lieutenant Robert Pierce watched them as they stepped off the Chinooks, wide-eyed after their first air flight. They were eager and excited, but also very apprehensive. Robby remembered his first impressions and understood the feelings. In his case, none of the men who came for the formation of the first brigade had any idea of what they had actually signed up to do. This bunch had read the extensive coverage the Rangers received in every paper in the country. There were even a few eyewitnesses to seeing the Rangers in action.

Robby chanced upon Sergeant Thomas Seacrest, the man who first interviewed him in Boston a lifetime ago. He was now Sergeant Major Seacrest, the top non-com in the brigade and working for the new brigade commander, General Forrester.

"You've come far, Pilgrim," said Seacrest. "I'm proud of you. Now you are going to have a platoon of your own to train. Who are your drill instructors?"

"Sergeants Wilkins and Thomas," said Robby.

"Good men," said Seacrest, "they'll keep the lads on their toes. They are old hands at this kind of work. Don't be too proud to ask for their advice."

"You can relax, Sergeant-Major, I hardly know what I'm doing here myself."

"New officers have a tendency to coddle their troops too much. Don't do it. Remember not all of your fifty men are going to make it through the training. You will lose about 20 percent, who just can't cut it physically or academically. When we get out in real action, you'll lose another 5 percent, at current numbers. Be tough, but fair, reasonable but demanding. You'll do fine."

Now the moment was upon them. He had 50 young boys standing in front of him in disorder. He walked out in front of them, his two sergeants flanking him.

"Good morning, recruits," he said. "I want you to line up in rows ten across and five deep. I want the shortest man in the front right corner as you face me, and tallest man in the back left row. Now move it!"

The men shuffled around, Wilkins and Thomas used their batons to help the pokey ones move with a sense of urgency. When the formation was finally formed, Robby went back to the front. "This is the formation you will have anytime you are ordered to fall in. Try to remember who's standing next to you, because if you get it wrong, you will have to pay a physical penalty in pushups."

"My name is Lieutenant Pierce. These are my bothers in arms, Sergeants Wilkins and Thomas. The three of us are Rangers. None of you are Rangers, and some of you will never be Rangers. For the next twelve months, you will be tested physically, mentally and emotionally. This is a volunteer army, you can quit and go home, whenever you like. In fact, we hope you do ring the bell in front of the mess hall and save us the trouble of having to write home to your family you got killed in battle because you were stupid, or got tired, or couldn't stand the stench of a battleground. The first words out your mouth when you speak to my men are 'Yes Sir, or No Sir, Drill Sergeant'. Do you understand?"

A loud chorus of "Yes Sir, Drill Sergeant," came from the recruits.

"I can't hear you," shouted the First Sergeant.

The recruits screamed at the top of their lungs, "Yes Sir, Drill Sergeant!"

"Our sergeants are not officers like me, so in real life they don't rate a Sir or a Salute, but you will see and take classes from a lot of other officers who do rate both of those. We just want to make sure you don't forget proper protocol."

"Now, the first thing we are going to do is turn you over to the medical people, who are going to vaccinate you for every disease we know about. After that, you'll go to the quartermaster to draw uniforms and equipment. Then you will be assigned your quarters, two men to a room, or two women, for you four. You'd better make up your minds with whom you are going to live with for the next year. After that, we will go to lunch. You will spend the rest of the day taking tests so we can find out who can read and write and separate you into classes. There is no shame in not being able to read and write. We guarantee you will be able to do both and a lot more before your training is over. Now we are going to march over to infirmary and get started. Move in single file, starting at this end and filling in when each rank has cleared."

The sergeants ushered the recruits into the infirmary. When the last had entered, they relaxed, knowing they would not see the recruits for several hours. They took the time to get better acquainted. "I'm John Wilkins, Lieutenant. Aren't you the one they call 'Hawkeye'"?

"That's me."

"It's an honor to serve with you, sir. Some of your exploits are legendary."

"If that were the case, I would be the General," smiled Robby.

"I'm Mathew Thomas, Lieutenant. I don't need to be told about you, I was in Veracruz when Willis Grant got killed. You may not remember me I was just one of the troops, but you saved a bunch of us that day, and the way you handled that cavalry outfit was really smart."

Robby looked at Thomas, "I thought you looked familiar to me. I'm glad to have such a veteran in my staff."

The sergeants picked up their platoon as they emerged from the quartermaster's building. They had all been to the barber and were pretty bald. They were now dressed in fatigues, and looked incrementally more like soldiers. They moved the men to the barracks. The recruits had all doubled up and so the Sergeants let them have ten minutes to admire their new quarters and wonder at the lights, mirrors, large beds, running hot and cold water and the flushing toilets. They dumped their piles of uniforms and equipment. Instruction of how to square away a room would come later.

Then it was off to the mess hall. Robby remembered how hungry he was when he'd gotten his first meal, and how surprised at how good and plentiful the food was. He didn't give them any more time to eat it than he had had. In exactly 45 minutes, they were moving in a line toward the classroom building and instructors took over to separate the men and women by education levels.

When the day was over another lieutenant came out to give Robby a report. "It's a about what we expected. About half the platoon is functionally illiterate. We can fix that in fairly short order with the computer enhanced learning programs. None of them has IQ's so low they can't learn. They are ignorant, and unschooled, not stupid. You do have some pretty bright people in your group, especially two of the women. We will push them along into higher studies as fast as they can absorb it."

The training got underway in earnest the next morning. Robby and his Sergeants drove the platoon very hard for a month. They were shaping up into a good platoon. When the specialized training began involving other instructors, Robby was sent to the Special Education center, which was also at Fort Liberty.

The elements of business, trade, commerce, and finance, diplomacy, and the history of the world, with special emphasis on Europe were presented in sections and he learned them. He became very proficient at operating a computer.

Part of the special education was a stream of information regarding the politics going on in Europe. Apparently, the American ambassadors to the major countries were able to stay in contact by radio with central command. The French and the Spanish were pushing hard to form a coalition with the great powers to mount an offensive on North America. The voice of caution was coming from the British, who had first-hand experience with the tremendous capabilities of the American army. All of the European powers were madly trying to regain what they had lost in the Americas by absorbing other weaker countries in the world.

A big part of Robby's education was learning the long strides being made in America. With the election of George Washington as President in November of 1776, he was able to organize departments to handle the many enterprises the country needed. Arcadia made sure money was not a problem, even though the flat rate system of taxes was working very well.

The most important projects underway were the development of bigger and more efficient steel mills. There were now half a dozen Bessemer plants in operation and specialized products of all kinds being manufactured in revolutionary assembly lines. Products coming out were tools of all kinds from hammers to saws to shovels all produced at a fraction of the price of what it had cost to hand forge these products.

The power for these mills and other factories was coming from improved hydroelectric plants. The simple generators Ben Franklin had seen were now being built in full sized versions and power was pouring out.

One of the priorities for the country was a working transportation system. The first rail line between Philadelphia and Boston was completed the same year Washington became President. At the same time, construction began on the first transcontinental railroad.

There was not a single unemployed person in the country and the biggest problem for many of the projects was a shortage of labor. Washington solved this problem by importing hundreds of thousands of starving peasants from Mexico, Central America and some of the Caribbean Islands. They were housed, educated, provided with ample opportunities to worship God in the Roman Catholic tradition, and paid more money each month than any of them had ever seen in their lives.

In return, the emigrants returned the benefits they were receiving by working very hard. Washington limited all workdays for the whole country to ten hours and everyone had no work on Sunday. This, in itself, was a big improvement in the working conditions people had previously known.

America adapted the steam engines from the locomotives to the shipping industry. The plants started turning out materials to build steel-hulled ships with powerful steam engines. Soon, a growing fleet of ships was coming out of the graving yards. They were stronger, faster, safer, and had a much bigger capacity for carrying cargo.

Another emphasized industry was textiles. The special education department got a few hints, here and there, from people disguised as students in the classes, but were actually trained technicians. In record time, the concept of the modern power loom came off the drawing boards. The British would not reach this level of sophistication for almost a hundred years. Cotton that would have normally gone to England to be turned into clothing and textiles, was now sent to plants located near the source. The southern states began to be the leaders in the manufacturing of cloth. Best of all, it was produced by former slaves whose standard of living improved along with the plantation owners. The introduction of the cotton gin significantly increased the amount of cotton grown and processed. The manpower for this expanding enterprise came mostly from Mexico and Central America. No new slaves were imported from Africa.

Much of this was still in development when Robby started in the Special Education school. It didn't stay that way very long.

Robby left the school after a month of intensive study and returned to his platoon to guide them through their year of training. They graduated 40 recruits and they went on to their permanent units for specialized training in the full range of Ranger operations. It was a fast year, and a second brigade of Rangers was just a year short of being operational.

Chapter 33
Innovation
The New District of Columbia, 1781

Arcadia stood in the center of her office and looked at the big model of Washington, D.C. It was almost a perfect copy of the real Washington she had known all her life, but was now just a smoking radioactive ruin in 2030. She had made a few small changes, but it was substantially the same Capital. Of course, most of it was still not built. She had a crew of 50 men who had come with her from Branson, all top-notch architects, contractors, electricians, plumbers, and top worker supervisors. To this, she added 10,000 workers. The first year they all lived and ate in tents until the building that would be the National History Museum was finished. It was large enough to house the work crews with offices for all the supervisors, and one for Arcadia.

The actual Capital was still in Philadelphia where Washington lived as President and Congress continued to meet in Liberty Hall and another building nearby. The government was still small, but very efficient.

The job of transforming a largely agrarian society into one with an expanding industrial infrastructure was daunting. Arcadia was pleased with the progress. People can do and accomplish amazing things when properly motivated. In the five years since the Rangers and the Navy consolidated the territory of the new United States, Arcadia had pushed forward on all fronts. She looked at the list showing her inventory. She had:

Six Bessemer Steel Plants

Twelve hydroelectric plants, each producing 250 megawatts per day

Ten modern textile mills with power looms producing 100,000 yards of cloth daily

One transcontinental railroad from New York to San Francisco Bay

An operational railroad running from Philadelphia to Boston

10 times as much land was under cultivation with the addition of the grain harvester, and power drill for seeds. One of the first outposts she established was in central Iowa, and she had 50,000 acres of corn in cultivation. The production of wheat in Kansas was turning out ten million pounds of flour every year.

There were a large number of manufacturing and fabrication plants building consumer goods of all kinds in assembly lines.

The oil fields in Pennsylvania and the associated refinery were turning out ten million barrels of diesel and aviation fuel a year. This kept all the Humvees, Bradley's, ATVs, and a fleet of helicopters running and flying.

Just before they made the time jump, a dozen communication and surveillance satellites were launched into orbit, grouped over North America and Europe. This was the secret of why the radios worked everywhere in the country and gave the government direct communications with the foreign ambassadors in the main European Capitals.

They had completed 10 steel, steam driven freighters with the keels laid and progress toward completion on 20 more.

Based on her understanding of history, Arcadia estimated the United States was now about 100 years ahead of the technology of any other country in the world.

After the establishment of the United States of America, the government established embassies in all the European capitals. The Europeans were pragmatic enough to realize America was a country, whether they liked it or not, and recognized its sovereignty. The ambassadors quickly reestablished trading relations with all countries. Trade steadily increasing. However, the trade was limited to the products the old colonies had always exported, cotton, tobacco, and food. The growing inventory of new and cheap consumer products, tools, textiles, and ships, were held back for a better time.

The ambassadors gave speeches all over each country inviting people to immigrate to America and promising several things. First, was credit for sailing and rail transportation, and a thing called the Homestead Act. This had actually happened in 1862, but Arcadia got it pushed through Congress early in 1781. It offered 160 acres of free land with a ten-dollar filing fee and a promise to work the land for no less than five years or until the bill for transportation had been paid. It was a seductive offer and hundreds of thousands of people began heading for the United States.

Despite all the apparent good will and increasing trade and immigration, Arcadia knew from the network of informants financed by the ambassadors, the French, Spanish, Dutch and, increasingly, the British were plotting a mass invasion of the United States and the return of all their holdings. Large amounts of money were spent to, secretly, build an enormous armada of war and troop ships, and assemble a huge professional army.

Of course, this took time. Arcadia figured the worst-case scenario was five years, which was the reason a second Brigade of Rangers were formed. The best-case scenario was ten years, which would allow the United States to build more infrastructure, stock up a bigger inventory of new products, train more workers, and allow the Special Education school to begin turning out more original work.

One of the products Arcadia wanted to sell in large numbers around the world was wagons, wagons of all kinds, freight wagons, coaches, and elegant carriages. She knew she could mass-produce large numbers of wagons using ball-bearing wheels with great strength and quality, cheaper than any in the world could. However, the feature making the biggest difference was rubber tires. This was one thing that the United States did not have. Knowing rubber originally came from South America, she sent big cargo ships and a team of experts to collect a large supply. The cargo ships were gone for months, but returned with cargos full of rubber. A regular shipment schedule was arranged.

With a supply of rubber stored in warehouses, Arcadia shipped some to the Special Education school, and with only a little help, developed vulcanization. That gave her what she needed and she subsidized a factory with the Pierce family in Concord, building wagons with steel hubs and rubber tires. Soon hundreds of wagons began pouring off the assembly line.

The Special Education school surprised Arcadia by adapting

rubber to many other uses. Soon she had rubber boots, rubber hoses, and many other applications. She set up more factories to produce the products.

Overnight, the United States was becoming a world power, but the rest of the world remained completely ignorant.

Arcadia originally estimated a five to ten year window before Europe struck back at the upstart Americans. As it turned out, she got nine years.

She had plenty of notice from the network of spies in Europe, plus the surveillance photos from the satellites showing large numbers of ships gathering at ports in England, France, Rotterdam, and Spain. At the same time, troops began to make their way to the ports. Arcadia, Washington, Jefferson, and Franklin sifted through the information. The obvious points of attack would be the principal American ports, Boston, New York, the Chesapeake Bay, Baltimore, Philadelphia, and further south at Charleston. The might even try to put a fleet into New Orleans. Washington considered that unlikely, but believed Havana, Puerto Rico, and Nassau were possible.

"I believe they will stick to the major ports," said Washington. They have to land enough troops and equipment to occupy the bigger cities and use them for bases to strike up and down the coast. What is your estimate, Arcadia of the number of ships our navy can intercept?"

"That depends on how they disburse the fleet. If they sail most of it in one convoy, it will be a turkey shoot. I don't believe that's going to happen. I believe we will see at least four major convoys, Boston and New York for sure, and probably Baltimore. However, I'm betting they put a good portion of their troops ashore in Charleston."

Why do you think that," asked Jefferson?

"Better weather, smaller population to overwhelm, and a straight shot up the coast to link up with a big force they put ashore in either Boston or New York."

"So how many ships will get through," repeated Washington?

"Maybe 200, or more, said Arcadia. There's a limit to what our ships can do. They have limited ammunition. The submarine can pick off 30 of the biggest ships. I would put it down in the Caribbean."

"That leaves us with 3 ships to cover five or six ports."

"Once the ships are within range of the helicopters we can do a lot of damage with those. If they get inside 10 miles, we can even use the

105s.

"Can we distinguish the difference between troop ships and battleships," asked Franklin?

"Yes, the battleships will show row upon row of cannons. The troop ships will have fewer guns to hold more men," said Arcadia.

"If I were in command of this force," said Washington, I would not want my troops scattered over hundreds of miles. I would concentrate on two main landing points and try to flank whatever forces were in between."

"So where would you land," asked Jefferson?

"I agree with Arcadia about a major landing at Charleston. The next port I would pick would be New York."

"We have a lot to lose in this," said Arcadia. We can't afford to lose our steel plants or all the factories around them. They're not far from Philadelphia. We have our big Textile Mills in Georgia, close to Atlanta plus we have a large civilian population to protect. When the armada actually sets sail, we'll have a good idea where they are going. A city we can rebuild, but we can't afford losing a lot of people. I think we need to plan to evacuate the target cities."

"I can organize that," said Jefferson.

"Forts Independence and Liberty will be empty, you can put at least 20,000 there," said Arcadia.

"We'll need big tent camps for New York and Charleston."

"Get with the permanent party at both Forts and see what you can arrange."

"It looks like we have done all the planning we can until we know more," said Franklin. "Let's go to dinner."

Arcadia hated it, but she had to agree. The waiting game was starting.

Chapter 34
Invasion

The Atlantic Ocean, 1788

The armada sailed for America on April 20, 1788. The Americans had the great advantage of knowing when European powers were sailing, believing they had the element of surprise.

"They have sailed," said Arcadia at the meeting in the big conference room at Fort Independence. "It looks like they have 1080 ships sailing from England, Rotterdam, Calais in France, and from Spanish ports. They have troop ships with 50,000 men on them. That's about 650 ships, and 430 battleships. They aren't moving very fast. We estimate about a month for the passage. Based on their tracks, the computers say Boston will not be a target. They predict New York for sure, with lower probabilities for Philadelphia and Baltimore. At least half the troop ships are on a course for Charleston. It looks like your original projection of concentrating their ground forces in just a couple of places was right, Mr. President."

On board the British flagship Citation, Admiral Malley was meeting with his staff. "Gentlemen, the signals from all the ships in the northern fleet tell us our entire fleet has sailed from the British ports, as well as Rotterdam, and from France. We can assume the Spanish have also sailed."

"Our plan remains the same. We want to strike at the heart of the American continent. Our principal target is the city of New York. There is more anchorage there than any other port and more places to disembark our troops and their equipment. We will bombard New York, inflicting the maximum damage on the population, then we will move inland and south toward Philadelphia and Baltimore. We expect the greatest opposition at this point. The Americans will have withdrawn to defend their biggest city. Of course, the element of surprise and the sheer size of our army should demoralize the Americans and reduce them to rabble."

"Admiral," asked one of the senior staff "is it possible the Americans have kept their force of Rangers intact? The reports of their effectiveness against General Howe are quite graphic."

"General Howe was led into an ambush and his force of less than 6,000 soldiers was harassed by militia fighting from tree to tree, until he was forced to surrender."

"I've read his official report and he states his entire army was decimated in less than 30 minutes by a force of demons, possessing enormous firepower."

"The Spaniards have given similar reports of an army of ferocious soldiers called Rangers. Their reports say entire companies of men ran away when they heard the words, 'The Rangers Are Coming'."

"What else would you expect from the Spanish? That is why we've given them the much easier target of Charleston, augmented by three of our best regiments. Besides, armies are expensive to maintain. I doubt the Americans can do that and have disbanded their entire force."

Day by day, the Commander in Chief of all military forces, President George Washington, watched the photographs from the reconnaissance satellites. Arcadia was his constant companion, as was Ben Franklin. The pictures showed two distinct groups. The computer track for the northern group still indicated New York was the target. The southern group was dead on toward Charleston with a squadron breaking off toward Havana.

"How is Jefferson doing in getting New York evacuated," asked Washington?

"Better than half the population has already moved to the tent camp, mostly women and children," said Franklin. "The men are rounding up as much of their valuables as possible, but they're ready to leave as soon as you give the order."

"And Charleston," asked Washington?

"It's my understanding from the Second Brigade," said Arcadia, "Charleston is a ghost town. They have a much smaller population to move and they have disbursed to friends and relatives a safe distance away."

"What is the distance of the armada as of now," asked Washington?

"About 600 miles, Mr. President," said Arcadia. "We will engage both fleets at 500 miles. The destroyers are trailing the fleet, just out of sight. They will start at the back of the fleet and move toward the lead ships. Mr. President, just how blood thirsty are we?"

"What do you mean, Arcadia?"

"Bloodthirsty was a bad choice of words. As I see it, we must inflict such a blow to the countries of Europe, they will think a very long time before they even consider invading the United States, like maybe permanently."

"I agree," said Washington. "What are you suggesting?"

"Our biggest and most lethal weapon is our Rangers. I think these foreign armies need to see them in action, up close and personally. We need them to be so afraid of the Rangers, even though we follow a strict policy of neutrality, they will always wonder what would happen to their country if we were to change our minds and let the Rangers loose on them."

"That seems like good insurance to me," said Washington. "What do we do?"

"We let the navy take out all the warships, except the ones with the big generals on them, and let the troop ships come ashore unopposed. Then we lure both armies onto ground of our choosing and let each of the brigades destroy them. We leave enough alive to sail back to England and France and Germany, and Holland, and Spain, with horror stories to terrify their governments."

"Do we have that kind of capability with just 6,000 men against 50,000?"

"It won't even be close."

"Then that is the way we shall have it," said the President.

Arcadia made a com call to all the Captains of the Destroyers, and the two commanding generals of the Rangers and laid out the plan. She could hear the grins on their faces as she finished the briefing.

It was several hours before the British or Spanish Admirals realized anything was happening. Finally, a lookout in the topmast of the flagship hollered down, "Big explosion dead astern."

The Admiral and the army generals went to the back of the ship and put their long glasses on the horizon. Even as they were watching, another explosion lit the sky. An hour later, a huge silver ship came into sight. Its speed was unbelievable and the long guns on the deck swiveled and pointed directly at the flagship. Then there was a pause and the gun swiveled to another of the battleships in the formation and blew it to pieces with a single shot. There were three other battleships in the group, and all of them went to the bottom with a single blast from the huge gun. Then the silver ship sped off at top speed and was out of sight in just a few minutes.

The flagship floated with just enough sail to maintain steerage. The Admiral was meeting below with his officers and the Army generals. "It appears that monster ship only attacked the warships, none of the troop carriers seem to have been hit."

"Our mission should go ahead," said the senior army general, our force of soldiers is intact. We will be in New York harbor in less than three days. We will go ashore under your cover fire and march on New York. When we've finished, we will march south to attack Philadelphia. The Americans will have to surrender."

The Admiral was beginning to have his doubts, but in the absence of a better plan, he agreed.

At the same moment, the Spanish Admiral was making the same choice.

Both fleets rendezvoused around the flagships. The 650 combined troop ships in the two fleets still made it look like a big armada. Admiral Malley could see the coast of New York in his long glass. It looked very peaceful. There were no ships visible as they approached the harbor.

Twenty at a time, the troop ships pulled up to the docks and the soldiers came running out. It took all day and into the night to unload all the men, their cannons and all their equipment. By this time, several thousand troops had entered New York City. They were very surprised to find it completely deserted.

British General Barton Sims was surprised too. Why would an entire population leave a city, unless they knew someone was coming, which was impossible? A little confused, Sims sent word his army would march out of town immediately and bivouac in an open area. The soldiers grumbled about not being able to loot the town.

The British army only went a short distance, since it was night, and made a quick, temporary camp to wait for morning.

With sunup, Sims called his regimental commanders together. "It was strange there was not a single person in the entire city of New York. There's no possible way they could have known we were coming."

"Perhaps there has been an epidemic in the city and everyone left to avoid getting sick," suggested a colonel."

"That was my thought," said Sims, "which is why we moved out of the city without delay. We will now move south on the main road. Keep the companies in close order with no straggling. The Americans have a reputation for attacking from cover, especially if they do not have an army to meet us in the field."

Another colonel spoke up, "Sir, it has been a number of years since the rebels fielded an army. Surely, they will have disbursed it."

"That is our belief," said Sims, "we shall march directly to Philadelphia, their largest city, occupy it, and set up operations to crush whatever resistance the Americans can muster."

The British Army, of 25,000 soldiers, plus artillery and wagons of supplies was over a mile long. Sims and his staff rode horses, near the front, with a company of scouts spread out along the point to avoid any ambushes.

In the afternoon, they turned off the road into a wide-open space and set up their camp. They remained there for two days, drilling the soldiers, and insuring the army was in the best condition for battle.

They saw no one on their way when they resumed their march. There were small farms, and tiny villages, all deserted, which the British looted for supplies, shooting the livestock, and burning the buildings.

In the afternoon of their first week, Sims was thinking of a finding a large enough space to stop for the night when his scouts came running up. "We found someone."

"A militia," asked Sims?

"It's a young girl, Sir. She's just ahead."

Sims continued on for half a mile and found some of his men standing around a girl, who could not be more than 10 or 11 years old. Sims got off his horse and walked over to the girl. She was wearing a gingham dress and had pigtails. As he approached the girl said, "Are you the army who landed in New York?"

"How could you know, girl," said a surprised Sims.

"You should turn around and go home," said the girl.

"Why would we do that," laughed Sims?

The girl looked at the general with serious eyes, "The Rangers Are Coming."

"Rangers, eh," said Sims. "Where are these Rangers, and how many of them are there?"

"I don't know how many there are," said the girl pleasantly, but they are camped off the road about three miles that way." She pointed south.

"We thank you for your information, young lady," said Sims, "now run along."

The girl curtsied and then turned and ran off into the woods. She disappeared in a few seconds.

"Send the scouts south and see if these Rangers have a camp," ordered Sims, "have the column, pick up the pace."

Soon the scouts were back with news. "There is open country ahead. There is room for the entire command to set up camp on top of a small ridge. On the other side, across a long valley, the land rises again. There are a number of tents set up on top of a small hill. We spotted at least a hundred men near the camp."

"Finally," said Sims, "the Americans have scraped together a few men. We'll move forward and set up our camp at the top of the ridge." Within an hour, the British wheeled off the road and set up their huge camp in an open area facing the valley, which was bordered by forest on the west. The slope rose gently to a smaller exposed area with a dozen tents set up. Sims could see men, wearing strange clothing standing along the top of the hill, watching the big British force flow onto the sizeable ground and begin setting up thousands of tents. The pushed their five-pound artillery pieces to the edge of the drop off to the valley.

"Just out of range, to hit their camp" an officer reported to the general, but if they move downhill and try to cross the valley, they will be easy targets."

"Typical amateur battle planning," said the general. "We hold the high ground and can set up five companies wide with a much easier slope for us than them on the other side. Tomorrow we shall see if they are willing to mount any kind of offensive. If not, we'll cross the valley and overrun their position."

"What strange uniforms they are wearing," said one of the Colonels looking through his long telescope.

Sims pulled his glass out to full extension and saw for himself. "They are wearing green uniforms with several shades of green in blotches from head to foot. Strange headgear, like iron kettles. They don't seem to have weapons. They are just standing there looking at us like we are a herd of cattle." He laughed at his own joke and his staff laughed too.

They would perhaps not have laughed if they had heard General Compton on the other side of the hill, looking at the British through high-powered binoculars.

"Just like a herd of cattle," he said. "The guy in the middle must be the big he-bull. He's looking at us with his one-eyed telescope. I'll bet he's telling his staff we're quaint novices who don't know how to pick a good battlefield."

"He probably thinks it's been a long day," said Compton's long-time chief of staff."

"Yeah, and it's going to be a long night too," smiled Compton.

The British sat up a standard camp with a traditional night guard detail. There was a sentry set around the camp at 200-yard intervals between guards. Altogether, there were 100 men on duty, not very alertly. They didn't expect any activity. There were half a dozen guards around General Sims Command tent in the center of the sprawling camp.

"Got your predator's set to go, Captain?"

"All set, General," said Robby. "There's no moon tonight. I think we can pull it off."

At exactly 3 AM, 150 men dressed in solid black uniforms, with hoods on their head and just a slit for eyes and mouth, wearing night scope goggles and armed with long knives, and razor sharp throwing stars, slipped across the field in a circle around the camp. They moved quickly and made no sound at all in soft soul boots. The men looked at their watches. At exactly 3:15 AM, they moved in one unit the dozen or so yards between them and the sentries. It was over in moments. The Captain said to make it bloody and gruesome, so the sentries died from slit throats, sliced from head to crotch and across their abdomens to spill entrails on the ground.

Robby led a group of ten men secretly from row to row of tents until they reached the command tent. The six sentries surrounding the sleeping quarters of General Sims went down almost simultaneously, without making a sound. They were cut up in the same manner as the sentries. Robby stuck a placard on the tent entry pole, and then he and his group faded into the night.

When light came with the dawn, men began moving around the camp. It didn't take them long to discover the slaughtered sentries. They looked with horror at the blood and gore, and began screaming.

General Sims came awake at the commotion and irritably put on a robe and stepped out his tent. He looked with wide eyes and an open mouth at the butchered guards in front of his tent. Men and officers came running up to make sure the general was safe. He ignored them and walked over to the placard stuck to his tent pole. He read it, and shivered a little in the cool of the morning. The placard said simply, "The Rangers Are Coming."

A thoroughly rattled senior staff of officers gathered 30 minutes later in the general's tent. "Report!" barked the general.

"Sir, our entire detail of sentries are dead, over a hundred men. They were all cut to ribbons like the ones guarding your tent. No one saw or heard anything. The carnage is ghastly.

"Get a detail of men to haul off those bodies before the entire command sees them," said Sims.

"I've already done so, sir, but a great many men saw the bodies. The camp is full of rumors and talk."

"We must take action immediately. Order three companies of the first guard to form, and march into the valley to the camp we saw yesterday. If we can catch them early in the day, we might surprise them. How soon can you form the troopers?"

"We can be on the march in a quarter of an hour, Sir."

"Fine. Give the order to muster. Tell the companies to cross the open space and if they are not engaged, move in broken formations through the forest."

In less than 20 minutes three companies of redcoats, 600 men were marching in long ranks down the hill and across the valley.

From the cover of the trees, General Compton had concealed 1000 Rangers. They had been there for a week working to set traps, built blinds, and camouflage their positions very effectively. Compton pulled the remainder of the brigade back from the forest and started moving them to their pre-arranged positions around the camp. The Bradley's were ready to slip from cover across the road. The Humvees were in position around two sides of the camp. The 105s were in position two miles behind the waiting Rangers in the forest.

Robby spoke into his mike, "It looks like they are only moving three companies, general. Probably all they could muster in a hurry. I imagine the British General felt he had to take quick action to keep his troops from panicking."

"I wonder what they are going to think when three companies just disappear," said Compton?

The British regulars moved across the valley. These were battle-hardened soldiers who were not easily rattled. However, after they crossed the valley and came up the slopes toward the tents, they began to move more cautiously and spoke words of courage to each other.

They reached the tents and rushed them. They were empty. The order sounded to move in open formations into the forest to smoke out the militia surely hidden there. As they moved between the trees, men started to disappear. There were no shouts, no musket fire, nothing, but a steadily shrinking number of soldiers. When they realized nearly all of their comrades had vanished, the remainder of the soldiers began to retreat out of the forest. A total of 16 men made it to the open field and began running across the valley back to the British camp. They came into the camp, chests heaving, and eyes wild with fright.

"What has happened," cried their fellow soldiers?

"We don't know," the men, cried, "when we entered that forest our lads just began to vanish."

"I saw Jamie just a few yards to my right," said one of the men. "I thought he stumbled or something, because he went down and when I ran over there, he was gone, musket lying on the ground."

General Sims was confused and irate, "Three companies don't just disappear, what sorcery is at work here. He was still talking with his staff when a soldier came running up, "Sir, there are men coming out of the forest and heading across the valley!"

"How many," demanded the general?

"At least a thousand, they are not in any kind of formation, but they are moving fast."

"Train the artillery on them!" screamed Sims.

The artillery batteries sprang into action, but before they could load a single round, huge explosions went off all along the artillery line. In less than a minute two dozen rounds had blown all the artillery and their crews to pieces.

"Companies to the front!" screamed the general.

As he was saying the words, six huge machines came up the slope on the other side of the road and began firing into the camp, blowing whole sections of tents and men to bits.

From the other side, out of the forest came more large machines with green-clad soldiers running beside them. The machines were firing bursts of rounds into the British ranks, killing them by the hundreds.

As the machines grew closer, three flying machines came over the horizon and began to strafe the British camp with mini-guns, firing 3,000 rounds a minute. Thousands of British soldiers went down. The 105s crept fire into the camp closer and closer to the central core.

As the confusion was at its height, the Rangers stormed into the camp, assault rifles blazing. Some of the British were able to fire their muskets at the men, who all had black streaks on their faces. The muskets did not seem to affect the soldiers at all. A few staggered, but kept on running and firing. The Humvees roared through the camp spreading death.

For an hour, the fight raged on, entirely one-sided. The British retreated to the center of the camp. Finally, when less than 2,000 soldiers were still fighting, General Sims ordered a white flag to be waved. The gunfire ceased at once. A loud voice spoke, "All soldiers drop your weapons and place your hands behind your heads fingers laced." The redcoats obeyed in an instant.

General Sims stood at the entry to his tent in shock. He was so shaken he could hardly speak. Through the ranks of massed Rangers who parted as he approached walked General Compton. He stepped up to Sims, pulled off his gloves and stuck out his hand to Sims. The general weakly put out his hand. Compton took it firmly and said, "May the Lord forgive us for this senseless loss of life today. I offer my humble apologies, general."

Sims was so surprised he could hardly speak. Finally, he said, "I don't know what to say. You have slaughtered nearly 25,000 British soldiers and yet you offer your apologies?"

"Most humbly and sincerely, sir," said Compton. "The fact is you've been deceived by your governments, who told you the United States could not withstand the combined might of all the great European powers. As you can see, we can defend ourselves and we did.

"However," continued Compton, "we bear you no ill-will. Your surviving soldiers, along with you and your staff, will be treated with dignity and compassion and returned to your ships in New York to go home. We will offer aid to your wounded and attempt to save as many lives as we can. Already our medics are moving through your camp treating your injured."

"I thank you for your gallantry, sir," said Sims.

"You should have listened to our little messenger yesterday. She told you to go home because the Rangers were coming. We left a similar message this morning, thinking invading your camp, eliminating your sentries, and leaving another message we were coming, would cause you to withdraw. Unfortunately, you did not believe us, so we had to attack. We would not have invaded your country; the United States is strictly neutral."

"When you get home, please tell the story of what happened here to anyone who will listen. Then give them this message, the United States is open for business. We will freely trade with any country who wants trade. We will also accept immigrants from any country in any numbers who wish to come.

"You knew we were coming. You knew everything about our campaign," said Sims. "How could you know this?"

"You will find when you begin trading, we possess many advanced products. Some of that technology was used in our defense."

"You must have a huge army."

"Not as big as you might imagine, but my brigade of 3,000 Rangers, was enough to do the job today," smiled Compton.

The end of the northern battle resulted in 21,500 British dead. There were 1,500 casualties, of which only 500 elected to return to Britain when given the choice to stay and become citizens of the United States. General Sims and his staff along with the 2000 soldiers who had surrendered, where taken by wagons back to New York and delivered to their ships with full stomachs, and real respect for their host Rangers. The British had to abandon most of their troop ships, taking only what they needed to transport the survivors. The United States had suddenly acquired nearly 300 brand new ships that were sold very cheaply to merchants, who made traders out of them.

Chapter 35
Grim Realities

Charleston, South Carolina

General Compton radioed the President, Arcadia and the senior government officials about the destruction of the northern army. He gave the grim figures with no sense of victory. In fact, the entire campaign sickened him.

"Mr. President, what is the current location of the southern army," asked Compton.

"They are still about a day away from Charleston," said Washington, "they had farther to sail."

"I'm wondering, Sir, if we can find a way to avoid the bloodbath we have just gone through?"

"If you have a better idea, now's the time," said Washington.

"The British commander, General Sims, was caught completely unaware of the trap into which he was marching. He was led to believe his offensive would be an easy one. The commander in the south, no doubt, believes the same. I wonder if we might be able to head off this sure slaughter, by negotiating with the commander of the southern army."

"How would you do that," asked Arcadia?

"I spent some time with General Sims and found him to be a smart and reasonable man," said Compton. "What if we were to transport him and some of his senior staff to Charleston and have him warn his counterpart what's waiting for him?"

"That might work," said Arcadia, "particularly if we could catch them before they were able to off load any soldiers and draw them into a parley. If it was safe, you could go yourself, Mr. President, and lay the foundation for the next part of our plan of being a big, friendly, neutral trading partner."

"I think we should at least try that approach," said Washington. "If it fails, we do have the alternative. Why don't you contact General Sims and see if he would be willing?"

"I'll do that, and call you back."

Compton immediately called his Chief of Staff, "Cal, where are you in getting the British back on their ships?"

"We just got to New York yesterday. We only have a few ships loaded with troops."

"Is General Sims aboard his flagship?"

"Yeah, he went aboard this morning. You never saw such as unhappy man."

"Can you go aboard and have a private talk with him?

"Probably."

"Then do it and here's what I want you to say." Compton laid out the plan for saving the lives of all the soldiers in the southern army, and the part Sims could play in it

"Sounds like a good plan to me," said the Chief, "I'll go ask him if he would be willing. I think he might be. He is truly grieving over all those dead men."

Compton hung around the radio for an hour before his Chief of Staff called him back. "General Sims is very eager to keep the southern army from being wiped out. He's quite angry with the bugle oil his superiors told him about the big, bad United States. What do we do now?"

"Have him and his senior staff get off the ship and take them out to where we can land a Chinook. We'll fly them to Charleston."

General Sims informed his staff of the intervention planned and asked if any one of them had any objections. None did. "Gentlemen, let us see if we can't save a lot of men. Remember we have three regiments of our countrymen in the force in the south."

The Chief of Staff got hold of three big carriages and loaded the British. They drove out of town just a couple of miles and turned into a field where a big Chinook was waiting for them. General Compton stepped out of the ship and went to greet Sims. "Good morning, General Sims," said Compton shaking hands with Sims. This time there was a smile on Sims' face and his handshake was warm and firm.

"I imagine this is going to be quite an experience for you," said

Compton. "We don't have the time to drive to Charleston, so we are going to fly in this."

"I have stopped trying to understand the wonders of your military," said Sims.

"If you'll just get aboard, we will get underway."

Sims and his staff walked up the rear ramp of the Chinook, looking all around as they went aboard. Ranger crewmen sat the men down in seats and showed the British how to fasten their seat belts. They explained some people got airsick and handed them all plastic bags for an emergency.

The engines of the helicopter roared to life and the whirl of the rotors grew louder and louder. Suddenly, the ship lifted off and every one of the British officers turned to look out the windows in wonder as the helicopter gained altitude.

The Rangers were smiling and polite. They were still wearing their outlandish uniforms of green, but they didn't have on body armor and had substituted their helmets for berets. They passed out big bars of chocolate and bottles of water to all the British. Sims sat next to Compton and found they could carry on a conversation as the Chinook slipped into a steady course.

"Have you started writing your report," asked Compton?

"I've started several drafts and torn them up because I found myself getting so angry," grumbled Sims.

"Can't say I blame you," said Compton, "if I'd been hoodwinked like you were. You had no idea what kind of a trap you were walking into."

"Is it really true you did all the damage you did with a single brigade?"

"Yep, 3,256 men and women to be exact."

"You have women in your army?"

"Sure do, we also have blacks, Native Americans, and some Mayans from Mexico."

"How do you keep order with such a collection of people."

"It's easy," said Compton, "we all surrender our wills to the love of Jesus Christ, who's Holy Spirit lives in each of us and guides our lives. For us, God comes first. We seek to do His will to the best of our ability and know our sins are washed clean by the sacrifice of Jesus in our place."

"Astonishing," said Sims, "yet you fight as none I've ever seen."

"Did not King Solomon, subdue and conquer all his enemies during his reign? But when his land was secure, he made peace with those nations around him and grew rich with prosperous trade and commerce. Remember, we did not bring this war to you, you brought it to us."

Changing the subject, Sims asked, "When we get to Charleston, what is your plan?"

"First we're going to try and keep Charleston from being reduced to rubble by cannon fire from the big warships leading the way into the harbor. We intend to fly white flags of surrender from every building. Then, when the ships dock at the harbor, we intend to walk out on the wharf, under a flag of truce and speak to their commanding General."

"What makes you think he will talk with you," asked Sims?

"Because you and your staff, plus me and my staff will be standing there to welcome him. Don't worry. We'll have snipers all over the place. If anyone wants to cause trouble, they won't get a shot off."

"Then what?"

"Why, we talk. You explain the reason why you're there, tell the exact story of your experience with your army, and say the reason you're here is prevent the same tragedy from happening to the army waiting on the ships in Charleston harbor. The fact your entire staff confirms all you say, will give their General pause for thought. He may not believe you, but he will hesitate to go further until he has more proof and information."

"And you have some kind of a demonstration planned, I suppose?"

"Think of it as a replica of your battle without the bloodshed."

The big Spanish warship came into view the following morning. It maneuvered toward the harbor of Charleston, with hundreds of troop ships spread out across the horizon. The Spanish General, whose name was Don Diego Estefan Ramirez, looked through his long telescope, and spotted the many white flags flying over the city.

"It appears the people of Charleston have no stomach for a siege. That will make it easier to carry off their wealth," said Ramirez with a snarling grin. "Proceed into the harbor and we shall tie up at the wharf."

As the ship maneuvered to a mooring berth, Ramirez was startled to see a group of men standing on the wharf. There was the unmistakable sight of British uniforms, with another group of men in very strange uniforms of mottled green and helmets standing next to them.

Ramirez was confused by the contingent, seemingly waiting for him. He called his own senior staff together, and they stepped off the ship, led by armed guards. General Sims came forward and doffed his hat in respect. "Good morning, General Ramirez," said Sims, "I'm sure you are surprised to see me here to greet you."

"Has your army robbed my soldiers of their victory," said Ramirez with some tone of annoyance.

"My army has met the Americans in battle," said Sims, "It is my duty to inform you my entire force was all but wiped out. We put our losses at nearly 22,000 men. I have come here today to save your army from the same fate."

"What madness is this," said Ramirez. His officers spoke out to each other and some of them laughed. But a British Colonel came forward and said, "General Sims, I am Colonel Howerton commander of the regiment of the Royal Black Guard. Surely, Sir, you can't be serious. Your force cannot have been ashore in New York for more than a few days. How is it possible to suffer such a defeat?"

"I will tell you the truth, Colonel," said Sims seriously, "my entire army was demolished in a single engagement lasting less than an hour. It was beaten by single brigade of 3,000 soldiers, called Rangers."

"So you are here as a prisoner of war?" said Howerton.

"Not at all," said Sims, "I am here on my own accord. I came voluntarily with my staff to bring you this news."

Sims own chief of staff spoke up, "Believe it, Colonel, we were all there and swear every word General Sims says is true."

General Compton stepped forward, "Welcome to the United States, General. I realize all of this comes as quite a shock, but we have arranged a demonstration for you I think you will find very enlightening. Under a flag of truce, I guarantee your safety and the safety of your entire staff. If you will just accompany us to a place not far from the city, I will be happy to show you how the British army was defeated."

Ramirez teetered in indecision. General Sims walked up to him and said, "I also pledge our sincerity and will accompany you."

"Very well," said Ramirez, "I agree to see your works of magic."

"Not magic, General," said Compton, "pure technology." He spoke into a short rod near his mouth, and around the corner came a string of carriages. The entire party of 30 people loaded up in the carriages and trotted off toward the edge of town.

They travelled along the road for half an hour and then pulled into a field, where a grandstand was set up on the top of a hill. The Spanish and the British Colonel sat at the top of the grandstand with the others in rows below. General Compton stood in front of the grandstand.

"First, I will show you a standard Ranger, A soldier walked up and stood next to the general. He is dressed in our basic fatigue uniform. It is in irregular green patterns, top, and bottom. This makes him very difficult to see in a green background, like a forest. His brown boots are made of a woven material that form fits to his feet. He can easily cover 30 miles in a single day.

"He's wearing our basic battle armor, which repels most fired missiles. For example, this flintlock pistol which is issued to your men. Sergeant, if you please. The Ranger backed off a few paces, and the general shot him in the chest. The Ranger barely moved. Now we have his helmet." The Ranger took off his helmet and passed it through the audience. "You will notice how light it is. It will also stop a musket shot, just as the body armor."

"Now we have the Rangers' basic weapon." The Ranger went over and picked up his M-14 assault rifle with grenade launcher. He turned to a dummy placed against a couple bales of hay about 50 yards away. This rifle is capable of shooting a single round at a time…" the Ranger fired a few rounds that hit the dummy and caused pieces to fly from it, "or it can be fired automatically." The Ranger turned on the dummy and 30 rounds came out faster than the first casing could hit the ground. The dummy was shot to pieces. "For targets in groups but still relatively close we have our grenade launcher." The sergeant raised his weapon and a thump kicked the rifle back a little. 100 yards away, another group of dummies were set up. They exploded in a huge blast, all in pieces.

"In the event our Rangers have no weapons, they become weapons of their own." Two Rangers came forward and put on a dazzling display of martial arts for several minutes. When it was over, the men were not even breathing heavily.

"These are the Rangers your soldiers face," said Compton. "That is, if they get close enough to engage them. In the valley below, you see an abandoned farmhouse, barn and several other buildings there."

From out of the trees came a Bradley Fighting Vehicle. At a half mile away its main gun fired and the entire farmhouse blew up in flash of fire and wood chips flying through the air. Next, a couple of Humvees came from the forest, roaring across the field at high speed. From the top, the 50 calibers opened up and the assorted buildings near the barn were shot to little pieces in less than 30 seconds.

"Notice the wagon sitting out in the field. We will now show you a demonstration of our artillery. You may have noticed it on the way out of town. It is seven miles from that wagon." Compton spoke into his mike, and mumbled, "Don't miss fellows."

They didn't miss. A whoosh went over the grandstand and the wagon was completely obliterated in an enormous explosion.

"Finally, we still have a barn standing, but not for long." He spoke into his mike again, "Scratch the barn." From over the hill came a Blackhawk gunship. It opened up on the barn from half a mile away. Its mini-gun giving out a steady stream of noise with tracers mixed in. As the chopper passed by the barn, the entire structure was filled with thousands of holes, and as the Blackhawk zoomed over the grandstand, the barn collapsed in a heap of shattered lumber.

"That, gentlemen, is what happened to General Sims' army a few days ago. And the same thing will happen to your army if you bring them ashore."

General Ramirez was speechless. He was a veteran soldier with many battles to his record, but this...!

"We have another brigade just itching to do battle with you, but under the circumstances," said Compton, "we were wondering if you might be willing to discuss an alternate course of action?"

"What alternative did you have in mind," asked Ramirez?"

"First, let's get out of this heat and go back to Charleston and have lunch," smiled Compton broadly.

The group of Spanish and British were more than ready to leave. General Sims whispered to Compton on the way back to the carriages, "It was much better to see it, than live through it."

Chapter 36
From Adversaries To Allies

Charleston, South Carolina

The Spanish and British were taken to a large banquet hall. Compton had the presence of mind to have several portable air conditioners installed in the windows, so the room was refreshingly cool after the heat and humidity of outside.

There were a dozen round tables set up elegantly in the hall, with room for six at each table. Generals Ramirez, Sims and their Chief of Staffs' set at the table in front of the short stage, along with Compton and a new General officer.

"This is General Riley," said Compton, "he's the commander of the 2nd Ranger Brigade. It was his men and equipment who provided the demonstration today.

Riley struck out his hand and shook with General Sims, and then with General Ramirez. "Pleasure to meet you gentlemen, I hope my boys put on a good show for you today."

"It was impressive," admitted Ramirez.

Lunch was served. It was pure Kobe beef, with twice-baked mashed potatoes and asparagus with Béarnaise sauce, sweetened iced tea in ice, and a fresh slice of peach cobbler. Nobody left a single morsel on their plates and marveled at the ice in the glasses. By the time lunch was over, the conversation between the British, Spanish and contingent of Ranger officers who came with General Riley, turned to somewhat personal things, and many compliments over the delicious meat. A box of Cuban cigars were passed around each table and the Spanish and British enjoyed them immensely. They hardly noticed none of the Americans was smoking.

At last, General Compton went up the stairs to the stage and stood in front of a single pole with a bar at the end. He spoke into it and the sound reverberated through the hall. Everyone except the Rangers looked around in wonder.

"Gentlemen," said Compton, "we did not offer a blessing before the meal. I would like to do so now, with your permission."

"We in our new United States have worked very hard to create this country. Through the years, we have had the spiritual leadership of a truly remarkable person, who has been an inspiration to us all in more ways than I can count. She is our greatest treasure. I am proud to present... Arcadia.

As she flowed onto the stage from the wings, there was an audible gasp in the audience. The Rangers smiled at this. Arcadia made a distinctive impression on everyone. She was wearing her, so unusual, shimmering silver-white gown/dress. The silver belt around her slim waist. Her flowing blond hair gleamed in the light and her noble, beautiful face was set off perfectly by her crystal blue eyes. Arcadia, bowed slightly to the audience and then said, "Let us Pray."

"Heavenly Father, we come to you today in humble praise of your majesty and our deep gratitude of the gift of your son, Jesus Christ, who came to earth to live as a man without sin and as an example of the love we can all show to one another. We thank you Lord for your wisdom of allowing Christ Jesus to give His life as a ransom for our sins and the promise of eternal life in the radiance of Your presence. May we join together today and may good will and strength of purpose be our guides as the old meets the new as brothers to the benefit of all. In the name of our Holy Savior, Amen."

She then repeated the prayer in perfect Spanish and French.

There was a murmur of "Amens" from the seated men, but all eyes were on Arcadia. She smiled and said, "When we founded this new Republic, we were determined to leave behind the old ways with so much grief, sorrow, war, and misery to this world. We asked ourselves, how could we make a different country and an example for others. We found the answer in the word of God, who proclaims every person is created equally, and is endowed by Him with certain rights that include life, liberty, and the pursuit of happiness. There are other rights as well, written in our Constitution, the law of the land. We believe the authority to govern comes from the people, and we have written our document in this manner, so no government can rule the people without their consent."

"We have now had two elections to provide us with leadership at the national level. One of the mandates of this national government is to provide for the common defense of our United States, which is now the largest country in the world. You have all seen examples of how we do this. By this time you, the British, the French, the Spanish, and the Dutch know we are unconquerable. However, you should also know we would not use this power against any other country. The United States was established with borders we believe are the correct ones for us. All people who live within these borders have the same rights as citizens. We have outlawed slavery and freed all. We ask you simply to accept us as we are now, and in return we promise to be a neutral power, taking no sides in global affairs."

"The war you brought to us is over. We do not hold any grudges and offer free trade to all. We also offer an open immigration policy for anyone who comes willing to accept our laws and the sovereignty of our nation.

"The reason, Admiral Ramirez, 25,000 of your children do not lay dead on our fields is we abhor what we were forced to do in the north. We offer you amnesty and the freedom to return to Europe without firing a single shot. If you permit it, we will accept as many of your soldiers as immigrants who wish to stay and to earn their citizenship, free land and a new life.

"As proof of our sincerity I would now like to introduce to you the President of the United States, who will confirm what I have spoken and deliver a written warrant of our resolve. Gentlemen, George Washington, President of the United States."

As Washington came on the stage it was General Sims who was the first to rise, followed almost immediately by General Ramirez. The Rangers snapped to attention as one, and the rest of the gathering followed.

"Gentlemen, we offer our sincere apologies for the lives we took in New York last week. We offer the hand of friendship to you all. I confirm and declare all the words spoken by our great lady Arcadia to be the truth, the whole truth, and nothing but the truth. I have documents here, which I ask you give to your governments upon your return speaking the same words of Arcadia and the true pledge of the United States. I say all these things in the presence of God, who is the true master of our people."

The applause began with the Rangers, but the entire room was soon applauding and even cheering.

The doors burst open and waiters and waitresses entered the room with huge mugs of really good beer. It was passed out and rounds of toasts began. The crowd toasted Washington, Arcadia, all the European countries, and especially the United States of America.

The party went on for the rest of the day and into the night. Washington spoke with Sims and Ramirez at length and they promised the events, which had occurred in America, would be known to everyone in the world.

Arcadia was mobbed by the Europeans and she chatted with them in French and Spanish fluently, much to their delight. Privately and publically, she was declared to be the most beautiful...and intelligent woman they'd ever met. Both Sims and Ramirez invited her to their homes in England and Spain.

At one point, Ramirez got Sims off to the side and said, "I don't know the words to express my gratitude to you, Sir. I grieve for your dead, but I celebrate mine who are alive."

"As do I, my friend."

Later, when everyone was bedded down for the night and Ramirez returned to his ship, Washington and Arcadia had a moment alone.

"Well, Arcadia, you managed to avoid another crisis and left us in a better position than I could imagine."

"It was quite a day, George."

"That's the understatement of the year."

"If you don't mind, I'm going to go to sleep. It's been a long two weeks and we have another dragon to slay tomorrow."

As she walked off, Washington realized in the past month, he couldn't remember Arcadia sleeping at all. He just shook his head as he strolled off down the streets of Charleston.

Chapter 37
Progress And Planning
Fort Independence, Virginia

The people of the United States selected Thomas Jefferson as the second President of the United States in November 1788. Washington served three terms, and was now happily retired to Mount Vernon. He remained active in government affairs, and his counsel was often sought.

Arcadia had now been living in the 18th century for almost 20 years. Her appearance was unchanged, as were those who had come through the Portal of God. It was an exciting, memorable time for them all. They'd been so busy and focused on the business at hand, few of them gave much thought to what they had left behind, and were as dedicated as Arcadia to following the guidance of God in altering the past in this way. She often wondered why God had let it occur this way in the first place, and why he didn't just make a different plan. When she had asked the angel why, he had just said cryptically, "They didn't have Humvee's in 1770." She now had an inkling of what that actually meant. It was the Humvee's and all the rest of the technology and mindset of went with it that was necessary to deflect the flow of free will of mankind in a different direction.

Well, she and her colleagues had certainly done that. Perhaps more importantly she had managed to gain the support and active assistance of the very men who'd made it all happen. The fact she had superior insight into what the future held for these men, and the difficulties it presented, required a change in the actual optics of the leaders. This was the difference in many harsh realities the country would have had to face. By taking the steps they had, the result was a United States of America able to change the rest of the world, just by being who they were.

Arcadia and the men and women of the 21st century would often have church for themselves alone. They would thank God for his mercy and blessings. If there was ever a group who relied on God so completely, they were it. In many ways, it was a crushingly lonely undertaking, and their faith in the love of God and his sure and steady grip on their lives, minute by minute, that kept them going.

In any case, the opening of the grand plan was coming to an end. Arcadia knew the changes in history they'd made would mean no war of 1812, no civil war, and no wholesale slaughter of the Native Americans. Those things alone were very good accomplishments. However, there were 310 years of history yet to unfold, and there was no assurance if they went back to their own time now, they wouldn't still find a shattered country and 150 million dead people.

She decided it was time to give more information, guidance, and direction to her original founding fathers. She contacted them all and asked if they would be willing to meet with her at Fort Independence. She sent helicopters to pick them up.

The group arrived two days later. They were, obviously, in very high spirits. They had accomplished more in less than 20 years than would have been possible in a hundred years. They worshipped Arcadia, and all were amazed she and the group from the future seemed completely unchanged. Arcadia said she had no idea how this was the case, but reminded them all this was God's idea in the first place, and He was in charge.

Washington, Adams, Jefferson, Hamilton, Franklin, and Madison were all there, and in the bloom of good health. 21st century medicine was able to work wonders. They sat in the big conference room with some of the key men from Arcadia's group, Generals Compton, and Riley, the chief of medicine, the key sociologists, engineers, and the top techs.

Arcadia went to the podium at the head of the room, and said, "All of you have every reason to be happy with what we have accomplished. I'm also happy, because we have bought ourselves some time and relative privacy from the big powers of the world. In fact, most of them now regard us as the big power. So much the better."

"However, 310 more years must pass, and if we don't conduct

our affairs properly, there is no assurance I won't go home to the same shattered country I left. I sincerely hope what we've accomplished in the nearly 20 years since we arrived, has bought us enough good will to continue our sincere efforts to guide history."

"It was Washington who spoke for them all, "I have to say, Arcadia, it's a little disingenuous of you to believe we, or America, would desert you now. We know a good deal of the near future, but only bits and pieces of the far future. If you will educate us, we will do our best to help you save an America that is yet to be.""

"Thank you George," said Arcadia, "it's not you gentlemen I'm worried about. It's the future generations of leaders who may have very different ideas of how America's business should be conducted."

She turned and lit up the center screen at the front of the room, "We've made this as short and succinct as possible. There are expansions of each section of history as we get to it, but in general, what you are about to see are the true events that will occur in the next two and a half centuries."

For the next four hours, a documentary of American history unfolded. Washington and the rest, could see, right away what difficulties, problems and misery was avoided by the quick and decisive defeat of the British, and the years of waste under the ponderous Articles of Confederation. As time went by, they saw the War of 1812 was simply not going to happen, and they were very grateful to see the Civil War would never bloody America because of the early emancipation and subsequent outlawing of slavery.

They saw the expansion to the west and the disgraceful way in which the Native Americans were treated. They saw corrupt and incompetent presidents. They watched the rise of the two party system and how, often, it was not in the best interests of the country. It was interesting to see the Spanish American war, and America taking most of what it already had from the Spanish.

Then they watched the great powers of Europe enter World War I, and how absolutely horrible it was, and how it was the Americans who turned the tide. But the Great War produced a deep depression in Europe and ultimately in the United States, a the principal reason for the rise of the Nazi's and Hitler to Germany. The holocaust was graphically shown. They saw the Japanese attack of Pearl Harbor, the long road back for America, and the end of the war by the use of nuclear bombs.

Afterwards, the Cold War, raged along with the near miss of a nuclear exchange in the Cuban Missile Crisis. With the collapse of the Soviet Union, the world looked safe again, but then came the rise of radical Islam, and the subsequent attack of 9-11.

They watched America drive God out of the schools and many elements of public life. They saw the huge growth of the Federal government and the entitlement mentality it produced, keeping the same kind of people in office with no term limits.

Then they saw the miracle of God in Branson with the appearance of the Park where the lion laid down with the lamb, and the resurgence of religion to America. It made the United States peaceful and prosperous again, but the hatred against America by the Islamists, overflowed and ultimately the bombs went off in Washington, New York, Chicago, Los Angles, Denver, and Houston.

When the documentary was over, Arcadia said, "Lots of us would often say the Founding Fathers would turn over in their graves to see how your principles were so disgracefully corrupted. Fortunately, none of you are dead, so I can ask you directly. Is this the United States any of you envisioned or intended."

"Disgraceful," said Jefferson.

"Idiotic financial policy," said Hamilton.

"I would be in the streets forming a new Revolution," said Adams.

"I told a lady," said Franklin, "when we came out with the constitution and she asked me what kind of a government we had given America. I said, 'a Republic, madam, if you can keep it. It looks like we couldn't."

"I would not put my name as Father of the Country on such an abomination," said Washington.

"Glad to see you agree with us. Perhaps now you can understand why my angel insisted on going back to the beginning to keep us from making all the same mistakes."

"Yes," said Washington, "I can completely agree with the solution he chose. I did not realize how large a part in the New Revolution you and your family has had. No wonder he picked you, Arcadia, you are truly the best of the best."

"Now you can see why I insisted on making the United States so big. In my time, illegal immigration is a terrible problem from Mexico.

Canada still only has about 30 million people, and 90 percent of them live with a hundred miles of our common border. I wanted all the Caribbean to forestall the Spanish American war and the rise of Communism and Castro in Cuba. I wanted a more placid central America where a few million less people would die under dictatorships. Best of all, I wanted the land all the way to the isthmus of Panama to have a free hand to build and hold a canal to make the passage from east to west so much easier."

"I also see you have made adequate provisions for the Native Americans, particularly the Sioux with a state of their own, " said Jefferson.

"That situation is not stable," said Arcadia. "We are going to have to help them along and honor our agreement. You see, there is a lot of gold in the Black Hills, their most sacred area, and we overrun them in my time."

"Very well," said Washington. "What are our most important steps?"

"One of the positive outcomes of producing a very strong Constitution was it provides a solid base upon which to build the government," said Arcadia, "Moreover, you can see the divisive nature of partisan politics. Even today, Aaron Burr is plotting to be Governor of New York and set up a political party to capture the Presidency. By the way, Alexander, he kills you in a duel, in our future. We will avoid that in this reality. We've decided there just can't be such polarized political parties. There will be disagreements on certain policies of the government simply because of the diversity of the population and their primary interests. Agricultural states have different priorities than industrial states, even though we have worked hard, behind the scenes, using the powerful tool of money to insure all states have a good mix of both. That's why the big textile mills are in the south."

"Our solution to this is to make the state primary election system where the real elections are held. They are very close to the people. All Congress will go directly to the capital without a partisan political agenda. Term limits for Congressmen and Senators without special privileges and high salaries, will keep the legislative branch from becoming a profession.

The President will be elected from the two top vote getters in the state primaries. A very good President can stay in office a long time. Poor presidents would be gone after a single term. My best-case scenario is to have a natural progression of office from the vice president to president. If we can expand this to include the very best men in the country and have, them work into the order through the Speaker of the House, so much the better. All these men, or women, need to be solid Christians , and all must buy into the future we are crafting to ultimately protect the United States. We will show them this documentary and let them see how much better things are by the successes we will have.

"There also have to be changes to the electoral process as far as voting is concerned. We need more informed and involved citizens. As each state organizes its school systems, we need to make sure several things crippling education in the 20th century don't happen. First, we must insure teachers receive a very good wage, and enjoy a high social standing in society, so they don't start organizing into self-serving unions. School needs to be a year round activity with breaks for planting in the spring, harvesting in the fall, and a relatively short break at Christmas.

"Thanksgiving has been a commonly celebrated blessing for a good harvest. In my day, its nothing more than the kickoff to the Christmas buying season. We need to make sure it's kept as a religious observance and held the first Sunday in November. Another important change to the schools will be a major concentration on civics and the concept of government ruling by the consent of the governed. It will be an easy sell to tell students in order to give their consent, people have a responsibility to be educated in how administrations and Congress govern. All students will be required to pass a test on that very subject in their final year of high school. The religious connection to owning their rights should never be far from the discussion on government. This firmly places God in the schools, and the subject of separation of church and state will never come up, as it relates to schools.

"A final improvement to the schools is to insure gifted students are treated differently. When the student is identified as gifted, it will be a great honor to a family to have their children given special education at centers eventually spreading around the country. Essentially, these will be facilities, where children live, and are provided everything they need to be happy and to immerse themselves in the subjects in which they excel. One of these schools will be just for promising government leaders. I'm hoping most of our future presidents come from this school.

"We have another problem on the domestic agenda threatening stability," said Arcadia. "When you take a census of the county in two years, you are going to find out you have about 30 million people living within our borders. Technically, all of them are American citizens. But really only in name and not practice. Basically, we need to redistribute the population, especially from Mexico and Central America and some of the Caribbean islands to some of the empty spaces in North America. We also need to break up the concentrations of blacks in the south, and the poor neighborhoods of the northeast."

"What do farmers want? Free land of their own. What do poor families want? Jobs improving their standard of living. We can do both.

"70 years from now, an American President will get Congress to pass something called the Homestead Act. This provides 160 acres of free land for any person with a $10 filing fee, and the promise to live on the land and improve it for at least five years. Offer that to the poor tenant farmers in Mexico and Central America, and they will come by the tens of thousands. However, we didn't wait 70 years the Homestead Act is a fact already.

"We need to rapidly improve the nations' infrastructure. That means more electricity to run factories. We get that by building strategic dams on some of the big rivers that flood every year. In order to do that, we have to have more railroads, highways, and heavy equipment. We have done a good job of building railroads in the last 20 years. We now have a rail system that runs north and south along the east coast, with several spurs that lead to our Mills. We also now have two transcontinental railroads running from New York to San Francisco Bay, and another that runs from Charleston to Southern California.

"In purely agricultural areas, will be produce food to feed the world. In areas marginal for farming, and there are places like that in every state, we build steel mills, and assembly plants for the many new products we are "Inventing." This will give us the diversity we need for the voting population and will homogenize our people so living next to a black person, who lives next to a Mexican, who lives next to a white man, is the natural order of things.

"One last thing, gentlemen," said Arcadia, "America has the biggest collection of natural resources in the world. We will exploit these to our mutual advantage, but not at the expense of fouling the land, the water, and the air. We will all be conservationists, or in our world, environmentalists. It simply means we respect our country. We also have some of the most beautiful places in the world. These will be administered by the Federal Government, and belong to all the people, as National Parks and forests. I have a list and a map of them all for you Mr. President."

"You certainly do know how to take charge," said Jefferson.

"Just the judicious use of the authority you have given me, Mr. President."

"Can we now turn to finances and trade," asked Hamilton

"Certainly," said Arcadia, "Let's take a look at to the business of making the United States rich.

"I admit we did most of the startup financing for a lot of our big projects, but the systems are operating correctly now. We have a flat tax of 10 percent on all income, individually and commercially. We are currently taking in about $6 million a year on individuals and $20 million on industrial and commercial business. It works very well, the employers hold back tax on income of their employees and send it in on one simple form along with their own business income. It's not an onerous tax, kind of like tithing to church. And we don't have a lot of other taxes to pay. The states have some taxes on sales, and on real property but, so far, not much.

"The government of the United States, is spending nothing on national defense, but still is collecting the taxes on income from the soldiers. The Federal government is currently sending $5 million to the states to pay for education. Other government costs last year were $11 million dollars. That means we have a $9 million surplus. However, real money is about to coming flooding in from foreign trade.

"All we have to do is wait. It's been six months since the intact and depleted fleets of the European powers returned to their homeports. The ambassadors in London, Paris, and Madrid reported there was unbelievable upheaval in each of the capitals. The response was predictable. At first, there was complete denial of the events, which occurred in the United States. Nobody in Parliament could believe General Sim lost an entire army in a single, one-hour engagement, despite the fact his staff all said the same thing, and all 2,000 survivors of the battle said they thought they were lucky to be alive and the Americans had treated them very well.

"Then came anger. The British talked about going back, but nobody wants to take on the Rangers. The French government has started to unravel, after the Constitution of the new United States is available to the people. Riots against the monarchy are growing. The Spanish were happy to get their troops and the troop ships back, but angry they lost so many capital ships. All the countries lost many ships, over 400 capital ships, which cost a lot to build. A continent-wide recession has begun because the treasuries are so depleted.

"Poor General Sims was so abused there was talk of trying him for treason. When the talk got serious, the American Ambassador to England took the general and his family into the embassy and found a way to sneak them all out of England and back to the United States, where General Compton welcomed him with open arms and put him to work getting caught up on modern warfare. He fits right in and now enjoys a pleasant and productive life.

"Finally came acceptance and the resulting crisis. In England, the situation is dire. The British has imported food for years because they can't produce enough to feed all their people. Now people are on the verge of starvation.

"When I heard that, I went to President Jefferson to tell him our big trading enterprise could begin. He ordered from the storehouses all over the country, an avalanche of flour, corn, barley, potatoes, and cattle. The cattle went on the new steel steamships."

"The rest of the food went on the original troop ships the British sent for the invasion. President Washington held back a hundred of these ships as government property and filled them all with the stored supplies. The satellites steered the fleet around the big storms in the North Atlantic and our losses were minimal.

"On a sunny day in Bristol harbor, the sails of a hundred ships were spotted. At the same time, the U.S. ambassador visited the Prime Minister and said the food and the ships were gifts from the American people. He also left a copy of a catalog with the P.M. that went into general circulation between the merchant and banking community. The publications are just a high quality catalog offering hundreds and hundreds of products from America at bargain prices. We produce them so cheap because of the benefits of assembly production. The same catalogs were distributed throughout Europe and within two months, the orders began pouring in.

"For the last 10 years, assisted by my cadre of specialists who came from 2030, we've been cherry-picking the best minds in America and driving them at top speed toward "discovering" some very advanced technology. Some remarkable results have been achieved. The independent discovery of the vulcanization process for rubber, for example. Then the super students went farther and began producing improvements for the process, like rubber boots and waterproof garments.

"All of this created new industries. Mass production techniques have created enormous surpluses of dozens of new products. The wheat and corn harvester was another outcome of the Special Education department. We have thousands of silos filled with grains.

"I'm still financing many projects, including the front money for producing the big inventory of products and putting them in storage. The workers and companies are happy, since they're being paid for the products. But, government warehouses are filling up with an astonishing range of products of all sorts. These were the products in the catalogs circulating through the business community of Europe. These companies and merchants could not believe they could buy these products for such low prices. In fact, we make twice as much money as the price for which they are for sale.

"Now the trade enterprise is paying off. We have foreign merchants pay their money to companies actually owned by the Federal Government. We will have a trade surplus of over $30 million this year.

"The gift of food and some very expensive ships retuned with no strings attached went a long way toward healing the wounds between the British and America. In ways, the food was the difference between living or starving in England. Parliament passed a resolution abandoning all their claims to the Americas, and the merchants are getting loans from banks to buy a lot of things, including more food.

"In Spain, there was enough food, but Spanish desperately needed all the tools and farm implements and many other products the catalogs offered. The problem for the Spanish was the banks had no money to lend to the merchants who wished to buy American products. We solved that problem by buying Spanish Reals and then lending them back to the government in the form of promissory notes payable in dollars at very low interest rates. In a very short period of time, all the governments in Europe will be making similar deals. It's kind of hard to cause problems with a country selling you everything you need very inexpensively, and to whom you also owe a great deal of money. In the case of Russia, America purchased Alaska for 10 million dollars in cash.

"Currently a long a stream of American merchant ships are crossing the Atlantic with an astonishing list of products. As we anticipated, one of the biggest sellers are the high quality wagons and carriages with vastly improved suspensions and rubber wheels. The leader in this industry was none other than the Pierce family who got a big head start from Robby Pierce, years before. The village of Concord has exploded into a medium-sized city to handle the demand for wagons.

"The entire system is not built solely on profits from trade. The United States needs things too. As merchant ships return to American ports, wonderful products are emerging. There is exquisite hand-made furniture, crystal, clocks and watches, fine wines, and lots more rubber, the list is endless. These products are purchased with much the same rate of exchange for what we are selling our goods, and are, therefore, much less expensive. The growing middle class of citizens in America are enjoying products they could never have acquired before.

"We now have and will continue to have the capital to build our infrastructure of railroads, roads, dams, more steel mills, a bigger fleet of steel steam ships and manufacturing plants."

"You want to know the best part of all this," said Arcadia? "We are doing all of this without giving up any of the secrets of how we are producing the products. The secrets of Bessemer Steel, electrical generators, assembly lines, railroads, concrete for building buildings, roads and so forth, are all isolated in the United States. We are about a hundred years ahead in technology for the whole world. Sure, they are going to develop a lot of this on their own, but by that time, we will be another hundred years ahead of them. So it will go."

"This is all very wonderful and makes me feel very secure," said Ben Franklin, "what I want to know is when the next global crisis is coming and what we are going to do about it."

"An excellent question, Ben," said Arcadia and it brings up the next big point of discussion. The next major global crisis will be a revolution in France. It will be a bloody mess. They will execute the King and most of the upper class in France by cutting their heads off with a guillotine, mostly in public to screaming masses. History says this will go on for several years before the rise of a man, a regular middle-rank artillery officer, named Napoleon Bonaparte. Napoleon is a military genius. He will unite France and form an army that will conquer Spain, Germany, Austria-Hungary, and attack Russia. Only England will be left to stand against him. His invasion of Russia will prove to be his undoing, plus the British Navy. America had little to do with that war, except to buy a big hunk of land from France. Its land we already hold and so Napoleon will not get aid from us in that way. This is the way we will have of demonstrating our scrupulous neutrality. We will continue to trade with any country with money, but we will not supply any weapons or military aid of any kind to either side. We just let them beat each other to pieces, and when the war is over in about 1815, we emerge as a real power, but one that maintains its neutrality, and encourages immigration. We need people to fill up our big country, lots of people. So that will be the big outcome of this crisis.

"However, the future is very fluid and all kinds of things we don't anticipate happening may surprise us. That is why the United States must operate the best intelligence service in the world. Basically, we have to flood the planet with thousands of spies. The secret of our communications system is our greatest weapon, but it's limited to the United States and Europe. So, we must rely on codes, people imbedded in governments, sleeper cells of spies, and we must be able to use this mountain of information to predict the threats, known, and unknown coming at us in the future. The farther we get into the future the greater the dangers, so we have a hundred years or so to develop the best intelligence system money can buy."

Chapter 38
You Want Cars?

<u>Washington, D.C.,1812</u>

Arcadia was extremely proud of the new Capital of the United States. President Jefferson, elected in 1788 and re-elected in 1792, 1796, 1800, and 1804, proved to be an extremely able, resilient, and prolific Chief Executive. In his 20-year administration, he built Washington, the District of Columbia, almost perfectly to what it had been before it was destroyed in 2030. It was designed to overwhelm, intimidate, and impress foreign dignitaries, and it certainly did that. The White House became the biggest home-court advantage in the world.

Jefferson followed the blueprint set by Arcadia to precision, not just because she said so, and had a huge pile of information to back it up; but because Jefferson believed in the plan to the core of his being.

The result of the Homestead Act was a massive relocation of peasants from Mexico and Central America. The mid-western states began to be more populated since they were good for agriculture and did not need the advanced irrigation systems. But the relocations made life in Mexico and Central America easier for those who stayed and were able to take advantage of the Homestead Act as well. Jefferson allowed most of the bigger ranches to remain intact as long as the workers were treated properly and paid a fair wage.

A great many blacks, former slaves, moved to the scattered industrial centers around the country and worked in the factories. Their lives improved a great deal and racial discrimination was the exception. The country continued to be devoutly Christian and this made integration of all groups go easier.

The government initiated vast programs of improved infrastructure building using the floods of money pouring in from international trade. There were now ports in both San Francisco and Los Angeles receiving trade from India, China, and Japan. The rail system grew to over 25,000 miles of track and there were few places in the country from Alaska to Panama not having access to rail.

Jefferson also started building roads. He used both concrete and asphalt, developed by the cleaver special education centers springing up around the country. New steel and concrete buildings were going up in the bigger cities. Larger cities, like New York, Chicago, and Kansas City were inevitable, but they were not ghettos. The expanded rail, and road system kept towns connected, but not over-crowded.

The wonders of electricity fascinated the research centers and enterprising reverse engineers figured out the secret of the electric incandescent bulb. Soon electricity was going into homes and the night became filled with light. The same process was underway with the Ranger's radios. That technology with printed circuit boards and transistors was still beyond the researchers, but not the concept of sound being capable of being carried by wire. Soon primitive, but quite effective telephones were popping up in offices, assembly plants, and some public buildings.

Jefferson multiplied by many times the amount of electricity produced by using steel and concrete to build bigger and bigger dams across unruly rivers flooding on an annual basis, but now backed up great bodies of water providing water and power to lands that previously had neither.

The innovative president had a dozen experiments of all kinds in progress at any given time in the White House.

The French Revolution occurred exactly as Arcadia had predicted and soon Napoleon was running roughshod over Europe. America maintained its strict neutrality, but continued trading food and non-military goods to any country who could afford it, or whom Jefferson was willing to extend credit. England was America's best customer with a steady supply of food. The United States expanded imports of rubber, rare minerals, and other exotic products fed into the voracious curiosity of the American public.

The United States maintained its two brigades of Rangers who saw action in an abortive attempt by Napoleon to attack Haiti and the Dominican Republic. It was a very short engagement and the Rangers were cheered all over the island state of Hispaniola. The Rangers were also kept busy putting down outbursts of outlaws in Central America and occasionally augmenting a local police force in dealing with crime. Usually, all that had to be said to restore order anywhere was, "The Rangers Are Coming." In fact, one enterprising Spanish General used that tactic to scatter three battalions of French soldiers. Jefferson, made it clear to the Spanish Government, through his ambassador, this was not the kind of threat the United States government appreciated emphasizing America was a strictly neutral, Christian nation.

The country was now completely used to, and approved of the basic primary election system to choose their delegates to Washington and to their state offices. The schools were doing their part providing excellent educations for students and instilling in them a sense of citizenship with what became known as the Master Civics Examination. Contests were held to see who was the best at basic government and current events questions, and the students with the highest scores in the test got trophies and adoration. The result was people intending to run for public office always faced a very informed and questioning public.

Jefferson took advantage of this improved way of electing high government officials by declaring his vice president. The implication was, "If you liked the way I ran things, you won't disappointed with my vice president. For the last three terms, Jefferson's vice president was Alexander Hamilton.

America was the most respected, honored, and envied country in the world. Each year the number of immigrants came pouring in, no less than a half a million. The requirements were simple. No matter what country the immigrant arrived from, they took an oath declaring unconditional loyalty to the United States, exclusively. English was the official language and everyone was required to learn it. Citizenship was provisional for a period of five years, at which time the immigrant was required to take and pass the current Master Civics Examination.

Arcadia was something of a problem for the country. In the beginning, she was the inspiration for a new nation. Now over 40 years had passed and she had not aged at all. That was the problem. Her unchanged appearance had the effect of making her seem "other-worldly." This was not the image she wanted for herself. She felt it might undermine the authority of the president, and she had worked too hard to make that an effective system.

Still, Jefferson, Hamilton, and Madison were constantly checking with her about current events and her forecast for the future. All her actions and predictions proved to be of enormous value to the foundation of the United States, and these men, were still from the original group. She had a large, very nice home in Georgetown, but it was difficult for her to leave it. All sorts of subterfuges were used to get her out of town to the estates at Monticello, and Fort Independence where her own team lived. They were also unchanged, but since they were mostly not public figures, they could come and go about as they pleased.

Actually, she liked going to Fort Independence. Not only were many friends there, but she loved to see the current crops of Ranger's in action. Many of the original Rangers had retired and lived comfortably on a generous pension in places all over the country. The new Rangers were every bit as battle ready as the ones who had taken to the field against the British. Their commanding General saw to that.

"Good Morning, Arcadia, " said the General when she was ushered into his office. " It's so wonderful to see you again.

"Hi there, Robby," said Arcadia," How's everything going with the wagon business?"

"Business is booming," said General Pierce, "My brother writes to me they're running three shifts of workers and still can't keep up with the demand. We have over 500 employees in the plant. I am constantly feeding my brother, who is in charge of development, little improvements based on having the Special Ed guys take one of the Humvees apart and figure out how they did something. As you know, the technology on those vehicles is very advanced and our people are just beginning to understand some of the technical circuitry. It will be years before they are able to reproduce it. However, there is one thing we have figured out and I need your counsel on it."

"OK," said Arcadia, "what's on your mind?"

"The techs are pretty good, and they've found out we don't really need all the special circuitry to build the engine. I understand it's called the Internal Combustion Engine. In different configurations, it's the key to making all our equipment run, from Bradley's to Blackhawks. They've constructed a prototype in the lab, and it works."

"Oh boy," said Arcadia, "you're opening an enormous can of

worms."

"How's that," asked Robby?

"About a hundred years from now, your engine is going to get adapted to a simple vehicle that can be mass produced and sold to the public at a price making it possible for almost all families to own. This will cause a worldwide revolution, with a lot of serious repercussions to it."

Arcadia pulled over a laptop and opened it. She entered the passwords that gave her access to the development of the automobile and the resulting benefits and problems, socially, politically, economically and environmentally to the use of oil, and the refinement of gasoline. "I need for you to watch this documentary of what really happens in the future, and then get back to me with your recommendations on what we should do next."

"Looks like I really hit a nerve," said Robby, "I've never seen you so serious."

"Imbedded in the documentary are the root causes for the destruction of the United States a little over 250 years from now. Keep this information to yourself and don't do anything until you talk with me. Take your time, but do a thorough job of studying this branch of our history. While you're preparing your report, I'm gonna go down to your martial arts school and knock a few heads around as the infamous 'Black Ninja'."

"I'll call the infirmary and tell them to expect some extra patients. Try not to kill any of my people."

"I'll be careful," smiled Arcadia.

After she left, General Robert Pierce, commander of the first Ranger Brigade, closed the door, and told his staff was not to be interrupted. Then he punched up the documentary and transferred it to the big screen in his office.

Over the next two days, Robby learned all about the development of the automobile. He also took careful note of where the supply of oil was coming from, and how damaging the burning of fossil fuels was to the environment, from the release of carbon dioxide into the atmosphere. He also learned the United States from Alaska to Mexico had enormous reserves of oil, coal, and natural gas. However, a lot of the supplies would be difficult to recover, and would require the application of technology which did not, as yet, exist. It was not lost on him the importation of large quantities of oil from the Middle East would put the United States on a collision course with the Muslim countries, which regarded Christians and Jews as enemies and already had the stated purpose, even in 1808 of killing or converting them all. He shivered at the prospects of what he was messing around with, and now clearly understood Arcadia's concerns.

He wrote a careful analysis of what he'd learned and made a long list of recommendations of what to do next. When he was finished, he put on his beret and wandered down to the martial arts training center.

On the wall of the training center wall, was a big permanent picture of Arcadia, clad in her Black Ninja outfit, which covered everything, and a large caption on the picture that said, "You will never be as good as the Black Ninja, but keep on working."

Robby stood in the back of the room and crossed his arms as he leaned against the wall and watched Arcadia working. She had 30 pairs of men and women spread out across the mats, and her current victim standing next to her. She explained the move she was going to do, and then demonstrated it at full speed. The student was an expert in his own right, but was helpless to counter the complicated maneuver Arcadia was teaching.

She helped her student to his feet, and then broke the routine down into its many parts in slow motion. She had the students work through each part of the exercise and practice it until they were able to do the maneuver perfectly. Then Arcadia stood back and watched her students practice it over and over again. Finally, she picked one student who seemed to be doing the routine the best and had him come forward.

"I want you to run this move on me," she said.

The student stepped forward with confidence and began the exercise. Everything went well for the first part of the sweeps and strikes, but suddenly, everything went wrong. Soon the student was laying on his face, slapping the mat in submission.

"This maneuver will work for you about 95 percent of the time, but sooner or later, you're going to find someone who has the defense for it, and then you'll be dead. There is always one more thing to do in martial arts. "Good work, today, Rangers." She bowed to the class, who responded by bowing even lower. She then left the building. Robby followed after her.

"I think you are losing your touch," he said, "the infirmary says there were only three sprained ankles, five sprained wrists, two broken ribs, and a broken arm."

"You do what you can," smiled Arcadia through her mask, "your troops are light years ahead of where they were when you and I went after it 20 years ago."

"Thanks for the compliment and for the training," said Robby, "the whole brigade is talking about it."

"How's your study going," asked Arcadia?

"Go into my private bath and get cleaned up, then we'll talk."

Showered and dressed in jeans and a sweater, Arcadia came into Robby's office, still fluffing her hair to make sure it was dry.

The general pulled up his report and projected in onto the screen. "The fundamental problem you have here is the interaction between the United States and the Muslim world. By importing their oil, you will not only make them rich, you will inevitably find our country in conflict with them. This must be avoided at all costs."

"I'm glad you have looked beyond all the wonderful advantages that cars bring to the people and have seen the real trap waiting at the end of it, "nodded Arcadia in satisfaction.

"We have a lot of oil in the United States, enough to be independent of any foreign oil for a long time. Unfortunately, some of it is going to be hard to get and I've no idea about the technology involved, even though I have seen it in your comprehensive documentary. It will be many years before we will have developed the technology to get at the oil imbedded in rocks."

"However, the automobile will set the population free and allow them to travel further, do more work, and actually provide a whole new industry of recreation and family pleasure. You saw the Grand Canyon on your trip to Veracruz, years ago, you've never forgotten it, or the big mountains. Think how wonderful it would be for our people to actually drive to those places and see them with their own eyes?"

"That would be wonderful," said Robby, "but as I understand it, the only roads you have built are between the big cities here on the east coast."

"That's true, and it's also the answer to the problem," said Arcadia. "We will be able to ration the use of this kind of travel by the rate at which we build roads, and the kinds of vehicles we put on them.

After the roads are built, the first vehicles we will use them for is commercial traffic. Trucks to transport cargo to and from the ports, and to and from the cities. We can still use diesel fuel for these vehicles. As the network of roads increase, we can start building them to some of our national parks and provide bus service to them, still using diesel and not significantly increasing our carbon footprint."

"Our what," asked Robby?

"The amount of carbon dioxide we dump into the atmosphere. Tell me, how close are your wonder boys to taking your prototype engine into a vehicle?"

"We could probably do that much today. The problem, they tell me is to recreate the shifting system and to figure out the way to stop the vehicles."

"All that takes is to reverse engineer the vehicles you already have. If we can get motorized vehicles on the road in the next few years, we will still be almost a hundred years ahead of the rest of the world. I'm going to send you some real mechanics to work with your teams. I want the first truck to roll out in a year. I'll send you the specifications for what the trailer should look like, along with the design for a bus. You can have your Dad's family send some trusted workers here and we'll build everything in a secret building. I want all of this kept strictly confidential while we're working out the details."

Chapter 39
The Year With No Summer

Washington, D.C.

Alexander Hamilton was elected President in 1808. In his first meeting with Arcadia he said, "All my proposals for a national bank and control of the currency were put into place from the beginning, so I'm a little confused as to why I am here."

"Because, Alex, you were one of the most brilliant men of the Revolution and would have been a great President if you hadn't have gotten killed by Aaron Burr in a duel in 1804. As it turns out, your paths have hardly crossed. Now you've been busy as Vice President under Thomas for the past eight years and are really ready to take the United States to the next major plateau of development."

"I believe your idea of putting the vice president in charge of education in general and the gifted schools in particular is a sound principle. I've been in a position to watch some of the remarkable things coming out of the special schools, and now that I'm president, I'm in a better position to implement the best of the things we are producing."

"That was the idea," said Arcadia. "Now do you see the results of the many developments and research projects developing?"

"Of course I see the financial picture first. The flat tax is producing $50 million a year, and business taxes last year were an astonishing $170 million dollars. Our trade picture is very strong. We export over $250 million dollars in products annually and import only about $50 million. Much of this money is flowing into private enterprise through your ongoing policy of taking the big developments in all fields by your jump-start you gave in technology through the government, and then backing the government out and forming private companies letting ordinary people buy stock. It's a huge advantage to investors. The average American worker has an annual income of $1,500 a year, and enjoys a standard of living, which is the highest in the world. Your goal of preventing the rise of trade unions is working since workers have benefits such as a 50-hour workweek, vacation, and sick pay. The major manufacturers have learned keeping their workers happy makes them infinitely more productive. We have a large and very productive middle class, who are using the investment strategies of companies who combine many different stock investments to limit risk. That's making it possible for people to multiply future income and use it for their later years when their productive work period has ended. Meanwhile, our unemployment rate is effectively zero, and the continuing dedication of people to the worship of God has made it possible for churches to pay relief funding for families who are in poverty or are otherwise disadvantaged.

"Our Federal budget is now $60 million a year. We have 10,000 Federal employees, and our surplus has grown to an astonishing half a billion dollars, all in gold reserves, and we are receiving about $25 million a year in interests payments for credits and loans we've extended to foreign governments.

"We currently have applications for immigration of over 2 million people, last year we only admitted 600,000 of them."

"That's because we are more cautious of those whom we allow to immigrate," said Arcadia, and we limit the numbers to what we can reasonably absorb into our work force."

"I must say I didn't entirely understand your institution of such an extensive intelligence system 20 years ago. It was, and is an expensive program, but our network of spies and intelligence gatherers, allows us to prevent the least productive people and common criminals from getting into the country. Moreover, it's very handy to identify the very gifted, who we are able to basically bribe to immigrate, by encouraging their research, and letting them teach, plus give them a decent salary."

"What about the expansion of our transportation system," asked Arcadia?

"Following the quarter century of Thomas' sound policy makes it easy to see where we go next. Let's summarize, we have now built over 50,000 miles of railroad tracks. The new trains running on diesel fuel with their special filters limiting pollution can reach speeds as much as 70 miles per hour. We are adding at least 5,000 miles of new track every year. The roads take longer to build and cost a lot more, but we've built highways between all the east coast cities and have three highways inching across the country. One to Chicago in the north, the farthest west is to Kansas City in the Midwest, and to Atlanta in the south."

"I know you've been sitting in on the meetings that give the reason for all these transportation systems," said Arcadia, "but I haven't kept up on the vehicle research like you have. What's the latest?"

"The engineers had to learn how to simplify their prototype vehicles. They were getting very frustrated over the advanced technology augmenting the systems in the Humvees. Finally, they decided to build the basic engine, transmission, and braking system without all the special features. They found out they didn't need all that to make the vehicle run efficiently. Then one of the bright lads decided to take a look at the much simpler ATVs. That was the breakthrough. The ATV's are easy to understand. So they built their own ATV and worked out the design problems as they went. They finally got one to run as well as the real ATV's after they figured out they needed a better fuel, a more refined product. One of the guys found a reference in the refinery schematics. This fuel is called gasoline, and it changed the entire situation. However, the bigger vehicles are going to run better on diesel, so a small model was built and they improved it gradually until they had a truck something between an ATV and one of those big trucks you showed us. Then..."

"Excuse me, Alex," interrupted Arcadia, "I kind of know all about these vehicles from my century. We could have built them for you, but the fundamentals have to be understood from the ground up by people from your century. Just give me the status of the project as of today."

"Of course," said Hamilton. "The shop at Fort Independence completed and tested the first big truck two months ago. It will carry 40,000 pounds, and will run 500 miles on a tankful of fuel."

"Wonderful," said Arcadia. "How soon can we start building trucks on an assembly line?"

"A year," said Hamilton. "Where do you want to build them, and who's going to do it?"

"The Pierce company has the best workers for wagons, so they will have the shortest learning curve to build trucks. They're used to working on an assembly line. When you survey the country, where is the place with the slowest economic growth?"

"Atlanta," said Hamilton. "They're stuck with a mostly agriculture economy and only have the textile mills."

"We have a highway, a modern road to Atlanta. That's where you should set up your factory."

"It makes sense, the city will be a boom town with a big factory to build trucks."

"New subject," said Arcadia. "So far we've managed to flood the world with great products without letting most of the secrets of how we make these products from other countries. How are we doing in keeping our edge?"

"Obviously every country would like to know how we build such advanced products at such cheap prices. We get a lot of visits from foreign dignitaries who bring their best scientists along in their official parties. They can't miss the subway system running under Washington, D.C., but they haven't a clue how we built it. They understand the fundamentals of electricity, but how we produce so much of it and then adapt it to trains running underground is a great mystery. Of course, the big power plants are always under heavy guard, so they can't see the generators. They marvel at our trains, but it would be quite a feat to steal one. We never give tours of our assembly lines, so that piece of information hasn't dawned on them yet."

"But there are smart people in every country, even though we try to siphon off their best, and use them ourselves. Nevertheless, other countries are making big improvements in their technology. Just knowing it exists here in the United States is a powerful incentive to make it. I think our goal of staying a hundred years ahead of everyone else is still true in nearly every area. In some fields, we are much further ahead medicine is one example. We're now routinely manufacture and distribute vaccines for diseases still killing millions of people. Our surgical techniques are so advanced people are not afraid to go to a hospital. In other countries, going to a hospital is like a death sentence, since most of the world hasn't figured out washing your hands, taking showers, using antiseptics and practicing personal and private hygiene actually prevent disease. Most of the other countries still are disposing of waste in their rivers without ever treating the contaminated water."

"I know about the great progress we are making in medicine," said Arcadia. "That was one area where we actually provided direct information, but tell me about the great revolution going on in education."

"Fundamentally, universities around the world are traditionally organized as institutions regurgitating knowledge. In other words, the teach only what is already known. With the establishment of your many Special Education and Research centers all over the country, the old university models are changing to the discovery of new knowledge. Now, all of the main universities we have had for centuries, Harvard, Yale, Princeton and so forth, are changing their curriculums to reflect original thinking. A lot of your research centers are expanding to become universities of their own. The result is an avalanche of all sorts of new ideas and new developments. The fact you have your own people secretly imbedded in these institutions means their storehouse of knowledge is growing faster and faster.

"Another key development is these universities are open to everyone, especially women. The fact you are still subsidizing these universities and making advanced education available to a much wider number of people is just staggering in the production of new things. All knowledge is now negotiable and in just a few years you will have students who are nibbling at the edges of technology in your own times."

"In general, I am aware of all this," said Arcadia. "It's not all good. In my history, sciences eclipses God and causes a lot of liberal thinking that sounds good, but which is actual very destructive. You've seen the master video, so you already know about the problems it produces. Your vice president, James Madison will be the last of the original founding fathers, which have seen the presentation. The president who comes after him will have to be the most carefully chosen person in the country. It will be my biggest decision so far.

"Speaking of that, Alex, how long do you intend to serve as president?

"I'm not going to do it for 25 years. As the country grows, this job gets a lot harder to do. It uses up a man pretty quickly. I would plan on two or maybe three terms for me and not more than that for James. He's already complaining about how hard he works."

"I agree with that," said Arcadia, "how do you think I feel? So it looks like I have less than 20 years to start growing myself a new crop of Presidents."

Arcadia spent a great deal of time reading history. The trick was decide which events in the world required the attention of the United States, and how. She was glad one of the first things she'd done was to establish the U.S. patent office. As new technologies were discovered around the world, she needed to be able to ward off any controversy and legal problems by being able to show the United States had already made and patented that innovation.

Her idea was to wait for someone to develop a new technology and then trot out the patent and all the improvements that came as a result and then offer to include this particular morsel of technology in the list of products the United States exported. She reasoned most people would not care where a super new technology came from they would just want it.

President Hamilton zipped through his first term, shrewdly doing one trade deal after another with dozens of countries. He finished 1812 with an even bigger surplus, and more importantly, major stock holdings in most of the big banks and corporations of the civilized world. His re-election was not even contested in most of the country.

Then in 1812, Arcadia went back to Hamilton and told him for the next four years, the United States needed to concentrate on growing food, and all buildings, and homes as possible be insulted for cold and a huge supply of coal built up in towns and cities all over the country. For the buildings already electrified and heated by electric radiators, and for the handful of big installations, like Fort Independence, heated by forced air pumped through the buildings on a supply of natural gas coming from the pipelines flowing from the oil fields.

Arcadia was adamant electrical lines be buried and not strung on poles. In the first place, she considered them very ugly. In the second place, they were very susceptible to breaking down and failing in high winds and heavy snows.

Hamilton wanted to know why the big emphasis on food production and cold weather production.

"Because, Alex, in April of 1815 a volcano named Mount Tambora in Sumbawa island will erupt. It will be the largest volcanic eruption in recorded history. It will wipe out the Tambora culture and kill at least 71,000 people.

"This eruption will create a global climate change known as "volcanic winter". In 1816, we will have a ' Year Without a Summer'. Unusually cold conditions will wreak havoc throughout the Northern Hemisphere. We need to be ready with at least a two-year supply of food, and a surplus we can donate to Europe and anyone else needing it. The same is true for building up a big stockpile of coal. The trains may not be able to transport enough to the cities, and the trucks couldn't carry enough to make a difference anyway.

"Obviously we can't announce this is going to happen, we just need to be able to get through it."

Hamilton went right to work, offering extra subsidies and high prices for all the corn, wheat, barley, and other grains the farmers could produce for the next three seasons. He also increased the production of coal and began storing it in huge piles scattered around all the big cities and towns.

The volcano blew up, right on schedule in April of 1815, and the dust cloud spread around the world in two months, blotting out the sun. Most of the crops in the United States, Europe and the Far East, failed that summer. The planetary temperature dropped 10 degrees. It started snowing in New England in August and it didn't let up until June the next year. There were no crops planted in 1816. It was just too cold.

The United States started digging into its vast reserve and no one starved. By the strong religious integrity of the country, there was no price gouging. Cries for help came pouring into America, and the United States responded by launching all its fleet of steel-hulled steamships filled with food supplies. The lifeline went on for two years, and the death toll was relatively small in Europe though strict rationing, and combining resources. The United States even delivered food to Japan and China as best it could without starving the American population.

In 1817, the dust cloud mostly disbursed and the weather returned to normal. But America was hailed as the savior of the world, since it had not charged anyone a dime for the food, saying only "it was the will of God for the United States to do all it could for its fellow men." Conversions to Christianity spiked significantly in the next several years.

Alexander Hamilton finished his fourth term, and then thankfully retired and turned the reins of power over to James Madison in 1820.

Chapter 40
A New Crop Of Leaders

Fort Independence, Virginia, 1818

James Madison was a small, somewhat sickly man who won the presidency mostly on his reputation as one of the original Founding Fathers, the author of the Constitution, and most of Federalist Papers. He was clearly past his prime when he took office and Arcadia knew she had two problems. One was making the President look good enough to take him through a second term, and the other was to find his replacement from a group of men nobody in the country knew anything about. He had to know about the Grand Historical Conspiracy, agree to its limitations, practice great Christianity, and also be a dynamic leader.

The Political Science and history academy was located at Fort Independence. Arcadia watched several men over a period of years and narrowed the list down to three candidates. During Hamilton's presidency, she sent all three men back to their home states to have them mount a campaign for Congress. As it turned out, two won seats to the House and one was elected a Senator. Even though the seat he'd won was from a term-limited man, the chances of a new face in the group winning the election from a man maneuvering to be the next Senator was formidable. Arcadia was impressed.

His name was Henry (Hank) Taylor. He ran with a slogan "Bank on Hank." He was a gifted speaker, and the records of his ten years in the Political Science Academy was spotless. He was consistently ranked near or at the top of his class. He was personable, intelligent, and tough as nails. He'd come to the Academy from the Rangers and had served five distinguished years in the ranks, before being spotted for bigger achievements and advanced to the school. At age 38, he'd served in the Senate for four years, starting in 1814, and was on two of the more important committees. Arcadia decided she had her man.

Hank Taylor was coming back to his office when a courier arrived asking him to be the guest of the President for a private meeting. Taylor had never met Hamilton in person, so he was very excited with the prospect. The invitation said 3 pm the next day. Taylor said a prayer of thanks to God for the opportunity and asked to serve the country to the best of his ability.

He was very impressed when one of the private fleet of Smart Cars from the White House pulled up to the steps of the Capitol and a driver opened the door for him. Private cars where very rare in the United States. Normally, Taylor took the Metro to work from his Georgetown apartment. He'd never ridden in a Smart Car before and it was exhilarating.

They passed through the guard gate of the White House without even stopping. Hank's driver pulled up to the main portico and escorted him into the Executive Mansion. Taylor had been there before, for a supper of all the new Senators and Congressmen, but that was five years before. The escort took him directly to the Oval Office and opened the door.

President Alexander Hamilton rose to his feet and came around the desk to shake hands with Taylor. "Glad to finally meet you privately Senator," said Hamilton.

"The honor is mine, Mr. President," said Hank.

"Do you mind if I call you Hank," smiled the President?

"Not at all, sir," said Hank. He looked deeply at Hamilton. He looked tired and worn. The challenges of the 'volcanic winters' had tested him deeply. Even now, in 1818, when the weather had returned to normal, he could see the residue of the crisis still remained.

Hamilton walked back to his desk and picked up a thick file. "I've been reading all about you," said the President. "You have a very honorable record."

"I have the Lord to thank for that, sir, He's blessed me greatly."

"Yes, of course," said the President. "They tell me you are a great student of history. Why don't you tell me the important figures of the American Revolution and the founding of the United States."

"Well, there was Washington, of course, and our mighty warriors of the Rangers, and also there was Arcadia whom is still revered as the inspirational leader of the whole movement. I've watched some videos of her speeches and sermons. She was quite a woman."

The President smiled, "Tell me, Hank, how do you suppose I was able to anticipate the volcanic winters and prepare the country for them?"

"Good and prudent planning, I guess," said Hank.

"Actually, there is another reason. It's part of a thing called the Grand Conspiracy. I hope you can be trusted with the truth, keep it to yourself your entire life, except for your successor, and lead the United States to a long planned future?"

Hank was taken aback by the enormity of words he'd just heard. His mind was reeling from the implications. "I don't know what to say, sir."

"You can swear before God you will take this responsibility and never waver in the common resolve all of us who have proceeded you have held as a sacred trust."

"I so swear, Mr. President."

Hamilton looked at Taylor for a long moment, his eyes locked on him. "I believe you," he said finally. "Sit down, Hank, this is going to take some time. The reason why I knew to prepare for the volcanic winters was because I was told to prepare."

"By whom," said Hank?

"By me," said a voice directly behind him.

Hank turned in his chair and then jumped to his feet, shaking his head in shock.

"I'm Arcadia, Hank. It's nice to meet you in person."

Hank looked at the woman before him. She was the perfect image of the Arcadia he had watched so often in the videos. She was tall, had flowing blond hair, and crystal blue eyes. She was young and beautiful. She was wearing the familiar silver/white, robe/dress going all the way to the floor and there was a silver belt around her trim waist.

Arcadia came across the room and shook hands with Hank, "Relax, partner, it gets rough from here on." She said it with a smile, and motioned Hank to a chair, while she sat in one facing him.

"There's no easy way to say this," said Arcadia, "so I will just blurt it out. I'm here from the future. In my world, it's 2030. The United States was attacked by foreign enemies with weapons beyond your wildest dreams. 150 million Americans are dead, our greatest cities are shattered and we are about to invaded by an army whose sole purpose in life is to kill every Christian on earth. I prayed to God for an answer to this tragedy, and He sent an angel to me and we talked, face to face, for a long time. The God of Creation has determined, he does not want this to be the fate of America, and sent me and a few hundred of my friends back in time to undo the damage and save our country. The correction in the time path had to begin in 1770. So that's where we started. We brought all our modern weapons from the 21st century with us, and the rest, as you have read, is history.

"Did you ever wonder where the Humvees, the Bradley's, the 105s, the Blackhawks, the Chinooks, your assault rifle, body armor and camouflage uniform came from?

"I enlisted the support and trust of Washington, Jefferson, Adams, Franklin, President Hamilton here, and James Madison. Madison will be President in two years. He is the last of the original Grand Conspiracy. Now we are going to have to go on with new men, men who have no idea of any of this. I've studied you and many more for years. You are my choice to become President when Madison retires and to serve for as long as you can be effective. The question is simple. Will you do it?"

"All of this true, Mr. President?"

"Every word."

"It sounds like an impossible job," said Hank.

"Oh we'll give you help. You and I are going to be together a lot. Also, you are going to go back to school and learn what our real history was, before Arcadia got here and started changing it. It's a fascinating and tragic story. What's more, we have to pray for guidance every day, or else by the time we get back to 2030, nothing will be different and the country will still have 150 million dead."

Arcadia smiled at Hank, "Look at it from the bright side. In a few years we will be sitting here telling this story to another person who will be your successor and will have the same look on his face as you do now."

Hamilton broke out in laughter, and patted Hank on the back. "It a lot like following a script, only you have to keep rewriting it."

The three spent the rest of the day strategizing on how to turn Hank Taylor into a household name over the next two years and set him up to succeed James Madison in ten years.

The next day Arcadia took Taylor to a situation room several stories below the White House and started him on the Master video of the old history of the United States. Taylor was used to seeing a video monitor, but he had never seen so many monitors of so many places in one place. In all, it took him three days to get through all the material.

Meanwhile, Arcadia was briefing incoming President James Madison on the choice. Madison took the news with calm acceptance and began to talk about the principal priorities of his time as President.

"You will preside over the period of history from 1820 to 1828," said Arcadia.

"Despite having to put so much on hold because of the Volcanic winters, we have still made a lot of progress on the building of infrastructure. We have added another 30,000 miles of track to our rail system. We have built another 5,000 miles of highways. We haven't gotten any further west, but we have connected a lot of cities without railroads with cities that do. We are now running a fleet of trucks from railroads to towns in many places heretofore isolated. We have 5000 trucks hauling freight."

"In the next 8 years we plan to concentrate on the highways and see if we can't complete one of them from coast to coast. We're going to fill in some more highways leading to some of our national parks, build some buses and start offering vacations for people.

"We don't want to start a big movement to build smaller private cars. We'll have a fleet for the White House and a few others for special use in Congress. Private cars are for the future, and I guarantee there won't be millions of them, like my time."

"We want to expand our energy infrastructure. We have two new dams under construction. They will turn out enough electricity to light the whole east coast. Of course we will bury all the power lines in steel tubes."

"One of the projects I'm very excited about is the tapping of our huge reserves of natural gas. The idea is to build pipelines to the bigger cities and then break those down to move into neighborhoods and hook up individual houses and businesses to gas and replace coal with furnaces with pumps to force hot air through the buildings."

"You already have a telephone you use to call the major offices and departments of the government. This system will continue to grow and expand. There will come a day in the future where there will be a telephone, electricity, lighting and heat in every home in the country."

"The next subject is just a little more tricky," said Arcadia. "New technology is being developed in other countries. They think they are coming up with something new. Obviously, we already have these products, and they are registered at the U.S. Patent office. Just before these new inventions come out, we are going to introduce them to the world, and start including some of those products in our list of trading goods."

"What sort of things are being developed," asked Madison?

Arcadia thumbed through a notebook. "In 1825, somebody is going to announce they've perfected the isolation of a new metal called aluminum. We've been doing that for a while, and will offer limited quantities for sale.

"Then we have Samuel Morey. He's an American who had several patents on steamboats. We managed to purchase these patents to clear the way for our steam ships. Now he's working on the concept of an internal combustion engine. We are simply going to file our patent first, under another name, and find a way to compensate Mr. Morey."

"In 1829, the first electric motor is going to get built in Europe. We've been using electric motors for years. We'll be filing for a patent during the next year."

"In terms of world activities, the United States is remarkably uninvolved in the next ten years. We think we have a nice window during your administrations to build our infrastructure, makes lots of money in foreign trade, and continue to improve the quality of life of average Americans."

"I'm grateful I don't have to face the problems Hamilton had," said Madison.

"The best thing you can do is to set up Hank Taylor to succeed you. We think he will have a nice long run, and there are a lot of fireworks coming up in the next 30 years."

Chapter 41
The Panama Canal

Georgetown, Washington, D.C.

The years of James Madison's presidency from 1820 to 1828, were used by Arcadia to consolidate all they had gained. In the 50 years since their arrival, the corps of workers from 2030 expanded in all directions. The quick jettison of the British from the colonies by a modern, high-tech army of Ranger's in 1776 bought Arcadia ten years. It also gave her a freehand to redraw the boundaries of the United States to make it the biggest country in the world, running from the Arctic Circle in Alaska to the Isthmus of Panama.

An advanced Republic emerged with all people regarded as equal. Slavery was no more, women had the right to vote, the Native Americans were in a state of their own with the rights of citizens. The population of the huge country had been stirred and interconnected with the Homestead Act giving free land to all willing to work for it. Racial discrimination was not only against the powerful Christian ethic, which dominated the lives of nearly everyone, it was also simply impractical.

For 50 years, modern schools with a quest for the advancement of knowledge, churned out gushers of new developments, technology and improvements in all areas of life. Just a gentle push here and there produced the world's biggest output of high quality, cheap steel. Oil and natural gas were being produced to power the growing number of engines, which went into continuously expanding machines from grain combines to asphalt pavers. In physics, chemistry, mathematics, engineering and medicine, the brilliant students were moving beyond their mentors. Routinely pushing into sciences that were excitingly new and progressive.

Railroads and highways crisscrossed the country like rivers, and transportation of products was easy and inexpensive with a big fleet of sleek trucks hauling consumer and manufactured goods of every description. The steam trains, which had seemed so modern 20 years before, were now being rapidly replaced with engines running on diesel powered by huge motors. Modern steel cargo ships were now being powered with liquid natural gas. This particular development was modern even by Arcadia's standards. A group of brilliant students in one of the research schools developed an effective way of adapting the process of putting this technology into ships. They were faster, and had three times the cruising range of steam or diesel ships.

Electricity was plentiful from the giant turbo generators at the big dams built with concrete and steel rebar, across chasms where wild waterfalls used to fall. This made every everything run from the subways in Washington and New York to the electric lights in every home and building. Nearly everyone now had telephones.

Arcadia was particularly pleased with the independent development of radio broadcasting. The early uses of radio were largely industrial, especially in shipping. However, it wasn't long before an enterprising pastor of a church found he could reach a much bigger audience by radio. The whole system made a huge leap forward with the nearly simultaneous discovery of the transistor, the key component to the modern computer. Another research center at one of the universities developed the compact battery, which made radios small enough to carry.

In the beginning, it was the government doing all the innovating and invention. However, Arcadia could see this was backwards to a truly Capitalistic society. As each new technology was perfected, Arcadia formed private companies and took them through the Initial Public Offering of stock process in these companies. The New York stock exchange traded these stocks to ordinary people who found Mutual Fund Companies waiting for them. The concept of watching a portfolio of stocks grow to provide healthy retirements was introduced to the American people.

Of course, the IPO's originated with the government and it benefitted from the creation of these new companies. The surplus of money in the federal treasury ballooned to stupefying amounts. It was Hank Taylor who announced, in behalf of the President, 1827 would be a tax-free year for all Americans and American business. The loss of income to the government was significant, but only a speed bump in overall wealth. It also did wonders for Taylor's image as a wonderful successor to the dour Madison.

The number of really wealthy people in the United States grew rapidly and was limited only by the hard work and enterprise of dedicated men and women.

The first company Arcadia privatized was the big network of the Emporiums, she used to break up the slave business. She was pleased to see many competitors angling to carve off a segment of the Emporiums business. Some were very successful, some failed. That was the natural nature of risk in a free market society. America was growing up.

Up was a good thing. Arcadia watched with interest as a couple of retired Rangers, who were helicopter pilots wondered if they could develop an aircraft with more range and carry more passengers. Soon they had a prototype airplane and wondered why it didn't work very well. One of the Arcadia's staff looked at their flat wings and suggested they study the wing design of birds. They did, and discovered the concept of lift from the airfoil. After that, it was easy. The boys looked around for something strong and light and another of the "advisors" talked about the existence of aluminum. They found a bank willing to back them in developing aluminum production and within two years, they had an airplane that would fly 500 miles and carry ten people. Then came the radial combustion engine running on gasoline, and an airplane that would fly 2,000 miles with 50 passengers aboard emerged.

That was the moment Arcadia waited for. By her reckoning, the United States of 1828 was now at about 1950 in most areas. It was enough for her to begin the really hard work of taming a very wild planet.

For the rest of the world, the United States was a huge mystery. Certain things were known. The country possessed an unbeatable army and navy. The Rangers were elevated to almost legendary status by the

British, French and Spanish who had seen the army in action first hand. This folklore had worked its way clear down to the common man on the street. America was simply left strictly alone except in all of its business enterprises.

The next thing the world knew about the United States was it produced products of unimaginable ingenuity and value. The equipment, tools, and bumper crop of basic and exotic foods at prices nobody could beat, made America the superstore of every country on earth. Arcadia's advisors told her they estimated the economies of the top ten countries in the world would collapse without trade from the United States.

This was about all anyone really knew about America. People immigrated, but nobody ever left. America was unique. It had embassies in almost every major country, but did not permit any foreign government to establish an embassy in the United States. These embassies were guarded by stern faced Rangers in full dress uniforms, adding to their formidable image. There were a few incidents in which off duty Rangers were confronted by tough guys in various places around foreign cities, looking to make a reputation for themselves. Despite all their efforts to avoid any problems, according to their orders, the Rangers were permitted to defend themselves if lethal force might be involved. Sometimes it was, and the Rangers beat the bullies to a bloody pulp. Even though they never killed anyone, witnesses to the exhibitions walked away telling everyone they knew the invincibility of the Rangers was real. Soon the incidents stopped and the Rangers became perfectly friendly ambassadors on their own, and always gave witness to God whenever the opportunity presented itself.

It was all tied up in the mantra of a strictly neutral, and isolationist political philosophy. America just didn't really need anything from anyone, and trade was mostly limited to exotic foods, most of the world's supply of rubber and shiploads of seemingly worthless rocks and minerals. Yet the United States held large holdings in loans and stock in a hundred foreign countries as a result of countries needing products and not having the trading materials or the cash to pay for them.

Arcadia pulled her first big international move in 1829, just a year after Hank Taylor settled into office as President of the United States.

Without any public announcement, men, equipment, supplies and heavy machinery began accumulating in the Isthmus of Panama.

A team of engineers, both from Arcadia's group, plus a large number of graduated engineers from American universities worked on the project for several years. They had to overcome the problems of disease, housing and feeding a work force of at least 10,000 men, and the colossal job of actually digging the canal. Huge machinery in dirt movers, big capacity scoop shovels, dump trucks, and railroad engines, had to be built and transported to Panama on ships. They used every scrap of useful information they had from the construction of the original canal. The locks, which had to be expanded in later years were designed bigger in the first place. Altogether, the original canal took the United States ten years, from 1904 to 1914, to build, and the French had done a lot of work before abandoning the effort in the late 1800's.

The American engineers believed they could do the job in about 15 years. In 1828, the work on the canal began in earnest. The engineers almost got it right. The Panama Canal was completed in 1843. Almost all the work was done in a near vacuum of publicity. The entire Isthmus was located inside the United States and the border with Columbia was heavily guarded by Rangers. This was according to Arcadia's plan. Her goal was to make a global statement, and use it to further her agenda of controlling world politics without violating the neutrality of the country.

Henry Taylor completed his fourth term as President in 1844. He presided over a rapidly changing United States. The advisors from the future, became mostly happy observers, except in some fields of astronomy, the development of modern rocketry, extraterrestrial space technology and microelectronics. Now, nearly all the new developments, of which there were many, were coming from the research facilities at the universities. The slow drip of information coming from Arcadia's team of experts gave the researchers a huge advantage. Just doing experiments trying to learn something would yield results. Knowing something existed provided a great many shortcuts leading to breakthroughs achieved in years, rather than decades.

He was often amazed to find some new wonder discovered, perfected, and brought to market. But Henry Taylor was the most proud of the monumental effort to build the Panama Canal. It was the summit of his 16 years as president. He would be happy to turn the reins of office over to his longtime vice president, Charles Gallagher, the first president to come from a state not one of the original 13 colonies.

Gallagher graduated from the Political Science school at age 21. He made an immediate splash in his home state of Iowa. He was regarded as an expert on everything agricultural, although he was thoroughly conversant in all the other components of government. He was elected to Congress at the minimum age of 25. He caught Arcadia's eye with his brilliant ability to find consensus and compromise to tough questions. She was very glad to see such an able man emerge when he did. President Taylor had chosen another man as vice-president when he took office, but he was tragically killed in an accident supervising the final months of construction on the Panama Canal. So Gallagher was only 35 years old when he became Vice President.

He went through the same process of learning of the Grand Conspiracy from Arcadia, who's memory was now regarded even more highly by the public as the Mother of America. His shock was significantly more profound than Taylor's, and his introduction to a living, breathing and unchanged Arcadia almost caused Gallagher to faint. Taylor enjoyed the moment immensely.

Gallagher went through the same extensive briefing and the viewing of the Master History video. So many things had changed, or never happened because of the 1770 intervention, Gallagher had a hard time believing the leaders of the country he loved had behaved in such foolish ways. Nevertheless, he was fully prepared to accept the actual nature of the United States as a clear and vast improvement.

The time came for the United States to unveil its new contribution to the world. A press release with lots of maps, high quality color pictures, and schematics of the canal was prepared by Gallagher, approved by the President and released to the world's newspapers, which did not have the capability of printing the color pictures, but could print the maps and the carefully drawn rendering of the canal. Taylor made sure his ambassadors delivered the full packet of photos and details of how the canal could be used, to the head of every country in Europe and Asia.

The announcement created global sensation. The British redoubled their efforts to build the Suez Canal and were fully aware the American effort was significantly more difficult. Nevertheless, they congratulated President Taylor, as did the other leaders of the community of nations. A fleet of ships about to depart from Europe to Asia and vice-versa, changed their sailing plans immediately and were grateful not facing the difficult passage around the South American horn, and the considerably shortened time to reach ports in China and other places along the Pacific Rim. They found the fees for using the canal high, but reasonable compared to the extra time it took to make the longer voyage.

Once more, the mystery and wonder of what was going on in the United States became the subject of speculation in every quarter from the head of government offices to the local pubs. The world got so many things from America...high quality goods of all kinds and at prices, no country in the world could match.

The anecdotal stories coming back from the crews of the trading ships sailing into the ports of America were often scoffed at. The idea you could travel the length of New York city in an underground train or that none of the buildings were made of wood, but were actually built with stone and steel. That the streets were all paved with a dark, hard surface; or lights burning without fire along every street and inside all the buildings, were generally discounted in the same category as sea monsters. If the people who were laughing only knew, the sailors were just seeing the tip of the iceberg.

As one of his last official acts in office, Henry Taylor presided over the official opening of the Panama Canal and the passage of the first ship, a large new American freighter. As Arcadia reminded him, "Make the first ship a freighter, not a warship. The symbol we want to convey is strength in peace, not war." Taylor thought this very sound advice. A long line of ships was waiting to pay their money and sail from the Atlantic to the Pacific Ocean in 20 hours, instead of two months.

Chapter 42
Indians And Innovation

The Great State of Sioux, United States

Arcadia's return to the land of the Sioux nation in 1844 was much different than her last visit in 1774. In that visit, Arcadia came to save the Native Americans. On this visit, she came to celebrate them. On her first visit, she descended from the air as the Spirit Mother. On this visit, she stepped off the train at the modern railroad station in Rapid City. When she had come before, she was wearing her ceremonial silver/white dress. This time she had on a pair of jeans and a short-sleeved polo shirt.

The last time the Lakota quivered in fear, this time they came forward with smiles and hugs. Arcadia greeted the Governor of Sioux in the native Lakota language. He laughed and responded in the same manner saying, "It's so gracious of you to return with the words of our heritage on your lips."

Arcadia laughed too, and said in English, "It's been so long since I learned Lakota, I was afraid I would mess it up."

"You were perfect, Madam Arcadia," said Governor Adam Blackthorn, also in English.

"Please, just Arcadia, and no Spirit Mother or any other ancient honorific," she laughed.

"Thank you," said the Governor, "when you called to say you would visit us while everyone else was preoccupied in Panama, we were honored."

"I had to make an inspection visit to make sure you guys are not causing trouble on the reservation."

"What a thing to say," groaned the Governor, "but I have read the history that no longer exists, and am happy to say we are doing quite well and I haven't lifted a single scalp all day."

The whole party of greeters and Arcadia had a big laugh at that, and headed off to the main street where a big crowd cheered as Arcadia came out of the train station. There was a podium set up and Arcadia joined the Governor on it. He held up his arms and said into a microphone. "It has been many years since the Spirit Mother came to our grandfathers and showed us the way to freedom and a better life. We welcome her back today, with joy and gratitude!"

There was a huge ovation from the big crowd. Obviously, Arcadia would have to say something. "Thank you all so much. I don't make public appearances anymore, but the people of the Great Sioux nation are wise. You know I appeared as a Spirit before, but know today I am only flesh and blood and are happy to help me keep my secret from the superstitious white men."

That got another huge ovation. Arcadia continued, "I am here today to celebrate your wisdom, your progress, and your success. There are no people in all this biggest country in the world with whom I am more proud!"

The Governor led Arcadia off the podium and escorted her to a large ATV. It was open at the top and she and governor drove slowly down the main street of Rapid City waving to the cheering people who were lined up four deep for a mile.

They reached the grounds of the state capitol and pulled around the curving entrance lined with flowers and a lush green lawn. The building was very different, uniquely Sioux, but it was beautiful. The pillars at the entrance were carved with intricate figures.

The governor's office was fairly traditional. It was large with a big table at the front and chairs and a couch facing his desk. He waved Arcadia to a seat. "I know you have paid special attention to us, and your letters and calls are very much appreciated. We have never had as much as we have today."

"You and your predecessors did a masterful job of convincing all the tribes to relocate within the state boundaries I set for you," said Arcadia, "I'm sure it wasn't easy, nor was it easy to become ranchers of buffalo instead of nomadic hunters. However, you are all alive and I thank God for that. Because you didn't fight a war you couldn't win, you preserved your population. Not having to worry about disease saved even more. The result is you have one of the most populous states in the country."

"We still think it was quite a wonderful thing when a very nice lady hinted we ought to scratch around in the Black Hills for hidden treasure."

"How much gold have you recovered," asked Arcadia?

"Oh only about $50 million dollars, worth," said Adam. "When you add in our meat production from several million buffalo, and the wonderful wheat and corn we grow along the Platte, using the irrigation techniques our children learned in the schools and universities, the State of Sioux is quite wealthy."

"What about alcoholism," asked Arcadia?

"Alcohol is illegal in this state, and our churches do a good job of keeping the evils of Satan from tempting the people. We still have some problems, but we manage."

"How many of your men have you managed to get into the Rangers," smiled Arcadia?

"Over 300, at the present time, but you already knew that," said Adam.

"And great soldiers they are. Some of them are serving at our embassies in Europe, the people are scared to death of them. Plus we put an entire company of them along the border with Columbia while we were building the canal. The racial similarities made for an easier time for both sides."

Arcadia spent a week in the big State of Sioux. She saw the huge herds of buffalo, being driven by men driving speedy ATV's. She saw the miles of corn and wheat crops. She saw a number of neat and tidy towns and villages, and she was very impressed with the capital of Rapid City with a population of over 75,000 people. The Sioux had made the most of their opportunity. They had excellent schools, and a thriving middle class. A big crowd turned out to send her on her way. She thoroughly enjoyed her ride on the train back to Washington. She received no more notice than any pretty, young blond woman would have gotten. Arcadia loved the anonymity.

Henry Taylor rode out of office with the respect and gratitude of the entire country. They had no problem is selecting his vice President Charles Gallagher as the new President in the November 1844 election. It was a custom, albeit secret, that all new Presidents go through a comprehensive planning session between the election and the January inauguration with Arcadia and her staff of experts. The purpose of the meetings were to review the historical records and to determine which events or discoveries, if any, had a direct impact on the United States.

Arcadia put the list up on the screen for everyone to review.

<u>1842: Anesthesia used for the first time.</u>

"I think we can add the family of anesthetics currently in use to our list of products that can purchased in trade with other countries," said Arcadia.

"You realize the anesthesia they are talking about is common ether," said one of the doctors. Our anesthetics are delivered by IV drip. The global medical community is still not even up to using needles. We would have to be able to demonstrate the entire process of introducing fluids to a body. Do we want to go that far?"

"That's a very good question," said Arcadia. "We would still maintain the integrity of the products, of course, the international medical community is not going to be able to synthesize the drugs, manufacture the needles, plastic tubes, or IV bags. However, we have come to our first crossroad of involvement by the United States in global affairs. Others will begin to come along in growing numbers in the near future, and we will deal with them on a case-by-case basis. As I see it, this one is easy. It's entirely humanitarian in nature, like the food we sent to the British a half century ago. However, the techniques and the training to use these products are going to have to be taught in person. We sure aren't going to bring doctors here, so that means teams have to go to Europe and teach the procedure at the big medical schools."

"I realize a lot of care must be taken by the docs not to reveal more advanced medicine than we want them to know," said the Director of Public Health, "Frankly, Arcadia, I've been waiting for an opportunity to put in a pitch for going public with the vaccines for the common diseases. These diseases are still killing a lot of people in the outside world. We can prepare a cocktail of vaccines delivered by needles that will cover measles, whooping cough, pertussis, mumps, polio, and Tuberculosis."

"I'm emotionally on your side, Doc," said Arcadia, "but the population of Europe is now over 200 million. We don't have the facilities for producing that much vaccine. If we made it a priority, we might be able to build the labs to turn out that much and more, but it looks like a 25 year job to me."

"I guess you're right," said the Doctor, "I suppose we'll have to put vaccinating the world on our 'to do' list. However, anesthetics are a much more manageable problem. We do have the production capabilities to keep up with that demand."

"How big a team do you need," asked the President, speaking up for the first time?

"Not too big. If we demonstrate the procedure in England, France, Spain, Germany, and Austria-Hungary, it will spread to the rest of the world. That means five teams of half a dozen docs; make it about 30 or 40 people."

"Why don't we just send one team to a medical school in England and let them spread the procedure," asked the President?

"Politics," said Arcadia, "None of these countries get along with each other very well in the first place. If we just gave the drugs and the procedure to the British, they might not share it. In any case, the other major powers would believe we were giving the British special treatment. We have to send our teams to all the big powers and deliver the new procedure at about the same time."

"Of course," said Gallagher, "the United States is strictly neutral and acting in the best interests of everyone."

"Right," said Arcadia, "I think we should put together all the pieces of this project, start producing a steady supply to sell to the Europeans, and assemble our teams. Let the President know when you are completely ready and then he can pass the word of our intentions to the Ambassadors."

"Are all our historical reviews going to be so complicated," asked the President?

"Not really," said Arcadia, "look at the next item on the list."

1843: The first wagon train sets out from Missouri.

"I guess we won't have to deal with that," said Gallagher. "Or the next one."

1844: First publicly funded telegraph line in the world—between Baltimore and Washington—sends demonstration message on May 24, ushering in the age of the telegraph. This message read, "What hath God wrought?"

"This was a big deal in early America, but now we do so much more. The event will never happen."

1844: Millerite movement awaits the Second Advent of Jesus Christ on October 22. Christ's non-appearance becomes known as the Great Disappointment.

"We'll broadcast this on the church channel. It will give our pastors lots of fodder for sermons that say the 'Second Coming of Christ' is none of our business."

1844: The Great Auk is rendered extinct.

"I don't suppose we can do anything about this," said the President.

"We could send a ship to see if there are any Auks left," said one of the staff, "and if there is we could maybe bring home a few to add to our national zoo."

"I'd vote for that," said the President.

"Then that is the way we shall have it," said Arcadia

1844: Dominican War of Independence from Haiti.

"This one would come as quite a shock to the state of Hispaniola," laughed the President.

"The next three are really not something we need to think about," said Arcadia.

She scrolled down on the screen and stopped at the next entry. "This one needs our attention," said Arcadia.

1845–1849: The Irish Potato Famine leads to the Irish diaspora.

"Something like five million Irish migrated to the United States as a result of this famine. A million in the first year of 1846," said Arcadia. "The Irish are one of the important groups of immigrants for our country. They will be good Americans, and make significant contributions to our society. The problem is dealing with the numbers. In real history, a lot of the Irish were shoved into substandard housing in New York and Boston and suffered from poverty, low wages, and disease. I think we need to take them in and then quickly disburse them in groups to several states. Most of them are farmers and the one thing we have plenty of is open land. Maybe we can grubstake them with seeds and equipment on credit. But we can't have them clogging up our cities."

The next item was, 1846–1848: The Mexican-American War leads to Mexico's cession of much of the modern-day Southwestern United States.

Events such as this just disappear into the river of time," said Arcadia. "Next item.

1846–1847: Mormon migration to Utah.

"It's OK for the Mormons to migrate to Utah," said Arcadia. "In real history they went by wagon train. Personally, I consider this religion a heresy, but at least it's based on the resurrection of Christ, which makes them a lot more attractive than Islam. I recommend the President contact Brigham Young and make a deal to send the whole bunch of them on trains. They can unload their wagons and finish the trip to 'the promised land' as best they can."

"I'll make the arrangements," said the President.

Arcadia scrolled the list.

1847: The Bronte sisters publish *Jane Eyre*, *Wuthering Heights*, and *Agnes Grey*.

"Nice."

1847–1901: The Caste War of Yucatán.

"Not relevant to our history."

1848–1849: Second Anglo-Sikh War

"Ditto"

1848: *The Communist Manifesto* published.

"An important book with multiple ramifications, but not for this century."

1848: Revolutions of 1848 in Europe.

"Don't even know what this is."

1848: Seneca Falls Convention The first women's rights convention in the United States and leads to the battle for suffrage and women's legal rights.

"Obviously, another historical relic"

1848–1858: California Gold Rush. 1849: The first boatloads of gold prospectors arrive in California, giving them the nickname 49ers.

Arcadia smiled, "The gold is going to be discovered. It's the best homogenizer of people I can imagine. Let 'em have their fun."

She scrolled on.

1849: The safety pin and the gas mask are invented.

1849: Earliest recorded air raid Austria employs 200 balloons to deliver ordnance against Venice.

1850: The Little Ice Age ends around this time.

1850–1864: Taiping Rebellion. The bloodiest conflict of the century, leading to the deaths of 20 million people.

1851: The Great Exhibition in London The world's first international Expo or World's Fair.

"I don't suppose we want to take part in this, asked one of the staff?

"Tempting, isn't it," said Arcadia? "However, the secrets of America are far too important to be fizzled away at a public exhibition."

1851: Louis Napoleon assumes power in France in a coup.

1851–1852: The Platine War ends The Empire of Brazil has hegemony over South America.

1851–1860s: Victorian gold rush in Australia

1852: Frederick Douglass delivers his speech "The Meaning of July Fourth for the Negro" in Rochester, New York.

1853: United States Commodore Matthew C. Perry threatens the Japanese capital Edo with gunships, demanding that they agree to open trade.

1853–1856: Crimean War between France, the United Kingdom, the Ottoman Empire, and Russia

1854: Battle of Balaclava and the Charge of the Light Brigade.

1854: The Convention of Kanagawa formally ends Japan's policy of isolation.

1854–1855: Siege of Sevastopol; city falls to British forces.

1855: Bessemer process enables steel to be mass-produced.

1856: World's first oil refinery in Romania

1856: Neanderthal man first identified. Age still unknown.

1857–1858: Indian Rebellion of 1857. The British Empire assumes control of India from the East India Company.

1858: Invention of the phonograph, the first true device for recording sound.

1859: Charles Darwin publishes *On the Origin of Species*.

1859–1869: Suez Canal is constructed.

"None of this is relevant to our current activities or technical progress," said Arcadia. "It's true the Industrial Revolution in Europe has a full head of steam. We would have to expect them to make progress in some basic areas, but we are so far ahead of them, we really can't risk revealing our true capabilities until we're ready. We have a full head of steam too, but our schools, research facilities, and labs are starting to turn out some technology rivalling or actually exceeding the technology of my time."

"Speaking of which," said President Gallagher, "do we have an inventory of where we stand today?"

Arcadia turned to her Director of Infrastructure and said, Got the report?"

"Mr. President, this is the report we deliver to the Chief Executive each year. It's fairly lengthy, as you can see. What it does is give you the current state of our infrastructure, technology achieved, financial numbers of our national wealth, and projections of where we are headed in the next five and ten year period. You can read the entire report at you leisure, but I have a synopsis I can give you now."

"Please proceed," said Gallagher.

A display appeared on the screen and began running numbers:

- Total current population of the United States 31 million
- Number of Federal employees 10,556
- 1844 Federal Budget $31 Million
- 1844 Revenues from Individuals $49 Million
- 1844 Revenues from Businesses $106 million
- 1844 Gold Reserve $1.2 Billion
- Gross Domestic product. Total of all goods, services, and incomes. $4.62 billion.
- Annual Corn Production 30 million bushels

- Annual Wheat production 40 million bushels
- Total electrical production from all sources 5 million mega-watt hours per day. Currently 65% of electricity is produced by natural gas, 25% by coal, 20% Hydroelectric.
- Number of power plants 452
- Total railroad miles constructed 106,000
- Total Highway miles constructed 98,000. 95% asphalt.
- Number of railroad engines 1152, 85% diesel.
- Number of diesel powered heavy trucks 12,786
- Total number of universities with research centers 132
- Total number of students in universities 140,523
- Number of steel hulled freighter ships powered by liquefied natural gas 315
- Number of Navy warships 3, original power source classified, 37 new, LNG powered with 73% of original firepower. 1 original submarine, power source, classified. New submarines 14, 61% of original firepower.
- Defense forces. 3 brigades of Rangers, total force 10,115 soldiers
- Number of airplanes, 250, with many more under construction. Mostly they are two engine planes with a passenger capacity of about 50, but the new planes, have four engines and will carry up to 250 passengers. We have airports at every state capital. There is word the technos are working on an entirely new aircraft engine using high-speed air pushed through a thruster. It's called a jet.
- Finally, we are making a tidy profit with Panama Canal. This year's revenue will exceed $10 million.

"Those are basic numbers, Mr. President," said Arcadia. "We have not included the heavy equipment such as we constructed for the building of the Panama Canal. We are still exporting ten times as much as we import. We have about 10,000 private companies in the country. Our crime rate is extremely low, I think mostly because we spend our Sundays going to church. The Christian ethic of the country is so strong we have not had to apply a single Federal dollar to the poor, the sick, and the helpless. The churches and their associated organizations like the Red Cross and the Salvation Army, handle it all.

In the past 50 years, the life expectancy of Americans has gone from 42 to 71 years old. We now have 30 national Parks open for business, and we offer low cost packages of train, bus, and guest accommodations for them all. We think Americans should be able to vacation as hard as they work. We've established a very active sports program. We have the national soccer team, basketball, and track and field. We run national programs for all those from grade schools to high schools to universities to professional teams.

We didn't make some of the same mistakes we did in the original history. We have a very good electrical infrastructure with four main grids, with all the cables buried in the ground and interconnected. We recognized the value of natural gas much sooner and we have the world's biggest reserve. Gas does not pollute like coal."

"In short, Mr. President, we have a 1950 economy for power, transportation, agriculture, and consumer goods. 90% of the homes in America are heated by gas and have telephones and radios. Our medical community is almost up to 2000 standards.

"Perhaps best of all, we have at least a dozen research centers at the universities working on micro-technology. The transistor is the basic tool for the computer. In the next ten years, the researchers are going to start figuring out how to miniaturize these circuits on boards, and you will end up with that," she pointed to the LED screen monitor on the wall, "available in increasing numbers."

"It all looks so wonderful," said the President. "And best of all, the rest of the world has no idea of what we have."

"That's our ace in the hole, Mr. President," said Arcadia, "and believe me, we are going to need it all, if we are going to prevent the horrendous world wars of the next century you've seen in graphic detail."

"How are we going to prevent it," questioned the President?

"I'll give you an analogy," said Arcadia.

"Suppose a race of peaceful beings from another planet discovered the earth in 1912, minus the power of the United States. What if their superior technology was so seductive the powers of the world knew two things. One, the aliens could physically prevent the great powers from warring with each other because of superior weaponry, and two, offered to share their technology with the world in exchange for a negotiated peace. What do you think the world would do?"

"I imagine they would think it over and take the advanced technology."

"That is my hope and prayer as well," said Arcadia. Only there will be no alien visitors, there will be the United States. We will be like a big, friendly elephant just leaning on the great powers until they go our way. Remember we have almost two centuries of peaceful trade and non-interference in global affairs going for us. The world is envious of us and curious as hell about how we supply such marvelous products, but we aren't anyone's enemy. We do not threaten the sovereignty of any country, but they all have the sneaking suspicion we could if we wanted to."

"Alright then," said the President, "I appreciate all you and your people do, Arcadia. I know God is watching us and I pray every day for His guidance and blessing."

"Me too," said Arcadia.

"I'll start the projects with the medical teams and their anesthetics, as well as devising a plan to deal with 5 million new Irish immigrants."

"I think that should keep you busy for a while, in addition to running the country," smiled Arcadia.

As the meeting broke up and the team filed out of the conference room, Arcadia stayed behind. "Have you given any thought to your new vice president?"

"I have a national search out for him right now."

"Don't forget half the people in this country are women. Now might be the time to pick one."

"I'll give it careful consideration. If the number one candidate turns out to be a woman, I'll choose her."

"Stay healthy, Chuck, your big moment will come when you are about 62."

Arcadia left it at there and didn't elaborate.

Chapter 43
The Medicine Men

London, England

St George's, University of London had its origins as a medical school in 1733. It was the largest and most advanced school in England in 1846.

Word came to the Chancellor of the school in late 1845, from the office of the Prime Minister for him go to Number 10 Downing Street for a special meeting with Robert Peel.

Chancellor Homer Dobkins was ushered into the office of the Prime Minister. Peel welcomed him and invited him to have a seat.

"Chancellor, I've called you here today to present you with a rather extraordinary proposal. Heaven knows the United States is the preeminent trading nation in the world, but they do not permit any one to establish embassies in their capital of Washington, so the world doesn't really know much about that huge country, and believe me we have tried to get more information. Their intelligence service is first rate and all our spy missions have ended up in failure. We have even had spies who have reported back America is a wonderful, magical country and they are going to stay. It is one of the world's greatest mysteries, this colossal United States."

"Now it seems the United States has gotten word of our development of anesthesia with ether for surgical operations, and are offering to send a team of doctors to instruct us in a more advanced form of anesthesia. The U.S. Ambassador would only say it was a purely humanitarian gesture by America, and one that would save many lives. They offer the instruction and demonstrations for free, along with an initial supply of their drugs and the manner in which they are administered."

"With respect Prime Minister, don't you think it's rather presumptuous for these Americans to lecture us about medical practices? England is the premier country in the world in medicine."

"But what if we aren't," said the Prime Minister? "Who knows what kind of magic the Americans are cooking up sealed behind their borders? And besides, they are sending medical teams to France, Spain, Germany, and Austria-Hungary at the same time. All in the name of fairness and equality. We would be foolish to not accept these doctors with open arms and seek to learn as much as possible from them."

"I suppose you are right, Prime Minister, but I'm not sure my colleagues will be as open and magnanimous. They are quite proprietary about their skills and training and you know as well as I do what inflated egos, most of them have."

"It will be your job to keep this hostility under control, and accept the teaching these doctors offer. It is not in the best interests of the British Empire to insult the Americans. Make that point clear to your fellow doctors."

"I shall endeavor to make their visit as pleasant and go as smoothly as possible, Prime Minister."

Doctor Dobkins left the Prime Minister's office with a flurry of mixed emotions. How dare the Americans presume to lecture us on medical procedures, he thought. Then he reasoned, but what if their techniques are of great value. We would be serving our patients most admirably. Anyway, once the Americans leave we can use their techniques or not, and claim the credit for them. That last part seemed like the best approach to his surgical colleagues, and he returned to the hospital and school and began bringing in a few of his most trusted friends first, and then widened the announcement to the entire staff of academic doctors. He even contacted a few key doctors from other medical schools in England and extended an invitation for them to view the demonstration.

Doctor Don Rippert had his team gathered in the wardroom of the 'Mississippi', just before they disembarked in London. The ship barely had the clearance to make the passage up the estuary of the Thames, but the alternative was to load all their delicate equipment onto carriages and endure the bumpy roads to the capital.

"All right, let's just make sure we're all on the same sheet of music. Our goal is to instruct these doctors in modern anesthesiology. We will use our standard masks and also the IV drip methods. Since none of these guys have ever seen a needle and don't really know the first thing about sanitation in an operating theater. We're going to have to give them some instructions in the importance of keeping the areas we are working sterile. This will no doubt cause a flurry of questions. Try and keep your answers confined to the procedures we are demonstrating. Most of the equipment we will be using will be foreign to them

"Bear in mind we are playing in their home court and I imagine there will be more than a little hostility over our being here. Just remember our mission is one of humanitarian support and treat the natives with dignity and respect, even though they are really no better than witch doctors, 3rd class.

"All our supplies are carefully packed to handle rough treatment and all you need to do now is to gather your personal effects. Remember there is Cholera in the city, so don't drink any unfiltered water, and use your hand sanitizers every chance you get. Here we go."

The team of six American doctors stepped off the ship. It was a steel ship and attracted a huge crowd of spectators, who had never seen such a ship before. They were met personally by Dr. Homer Dobkins, "How do you do gentlemen, welcome to London. I am Dr. Homer Dobkins, Chancellor of St. Georges."

Dr. Rippert shook hands with the doctor and said, "We are grateful for the opportunity to collaborate in the world of medicine with such a distinguished person such as you. Thank you for your hospitality."

"Not at all," said Dobkins pleasantly. "We've made special arrangements to insure the safety of your equipment and its safe delivery to the hospital. If you and your team will step this way, we will handle your luggage and proceed to your quarters at the school."

The first thing Rippert noticed when he got off the ship was the smell. London fairly reeked of garbage and human waste. The humans themselves didn't smell a lot better. Everywhere he looked, he saw muddy pools looking like petri dishes filled with the worst bacteria in the world.

They had their luggage taken and stacked on a wagon, while two large carriages, pulled by horses were for the team of Americans and their host. They wound their way through the crowded streets of London. The sight of so many ill-fed and sickly looking people made Rippert sick, and the air was filled with the smoke of factories pouring out black smoke from coal-fired steam engines.

Finally, they pulled through the gates of the hospital and school. At least this had a more healthy look. There were lawns and flowers and the driveway was paved with stones making the ride seem smoother, than the jolting and bouncing they experienced on the streets of London.

Dr. Dobkins led them into the wide entrance of the main building and up two flights of stairs to a long hallway. He stopped at the first door and opened it, handing the key to Dobkins. "These are your quarters, Doctor," said Dobkins. "Your colleagues have rooms along this hall. When you are settled, please come back to the main floor, we have prepared a luncheon for you and some of the medical staff of St. Georges."

Rippert stepped into his room. It was an oversized area, with a table. Obviously, this was where Rippert would hold meetings. There was a bed in the alcove around the corner, a chest of drawers with a large bowl, and a porcelain pitcher of water. There was also a bucket Rippert supposed he was expected to use as a toilet. At least the room seemed clean but had a musty smell.

He unpacked his suitcase, and put away his clothes, after wiping down the drawers with a sanitizer. He also wiped down all the surfaces he might touch with sanitizer. Now, at least the room smelled fresher.

After he'd unpacked he left, locked the door and wandered down the hall to the next room. When he knocked, Bob Peters opened the door. "I suppose you got a room of your own. I'm stuck with Eli here and we all know how he snores."

Eli waved a container, "I thought I was being extravagant bringing so much sanitizer, but I bet I used half a bottle wiping down this place. Did you ever, in all your life smell such a rotten place as London? I thought half the people were going to die just by driving past them. And look here, I've got a bucket to crap in, and one lousy bowl to wash my hands."

"We can slip back to the Mississippi for showers when it gets so we can't stand it," said Don.

"Really, Don, is this such a good idea? These guys are so ignorant and primitive, I'm not sure they will know what we're talking about.

"Not much we can do about it now but try and make the best of it," said Don. "Let's get the others and go down to lunch. Don't forget your water bottles."

The team went down the stairs to the main floor and found Dr. Dobkins waiting for them. "Splendid," he said, "my doctors have all arrived and are eager to meet you." He led them down another hall and through big double doors to a dining room with one long table. Dobkins led the way to the head of the table and signaled Rippert to be seated on is right. The rest of the team were sprinkled down the table with British Doctors sitting next to them.

Waiters entered the room carrying platters of food. The British doctors immediately started grabbing platters and starting serving themselves.

"Excuse me, Doctor Dobkins," said Rippert rising to his feet. "In America it is our custom to thank the Lord before we begin eating a meal."

"Of course," said Dobkins, forgive me and please proceed."

"All six of the Americans stood and put their hands together. " Heavenly Father, we offer you our praise and honor for a safe passage and an opportunity to meet with companions in science and medicine. We ask you to bless our efforts and our work here to your glory. We ask thanks for this meal in the name of our holy savior, Jesus Christ, Amen."

"Amen," came a chorus of the men at the table. The Americans sat back down and began studying the food, trying to figure out what they could eat that wouldn't give them dysentery.

"I understand," said a portly British doctor to Bob Peters American Medicine has discovered the use of ether as an effective anesthetic?"

"We have been aware of ether for some time," said Peters, "However, today, ether is rarely used. Diethyl ether was found to have undesirable side effects, such as post-anesthetic nausea and vomiting. Modern anesthetic agents, such as methyl propyl ether and Penthrane reduce these side effects."

The British Doctor blinked and cleared his throat into his napkin.

Rippert caught the exchange and said loudly enough for the rest of the room to hear, "Actually, we have developed an entirely new and different procedure providing us with a large number of options when we are conducting an operation. This is the reason we've made this trip to Europe. As you know, we have four other teams who are currently in, or arriving soon, in France, Germany, Spain, and Austria-Hungary."

"How soon will you be able to provide us with this demonstration," asked Dobkins?

"Has all our equipment arrived the hospital?"

"Yes, it came with you this afternoon. We placed it all in our largest surgical observatory."

"Then give us a day to get set up and we'll be ready to start," said Rippert.

"I, uh, am reluctant to bring it up, but finding volunteers to undergo your experiments are somewhat difficult to find."

"That won't necessary," said Rippert, "three of my doctors will serve as patients, and these are not experiments, they are standard procedures for all our operations in the United States."

"Well, that is very good news," said Dobkins. "I notice Doctor you are not drinking anything except water from those strange bottles. What is the reason?"

"Damned good reason," said Eli, from the other end of the table. London is currently experiencing another outbreak of Cholera. Since Cholera is a water-borne disease, we are only going to drink water we know is safe,"

Rippert cringed at the other end of the table. He knew Eli was only speaking the truth, but the truth was nobody in the world knew Cholera came from drinking contaminated water. He hoped Eli had not opened a can of worms.

"Are you saying Cholera is caused by drinking water," asked a shocked doctor sitting across from Eli.

"Contaminated water," said Eli," when you mix fresh water with water containing human or animal waste, or anything rotten you introduce the Cholera bacteria into the water. People drink it and die basically of dehydration."

"That is astonishing information," said the British doctor. We have observed Cholera does not spread from person to person."

"Of course not," said Eli, "Cholera is not an air-borne disease."

"How do you prevent its spread, asked the doctor?

"Separate your fresh water supplies from your sewage, like not dumping your sewage into the river. It will make London smell better too."

"And how do you make suspicious water safe to drink," asked the doctor?

"Boil it," said Eli, "that kills all the pathogens in the water."

"Very interesting observations, Doctor," said Dobkins.

The meal finished with very little conversation.

The team moved into the operating theater the next day.

"Will you look at this," said Bob, "it's nothing more than a classroom with auditorium seats. The doors go right out to the street. So much for a sterile atmosphere."

"We aren't doing open heart surgery," said Rippert, "all I'm going to do is poke you with a needle. I'll still take all the precautions."

They rolled three tables into the open space at the bottom of the room. Rippert ordered three large porcelain jars be brought in with boiling water in two of them. He sat these on another table across the room with a deep bowl in the center. He got out a frame for the IV bags, with a hook at the top. On this, he hung a bag of common saline solution and attached the bag to a plastic tube. The tube had a port in it to inject whatever drug he chose. At the end of the tube was a connector for a needle. He sat out some small bottles containing a variety of anesthetics, and some syringes with covered needles. "I think that about does it," said Rippert, bring in the audience. He and Eli put on the long white coats of doctors.

Over a hundred doctors rushed into the room filling all the seats and gabbling as they sat down.

Rippert turned to the audience and said, "Whenever you are working or operating around a patient, great care must be taken to insure no bacteria of any kind be introduced to the patient's body. We take our first precaution by what is known as 'the scrub'." He walked over to the porcelain jars and poured boiling water in the basin, adding a small amount of cold water. "This water is as hot as I can stand. Ideally it should be running." Rippert took the soap bar and a stiff brush and began to industriously, scrub his hands, and up his arms. He did this for several minutes, throwing out the water in the basin and adding more. Finally, he washed off his hands and Eli handed him a towel to dry his hands. "This towel is from our supply and I know it is sterile. It was washed in boiling water and a strong detergent, dried and stored in this bag. I am now drying my hands."

Next Eli pulled out two plastic surgical gloves from a clear container and with gloves already on his hands; held the gloves for Rippert to shove his hands into each of them. "There is powder inside the glove to make it easier to put on." He held up his hands to show the audience. "We now have taken the second precaution to maintain as sterile an environment as possible. More patients die of bacteria introduced into their system by the surgeon, than do of the reason they came to the doctor in the first place."

Eli then placed a surgical mask on Rippert and tied it up. Rippert did the same for Eli. Then, speaking through the mask Rippert said, "A third precaution we take is to wear surgical masks. This keeps us from breathing or spitting any bacteria into the patient. Everything I have done should be standard procedure for any operation in which the patient's skin is broken. It is a sacred rule of the oath we all took, 'First, do no harm.' Bring in the patient."

Bob Peters came walking into the room. He was wearing jeans and a short-sleeved shirt. He lay down on the table with his head facing the audience, which was a silent as a tomb. Rippert rolled the IV stand over to the edge of the table and pointed his gloved fingers to it. "This bag contains nothing more than a common saline solution. The human body is 90% percent water the same as seawater. This plastic tube is connected to the bag. In the center of the tube is a port, by which I can inject anything I want into the patient. This is done by injecting the end of the tube, which has a needle attached to it, into the arm of the patient. This is a very sharp, thin piece of hollow metal that is sterile because of the covering on it. I will now remove the cover and pass some samples around the room. As you can see, the needle will allow the solution to pass through it into the patient's body."

Rippert put a plastic band around Bob's arm above the elbow, and said, "I am doing this to slightly constrict the blood flow and let me better see the veins in Bob's arm here. We take the needle and insert directly into the vein." He swabbed Bob's arm with an alcohol wipe. "This is just alcohol to sterilize the skin where I am going to make the injection. It keeps any germs on his skin from going in with the needle."

Then he gently shoved the needle directly into a vein. He lifted the tube a little to show blood was flowing. He then turned and picked up one of the small bottles. "This bottle contains our anesthesia. I am going to use this syringe and withdraw a small amount from the bottle. I don't want Bob to sleep all night and miss dinner."

Rippert stuck the needle in the bottle and drew out a small amount of clear liquid. Then he injected it into the port on the plastic tube. "Bob, start counting backwards from a 100!"

Bob called out "100 -99-98-97-96–nine." And that was it.

"Bob will out for approximately one hour. He will awaken feeling fine and be ready for dinner. Can I have my next two volunteers? This is Doctor Clay and Doctor Harris. Which one of you brave souls is ready to come down here and do what I have just done?" Rippert waited for a bit, and then said, "Come, come, gentlemen. This is very basic medicine. There must someone willing to give it a try."

From about the middle a gallery a middle-aged man stood up. Dr. Rippert, I think I speak for us all when I say we have all just taken a giant leap into the medical future. I admit, I am afraid, but with your help, I'm willing to be taught."

"Good show, old man!" said Rippert, Come on down here and walk into history."

Rippert got fresh boiling water and supervised while the doctor, whose name was Crane, scrubbed up. He had to do it three times before he passed Rippert's inspection. Then Rippert handed him a towel to dry his hands, put on a new pair of gloves, and held another pair instructing Dr. Crane to push his hand into the glove smartly to make sure of a good fit. He tore up two pairs of gloves getting the hang of it. Then Rippert put on Cranes' surgical mask and one of his own, explaining as he did you always use new gloves and new masks every time.

Dr. Clay came into the room, smiling, and lay down on the table. Rippert rolled the new IV bag over to the edge of the table with a new plastic tube, port, and a shielded needle at the end.

He had Crane, tie the elastic round Clay's arm, and swab him with alcohol. Then both of them got close and Rippert pushed gently on Clay's arm. "See the vein," said Rippert, "Put the needle right in the middle of it."

Dr. Crane would be forever grateful his hand was steady and he hit the vein on his first try. Then he got the second syringe, and drew out the exact amount Rippert said to take. He pushed the needle into the port and said, "Count backwards from a hundred." Crane only got to 98 before he was unconscious. "This anesthetic is for use when time is short, like you have a man with a belly wound and he's about to bleed out on you."

He held up the syringe and said, "Whose next?" This time there were several volunteers. Ripley picked a young man and sent him through the entire routine until Dr. Harris came into the room and went out cold, right on schedule.

"I don't think we will have trouble getting volunteers now," said Rippert, "tomorrow we will begin again, and each of you will do this routine until it becomes like second nature."

Rippert was mobbed by applauding doctors who wanted to get their hands on all the strange equipment they'd seen. They asked a hundred questions, oblivious to the three sleeping men on the tables.

The stiff British reserve was gone. Dr. Don, as he came to be called, and the rest of his staff worked diligently for two weeks to insure no less than 200 doctors mastered the technique and learned to wash their hands before they operated. They worked in harmony and an air of the unknown. Exactly what was the nature of medicine in the United States if the docs could answer any question put to them, no matter what the subject? It gave the British physicians a profound respect for what America must be doing in other areas if they had come so far in medicine.

The American Ambassador to England dropped by one day to say the results in the other countries was much the same.

When the mission was over, a great party was held. One of the highlights of the party was Dr. Don drinking a glass of water Dr. Dobkins gave him. He said it was part of a batch of water boiled especially for the occasion. The water wasn't cold, and there were no ice cubes in the glass, but it was a very satisfying drink for Dr. Don.

The team left ample enough supplies to conduct several hundred operations. The British government ordered an entire shipload of the things they needed to keep the anesthesia running. All the other countries did the same, and a pharmaceutical company in Virginia had a windfall of profits.

Chapter 44
Setting The Stage

<u>**Washington, D.C., 1850**</u>

Arcadia sat at her computer in her big Georgetown house. The computer was transferring the image onto the big monitor covering most of a wall in her large office. The other walls were a collection of photographs of the important events of America, going back to 1770. Now, in 1850, Arcadia was reviewing the land use planning maps she and her urban designers conceived when the North American continent was secure.

The nice thing about having a big empty space like she did with Alaska, Canada, the original United States, Mexico, Central America, and the Caribbean, as a palette was the planners could make the most efficient use of the land for all the purposes emerging in a modern country. In the original United States, growth produced a hodge-podge of land uses putting industrial areas too close to residential areas, did not make the best use of the agricultural lands, or provide for the proper growth planning emerging with population growth.

The states had mostly the same boundaries as before, with some major differences. California, for example, became two states, north, and south. Of course, the state of Sioux had wiped out North and South Dakota and Nebraska and increased the size of Kansas. The National Parks and Federal land in forests and unique geographical places were kept clear of all development, except the service centers for visitors. Transportation corridors for rail, and highways, were also planned for expansion and growth as the population increased. The electrical power grids were interconnected and all buried in steel pipes. The dams built, took into consideration the environmental impact along with the commercial uses in hydroelectric power, and the land turned into agricultural uses, along with their natural flood control component.

As immigrants were admitted to the country, they could be disbursed to the regions, most like their former homes. They were kept in large enough groups to help maintain their culture, but not big enough to dominate a region.

Thus, when the flood of Irish began to arrive because of the potato famine, they found themselves divided by their work skills, and transported to the part of the country where that activity was underway. Farmers went to farmland and received free land, factory workers went to the one of the many assembly line production centers. It was not unusual for groups of Irish to end up in the state of Alberta for farming, or Guadalajara for work in an aircraft plant.

The school system was completely accustomed to bringing in illiterate people or those who did not speak English and transform them into useful workers, farmers, or students in just a couple of years. At the heart of all things in America was the Christian ethic asking people to live their lives as much as possible as Jesus did, with love, charity, and moral integrity in regards to honesty and strong family units.

With the titanic industrial, scientific, and agricultural output of the United States dominating the world marketplace, America grew more prosperous and poured the money back into more infrastructure, research and development, and the quality of life of the people. The flat tax system brought in more than enough money to fund all government activities. The actual size of the Federal government was kept small and the states played a bigger role in the administration of their business. However, the states themselves left a great deal of latitude for individuals to prosper and excel in whatever enterprise they desired.

The states followed the lead of the Federal government in preserving important sites, and making sure large parks, walkways, and recreational areas were in plenty.

President Charles Gallagher proved to be a very able leader.

Arcadia believed he understood the "Big Picture" better than anyone who ever held the office. He was constantly consulting with Arcadia over some adjustment he could make in policy today that would be valuable a hundred years from now.

"The problem, Chuck," said Arcadia at one their private meetings at the White House, "are the radical Muslims. However, they aren't radical yet. Most of the Middle East is still dominated by the Ottoman Empire or the Europeans. The issue of oil is not yet an issue. There are plenty of Jews living in Palestine, but they are at peace with the Palestinians. The real boundary lines of all the countries in the Middle East haven't even been drawn yet."

"Looks like your current plan of trying to reset history by working through Europe is still the right plan," said the President.

"The wave of nationalism among the major European powers begins about 1870. Not only do the Europeans start trying to see how much of the world they can annex to each country, they will get the idea their country, their culture, their politics, their national priorities are better than any other country. It's like 10 big bullies living on the same block. They hate each other and often fight one on one. Then five bullies get together and start picking on the others individually. Of course, the remaining five bullies make an alliance of their own, and the two gangs fight it out, regardless of the collateral damage to the neighborhood or its poor people. That's the situation forming in Europe. It's currently 1850 we have 20 years to become so strong, a gentle suggestion by us is translated into an order for everyone else. Moreover, we have to do this without taking a single action outside our borders."

"Most of the Europe nations are so dependent on our trade now, we can call the shots," said Gallagher.

"That's actually not true," said Arcadia, "if we cut off trade to any block of countries, we invite an open invasion of the United States. Bear in mind, we have more borders to guard than any one, are protected by one division of Rangers, and are outnumbered ten to one by the Europeans. We need to convince them what we have is so valuable they will pay any price get it. We need to kill them with kindness and generosity. They need to admire us so much they want to be like us."

"How much do you think we can accomplish in 20 years," asked Gallagher?

"A lot, an awful lot," said Arcadia. "We are pouring money and resources into our research and development centers at Universities and some of the bigger companies. There are two main areas where we can make the biggest difference...microelectronics, and the generation of power independent from oil. We are closest in electronics. The discovery of the transistor has started several companies working on ways to miniaturize the transistor and then to mass-produce them into what are known in my time as 'Mother Boards'. That's the technology you see with our big LED screens and the computers running them. If we can get that done, then we can put LED screens in every home in America and broadcast live programming, entertainment, education, news, weather, whatever you want. Moreover, we can produce real computers for personal use. This technology is only about a hundred or so years away. I have been getting regular reports and the news is very encouraging. Best of all, it is real Americans, not my bunch, who are making the discoveries."

"Amazing," said the President, "What about power?"

"You would ask that question," said Arcadia. "What I am proposing we do is develop technology which doesn't even exist in this form in my time. Fortunately, we don't have to complete this project, just demonstrate its existence, and mobilize the rest of the world to help us complete it."

"What is it," asked Gallagher with eagerness?

"Solar Power," said Arcadia. "Eventually the world will turn to this anyway."

"I don't understand," said Gallagher.

"Look out the window, Chuck," said Arcadia. "What's the biggest thing in the sky?"

"The sun?"

"Right, the sun shines all the time, and delivers an endless supply of energy to the earth. We collect solar power in my time with big panels turning the power into electricity. If we had the means to collect solar power all the time, we could deliver an unlimited amount of power to every corner of the earth."

"How would you do that," asked the President?

"By collecting solar power in space and broadcasting it back to earth and into our power grids. Trust me the technology exists to do this in my time. It's just no single country can afford it. We can't either, by the way, as rich as we are. However, there is something we can do to fire the imagination of every person in the world."

"I have a team working down in Florida. You know on the 4th of July we launch rockets flying into the air and blowing up in pretty patterns?"

"Yes, of course," said Gallagher.

"That's what these guys are doing. They're building rockets, bigger and bigger and launching them into space. In 20 years, they'll have a full blown space program developed and we will launch one of those rockets, with men aboard, to fly to the moon."

"Are you in earnest," said the President, or is this a joke?"

"No joke, Chuck, I'm deadly serious. Furthermore, people in America will be able to watch the whole thing on television screens."

"It can't be possible," said the President.

"We've already done it," said Arcadia, "starting in 1969, just a little over a hundred years from now, we sent several manned missions to the moon, and brought the men all back alive. We have walked on the moon."

"That would be quite something to see," said Gallagher.

"How impressive would it be to a European leader who has never even seen a diesel locomotive or a truck driving on a highway at 70 miles an hour," asked Arcadia?

"Offer them a piece of the good life of America and throw in a mission to the moon, and I think we can convince any country to do whatever we have in mind," said the President.

"See how busy we are going to be the next 20 years," laughed Arcadia.

The electronics piece came together in spurts and periods of frustration. The breakthrough came from the research lab at General Telephone. The President broke up their monopoly of phone service in the country by making them share all their network of lines with other companies. It meant people could buy their telephone service from several choices, all competing with different kinds of services and prices. What the President did not do was to break up the research arm of General Telephone. In fact, he offered government contracts to develop the kind of microelectronics Arcadia wanted. It took them five years to develop a silicon board with grooves, into which tiny transistors could be soldered into circuits. Having an example from a cannibalized computer was a big help. They knew it could be done. They only had to figure out how and have the precision machinery built to assemble the boards and connect them in a series to talk to each other in the standard binary code of 1 and 0. Then they had to learn to write codes to make their computers do the things they wanted. The first thing they developed was a code to do writing on a screen and a complimentary piece of independent design to make a printer. The elementary computer typewriter was the gateway for dozens of other applications. Soon they had a computer making complex calculations, drawing figures, communicating with other computers, and making a combined system to fit in a small box.

The first time Arcadia saw the prototype she asked her computer tech, "How much of this did you give them?"

"Just the basic computer," said the tech, "They did all of this on their own by reverse engineering the whole instrument."

"Start them working on navigation," said Arcadia. "One of these babies has to find its way to the moon and back."

"Do you have a reliable rocket," asked the President, when she told him?

"We launched a 100 pound pod with a radio beacon into orbit last week."

"Boy, Arcadia, I'm beginning to believe we're going to pull this off."

"We only have ten years to go, 1870 will be here before you know it. Just so, you know, I have Tony Carter working a separate plan with the Ottoman Empire to run concurrently with our big project to consolidate the European powers. My hope is both plans come together about the same time."

"Nobody ever said you weren't sneaky, and think in networks," smiled Gallagher.

Arcadia encouraged the President and he drove everyone else. In addition to the electronics, he was having companies build luxury buses, more roads, faster locomotives, and more power plants using natural gas being pumped and refined in a half dozen new refineries dotted around the continent.

The schools were drumming into their student's minds the rest of the world was in darkness and it was the responsibility of America to bring them light and enlightenment to turn away from war and misery. The students worked very hard, and went smoothly into the fields in which they were the most qualified, and started making contributions of their own.

The cities were made beautiful with concrete, steel and marble. They gleamed with colorful lighting. The cities were compact to allow the general use of mass transit, but the homes of the people were spacious and comfortable.

In the 1860s when American history had 600,000 men dying in a civil war over slavery, Americans where using the great transportation system available to them and spending their free time in seeing the wonders of America from half dome at Yosemite to the geysers of Yellowstone, to the breathtaking wonder of the Grand Canyon. The price they paid was they worked hard, very hard, and felt they were serving the Lord on a mission of mercy involving the entire world.

Chapter 45
Operation Awakening

Washington, D.C.

It was Christmas time 1869, and most of Europe was celebrating the Holidays, in happy parties and merry spirits. It was at this moment 62 year old, President Charles Gallagher chose to begin what was called "Operation Awakening."

The Ambassadors of every major country in Europe, and Asia, including China and Japan, started the long awaited ball rolling. They were all completely prepared, and eagerly delivered their messages to the Prime Minister's, Chancellors, Kings, and Heads of State of every country. The list of recipients was carefully assembled to create the biggest impact on each country. The message was personally delivered.

The Honorable Charles Gallagher, President of the United States is pleased to make the following announcement.

For nearly a century, the United States has been intimately involved in the economy of your country. You have benefitted greatly with peaceful trade with our country. We realize even though this process has been lively and active, the United States is still one of the great mysteries of the world. Our policy of privacy regarding our business and the means by which we manufacture the goods you enjoy has always been of great interest and speculation on your part and the part of your citizens.

As we celebrate Christmas this year, I have a personal gift for you and your family. The time for secrecy has come to an end. The United States of America will now be open

for your personal inspection. We extend an invitation for you, and your family to pay the United States a visit and see, what we have hidden for so long.

We guarantee several things. First, your personal safety. Next, an opportunity to view with your own eyes the rather extraordinary wonders we have accomplished. Next, we offer prospects for improving relationships with all your neighbors and delivering an incredible benefit in your national pride and honor. Finally, we will be pleased to provide you with one million dollars in gold for your personal use.

The United States is vast. You can expect to spend 30 very busy days with us. We will provide personal guides to show you and your family different aspects of our country. This will be barely enough time to show you just a portion of what we have accomplished, and for you to witness sights beyond your wildest imagination.

Our open house will begin on June 1, 1870, at the White House, the Executive Mansion of the President in Washington.

We will be pleased to provide you with special transportation to the United States.

Please respond your willingness to attend our Open House via our Ambassador. He has all the details of the protocol of your visit.

Welcome to the United States of America
Sincerely,
Charles Gallagher,
President of the United States.

The invitation was artfully written. It came as a personal invitation, indirectly sent to the one person who could claim preeminence in his country without mentioning the same message was sent to at least 25 other world leaders. It was incredibly seductive. If there was one subject dominating gossip in the world, it was the mystery of the United States. Now came a carte blanche invitation to see everything. The dignitary need not share the experience with anyone except his personal family. No fawning ministers or other members of the court need be included. Of course, there was also the money.

Almost immediately, Gallagher started hearing back by radio from his Ambassadors. The initial response was shock and surprise. Gallagher had many conversations with his ambassadors.

"Mr. President, the Prime Minister wants to know why he has to travel with his family to a remote location in France to take advantage of this special transportation we have arranged."

"What did you tell him," asked Gallagher?

"The prepared script, Mr. President, I told the Prime Minister after a century of secrecy he should be prepared for anything from the United States. I have assured him he and his family will be completely safe and the experience we offer will be a very exhilarating."

"No doubt about that," chuckled the President, "any other issues?"

"He's completely befuddled with the clothing list," said the ambassador. "I gave him the list for him and his wife and children, and was astonished I am going to provide these clothes in the exact size right down to the smallest daughter. He is certain this wardrobe will not be nearly enough for a full months' travel. I have assured him this will be entirely adequate, and also we have space and weight limitations. He's not very happy, but he and his family are too excited to do more than complain. I hope they still feel the same when they see a big airplane."

"You have it hidden behind the covering curtain with only the stairs and the entrance showing, haven't you?"

"Yes sir, we were very careful about that. What I'm really worried about is who else they see getting on the plane."

"In the outfit we are giving them to wear, they might not even recognize them," said the President. "Relax, Carl and enjoy the moment."

Gallagher had quite a few conversations of the same kind. He and Arcadia enjoyed them immensely.

"I'm glad the total party of country leaders and their families will all fit on one airplane. Still, it's 320 people, plus the crew. The flight attendants will have their hands full."

"I'm glad we were able to get the 747 out of mothballs and prepped to fly in time," said Arcadia. "It will make the flight to Washington only about 8 hours."

❖

William Gladstone, Prime Minister Great Britain, his wife Catherine, and their two youngest sons, 18-year-old Herbert, and 16-year-old Henry, were all uneasy. Gladstone was wearing a brown suit with a yellow tie. He'd never worn such an outfit before, but the shoes were very comfortable, as were the clothes. Catherine was wearing a white blouse with a coat over it, and a slim gray dress with no petticoats. She felt very undressed. The boys were wearing Dockers and light sweaters. They had on very comfortable tennis shoes. They didn't feel uncomfortable at all.

The U.S. Ambassador escorted them personally.

The family endured the boat ride across the channel and were met by a good carriage taking them west and south from Calais and down into Normandy. They turned off the road and on to another road with a gray, hard surface leading to a large curtain with a flight of stairs and a door with a curved surface as the top of the stairs.

Men came forward and took the single bag each member of the Gladstone family had with them away. They were left with small shoulder bags the ambassador handed to them. "For your journey," he said with a smile. "If you will just go up the stairs, an attendant will show you to your seats."

The family climbed the stairs, and went through the door. A pretty young woman checked the paper the ambassador had given Gladstone as he said goodbye and shook his hand.

"If you will just pass to the other side, you are in rows 10 and 11, seats A and B. Welcome aboard,"

The Gladstone's looked down a long row of seats, there were two seats on the side, four seats in the middle, and on the other side of the craft was another aisle way with three seats against the wall. There were windows all along the craft. The family walked down the aisle and located their seats. The boys went to the second row and Gladstone helped his wife across to the window seat. Then he sat down in the soft chair. He examined the shoulder bag. It held a newspaper, a book, a bottle of water, a tin of pills, and two large chocolate bars.

Other people were already onboard. Gladstone thought several of them looked familiar, but since everyone was wearing variations of the same outfits he was wearing, he couldn't exactly place them. Everyone on the craft had the same looks of nervous anxiety and excitement.

In a few minutes, the entire cabin was full. There were many kids of all ages, with the wives of the political leaders. Gladstone thought this herding of people was slightly insulting, but there wasn't anyone to complain too. He glanced at his watch. It was just 8 AM.

A smiling woman took an object on a cord and spoke into it. Her voice could be heard throughout the cabin. "Welcome to all of you distinguished guests. As of this moment, you are the guests of the United States of America. I know you all have many questions, the main one probably is if the Open House is to be held at the White House in Washington on June 1, then why are you here on May 31? Well, the answer is very simple we will arrive in Washington about 8 hours from now."

There was a murmur through the cabin, but the woman went on, "My name is Mindy and I am the senior attendant. You probably have noticed you are sitting on belts like this." She held a small version of the belt in the air. "This is your seat belt. It goes around your waist and clicks together like this. To remove the belt you simply pull up on the tab, like this. Above you is a lighted sign saying please fasten seat belts. Please do so now."

The Gladstone's fumbled around a bit, but managed to put on their belts. As they were clicking their belts, a whining sound filled the cabin, and grew louder and louder. Henry looked out the window and could see a wide wing of shiny metal sticking straight out. There were two big bulges in the wing. The curtain had concealed this before.

As the roar grew, the entire craft began to move, slowly at first and then faster and faster. Gladstone felt himself pushed back into his seat. Catherine reached over and took her husband's hand.

Suddenly the entire craft lifted off the ground and began to climb into the sky. Gladstone looked across his wife and saw the trees and the ground getting smaller and smaller. The entire cabin was in an uproar.

A deep voice of a man was heard through the cabin. "Good

morning, Ladies and Gentlemen, boys and girls. My name is Captain Martin and I will be your primary pilot on our flight to America." A screen lit up on the seat back. "Our route will take us over the coast of France and out over the Atlantic Ocean. We will be flying at an altitude of 35,000 feet, with an air speed of 560 miles per hour. Our expected arrival in Washington, D.C will be 10 AM this morning. The difference in time is because Washington is actually seven hours earlier than Europe's time. We will be serving a meal in a few minutes when we've reached our cruising altitude. Now I realize this is the first airplane flight for all of you. This is routine and we expect no difficulties. There may be minor air turbulence, but I assure you this is completely normal. After you have eaten, you're free to leave your seats and to move around the cabin. I would imagine you have quite a bit to talk about. The lavatories are located in the front and rear of the cabin. If there is anything we can do to make your flight more enjoyable, please don't hesitate to ask."

The Gladstone's relaxed a little. The sound of the engines fell so normal conversations could be held. Are you alright my dear," said Gladstone?

"I think I am now. This is such a remarkable experience."

"I think it's great," said Henry. "Me too," said Herbert, "I've read stories about someday man learning how to fly. I guess this is the day."

"Indeed," said his father. "If the United States has achieved the ability to transport this many people at over 500 miles per hour for eight hours and cross the entire Atlantic Ocean, I can hardly imagine what we are going to see when we arrive in America."

A woman pushing a cart came up and said, "May I offer you something to drink?"

"What do you have," asked Gladstone.

"We have an assortment of spirits, wine, and soft drinks."

"I'll have a brandy," said Gladstone. "May I have white wine," asked Catherine?

Gladstone got a very generous snifter of brandy and Catherine a big glass of wine.

"What about you boys?"

"Nothing strong, maybe something sweet," said Herbert.

"I've got just the thing for you," said the girl and set two big glasses on the tray she let down for them. She filled them with ice, and then opened two big bottles of Coca-Cola. She poured them, and waited for the boys to try it. They both smiled and smacked their lips.

The brandy and the wine settled the Gladstone's nerves and they began to relax.

Just then, breakfast arrived. It was eggs and bacon. There was also a roll and excellent coffee. For many minutes the Gladstone's ate and enjoyed the food. The boys polished off the dinner and were tearing open their chocolate bars. They loved chocolate but it was so expensive they only saw it at Christmas.

Gladstone decided to get up and use the lavatory after his dinner plate was cleared away. He had to wait in line behind a man with a thick beard. Gladstone looked at him again and tried to remember where he had seen the fellow. Finally, he said to the man, "Excuse me, have we met before?"

The man snuffed arrogantly and said with a thick accent, "I am Wilhelm."

Gladstone then recognized him immediately. He was none other than the Kaiser of Germany. "Excuse me, your highness, I am William Gladstone, Prime Minister of Great Britain."

Wilhelm looked at him a moment and then laughed, "Who could recognize anyone in these ridiculous clothes?" Gladstone laughed too. "I wonder if that was part of the American's purpose, to make us all look like fools?"

Just then, the lavatory door opened and a man with long sideburns and a heavy moustache stepped out. "Strange room," he said, "but it has running water." Gladstone knew this man. He was Phillip the VII, King of Spain. "Your highness?" The man looked for a minute, "Gladstone?"

"In the flesh and up in the air with everyone else," laughed Gladstone.

Before long, half the airplane, well plied with more alcohol, was playing the guessing game of "Who are you?" The kids mixed with others their own age, drank two or three more of the delicious Cokes. Wives chatted and more often than they would admit, everyone looked out the windows to see the big clouds below and the swirling waters of the Atlantic Ocean.

"I don't feel so out of place now I see all the other ladies dressed much like me. I had such a nice talk with Marie Louise; she's the wife of Moncrieff, the premier of France."

"It's strange how much different people are when they are separated from their throne rooms and courtesans," said Gladstone.

The captain popped his head out of the cockpit and waved at Mindy, "How's it going?"

"It's just like they told us it would be. A good meal, plenty of alcohol, plain clothes, and they're all gabbling like tourists."

"The President really knows what he's doing. We'll be on the ground in an hour, right on time," said the Captain. He slipped back into the cockpit.

It was a bright, sunny day in Washington. The Captain made sure the flight attendants got everyone back in their seats and buckled up. His orders were to make their arrival in Washington very colorful, so everyone could see the capital from the air. He swooped along the Mall at 1000 feet, and then turned and went back to make sure people on both sides of the ship got a good look at the sparkling city. He imagined there were a lot of oohs and aahs in the cabin and he was right. Then he turned on final and landed at the airport. It was in the same place as Ronald Reagan airport had been in 2030. The plane made a smooth landing and taxied to the edge of the tarmac. There was a crowd waiting for the plane to come to a stop right in front of a red carpet. The doors were opened and a set of stairs were wheeled up. There was no particular order to the way the passengers disembarked. They were guided to a set of bleachers near the plane in front of a podium with a microphone set up. It was quite hot and humid. A man stepped forward. He was clearly an older man, but he seemed especially fit as he bounced onto the podium and up to the microphone. He was dressed exactly like all the Europeans.

He smiled and raised his hands. "Ladies and Gentlemen, boys and girls, I am Charles Gallagher, President of the United States. Welcome to America! You are going to have such a wonderful time this next month. You're not going to want to go home! Here is our schedule for the rest of the day. Your first stop is your rooms where you will stay when we are in Washington. You have the rest of the day to relax. Dinner tonight will be at the White House at 5 PM. If you are wondering why so early, it's because 5 PM is Midnight back in Europe. You are still on that time. We are going to eat early and then send you back to your rooms for a good night's rest. Tomorrow we will tour Washington. The schedule for the rest of your time here in the United States is waiting for you in your rooms. You will find on many days there are choices of activities you can choose. The young people will want to do different things than their parents. We promise you will never be bored. This is a great time for us. We have worked very hard to make a good country here. It is our pleasure to show it to you now. Thanks for coming. I'll see you all tonight."

As the Gladstone family went through the entryway, a young man, probably only a few years older than Henry or Herbert approached them. "Hello there, you must be the Gladstone family."

"We are," said William.

"My name is Cary Richardson and I will be your guide and companion during your visit to the United States. We are so glad you're here. Please call me Cary."

Henry asked, "Is it always so beastly hot and humid here?"

Cary looked around, "This is just the beginning of summer, are you all uncomfortable with the heat already?"

"It seldom gets this hot in England," said Gladstone.

"I will do everything I can to make you comfortable," said Cary. "Our first job is to find your luggage, four pieces, right? Did you use your tags to mark your bags in London?"

"We did," said Gladstone. "It seemed a little silly at the time, but then we did not expect to be travelling with such a large group."

The luggage was all lined up along the sidewalk. The Gladstone's walked along until they found their four pieces.

"The reason why you were all limited to one bag is because of the weight limitations on the plane, and also because we will be travelling a lot in the next month and hauling around luggage is such a pain. But it's easy." He grabbed one of the bags and pulled the handle, which slid out of the bag. Then he turned the bag up on its end and wheels underneath the bag made it simple to pull it along. "Try it," he said.

They all extended the handle and pulled their bag along. Gladstone thought it was very ingenious.

"Next, I have for you all an identification badge." He showed them bright blue badges with their names on them and a big number 2, in the corner. The badges were attached to lanyards. "Put these around your necks and wear them all the time," said Cary, "it will help all the people you meet to know you are our special visitors group. With these badges, the whole country is open to you. It will get you free food everywhere you go, admit you to any place, and if you see something in a store you like, just take it. You are not allowed to pay for anything while you are with us. If you are ready, I'll take you to your bus."

Cary took off with the Gladstone family following him. They were all amazed at how easy the bags were to handle.

Outside the gate, there was a parking lot with seven big buses lined up in a row. They all had numbers on the front. The Gladstone's looked at the buses in wonder. They were all at least 50 feet long, perhaps ten feet high and had clear windows that ran in one continuous, unbroken sheet along the top of the bus. "Wherever we go, just look for bus number 2."

They walked over to the buses, which were rumbling as if they were alive. Porters took the Gladstone's bags and put them in large open bays at the bottom of the bus. Then Cary pointed the way to the front and had the four climb aboard. "Pick any seats you like," said Cary. "It's just short drive to the resort.

The family chose seats near the middle of the bus, which was already half full of families, who were looking out the clear windows and up to the sky. Henry noticed the bus was decidedly cooler than the outside.

When the bus was full, the guides, apparently one for every family, stood in the aisle and raised their hand to signal their group was properly loaded. The door in the front closed and the bus pulled out to line up second in the line that rolled away from the airport.

"What is the means of propulsion for this vehicle," asked Gladstone?

Cary spoke immediately, "The buses are powered by V-8, 400 horsepower, diesel engines. They have a range of 1000 miles on one load of fuel and can travel at speeds up to 75 miles per hour."

Gladstone did not understand all Cary had said, but he sure heard the speed and range of the bus. They glided along the smoothly paved streets past monuments, great buildings, and a long pool leading to a very tall obelisk. Then there was wide park of grass and at the end was a huge and magnificent building with a dome on the top.

"Is that a church?" asked Gladstone, since it reminded him of St. Paul's in London.

"No sir," said Cary, "It's the Capitol, where Congress meets. Think of it as the Houses of Parliament."

"It's beautiful," said Catherine.

The bus made a turn at the Capitol and went two streets where they turned into a driveway with a tall and very elegant building in front. There was a fountain in the open space from the entry drive to the front of the building. Gladstone estimated it was at least ten stories high. The bus came to a stop and Cary said, "Here we are, Home Sweet Home."

The family disembarked the bus by the back door, and found porters were already unloading the baggage. "Don't worry about your bags," said Cary, "They will be delivered to your rooms. Shall we go inside?"

A big crowd filled the entryway and looked in wonder. The center of the building was a huge open space. There were trees, flowers, another fountain, tables and chairs and comfortable long couches spotted here and there. On each end of the building was a glass covered lift moving up and down. Each floor of the building had an ornate railing covered with long boxes filled with blooming flowers.

When Cary thought they had gawked long enough he said, "I'll take you to your rooms now." They followed him along the richly carpeted and wide walkway to the end of the building and turned left to stop in the center. "Watch this," he said, "to call for the elevator. The top button means up, the bottom button means down." He pushed the up button and shortly a door slid open. They all stepped in and could see through the glass. "You are on the 9th floor," said Cary, "See the row of buttons on the panel? Push the number 9." Herbert did that, the doors closed and the elevator started up. It was such a sight to see the floors going by, the people below getting smaller. The elevator stopped when the lighted number in the row reached 9. "In order to go back to the ground floor, you just push lobby," said Cary.

The door opened and Cary headed out and to the left. They turned the corner and went down the hall about half way. "Run your card along the slotted panel," said Cary, "any of your cards will work for this door, and this door only. Mine does not open the door, so one of you has to slide your badge for us to get in. Henry used his badge and the handle on the door clicked. He pushed the door open.

The room they entered was like a very well decorated living room. It was spacious and there was a closed curtain across the back wall. Cary reached over and pushed the switches on the wall, and the room was suddenly filled with light from several lamps. The Gladstone's seemed to be in shock at the never-ending string of miracles they were experiencing. To the left was a door and to the right another door. "You guys have the room to the left and you Mr. and Mrs. Gladstone have the room to the right. There are things in these rooms that need explaining, so I will start here. Over on the right is the service bar, it has a refrigerator to keep things cold, and is filled with all sorts of goodies. Use it all you want. We refill it every day."

Cary walked over to the closed curtain and pulled the cords to open them. The Gladstone's gasped as the view unfolded before them. They could see the entire Mall, the reflecting pool with the big monument at the end, the tall obelisk, and the Capitol to their left. Cary pulled open the sliding doors and let the family walk out onto the long deck. There was a table and chairs out there, along with a couple of long lounges. The view was spectacular, but it was Henry who said, "It's really hot out here."

"Then come back in and I'll close the doors," laughed Cary.

The cool of the room enveloped them. "You can regulate the temperature of the rooms." He stepped over to a panel behind the service bar. A lit panel showed the number 72. "This is the current temperature the room is set for. To make it warmer, you push this button up or down." He demonstrated and the number changed to 71. "There's one of these in each of the rooms for your comfort. Now shall we look at the bedrooms?"

He led the family into the master bedroom. There was a king-sized bed in the center, a chest of drawers on one wall and a large oaken cabinet on the wall facing the bed. There was also an easy chair and a small table with two chairs nearby. Cary moved into the bathroom. There were two sinks along one wall and a frosted glass enclosure on the other wall. At the end was a small room with a porcelain stool. There was a sliding door to that room. "This is your toilet. You do your business, use the paper from the roll, and then push this handle." He demonstrated and the toilet recycled. Cary went to the sink and lifted a handle water started flowing out. "For hot water you move the handle to the left, for cold water, the right. Somewhere in the middle will be the right temperature to wash your hands."

He turned to the shower and opened the door. He turned the same kind of handle that was on the sinks. Water came flowing out from the ceiling and from three places on the side. "I have it just turned on a little to show you how it works," said Cary, "but pull the handle back and you'll get a lot of water. Again turn the handle to the left for hot water, and to the right for cold water. I'm not sure what you have heard, but getting completely wet is not bad for you. In fact, it's very healthy. Most Americans shower at least once a day."

They returned to the main bedroom. Cary opened the doors to the oak cabinet. Inside was a flat screen that was dark. Cary picked up the remote and handed it to William Gladstone. "Push the red button to turn it on." Gladstone did that and a crystal-clear image appeared on the screen. "There are several channels from which to choose," said Cary. "This one gives you a tour of Washington and all our attractions. Push the button on the side." The picture changed to views of beautiful sights...canyons, great mountains, flowing geysers, Great Plains of wheat and corn growing. "If you watch this channel, it will give you a look at the sights you can see in America. Each of you can pick up to four destinations, and we will make arrangements for you to see them in person."

He pushed another button, and a list appeared on the screen. This is the entertainment channel. It's like going to see a play, only better. If you push the button on a title that interests you, an information screen will appear with the synopsis of the program. If you want to see it, there's a button for that, and another to return to the list to pick something else. We also have a religious channel where you can hear the word of God, and the next four channels are music from classical to popular, American Style."

"I think that covers everything," said Cary. He looked at a watch on his wrist. It is now 11:30 AM. You are free to do whatever you like for the balance of the day. If you wish to visit anything in Washington, be my guest. You can get around easiest by using the Metro. That's an underground train that goes all around the city. The signs will show you the next stop. The closest Metro entrance is just outside the hotel, on the corner."

Dinner at the White House is 5 PM. The buses will pick you up at 4:30. The dress for tonight is semi-casual. You will find clothing in your closets, a Blazer, short-sleeved shirt, no tie and dark pants for the men, a simple dress for the ladies. As you have already noticed, it's a little hot. We want you to be comfortable."

There was a knock as the door. "Perfect," said Cary, "that will be your luggage. Enjoy yourselves, take a shower, eat a snack, take a nap, go for a walk. I'll be back to get you at 4:30." He left as a man came in with the luggage.

Chapter 46
Absorbing America

The Gladstone family was in a state of shock. It was impossible to sort out the events of the past day. It was as if they had been magically transported to some kind of utopian paradise. William Gladstone sat down heavily on the couch and looked out at the sight of Washington. The clean lines and perfect symmetry of the great, stately buildings arranged around the central Mall, made London seem quaint and a little grubby.

In any case, he had no idea what to do first. "I'm hungry," said Herbert. "Me too," said Henry. As if their speaking had set off an alarm, an instrument on the service bar was ringing. Gladstone went over and looked at the instrument. It seemed to be some kind of communication devise. He picked up the receiver, and a voice spoke into is ear. "Greetings, Prime Minister, would you and your family care to have a light lunch?"

"That would be nice," said Gladstone.

"We'll be right up," said the voice, and the earphone clicked. Gladstone returned the telephone to the receiver.

"William, come in here," said Catherine. He got up and walked into the bedroom. Catherine had opened her suitcase and hauled out the clothes she found inside. "I've never seen such a collection of clothes such as these."

"That dress looks very nice," said Gladstone innocently. Charlene nodded, "Yes, it's beautiful and made from a fabric that is like silk, but a little heavier. But, look at the rest of this." She picked up a pair of jeans, "Do they honestly expect me to wear these? The very idea, pants for a woman. That's outrageous." She poked around the rest of the clothes. There were several very elegant blouses, some sort sleeve shirts both with buttons and without. Two pairs of shoes, one of which looked more like short boots. There was also some very odd lingerie. She handled the bra with curiosity, several pairs of undergarment pants that were soft and sleek. There was also another pair of pants, cut off at the knees. She picked up a dark blue, one-piece garment that would only cover her body from neck to thighs. It stretched as she pulled on it. "I've no idea what this is." The last thing she picked up was obviously a nightgown. "This is very nice. It's for sleeping I think." She sighed and started putting clothes in the chest of drawers.

As Catherine was busy with the clothes, there was a knock at the door. Gladstone opened it and found a pretty woman with a uniform at the door pushing a cart full of food. Gladstone made way for her and the girl pushed the cart to the table. She began setting out covered dishes around the table. The boys heard the commotion and came out of their room, stopping in their tracks when they saw the girl. She wasn't just pretty she was ravishingly gorgeous. She was wearing a tight sweater with short sleeves that emphasized breasts that didn't need it. Moreover, she was wearing a pair of those short pants. Her long legs went down to a pair of comfortable tennis shoes. She pretended nobody was watching.

When the table was set, the girl did a little bow and pushed the cart out with her behind it. The boy's eyes were fixed on her behind. "Bon Appetite," she said as she closed the door.

The family sat down and looked under the coverings. On two of them were round sandwiches that seemed to be filled with a piece of meat, with cheese on top. There were also long thin potatoes, and garnish of onions, lettuce, tomato slices, mustard and ketchup. "This must be for us," said Henry lifting the top bun and starting to pile things on it. He tasted the mustard. It was spicy and tasty, so he put on quite a bit. There was salt and pepper on the table and they sprinkled that on their cheeseburgers, also. They dug in and soon were grinning as they ate.

Catherine had a plate of exotics fruits, some of which she didn't recognize, but which tasted delicious as she ate them. There was also a bowl of cold cottage cheese.

William had a large ham sandwich with onions, cheese and green peppers. He also had a pile of chips he nibbled and then ate enthusiastically.

There was a large pitcher of water with ice, and big glasses filled with a dark fluid. When the boys tasted it, they smiled. It was the same drink they had on the plane, only this was better.

When the meal was over, Catherine said, "It's as if they knew what we liked to eat. Is that possible?"

"At this point I am beginning to believe anything is possible," said William.

"We are going to go for a walk," said Henry.

"Keep track of the time and be back in time to dress for dinner," said their father.

Catherine explored the bath and looked at the shower. She really wanted to freshen up, but was worried about her hair. She went back to the living room and stared at the phone. There was a small sign on the phone that said, "Questions? Dial Zero." She picked up the phone and pushed the button. A voice answered immediately, "Good afternoon," said a women's voice, "How can I help."

"I am going to dinner tonight," she started.

"To the White House, Mrs. Gladstone, and you want to look your best. I'll bet you want to take a shower but are worried about your hair."

"How did you know?"

"Yours isn't the first call. Want some help?"

"Oh could you, I would be so grateful."

"I'll be right up."

When Catherine came back to the bedroom, William was laying on the bed and watching the TV with the highlights of America showing. "This the most comfortable bed I've ever laid on," he said. "I was just looking at some of the wonders of this country. It will be hard to pick just four."

"William, a woman is coming up to help me get ready for tonight. Would you mind watching that in the living room? I'm sure the screen has the same programs."

"I can do that," he said happily, "are you going to take a shower?"

"I am."

"Then you can give me instructions on how it works," he said going out of the room. He had gotten to the couch when there was a knock on the door. He opened it and a middle-aged woman was standing there. "Good Afternoon, Prime Minister, your wife called about some help in getting ready for tonight."

"Yes, of course," said Gladstone, "Come right in, Catherine is in the bedroom."

The woman went to the bedroom and closed the door.

Gladstone resumed his tour of America and began to narrow down the choices. He definitely wanted to see a place called Yellowstone and see the mountains called the Grand Tetons. After that he was torn between the giant Sequoia trees, the big cave at Carlsbad, and Niagara Falls.

He walked to the bedroom door and could hear laughter inside the bathroom.

Catherine giggled at the experience of the wonderful shower spraying hot water at her from all directions. Her new friend, Grace, explained it all, and gave her wonderful shampoo and conditioner for her hair. She sat in a chair while Grace dried her hair with a blow dryer, and used a curling iron to give here the most beautiful hairdo she ever had.

"Grace," said Catherine, "I saw the most outlandish clothing in my luggage today. I don't even know what some of it is. I certainly can't imagine ever wearing pants."

"You mean the jeans," said Grace? "Honey, I've got to tell you they are the most comfortable clothes you'll ever wear. You'll see a lot of women in America wearing them."

"Really," said Catherine, "and what about those pants cut off at the knees. Our server for lunch was wearing them."

"There called shorts," said Grace, "In case you haven't noticed, it's kind of hot and humid around here. It's even worse down south, and out in the desert in the west there's not much humidity, but the temperature is as much as 120 degrees. You will be happy to shed your clothes along with your modesty when you get out in that weather."

"We are overwhelmed with what we have found in America. You have great wonders. Are the people all as happy as they seem?"

Grace looked Catherine right in the eyes. "We are blessed by God.

Every day for us is a miracle and we never forget to say thanks to the Lord. We get it wrong all the time, but that doesn't keep us from holding the love of God in our hearts. The fact is we've kept the world at arm's length for a reason. We wanted to build the kind of society the rest of the people on earth will want to join. You tell your husband to listen to Charlie Gallagher he has a wonderful plan.

Catherine Gladstone came out of the bedroom with Grace, wearing her dress for the evening and looking beautiful. William jumped up and said, "My dearest, you look like a dream."

"Thank you, I couldn't have managed without Grace." The two women hugged each other and Grace left.

"Come along, stinky, I'll show you how the shower works."

Gladstone enjoyed his shower so much he didn't want to get out. Catherine showed him how to work the hair dryer. He liked the way his hair turned out. Catherine told him a lot had to do with the shampoo and conditioner. He found deodorant in the medicine cabinet, and stared for several minutes and what appeared to be a razor. He found a can saying shaving cream and pushed a button and a lot came out. He used the razor and was dumbfounded at how easy it was, without a single nick. He finished up with some wonderful smelling after-shave lotion. When he came out of the bathroom, Catherine had laid out his clothes for the evening. When he put them on, he decided he liked the way he looked. Catherine said he looked very nice.

As they were congratulating themselves, the boys came rushing in with stories of the view from the top of the Washington monument and the marvelous Metro. "It's an underground train, father. It was so much fun."

"I'm glad you enjoyed yourselves. Now you just have time to shower and dress for dinner, so off you go."

Apparently the shower was not the mystery to the boys it was to their parents, although William had to show them the hair dryer. In record time, they were clean, dressed and ready for the big evening.

At exactly 4:30 there was a knock at the door and Cary was there to collect them for dinner. He was dressed as they were, but his blazer was green.

They flowed through the hotel, greeting smiling people as they went. Apparently, the rest of the Europeans had enjoyed their afternoon as much as the Gladstone's and were laughing and in good humor as they rode down on the elevators, and boarded the buses. Gladstone spotted Kaiser Wilhelm and hardly recognized him without the beard. "Your highness, you look so different, I hardly recognize you."

"It's those marvelous razors," said the beaming Kaiser, "I had a fellow come help me with the shower, he speaks fluent German, and said he thought I would look better without a beard. I told him I hated the beard but my skin is so tender I can't shave every day, without nearly bleeding to death. Then he cut off my beard, put a lotion on my face and shaved me with that new razor. I feel wonderful!"

"You do look handsome and much younger, "said Gladstone.

"That's what my wife said," laughed the Kaiser.

It was a noisy, happy bus winding its way with the other buses like a conga line in the hot afternoon in Washington headed for the White House. The buses pulled through the gateway and the expansive lawns surrounding the Executive Mansion and came to a stop at the South Portico.

Not standing on ceremony, President Gallagher, and his wife, Emily with the faithful First Pet, a large beautiful collie, named Kodiak greeted each of the guests in their own native language. The assigned guides led their charges on a small tour of the White House before taking them to the big ballroom where round tables for eight had been set up. Cary led the Gladstone's to their table somewhere near the middle of the room.

They were soon joined by Leopold II, King of Belgium, his wife, Marie, 12-year-old Louise, and six-year-old Stephanie. Gladstone knew the King and rose and bowed, introducing his family in the process. Fortunately, Leopold spoke good English, so his guide did not need to translate. The King seemed to be in a very reflective mood, but was pleasant, as was his wife, who was quite happy. They all sat down. Cary and the other guide said they would be back to get them after the evening dinner and program, and left the room. Gladstone could see the other guides doing the same.

President Gallagher came out on the platform at the end of the room and spoke into the microphone. "I hope you all found your rooms to be comfortable and your afternoon enjoyable."

- 314 -

There was loud applause to this, and Gallagher breathed a sigh of relief inside. The first step was a success. Not only that, but the crowd seemed to be in very good spirits. He knew jet lag was going to catch up with them all in just a couple hours, and had planned the evening to end early. He smiled and said, "Before dinner is served, it is our custom to thank the Lord." He closed his eyes, put his hands together and prayed, "Heavenly Father we thank you and praise you for allowing us all to be together here tonight. We ask your blessing for our meal. We are your children in the universe of your creation, and thank you for your eternal love, Amen."

There was a chorus of Amens through the audience, and, almost immediately a swarm of wait staff came pouring into the room, and the orchestra began to play.

Gladstone wondered what the meal would be and was pleasantly surprised to find it was Prime Rib, somewhat rare, with a big potato, smothered with butter, and asparagus with béarnaise sauce. It was his favorite meal. He looked around the table and saw the looks of satisfaction on the faces of all the people. Each had a different meal, but it appeared to be their favorites as well. Gladstone glanced around the room and saw a very wide variety of foods was being served. The Prime Minister was smart enough to realize all of this was by design, and he shook his head in admiration for the intelligence services of the United States.

The music being played by the orchestra was definitely up-tempo and foreign to Gladstone but he enjoyed it very much. The rest of the people in the ballroom seemed to feel the same. They were tapping their feet, and the youngsters were clapping their hands. They had no idea they were listening to a carefully chosen program of music Arcadia had selected herself, and represented the very best melodies and songs from a hundred years before Arcadia was even born. It was happy music typical of Walt Disney productions. Every few songs vocalists or groups came out and sang a song or two. They had lovely voices and the harmonies were flawless.

As pleasant and enjoyable as the entertainment was, Gladstone suddenly felt very tired. Almost on cue for that, President Gallagher came back to the microphone. "I hope you enjoyed your meal and the music," he said, "The fatigued feeling most of you are experiencing now is caused by the big time change you had in coming here from

Europe. That's why we scheduled dinner so early and are going to call it an evening now. Tomorrow, breakfast will be served from 6:30 until 9 AM in the restaurant at your resort. Our plans for tomorrow include a tour of Washington beginning at 10, when you will board your buses. Until then, I wish you a pleasant night's sleep and once again we sincerely welcome you to America. Good evening."

Gallagher bowed and left the room. The guides flowed back in and escorted their families back to the buses. The trip back to the resort hotel was short and Cary made sure the Gladstone's got safely to their rooms. He thanked them, and said good night.

The family was happy, commented to each other about the splendid meal and entertainment, but were definitely ready for bed. They all went to their rooms, put on the pajamas. Their beds open and inviting and the temperature of the rooms dialed down to 68 degrees. Gratefully, the Gladstone's climbed into their very comfortable beds, turned out the lights. They were asleep in minutes. It was just barely 8 PM.

In the big restaurant downstairs, the guides met. Their supervisor asked if there had been any problems. There were none that hadn't been handled. "It looks like the first, very critical 24 hours have gone exactly according to plan. No matter how exalted this big collection of great leaders are, they were overwhelmed by the circumstances we put them in. They didn't have time to think about anything except what we put in front of them. I think they're now all relaxed and comfortable. They certainly seemed to warm to each other despite the politics of Europe. Let's keep it that way. Most of them will sleep at least ten hours and wake up ready to be super visitors. We have a rather easy day for them tomorrow. We've put in just enough exercise to wear them out. Make sure they drink lots of water."

"We have an informal meal in the restaurant tomorrow evening, cafeteria style, so everyone can try a large variety of foods, most of which they've never seen. After that will be the big presentation of our America the Beautiful video, and we'll ask the visitors to begin choosing the places they want to see. If they can narrow it down to a half dozen, it will make it easier to plan the logistics when they have to pick their four top attractions."

"Today is Wednesday, tomorrow we do Washington. On Friday we fly them down to the Cape to tour the facilities and see the infrastructure for the space program. On Saturday morning, we have the launch of the 'Enterprise' for the moon. That should get their attention in a big way."

"We fly back to Washington Saturday night, for the big soccer match, and then on Sunday we show them how we spend our Sabbaths."

"All of you have done a great job, and I thank you for your hard work. Now get a good night's sleep, and we'll see you for breakfast."

Chapter 47
Capital Hospitality

Washington, D.C.

William Gladstone awoke and stretched luxuriously. He couldn't remember having a better night's sleep. As he pulled back the covers it seemed a little cold in the room for him. He walked over to the pad on the wall and pushed the button to show 72.

Then he walked into the living room and opened the curtains. It was a beautiful, sunny morning, and Washington shined in the early light. He glanced at the clock and saw it was 6:30 AM. He opened the sliding door and walked out onto the balcony. It was not very warm yet, and he sat in a chair and admired the view.

In a few minutes, Charlene joined him. "Good morning, dear," said Gladstone, "How did you sleep?"

"I don't think I moved all night. The bed was so comfortable, and I slept very well indeed."

"So did I," said Gladstone. "That's quite a view."

"Spectacular, I'm looking forward to seeing the city today."

"As am I."

A small bell rang on the television monitor. Gladstone picked up the controller turned the monitor on. The screen lit up. It showed an image of Cary. He smiled, "Good morning! I didn't know if you were awake yet, but I hope you slept well. When you are ready, come down to the lobby and follow the signs to the restaurant. It will be about the same weather today as yesterday, so wear light clothing. The men will be comfortable in the light brown pants, and short sleeved button shirt. Mrs. Gladstone, I suggest a light skirt and a short-sleeved blouse. All of you should wear the comfortable walking shoes, because we are going to do a lot of walking. Don't forget your shoulder bags, you might find something you want, and don't forget your badges. I'll meet you in the restaurant."

The image flicked off. "I certainly don't know how they do that, but it's a great tool," said Gladstone. "Why don't you wake the boys? I'm going to shower and shave."

In less than an hour, the family was ready to head for the restaurant. Henry and Herbert had opted for t-shirts and were wearing shorts. Gladstone just shook his head, and said nothing.

They went to the elevator and pushed the button that said, 'lobby'. There were signs pointing them to the restaurant. As they came in, they found a very large room, and Cary, waiting at the door. "Good morning, Cary," said Charlene, Henry and Herbert shook hands with him. Not to be rude, Gladstone also shook hands with Cary.

Cary pointed at the long cafeteria line. "We have a lot of choices for breakfast. Just take whatever you want. There's a cook right after you pick up your tray and utensils who can make you eggs or an omelet. He's a great cook. After that is everything you can imagine eating. I recommend the hot cakes with butter and pure Maple syrup. It's delicious."

The family went to the first stop and got a large plastic tray with compartments, and picked utensils out of a containers. Gladstone asked for a cheese and ham omelet, Charlene passed on the eggs, but Henry and Herbert had scrambled eggs, and eggs over easy respectfully. As they pushed their trays along the rail, they realized Cary had not exaggerated. The breakfast bar was loaded. Gladstone took both bacon and sausage patties, and Cary's recommendation of hot cakes with a big pat of butter and a generous helping of Maple syrup.

They looked around and found an empty table for four. As they sat down a waiter came up and asked, "Tea or Coffee?" He said, "You already have water, but we also have a good selection of juices. Have you ever had orange juice?" None of them had so the waiter brought a carafe and four glasses.

The Gladstone's thoroughly enjoyed their breakfast. Gladstone thought his omelet was the best he'd ever eaten. He really liked the hot cakes and the tasty Maple syrup, and everyone loved the orange juice.

As they were finishing, Cary came up to the table with a bag. He handed each of them a large bottle of water and said there would be more on the bus, which was ice cold. He then pulled out baseball caps. These are for you to wear to keep the sun off their heads. He also handed them each a pair of sunglasses. This is to keep the bright sun from blinding you. Gladstone took off his own glasses and put on the sunglasses. As he half expected, the sunglasses matched the prescription for his vision, made it a little better, actually. "You chaps seem to know a great deal about us."

"We can't have you not being able to see the sights when you're wearing your sunglasses," said Cary, with a merry grin. "How was breakfast?" The whole family chimed in with compliments for that. "Isn't that Maple syrup the best," said Cary?

"Yes," said Charlene, but the highlight was the orange juice."

"Are you ready to go to the bus," asked Cary.

"Lead the way," said Gladstone.

As they went, the family stopped off at the restrooms, and picked up their bags.

When they got out outside, Gladstone saw a sea of baseball caps, nearly everyone had taken their guides advise and worn comfortable clothes. Gladstone saw many pairs of shorts in the crowd, and not all of them were on children. The Minister of France was wearing his and seemed pleased with his choice.

The tour of Washington took only six hours. It could have been much longer, but Arcadia knew the endurance of her visitors. They did see the Capitol and the Houses of Congress. They went to the top of the Washington monument, visited the Jefferson memorial, and the big square memorial that would have been dedicated to Lincoln, but instead had a tall statue on a pedestal of a beautiful woman in a sleek gown with a silver belt around her slim waist. Her long blond hair was intricately carved. The inscription just said 'Arcadia'. There was a carved panel with one of her greatest speeches cut into the stone. There was another inscription on the other side that simply said. "To the inspiration that made us a nation, we dedicate this memorial to the "Mother of America."

Gladstone read the panel. "These are great words," he said. "I wish I could have known her."

The last stop was a big store near the big train, and metro station. It said, "Emporium" on the front. As they were going in, Cary said, "You will have several other opportunities to come back here, so don't feel you have to do the whole store at once. Take what you like, but remember it has to fit into your luggage for the plane, or else you will have to wait a month for it to come by ship. Please meet me here to get back on the bus by 4:45PM. Now go and enjoy."

Gladstone and the boys were not big shoppers, but were more interested than they thought they would be. Both the boys picked up wristwatches like Cary had. Gladstone could not resist a wonderful reproduction, in marble, of an "Arcadia" statue.

For Charlene the experience was mesmerizing. She saw clothing of all colors and designs. A saleswoman helped her pick out a really elegant dress, in the style she had worn the night before, but more beautiful in every way. She saw the price tag and gasped. However, the sales woman just smiled and wrapped the dress up for her. "You folks are most welcome in America, take it with our best wishes."

Charlene thanked her profusely, and for the magic badge around her neck.

The short ride on the bus back to the resort had everyone on the bus showing each other what they got at the Emporium. Without realizing it, the barriers of country, politics, and social differences were starting to melt away in the great stirring pot of America.

Dinner was at 7 pm. It was the same cafeteria style as breakfast, but the menu was very different. Henry and Herbert discovered something called "tacos and enchiladas." They whistled for Cary for an explanation. Cary expertly assembled a big taco for them. He took the corn tortilla, filled it with ground beef, added, onions, lettuce, cheese and a red sauce, and handed it to Henry. "Take that back to the table and try it. If you like it, you can come back for more. Henry and Herbert were back in about two minutes and put together a half dozen tacos each, with more hot sauce.

In the middle of the big room was a stage and the same group of musicians as the night before. Once again, President Gallagher came out without any pomp and circumstance and no introduction. Nevertheless, he got a very warm greeting of applause. He smiled and said, "I hope you enjoyed the short visit to our Capital today. You didn't see it all, just the highlights. I would imagine most of you ladies enjoyed the Emporium." Big applause came from the ladies.

"Tonight we have something special for you. As you've already been told by your guides, during your stay with us we want you see some of the natural wonders of America. We've prepared a special video for you showing many of our biggest treasures. Some of them can be seen on the travel channel in your room monitors. This is a bigger presentation. It is recorded in English, but your guide has a pair of headsets you can wear playing the same narrative in your own language. When the show is over, you will be able to mark your top six choices on the sheets of paper now being given you by your guides. Everyone should vote, even the smallest children. This will help us plan your visits to these places. In the end you will have to narrow your list to four. This is not to be stingy or cheap on our part. Remember, you are in the biggest country in the world and some of these attractions are separated by thousands of miles. So, it's simply a matter of practicality for the time you have. Now, let's get on with the show. "

The hour-long travel video the Europeans saw had taken over two years to produce. The music was specially written for the work and the narration was done by both a man and a woman, both of whom did a magnificent job.

Arcadia was deeply moved every time she saw it. She'd seen the video several times.

With stirring music and very informative narration, the Europeans saw the best North America had to offer. Many of the national parks were featured, along with some strategic locations that were beautiful, but safely reachable. When the video was over, there was a loud ovation.

The music began to play while each family and sometimes several families, regardless of nationality, discussed their favorites. The kids liked the idea they had a vote too. With a lot of discussion, the families began to mark their favorites. Cary and the rest of the guides explained groups would be assembled by the attraction, not the family. They made it clear breaking up families to see different places, was not a problem and each person would be perfectly safe. That made it easier, Henry and Herbert agreed on two places, but not six. William and Charlene didn't really agree about anything.

President Gallagher came back to the stage and whistled for attention. The 300 people finally quieted down. "Well, that was fun wasn't it?" Everyone laughed. "Let's get a kind of an idea which places are the most popular. Raise your hand a cry out when I mention some of your favorites."

When the straw poll was over, the clear winners were Yellowstone and the Tetons, Grand Canyon, Banff and Jasper national parks in Alberta, Niagara Falls and oddly for Gallagher, Mesa Verde national park and the home of the ancient Anasazi Indians and their cliff dwellings. At least 25 men and older boys wanted to shoot a buffalo. There were several other places getting votes. The teams watching the surveillance cameras started finalizing some basic planning. They had anticipated most of the favorites and had done some work preparing for visitors.

Gallagher called for attention again. "We need you to pick your top four by the first of next week, then give us another week to make camps for you and all of you will be on your way.

"Let me tell you about our schedule for the next several days. Tomorrow, we are going to board another plane and fly south to Florida to a place called Cape Canaveral. It's at this place our most ambitious project to date is about to happen, and you get to witness it. One of the biggest debates we have had is when to tell you what you're going to see. The majority thinks we should tell you now, what this is all about, so I am going to tell you and let you anticipate this as much as the rest of us are.

"Down in Florida, we've been working on a big project to build rockets. All of you have seen rockets you fire off by lighting a fuse and watching the rocket fly up and make a pretty flash. We are going to do that, however on a much larger scale. On Saturday morning we will launch a rocket with 8 men aboard. Their destination is the moon. Two of our men are going to take a smaller rocket down to the surface and walk on the moon."

There was a stunned silence in the room, than an outcry of emotions as people began talking to each other. Gallagher shouted, "This is a tremendously dangerous project for us, but we would rather have you see us try and fail, then to keep the secret from you. I promised no more secrets to each of you, and this one is our biggest. The buses leave for the airport at 9 am. See you in the morning."

He left the stage and the room and the orchestra started to play. The music soothed the crowd, but not the lively conversation. Most of the people had seen enough wonders so far to believe the United States might be ready to attempt such a death-defying stunt, but it was so far away from anything they had expected, they were at a loss to express themselves clearly.

After a while, the music began to encourage some couples out onto the dance floor to dance. Some of the male guides were dancing with the female guides, a bouncy step, and many of the younger kids wanted to try it. The waltzes were the most popular with the older people. Everyone enjoyed themselves, despite the huge announcement.

The Gladstone's talked about the day, their choices of places to visit and the news about the voyage to the moon for a couple of hours, before retiring for the night.

Chapter 48
To The Moon

Cape Canaveral, Florida

The buses took the 320 visitors to the airport at 9 am and they were in the air in half an hour. There was another airplane filled with Americans, including all the guides, flying in formation with the Europeans. It was a three-hour flight. They landed on a big runway near the shuttle pad, and all of buildings part of the complex.

They spent the rest of the day on tours through the assembly building where they saw mock up reproductions of the big rocket, and the shuttle attached to it. They were able to actually enter the shuttle, see the control cockpit and the shuttle bay.

Outside the shuttle was a duplicate of the command capsule with the lunar lander attached to it. Some of the men wanted to sit in the command console and take the ladder down to the lunar lander. They loved the experience.

The techs showed how the command capsule and lunar lander was installed in the shuttle bay and how the control arm of the shuttle would take the command capsule and lunar lander out of the shuttle and then retrieve it. The shuttle would then fly back to the earth and land on the same runway the airplanes had landed on. Arcadia's team got the idea to build a shuttle because the rocketry was more advanced and they could fly the shuttle to the moon with more safety and comfort than the way the original lunar missions had flown. With the shuttle in orbit around the moon, they could launch the command console and the lunar lander and let them maneuver for a landing. One of the biggest moments for the Europeans was when they got to meet the astronauts going on the mission, and the two men who would actually take the lander to the surface. Even great leaders can be impressed with an authentic hero.

The project had been underway for 20 years. Several test flights of the shuttle had actually flown the entire mission to the moon and back, twice, successfully. However, they were not going to tell the leaders of Europe that. As far as they were concerned this was the maiden flight of the 'Voyager'. As Arcadia said, "We may be reckless, but we're not stupid."

In any case, the whole complex and all the intricate machinery was enormously impressive to the Europeans. When the buses, duplicates of the ones in Washington, took them around to the big control room, the mission control center, with its rows of monitors, and dozens of technicians wearing white coats and headsets at each of the stations, they were speechless.

President Gallagher was a little concerned about the somewhat Spartan accommodations for the Europeans in Florida. They were not up to the standards of the resort, but Arcadia said, "Look, they're going to have even less when they get out to Yellowstone, Grand Canyon, and some of the other places. We might as well start getting them used to what they're going to have to tolerate with this place. It's not so bad. I'll bet some of these leaders don't have much better at home."

Arcadia was right. None of the leaders complained about the quarters in Florida. They still ate very well. The kids didn't seem to notice the difference at all, and the older young people regarded the whole thing as a huge adventure.

The following morning, everyone was made to rise very early to match the launch schedule. Breakfast was served at 5 AM. The buses took the leaders to the grandstands only four miles from the launch pad at 6 AM. Then loudspeakers ran the conversation traffic between the launch pad and mission control. The entire launch cycle was heard by everyone.

At the end, came the final tense minutes while the last commands were being sent to the launch pad. Then the final 30-second countdown began. At the ten-second mark, the engines on the rocket were lit and huge plumes of fire began to come from the bottom of the rocket. The last countdown was heard...5 – 4 – 3 – 2 – 1 "lift off, in progress."

The rocket shuddered on the pad, the noise was deafening. Slowly, the rocket began to lift from the pad and climb. Faster and faster it went as it climbed into the sky. "Roll program, executed," said mission control.

The people in the grandstand's attention was shifted to the wide monitors connected to the big telescopes monitoring the launch. They watched as the first stage rockets separated from the main rocket, releasing the shuttle. The shuttle engines fired and mission control reported that all systems were normal and it was moving at 18,000 miles per hour. Earth orbit was achieved.

Everyone started breathing again. The experience was thrilling for every person, American or European.

At lunch, the Europeans mixed with flight directors from mission control and asked endless questions of how this amazement could happen. The scientists and technicians answered every question honestly and completely. The leaders appreciated that, even though they didn't understand all they heard.

On the flight back to Washington, the seat belt had barely clicked before people were travelling around the cabin and sharing their thoughts on what they'd seen.

"As usual, the Americans have presented us with another incredible experience," said Gladstone to a group of leaders from Prussia and Austria-Hungary. "If I have learned one thing it's anything can happen here, and our lives from now on will be forever changed."

None disputed this great truth.

They got back to Washington in time to rest a little in their rooms at the resort, and then Cary came to get them for dinner at 5 PM. "We have a wonderful treat for you tonight."

"What's that," asked Henry?

"Well, it just so happens the national finals of the soccer championship will be played tonight and you all have wonderful seats, meaning I have a wonderful seat. Usually, for the championship you can't get tickets at all."

"You play football here," asked Herbert enthusiastically?

"It our most popular sport," said Cary. "It's played in all the schools from the little kids, all the way up to the big University teams. However, the teams who are playing tonight are professionals, who more or less play soccer, or football to you, a fair amount of the year. A lot of them are Rangers, since they are usually our best athletes."

"I was beginning to wonder if we were going to see anything of the legendary Rangers," said Gladstone. "Now we find out we get to see them playing games."

"I can't wait," said Henry, "I play football at my school, and Herbert was a starting forward for Queen's college.

The buses came for them at 6:30 and drove them across town where there was a big stadium, all lit up, with buses and the metros coming in jammed with fans, wearing all sorts of flashy team colors and singing songs.

The Europeans were swept up with the crowds and into the stadium. Gladstone had never seen such a big stadium, unless you counted the Coliseum in Rome. It looked about the same size. He and the rest of the family were given tickets by Cary who guided them through portals and wide causeways inside the stadium, selling all sorts of souvenirs and food. "How about some popcorn and a Coke," said Cary?

"Great, said the boys."

"Then come on along and help me carry everything."

They disappeared into a line at a snack bar and left William and Charlene alone. "Tell me, my dear, did you have the least idea of what we were going to see and experience on this trip," asked Charlene?

"Not a clue," said the Prime Minister. In my work you sometimes here rumors, but you usually discount them as idle gossip. The reality is impressively different."

Cary and the boys came back, loaded down with drinks, bags of popcorn, and sacks of peanuts. He passed them out and then led the family through a portal to the stadium interior. It was ablaze with lights on a very green field with the traditional soccer markings. The teams were warming up on the field.

The stadium itself was an enclosed oval with seating all around. Gladstone was surprised. "How many people be seated here," he asked?

"Oh, about 40,000 said Cary. You can bet every seat will be filled tonight."

Cary wasn't kidding about the seats. They were in the middle of the field and along the first deck of seating. They had a perfect view of the action.

There was a ceremony before the game. A gang of people spread out a huge American flag over the field, with its many stars and stripes. The first thing was a voice asking everyone to rise for the benediction over the very clear and loud sound system. A pastor was praying for a good game in which God let every man do his best and play without injury. Then another voice said, "Please remain standing while the band plays the national anthem." A big band was marching around the field, playing music as they performed complicated formations. Now they stood in a big square and the Star-Spangled Banner was played. Everyone sang it and held their hands over their hearts, usually with a hat in their hands. Gladstone saw everyone had taken off whatever headgear they were wearing and he nudged his family to do the same. They snatched their baseball caps off their heads and stood reverently while the nation anthem was played.

When it was over, the crowded roared. Another voice said, "Ladies and Gentlemen, we are pleased and honored to welcome tonight the Monarchs, Royalty, Heads of State and their families from most of the countries in Europe, who are enjoying their first visit to the United States. Will they please stand, so we can welcome them."

There was a thunderous ovation, and all the leaders and their families stood a little taller and waved at the crowd.

Then they sat down for the serious business of the soccer game. The teams came marching out onto the field and stood in a line facing the audience. President Gallagher came out of the runway to a huge round of applause and went down the rows of both teams, separated by the officials and shook hands with them all.

The announcer said, "Tonight we have the pleasure of presenting the champions of the National League, represented by the Sioux Warriors and American league, Atlanta Falcons, playing for the National Championship, and the Washington Cup.

"The Falcons are the defending champions," said Cary, "They always have a good team, but the Warriors have been great this year. It should be quite a match.

It was. All of the leaders of Europe had seen soccer played in their own countries, especially the British, who invented the game and wrote the official rules. Gladstone wondered if that was how the game would be played. It only took him about two minutes to realize he was watching the best soccer he'd ever seen. He was particularly impressed with the big jumbotron on one end of the field allowing them to see exciting plays replayed to enjoy again. Atlanta scored two goals in the first 15 minutes, and the Gladstone's started rooting for the underdogs. They jumped up and cheered when the Warriors scored on what looked like an impossible goal in the 35th minute.

Halftime came with score still 2 to 1. "How about some hot dogs and more Cokes," said Cary? The whole family went with him to use the restrooms. Gladstone was surprised how clean and efficient they were. He reminded the boys to wash their hands before they left.

Meanwhile, Charlene visited the ladies room, while Cary was standing in line for the food and drinks. The Gladstone's joined him and looked curiously at the hot dogs, since they'd never seen one. Cary showed them how to put on mustard, ketchup, onions, relish, or cheese. The boys loaded up while Gladstone just added some mustard, cheese and onions. He gave one to Charlene without the onions. They went back to their seats and saw a lot of their group had done the same, plus adding more popcorn and pretzels.

The boys gobbled down their hot dogs and ran back for more before the second half began. This time they both came back with two hot dogs each.

The second half was very exciting. The Warriors tied the game in the first five minutes and then scored again on a beautiful three on two a few minutes later. The teams battled each other hard. The Falcons tied the game in the seventy-third minute. Then there were a bunch of near misses, a few fouls, and a couple of yellow cards as the referee labored to keep the game under control.

All the Europeans were cheering as loudly as the Americans at the wonderful game, they were witnessing. In the final minute, the Warriors mounted a final offensive and scored with a kick in which the player had his back to the goal and threw his legs over his back and shot the ball into the goal. Gladstone jumped up and cheered. He was certainly not alone.

It was a splendid experience. The buses were buzzing all the way back to the resort. Some of them had acquired team banners and some team scarves. Cary escorted the family back to their rooms. "Tomorrow is the Sabbath. There's no work. Church is at 10:30 for you at the Good Shepherd Assembly of God. It's a protestant service I think you will like. The Catholics will go to St. Paul's. You don't have to dress any different than you did tonight. We don't dress much for church. The Lord loves us from the inside out. Besides, most of us don't want the inconvenience of having to go home and change. We would miss too much fun. See you for breakfast."

The family was surprised to find their beds had been changed, all their clothes cleaned, pressed and hanging neatly in the closet. Their rooms were spotless. As Gladstone stepped into the shower he wondered if the perfect showers were causing him to shower more or if it was him changing. In England, a weekly bath seemed plenty. Charlene was showering twice a day.

They went to bed and had another perfect night's sleep.

After the usual banquet breakfast, the Gladstone's boarded the bus for the drive to the Good Shepherd Assembly of God. Cary was right nobody was dressed up. The service was lively as they mixed with the Americans, who filled the big church, and all of whom seemed eager to greet the family. The message was a recorded sermon given by the legendary Arcadia, many, many years before. It was a tremendous sermon. Gladstone considered it to be very inspirational, and he realized why the country regarded Arcadia as the "Mother of the Country."

After church the buses took them to the big grass Mall near the Capitol. It was filling up fast with families who had an assortment of games, food baskets, and their pets. Cary had a big blanket open under a tree and a whopping basket of food. For the remainder of the day, the people engaged in impromptu soccer matches, with both Henry and Herbert taking part. Gladstone went over and learned the fine art of horseshoe pitching, and Charlene played croquet with a mixture of American and European woman and girls. Later, there was a fine meal of sandwiches and fried chicken, with sweet tea. Then quite a few people settled down for naps, while small groups of men and women visited about life, God, children, home, work, and play. Some of the older boys and girls were spending time getting better acquainted. Herbert, as the older, seemed to be smitten by a green-eyed beauty from Washington. They talked for a couple of hours, laughing a lot.

Gladstone looked up from a group with who he'd been visiting, and realized there were many such groups of men and women, and that it was almost impossible to separate the Americans from the Europeans, except for the black people, of which there were quite a few. They fit right in with everyone else. Gladstone may not have realized it, but it was at that moment his world-view changed. This was the way people should live.

The family went back to the resort at dark and turned on the monitors to get an update on the mission to the moon. The shuttle was over half way there, and there were pictures and comments from the very men they met at Cape Canaveral. An announcer showed a slick graphic on how the mission to land would be completed.

Everyone showered before they turned in for bed. Gladstone spent a few minutes alone on the balcony looking at the lights of Washington.

Chapter 49
American Industry
On the Road to Three Rivers, Pennsylvania

When they got to the Restaurant the next morning, Gladstone looked around the room. He couldn't believe the changes the great leaders of Europe had undergone in less than a week. Actually, he couldn't believe the changes in him.

Now it didn't matter with whom you ate, or who you sat next to on the bus. They had all become some kind of an exclusive club to which nobody else in the world belonged. The collection of clothing they wore was a hodge-podge of different tastes and adjustments in the name of comfort. He noticed many of the women had taken to wearing jeans, or even the shorts they considered so outrageous when first they saw them. They had picked up a variety of extras, like wide belts that had a holder for a liter of water, or a pack that contained sun tan lotion, extra sunglasses, and chewing gum. Of course everyone wore their baseball caps. Even Charlene was doing that. Gladstone chuckled at the boys with t-shirts, shorts and their baseball caps often worn backwards.

Breakfast was leisurely today. Cary said President Gallagher was coming to visit with them. They didn't have long to wait. The President arrived just as Gladstone was finishing his second cup of coffee.

Gallagher jumped on the stage and took the microphone, "Good Morning, my friends."

He got a lot of hello's, some applause, and a few wisecracks. He beamed, "You folks are acting more like Americans every day."

"Wasn't that the whole idea," said the King of Belgium? "I can't speak for anyone else, but I'm having more fun than I've had in years."

That got a roar of consent from almost everyone.

"I know a lot of you heads of state have been wondering where all this marvelous technology comes from and how we make it. Well, beginning today we're going to show you exactly how it's done. It all begins with raw power, from electricity and petroleum. Once you have a way to make the wheels go around and the switches turn on and off, the rest comes from a lot of smart people finding ways to play with the power in different ways. Today you are going to see the real secret of America, our schools. We will leave from here and take you to one of our larger schools. Larger in that it has classes for very young people, all the way up to the University level and attached to one of our big research and development centers. The school is located not far from here imbedded in a large residential area where the people live. So, go back to your rooms and gather your stuff. Oh by the way, on your tables are the top vote getters for places to see in North America. If you don't see your choice it's because you were the only one who wanted to go there, or the numbers were too small to make up a trip. You need to pick your top four and give them to your guides when you get on the buses. See you all in 15 minutes."

On the elevator to their room, Henry asked his brother, "Which four did you pick?"

"I picked the buffalo hunt, Yellowstone and the Tetons, Grand Canyon, and Mesa Verde," said Herbert, "What about you?"

"I chose Yellowstone and the Tetons and the Grand Canyon, but I picked the big trees and Carlsbad Caverns."

"What did you choose, Charlene?" asked William.

"I picked Niagara Falls, Yellowstone and the Tetons, Banff, and the Grand Canyon."

"What about you father?" asked Henry.

"I asked Cary to book me a ticket on the Transcontinental Train. I want to see the whole country from sea to sea."

"That wasn't on the list."

"Nevertheless, they're going to accommodate me."

When they arrived at the sprawling campus of the school, located several miles outside of Washington, the visitors divided into smaller groups, and toured the classes from the youngest to the oldest in high school. Then, they looked into several university classes and on to the research center.

At dinner that night, the leaders from Prussia, France and England were sitting together. Cary had stayed on to answer any questions they had.

"It took me all morning to figure out what was different about your schools," said Moncrieff, "Your schools don't spend a lot of time in learning the classics, everything seems to be about thinking of new things."

"That's right," said Cary, "We're not much interested in learning what was taught in the past, the accumulation of knowledge. Our emphasis is on pushing the boundaries of new ideas, new concepts. We expect our kids in grades 1 through 6, to learn all the basics, after that the whole idea is to develop along a much different line. You see we want to develop, self-aware, self-reliant, self-actuated people whose minds can soar with an exaltation of intellect, an ennoblement of desire, an enrichment of thought, an invigoration of higher aspirations, a proclamation of discovery and the mighty mobilization of individual souls to reject the human tendency to selfishness, evil and sin.

"What's more," said Cary, "education describes efforts largely self-initiated for the purpose of taking charge of your life wisely and living in a world you understand. The educated state is a complex tapestry woven out of broad experience, grueling commitments, and substantial risk taking. To be educated is to understand yourself and others, to know your culture and that of others, your history, and that of others, your religious outlook and that of others. If you miss out on this, you are always at the mercy of someone else to interpret what the facts of any situation mean."

"That's unprecedented," said Gladstone.

"The results are right in front of your eyes," said Cary.

"I didn't understand most of what I saw at the research center," said the Prussian Monarch. "I saw people writing complicated mathematical formulas and others seeming to apply the formulas to beams of light."

"Frankly, I don't understand it either, other than the general goal to develop a high powered beam of light, called a laser, which will cut metal."

"What happens to all this information," asked Gladstone?

"An excellent question, Prime Minister," said Cary. "We have another research center that monitors all the other research centers. It's no secret to any of you now we are using machines, called computers, to compile, correlate, interpret, and then apply information of all kinds. The combined work of all the research centers in the country are downloaded to a master computer on a daily basis. This gives us linkages impossible for humans to interpret. The master computer is capable of billions of computations a second. It analyzes the fragments of work being done around the continent, and then combines it into usable avenues of continuing work. It then sends the new data to the research center working on that particular area of work, and gives the researchers the benefit of everything anyone else has learned that might apply to their projects. We are coming up with new things all the time."

"Astonishing, "said Gladstone.

"As the President said, it's the greatest secret we have. We've been working in this way for almost a hundred years. The results in new products are sent all over the world in our trading network, and each of your countries benefit from the solutions."

The conversation had drawn a lot of people to listen in to what was being said, and the look on their faces showed a dawning understanding of what a motivated and interconnected group of people could accomplish.

The next morning the buses were loaded and the convoy left Washington, driving on a smooth sheet of wide asphalt to the west. Gladstone was amazed at how fast the buses could move when they were put to maximum output.

They drove across the colorful and beautiful country of the Appalachian Mountains and down into Pennsylvania. The first stop was at a huge industrial complex.

"This is one of our oil production centers," explained the President as the buses were parked on a hill overlooking a big valley. "We have at least a hundred wells for oil drilled down there. They can produce about half a million barrels of oil a day. We have an equal number of wells that are extracting natural gas. The entire output goes into that very large refinery you see located in the center of the producing fields where diesel, gasoline and aviation fuel is refined from the crude oil. The heavier waste is processed into tars, which are combined with sand and rocks to make the surface of the roads on which we have been driving."

"There are pipelines leaving the refineries to deliver fuel to stations scattered all over the Eastern Coast. Other pipelines spread out to the cities where they deliver natural gas to disbursement centers and smaller and smaller pipes until they reach homes and buildings. The heating and air-conditioning of your resort comes from here.

Further down the valley were two big buildings with a light smoke coming from stacks. The buses unloaded and the groups were taken inside.

"These are power plants," said Gallagher. "They are run on natural gas, and produce electricity. The heat from burning the gas run those turbines and generates electricity. These two plants produce about a million giga-watts of energy per day. The electrical lines are all buried and the wires are encased in steel pipes. That way they are not subject to being knocked out with high winds or snowstorms. These two plants power Washington, Baltimore, and Philadelphia."

"We currently have about 500 of these plants running across the continent."

"Where do all the people who work at these facilities live," asked someone?

"Good question," said Gallagher. We have two high-speed trains running out of this industrial valley, over the hill and down into another valley. We have a complete city there. It's quite pretty and quiet. The workers come back and forth on staggered schedules, which make the commute from home to work, just 20 minutes."

"Our next stop is Three Rivers, a city that got its name from the three rivers that converge."

It was another hour to the city of Three Rivers. At the confluence of the rivers was the city itself. It was a lovely designed community spreading out from the commercial and recreational center, lined with parks.

"You would never know from looking at Three Rivers, an enormous industrial plant is located that way, beyond the line of forest.

Again we run high-speed trains to let the workers commute."

They skirted the city on a smooth road and approached a really gigantic complex of buildings. The largest of which was in the center. Other long buildings fanned out from the central building. A network of smaller trains moved all over the area, carrying people and products. The buses were able to inch their way along between the buildings and stop at the entrance of the huge, very noisy building.

"If you expect to hear anything I say, you will have to wear these headsets," said Gallagher, "Also, for safety reasons, we ask you all to put on a yellow hard hat."

The group filed by a distribution point and donned headsets and hard hats. They could hear Gallagher talking, and the headsets drowned out the roar of the building itself.

They walked along a catwalk over-looking several huge containers, full of hot molten metal.

"This is our largest steel mill in the country," said Gallagher. "In the beginning we used what you have recently developed, the Bessemer method of producing steel. Later, we switched to the Open Hearth Method, which is more efficient and produces a better quality steel with fewer impurities."

One of the open hearth containers was dumping it's load, just then, and Gallagher paused to let people see the process. The molten steel went shooting off into at least a dozen troughs that went in all directions, out of the building. "The open hearths run 24 hours a day, six days a week," said Gallagher, "We produce a million pounds of steel every day."

"Now let me show you the genius of our early designers," said Gallagher. "We kept the assembly plants for products right next to the source. It means we don't have to reheat the steel to make things. Follow me and I will show you one of the assembly plants.

They walked several hundred yards and entered a building. The steel was enclosed in a long, square box on the way to the assembly plant and was now cool enough to work.

As it entered the assembly plant, the steel was divided into various sized long squares and these were cut into different sizes and fed into big stamping machines. Gallagher led them down the line and the people could see shovels, rakes, hoes, pickaxes, sledgehammers, and the frames for wheelbarrows coming out the other side and down into water that steamed as the metal cooled. Men were waiting to attach the handles, and attachments to the tools. A machine took away the completed tools, men neatly stacked them in wooden boxes, stamped, "Rome" and trucks hauled the boxes away headed for a port and a ship that was being loaded for Italy.

Gallagher picked up a hammer from the finished pile. "We just made this high quality, last forever, hammer in five minutes. It cost us about 50 cents to produce the steel and a quarter for the materials and labor to make it a complete hammer. It will cost about a quarter to deliver this hammer to a port and put it on a ship, and another quarter to ship it to Rome. We can make and deliver it for $1.25. You think you are getting a wonderful bargain for buying it wholesale for $6. You sell at retail for $12, and it's the best hammer in your store, for the least amount of money."

"We can receive an order, refit our machines for whatever you need, built and turn it all out in less than a week. There is a complex of 12 assembly plants, surrounding the steel mill where each man does a particular job in an assembly line. We have 10 such complexes sprinkled around the country making everything we export, plus a hundred specialized mass production facilities that build products for us and for you. The only thing people complain about is not being able to get enough of what we make."

"This is just an example. Today we wanted you to see the power source of our electricity, the source of our steel production, and examples of our assembly lines making products. I'm sorry you ladies didn't get to see the textile mills and the plants making all the clothing we ship abroad, but they are clear down in Atlanta and we just didn't have the time."

"As it is, it will be late before we get you home tonight, but I think you are going to enjoy it. The Voyager has reached the moon and is now in orbit. This evening you will get to watch the first men in history walk on the moon. So, if you are ready, let's drive back to Washington."

They got back to Washington in time for a late supper. Everyone was hungry and the food was particularly good. The Europeans had seen an eyeful that day. All of them had wondered how the United States generated the titanic industrial production they did. Now they knew. Every leader was thinking of ways to increase their own country's production, using some of the wonderful innovations they'd seen today.

After dinner, the big screen covering most of a wall lit up and live coverage of the moon landing got underway. The Command Capsule and the moon rover safely lifted out of the shuttle bay. The three man crew aboard reported that everything was a "go" for orbiting and detaching the moon rover. The cameras showed the command capsule maneuver to a lower orbit, and the moon lander broke away with its two-man crew.

Within an hour the powerful cameras showed the lander make a soft landing on the moon with puffs of moon dust floating up. Soon the astronauts were climbing down the ladder and stepping onto the surface of the moon. "That's one small step for man, one giant leap for Mankind," said the astronaut. Arcadia had insisted on those words.

The entire North American Continent, every citizen, American's all, swelled with pride at the sight. The remainder of the world was represented by 320 Europeans, who had the same feelings.

It was late when the show was over. President Gallagher thanked the visitors for being there to see this event with him. "Tomorrow is a day for rest and recreation. We've driven you nice folks pretty hard the last ten days, so I think you need a day off. Go swimming in the pool, sleep late, go shopping, visit the sights of Washington you've missed. Do whatever you want, because the day after tomorrow you'll be leaving on your tours to see the wonders of our country.

The group took him at his word and scattered. Charlene and a bunch of ladies headed for the Emporium. Henry went to see Mount Vernon, the home of Washington. Herbert had a rather special offer from a certain green-eyed girl to spend the day with her, go to the National Zoo and have dinner at her home with her family.

William Gladstone, decided to try the swimming pool, which he enjoyed very much, especially the hot tub, he read a newspaper, sampled one of films on the movie channel. It was called Robin Hood, starring Russell Crowell. He really enjoyed that experience. Then he took a nap.

The following day, the Europeans split into small groups, and took off by plane, train or bus, to see America.

Charlene and three other ladies plus four teenage girls went by bus to Niagara Falls. They went first to New York City and stayed to sightsee and shop for three days in America's biggest city. Then it was on to Niagara Falls, which they all enjoyed very much. Next, they got on a train and went west through the Canadian States and saw Banff and Jasper national park. Even though she had done different things then were on her list, Charlene could not have imagined a more enjoyable time and became fast friends with her travelling companions from Austria, Prussia, Italy and Spain.

Herbert had a thrilling time with the Lakota Sioux, and enjoyed the traditional ceremonies they presented. However, the biggest thrill was racing across the prairie in an ATV and shooting a big buffalo from amongst a herd of millions. He went on to Yellowstone to see the geysers, and the big falls. The Grand Teton's, were like magic. One of his French friends told him Teton was French for breasts.

Then they flew to the Grand Canyon. Herbert was offered a four-day float trip on a big raft down the Colorado, instead of his last choice, and he was never more glad to have made that choice. The wild ride on the rapids of the river was unforgettable and he actually enjoyed sleeping on the ground in a tent, by the flowing waters.

Henry saw Yellowstone and the Tetons. He was overwhelmed by the Giant Sequoias. He loved the Grand Canyon, but only took a burro down to the river and back. He thought the highlight of his trip was a visit to the mysterious cliff dwellings of the Anasazi, the Ancient Ones, at Mesa Verde.

William Gladstone took ten days to make the trip on the railroad across the entire continent. He stopped in a small town in Iowa. He got there on Sunday, and was enchanted with a repeat of the Sabbath activities, on a smaller scale. He was deeply impressed with the people's dedication. He ended up in San Francisco, enjoyed that boisterous gold-happy boomtown, and took a plane back to Washington.

When the entire group was joined together again at the resort, almost two weeks later they had a grand banquet in the restaurant with a thousand tales to tell. They were sunburned, had all sorts of scrapes and bruises, their clothes were torn and tattered, but they came to the dinner, the way they came back and wore all their experiences like badges of honor.

Wonderful new friendships were made; bonds of comradeship that would never break were forged. There were now six new couples among the group of young men and women who had found love in their time together. Actually, the number was seven. Herbert invited his green-eyed beauty to have dinner with them. Her name was Andrea Marie. They were clearly in love and agonizing over what they would do when the time came for Herbert to go home.

The orchestra was back, as was the President and all the guides. Gallagher went out with the groups and managed to see most of the visitors at some point on their adventures. He hopped up on the stage, grabbed the microphone and said, "Well, what do you think of the United States NOW?"

The yelling and foot stomping and applause went on continuously for ten minutes.

Chapter 50
Celebration And Deliberation

Georgetown, Washington, D.C.

Arcadia met with President Gallagher often during the previous three weeks the Europeans were in the country. They reviewed a hundred hours of surveillance tapes capturing the secret conversations going on among the families. They also had tapes where groups of men and women were together.

"The whole point to showing our hand here is to overwhelm these galoots with a world they don't know exists," said Arcadia. "I would say we have accomplished that beyond our expectations."

"The status of women in our society hasn't been lost on the European women," said the President. "Most of them are badgering their husbands to give them the same rights."

"Listen to this piece of conversation between the Czar of Russia and the French Chancellor," said Arcadia. She punched up the conversation and they watched.

"There is no way we can compete, catch-up, or conquer the country," said the Frenchman.

"They must have some motive for revealing all these wonders to us," said the Czar, "I wonder what it is."

"Obviously, they know we're going to want everything they have. I can't imagine what the price will be."

"Nothing short of overhauling all our countries, I would guess," said the Czar.

"The trouble with that," said the Frenchman, "is that I don't think it's such a bad idea."

"That's pretty typical of what we recorded," said Arcadia

"We are enjoying a period of good will among these nations

they've never known," said Gallagher. "The idea of going back to the plotting, scheming and warfare is something none of them really want to do. However, so far, only Gladstone has had a glimmer of the idea, we're planning to give them a better choice. He said it the other day, "Wouldn't it be sensible to turn all this good will into a way to get together and talk about our differences? How can one look on all this and remain unchanged?"

"He's getting close," said Arcadia. "When the time comes to roll out our plan, he might be the first to endorse it."

"Okay," said Gallagher, "One more giant ego boost the day after tomorrow and then we will get down to business and see if we can pull this off.

The ego boost was the successful return of the astronauts from the moon and a big ticker tape parade down Broadway in New York. The media played up the fact it was actually the Europeans who were there to send them off. Therefore, as a special treat for America, a chance to see all the great leaders of Europe together for the first time riding in the parade on special floats built for the occasion.

At dinner the night before they flew up to New York, the Europeans talked about what they should wear on an occasion of such pomp and circumstance.

"I'm wearing my buffalo hat, the Lakota gave me," said Herbert.

"I'm wearing my new dress, I got at the Emporium," said Charlene.

"I'm wearing my shorts and my USA shirt," said Henry.

"I'm certainly not going to dress up," said Gladstone. "I'm hoping to look like a typical American. It's the very least I can do."

The same kind of sentiment filled the room. People collected special articles on their visits and were wearing them. There would be lots of shorts, even among some of the men, and a lot of the women took a liking to the sleek jeans. The Europeans dress would be varied, but colorful.

It was a lovely day in New York when the plane landed and the buses took the Europeans to the place where the parade would begin. They had a joyous reunion with the astronauts and words of praise for their achievement and bravery. President Gallagher made a little speech.

"You folks were the only crowd to see our fellows off, except the ground crew, plus you've been travelling around the country making lots of friends, but the country hasn't seen you altogether or in person yet. So we're making this a special double occasion. I hope you all enjoy yourselves."

Gallagher got a cheer. He walked over to the float representing America. Actually all the floats were covered trucks pulling a flatbed with a scene built on it by volunteers. It was very colorful, but so were the floats for each of the countries represented from Europe. They were told America would go first, but that all the other countries were fairly represented in alphabetical order, and the people along the parade route knew that.

With so many immigrants from Europe, there was a sizeable contingent of rooters from every country.

A company of Rangers let the way in dress blues and with the flag of every nation represented. Arcadia wisely ordered Rangers to line the parade route and be on the lookout for anything that might be embarrassing. She thought that was enough. Nobody, including ordinary Americans, were anxious to cross a Ranger.

The parade began. People had streamed into New York for days for the big event, so the route was jam packed for two miles with tens of thousands of people and hundreds of buckets of ticker tape ready to shower the procession.

The Rangers clicked into order and began to precisely march. The American float with the President and the Astronauts came next. Then the colorful European floats flowed down the parade route. Gladstone's family was sort of in the middle as Great Britain. They marveled at the crowd and the piles of ticker tape flowing down. They smiled and waved at all. Herbert kept taking his buffalo hat on and off. Charlene was really lovely in her purely American peach dress. Henry got lots of applause with his shirt made to look like a flag. William Gladstone wore a simple pair of trousers and had on a t-shirt that said "Thank You, America" on it.

When the Gladstone's passed the section filled with those who had immigrated from Britain, there was a huge outburst of applause and cheers. There were more British than any other group.

The other delegations received similar applause from their

countrymen. They waved and smiled happily. It was just a great day.

The group flew back to Washington and watched themselves on television on the news reruns and specials at dinner in the restaurant on the big screen. There were lots of jokes and good-natured comments on how everyone looked.

President Gallagher came up, took the mike and said, "Before the orchestra starts playing, I want you to know we are going to teach you all a special American Dance. It's called a line dance, and you do it in rows of 20 across. The staff are pushing all the tables to the side so there will room for you all, young and old. I want you to know how proud I was of you today. Give yourself a round of applause."

The group did so and added a bunch of cheers.

"The last thing I'm going to say is this. We are coming to the last part of your trip to America. I know a lot of you have been wondering why we did this. Well, I have some things to say about that. I have a little business to discuss with you. We'll do that tomorrow morning starting at 10 AM in the Capitol in the House of Representatives. This meeting is for everyone, except the small kids, so don't sleep in. Goodnight. See you tomorrow."

He left to applause. A woman jumped on the stage and said, "You're going to love this. She then organized the group into lines of 20 wide and 16 deep, with an arm's length between them all. Then she taught them a lively, but fairly simple line dance, complete with foot stomping, handclaps and Yehaws.

Gradually the band started to join in and keep time as the group went through the routine. In a few minutes, they had it down. The band made up of guitars, drums, a few horns, fiddles and a real western beat, paused for just a minute and then began to play the fun, tuneful, and happy song. The instructor held up her hands and yelled into the mike, "NOW! She was joined with a group of singers and the dance was on.

The crowd didn't want to quit after they had done the dance three times. They were really getting the hang of it now, and having the time of their lives. They were still going strong half an hour later.

Arcadia and Gallagher watched them through the monitor. They were now a precision team to match the Bolshoi. In perfect unison they stomped and clapped as if it was a single sound. Arcadia smiled,

"Remind them of their unity and precision tonight, tomorrow."

"I will, indeed, Arcadia," said Gallagher. "I don't know when you thought this one up, but it's perfect."

"As Gladstone was getting on the bus to the Capitol the next morning, he said to Leopold of Belgium, "I wonder if this is when we get the check for the party?"

The buses pulled up to the Capitol and everyone went in. Their guides escorted them to the House of Representatives. In the center, there were nameplates on desks. They were in alphabetical order, so Gladstone and his family found themselves once again in the middle.

Across the front of the big podium was the flag of every nation present, with the flag of the United States in the center.

President Gallagher came out a door on the side and up to the podium. He was smiling as always. "I thought you might like to how much fun you were having last night. He picked up his clicker and the big screen in the front of the room came on.

Every one sat forward and smiled as they saw themselves moving in perfect unison as the music played. There was not a person in the room who did not laugh and point at themselves as they sashayed with the best of them. They stomped together, they clapped together, and Yehawed together as the music pierced them to the core of their souls, as it had the night before.

"Quite a show, don't you think," said Gallagher? "When was the last time any of you can remember doing anything together so well?" He paused to let that settle in.

"Is there anyone here who would like to have all we have for your country?"

The audience, used to responding to Gallagher, shouted out "Yes! and Of course we would"

"OK," said Gallagher, "How would you feel if we gave the wonders of America to only a few of you, we'd determined were 'special'?"

That caused the audience to squirm a little in their seats.

"To carry this line of reasoning a little further, how would any one of you feel if we were to move into your country, use our technology to take over and start telling you what to do and how to live?"

This was definitely something nobody liked.

"You would have the advantages of all the wonderful toys you have enjoyed this past month, but the goodwill in which you received it would be gone. You would resent our imposing an authority over you."

"To state the obvious, what is the difference with us doing that, then what you are doing today in the Congo, in South Africa, in Morocco, in India, Kenya, Tanzania, China or a dozen other cultures in the world? You are the superior power with the better technology. You say you are bringing these people better lives, and you might be, but you are also stripping these countries of their wealth in natural resources, and have to station armed forces in these countries because the people resent what you are doing and resist."

"This policy, used by every nation in this room, has additional complications. You resent your neighbors gains, and do everything you can to prevent any of your neighbors from getting an advantage over your country."

"So what is the result? In the last 70 years of the 19th century, you have fought 37 wars with each other, and killed 20 million of your fellow human beings. I'm afraid I would have to say the Lord does not honor this."

"To add more, each of your countries is spending a significant portion of your annual income in developing weapons and maintaining a large armed force.

"Doesn't it occur to you there is something wrong with this?"

While the European delegations where eyeing each other to see if what Gallagher was saying was having the same effect on them. Gallagher ran the video again of a happy, unified group of people marching in unison.

Gallagher challenged them all. "If you would rather have this," he said loudly pointing to the screen, "rather than what is waiting for you when get home, please stand up."

The President was not at all surprised to find the first people out of their seats were the woman and the older children. Gallagher waited patiently. As he expected, the first real leader to come to his feet was William Gladstone, the most powerful country in Europe.

All of the leaders eventually stood up. Again, Gallagher was not surprised to see the last to stand were the actual Monarchs of their country.

"Congratulations, my friends," said Gallagher, "You have just taken your first vote as a United Nations. This is, and has been, the ultimate goal of the United States. America is a neutral nation. If one of your countries' receives a piece of advanced technology, all of you will receive the same technology at the same time. Furthermore, we are prepared to begin to share everything we have with all of you immediately."

"We have guidelines for this. We ask each of you establish a residence in America; not an Embassy, which is nothing more than an isolated island of each countries' sovereign territory, but a home among us."

"We ask all of you return to Washington, for two days each month for the next six months, and after that for one week, every six months. The purpose of your time here will be to act as United Nations to discuss disputes and disagreements you have with one another."

"Further, we ask that none of your countries fire a single shot in anger, until you have spoken to each other here in America."

"If it is your wish, the United States is willing to serve as a fair broker to arbitrate your disagreements. We have no vested interest in any country in the world."

"In return for your agreement to these modest requests, all you have seen, all the technology you have enjoyed, while being our guests in the United States, will begin to flow to your ports starting today. We will send technicians with the materials to teach your workers and scientists to help you bring these products on line as soon as possible."

"Does anyone have any questions?"

Charlene Gladstone raised her hand, "President Gallagher, I gather you will now allow each country to speak with each other regarding your very generous offers. My question is this, Are the women present here today permitted to raise the issue of extending equal rights to women, as you have in the United States?"

"We believe all men and women are created equal. We have no slaves; our population of Native Americans enjoys the same privileges of citizenship as I have. What is fundamental in our philosophy, is all have individuals have natural rights, which are given to them by God. Therefore the rights of government are derived from the governed...the people."

"If that is the case," said Charlene Gladstone, "I hereby move the first order of business of our United Nations is to extend equality and voting rights to all adult women."

A big rumble of conversation broke out among the Europeans. Before it got very far, the wife of the French Chancellor stood up and said, "I second the motion of my good friend from England."

Arcadia was watching the proceedings from her home in Georgetown. When he heard the women speak out, she slammed her fist into her hand and said, "Yes! Membership in the United Nations will require new applicants agree with international laws. This is our portal into the heart of Islam, and the beginning of their marginalization. "

Back in the House of Representatives, the President gaveled for order. He held up a big piece of paper. "Ladies and Gentlemen, just to set the record straight, everything the United States has pledged, has been unanimously approved by the Congress and I hereby add my signature to this document." He signed the paper with a flourish. Aides passed through the group and gave a copy of what he just signed to each person, man, and woman. The document said everything Gallagher had said and added a few other benefits as well.

"I think you folks have some things to discuss," said Gallagher. "I will leave you to it. Lunch will be served in the cafeteria, when you want to eat, and the buses will pick you up at 5 PM."

Gallagher and every American left the room and the Europeans were alone.

Chapter 51
Forging A United Nations

<u>U.S. Congress, Washington, D.C.</u>

For a very long time, there was silence in the House of Representatives. People were reading the manifesto of the government of the United States. It repeated exactly what President Gallagher had said.

It was William Gladstone, who finally rose to his feet. He looked over the people he had come to know and like so well in the last month. He could see Gallagher's words deeply impressed them. He approached the problem from the back door. "Is there anyone in this room who rejects this proposal entirely and is unwilling to discuss its properties in open debate?"

There was silence. "That is a very hopeful sign to me," said Gladstone. "We are being presented the biggest blank check in history. Now we must decide if we can cash it."

The wife of the French Chancellor stood up and said, "There is a motion on the floor with a second. I want this matter debated here and now. We women either, have a stake in this or we don't. If we do, I want to be able to vote on the proposal. If we don't, then the women are wasting our time, because you men were just on vacation and were oblivious to everything you've seen and heard in the past month."

"Make your case, madam," said Gladstone.

"Very well, in the past month we've witnessed, first hand, a civilization in which women function in every position in society. We saw them in the schools, in the factories, driving the buses, serving as our guides. The men in America are neither afraid nor intimidated by their women and give them the respect they certainly deserve.

"You might recall the only thing the government fears is an uninformed electorate which is why all citizens are required to pass a Master Civics Examination before they are allowed to vote at age 21.

This applies to both men and women. You men have been telling women for years we do not possess the sophistication or insight into government or business to be able to exercise the mandate to vote. As we have clearly seen here, that is not the case at all.

"As President Gallagher said, "We hold these truths to be self-evident; that all PEOPLE are endowed by their Creator with certain inalienable rights and that the power to govern is by the consent of the PEOPLE.""

"Madam Moncrieff," said Leopold, "the fact of the matter is we do have a considerable number of women who are not qualified. We might exclude the present company, but back home it's just not practical."

"Back home, only men who own land are allowed to vote, and none of the women. The United States is offering us a way out of this sorry condition. Nobody is saying it is going to be done overnight, and the Americans understand that. However, Leopold, you correctly said present company was excepted. I agree with that. If we accept the United States' solution, I want to have a say in that decision."

Her last remark seemed to stir up a good many of the women, and for half an hour, they dominated the debate. The men were confused and flustered. Most of them did not want to give the vote to women, but most of them included their own wives in their reckoning. A good many of them consulted their wives on matters of state on a routine basis.

Charlene Gladstone held up her hand and rose. "Very well, I amend my motion to say that for the purposes of this debate and the issue at hand, all persons over the age of 21 shall be entitled to a vote."

"Second," said Madam Moncrieff.

"I call the previous question," said William Gladstone. All persons in favor of suspending debate and moving to a vote on the motion raise your hands."

It wasn't even close.

"Therefore, the question being called, all persons who believe for the purposes of deciding on the offers of the United States should include all persons over the age of 21, raise your hands."

Arcadia took a deep breath. There was no question in her mind the practical minded women in the group would push the

American proposal to acceptance. She also knew how to extend a victory for these women was the same as giving it to all women. Give her five years in the schools and women would be passing the Master Civics Exam faster than men.

"I do not like war," said Moncrieff of France. "It always brings tragedy and the need for higher taxes.

Giovanni Lanza, Prime Minister of Italy said, "It's so simple a plan. When Gallagher said it, I wondered why I hadn't thought of it before. Certainly, the benefits are worth more than mustering an army and going off to capture a weaker country, just because they have a gold mine."

Count Alfred von Potocki-Pilawa, Minister-President of Austria, brought up the crucial question, "Over half of Europe is ruled by Kings and Monarchs, most of whom are related in some way. When we begin bringing in the American improvements it will significantly improve the standard of living for the common person and will produce a robust middle class. This group has sought a more representative form of government and a bigger say in the affairs of their countries for years. Now they will have the numbers and the influence to get it. The Kings who are still real kings and not constitutional Monarchs know their days are numbered, but will, nevertheless resist with all their strength. Our King Franz-Joseph could not be bothered to come to America, so he sent me. How do you think he will react when I go home and tell him Austria-Hungary, has just joined a United Nations and this group will interfere with his sovereignty, particularly as it relates to waging war?"

"Perhaps you would like to hear from an actually reigning Monarch," said Alexander II, of Russia. He went on, "I agree with Alfred. He and I have spent a great deal of time together in America, and I told him the time of Kings and Czars are ending. It was actually the United States who started the movement, gaining independence from England, the world's greatest power, then and now. I don't have to tell any of you the United States has made the most of its independence. They have wisely refrained from getting involved in any foreign matters."

"For the remaining Monarchs, we spend all our time fighting with our own people. There have been three assassination attempts on my life in the last two years. I must tell you the time of the people is coming, sooner than you might think. They are no longer willing to be poor serfs with no futures.

"This proposal from the United States does several things. First, the flood of technology of the kind we have seen here will make any government very popular with their people. Next, we can institute real reforms. I suppose I will have to imprison or execute several thousand major landowners, but after that, I can continue to improve the lives of the people and give them what they want, a real republic, like this one. Maybe we can copy their constitution. The best thing of all, is I get to be a constitutional Czar with no real power, but the undying love of the people. I can retire and spend my time visiting hospitals and dedicating new bridges and dams, as fast as the Americans can show us how to build them."

"I'll tell you one thing for sure. This is not the last time I'm coming to America."

"Think how much money we can save by cutting our military budgets down to a bare minimum, "said Gladstone. That will free more money to buy more from the United States. I can tell you it will be a great comfort not to have to worry about wars."

"How would we handle the admission of new countries into our United Nations," asked the Greek Prime Minister.

"I should think," said Gladstone, they would have to agree to the terms of the charter. That would mean universal suffrage, no fighting of wars. It would be diplomacy, negotiation, and if necessary arbitration. I don't have many problems with letting the legal system in the United States rule on tough issues. After all, they have a hundred years of disciplining themselves with strict neutrality. If we can't count on the Americans to be fair, as they have been in all their dealings with all of us, then who else could we trust?"

It took three days for the delegates of the European powers to come to a unanimous agreement. There were some very tough negotiations, a few of the leaders were a little hesitant to give up their intense nationalism and dreams of colonial rule, but the American Pot of Gold at the end of the rainbow was a powerful incentive.

Count Alfred von Potocki-Pilawa, President of Austria went to President Gallagher privately and told him that King Franz-Joseph was going to be one tough nut to crack and wondered if Gallagher could help him. Gallagher got on the phone to his ambassador in Budapest and had him call on the King. It took him two days of intense talks and the threat of getting no trade from the United States at all before the King agreed. He was probably the most impressed by being able to talk to his Count personally on the phone and give his blessing to the United Nations.

President Gallagher had to handle one problem he had not truly considered. It came from Gladstone who visited the Oval Office. "Mr. President, other countries are going to want to join this special club of ours. We have worked out the details for them becoming members. However, with the drastic reductions in our military forces, what is going to keep a big nation, like China from invading Russia or other such rogue nations. I believe the United Nations should have a military arm of its own to protect our members."

Gallagher had to go to Arcadia to get an insight into that. "The United Nations of my time is nothing like the one we are forming will be. They have a military arm. They are called Peacekeepers and they are only used to keep two sides from fighting. It doesn't work. I agree the member nations need to feel more secure. Tell you what, if we have a problem like that we will tell the belligerents, 'The Rangers Are Coming'. That ought to squelch most of the problems. If not, we can always make an example of some country that won't behave."

Gallagher passed on the solution to Gladstone, who shuddered, "The British have first-hand experience of what it's like to face the Rangers. Even today, their reputation throughout the world is legendary."

"I can assure you, William, the Rangers are more lethal today than they were a hundred years ago. We considered having them put on a firepower demonstration, but decided against it. The whole idea of this visit was to make peace, not war."

The time in America for the Europeans was running out. None of them were looking forward to going home. They had changed so much. They had gotten very accustomed to the casual luxury of life in the United States. All of them had made friends with Americans. Some more than others.

"Father, I need to speak to you on a very serious matter," said

Herbert to his father.

"What would you like to discuss Herbert?" said William, who pretended he didn't know what was coming.

"I would like your permission to remain in the United States permanently."

"Your life is in England, son, your friends, and your school."

"I know that, Father, but Andrea Marie is not in England, and I could not consider asking her to leave America to live in London."

"Ah," said William, "So it is a matter of the heart?"

"Yes, indeed, father, we are very much in love."

"How does her family feel about this?"

"They want us to finish school, of course, but I think they approve of me."

"They do, indeed, Herbert," said William. "I had a most interesting conversation with Mr. Franklin, just last night. The general consensus is you and Andrea Marie were made for each other. Mr. Franklin believes you will make a cracker-jack addition to his company."

"You have spoken to Mr. Franklin?"

"More than once," said William. Once your mother spotted the stars in your eyes over this girl, we felt it necessary to speak to them and find out if they approved of you, 'Herby'."

"That's what they call me."

"Well, she's a lovely girl, and we approve of her. President Gallagher says you can take your tests next month to see where you fit in Washington University. I would imagine you are destined for the Political Science research center."

"I've invited their family to the banquet tomorrow night."

"We will miss you, of course, Herb, but I expect to see you often with my visits to Washington on official business. Benjamin Disraeli will be the next Prime Minister of Great Britain. I will be his official representative. I expect the whole family will move here within a year or so."

"That's wonderful news, father!"

"We have fallen in love with America, too."

The final banquet of the Europeans was scheduled on the evening after the formal signing of the United Nations Charter at the U.S. Capitol.

President Gallagher presided over the ceremony. The formal document was a statement of peace and purpose meant for the whole world. The United States would be the official headquarters of the United Nations and was charged with the responsibility of being the neutral court to handle disputes, and to provide security for members. The charter incorporated the bill of rights from the U.S. Constitution. Arcadia wanted all people to have the right to bear arms against tyranny.

In a grand ceremony each nation signed the document, not only each nation, but also all the people who had a part in its creation. 153 women signed the document.

Then it was time for a party.

The ballroom at the resort was the only place large enough to hold the big crowd. The temporary walls were pulled back to make the room almost twice the size of what the Europeans were used to. Most of them didn't know the room could be expanded so much.

Not only were all the Europeans there, but for the first time the government of the United States was also invited. The President's entire Cabinet was there, plus half the Congress came in for the event, and some of the senior leaders of business companies were invited. All of them were intensely interested and supportive of the President's grand strategy, but avoided getting involved for fear of complicating the process. Now they were delighted with the accomplishments.

The Americans mixed freely with the Europeans. They received private and thorough briefings on what was being attempted. Now they not only congratulated and praised the European delegation for their good sense and farsighted discernment, but also began the process of implementing the U.S portion of the deal.

"As we see it," said the Head Master of the Political Science Research Center, "the biggest problem you are going to have is being believed. Tell me," he said to Giovanni Lanza, Prime Minister of Italy, "would you have believed what you have seen in America if you were not here to witness it with your own eyes?"

"Obviously not," said Lanza, "The wonders of the United States are so vast, your technology and science so advanced, I'm not sure I believe it now."

"We have planned this for a long time," said the Head Master. "At this moment, in all the major harbors of Europe are cargo ships we sent in advance. In them are some advanced generators, very large LED screens, big enough to fill the stages of your largest opera houses. We have done a good job of recording and documenting your visit. We have techs to install these big screens and get them ready to work. You should open the doors of your theaters and start running the videos around the clock, every day. Make the first showing a gala event for your government leaders and other important people, and then run the videos for the people, free of charge, of course. The videos also contain special features showing our technology in detail. You simply say your country is going to get all of these marvelous things and you have devised a means of preventing armed conflicts in the future through the United Nations."

"We have workers and equipment on those ships to start building roads, dams, providing electrical power plants, and steel mills immediately. We will give jobs to many people."

"In other words, we intend to prove the videos they see, which will be amazing in themselves, are not just pictures, but can be put into practice immediately."

"At the same time you are doing this, we will be flying all your great scientists and key leaders from all over Europe, to America to give them the same treatment you got, probably minus the vacations to our national parks."

"One of the major advantages you will have over others in your countries will be the use of this," the Head Master pulled out a black, rectangular object with a keypad on it and an antenna, "this is how we keep in contact with our ambassadors in Europe. It's a communication devise, like the phones you've been using. This one will allow you to call us from Europe. It runs on batteries, which can be recharged by plugging it into an electrical outlet. You won't have electricity for a while, but the American ambassador has a way to recharge your battery. Here's a little pamphlet telling you all about it, and a list of numbers to reach people in the U.S., including the President. You can also call other leaders who are here. They are also getting phones. Their numbers are in the pamphlet. Good communications with others will give you a great advantage."

"Thank you," said Lanza. "I'm sure this will be a great aid."

"If you will excuse me," said the Head Master, "I have more phones to pass out, and the same speech to give to the rest of the leaders I haven't spoken to yet."

William Gladstone had already received his phone. He was having dinner with the Franklin family and getting to know them better. He liked both Ben and Marie Franklin and learned Ben was named for his grandfather four times removed, the famous Founding Father. The two lovers, Herbert and Andrea Marie were sitting together and carrying on a private conversation, holding hands under the table. Both families though it was a good match.

"I have to say," said Charlene to Marie Franklin, "I never expected anything like what's happened to us this month, especially leaving Herbert behind. However, I am happy for him. He and Andrea Marie seem well matched."

"We think so also," said Marie Franklin. "Although I don't think Herby knows what he's about to experience at the university. It will keep him so busy, time together with Andrea will come at a premium, even though they are in the same school. But we will take care of him and make his transition as smooth as possible."

"You are so kind," said Charlene with real sincerity.

President Gallagher was busy with more important business. He was off to the side with the German Kaiser and the French Chancellor. "Otto Bismarck is about to pull the trigger on a war with France. His goal is Alsace-Lorraine. Frankly, most of the territory is traditionally German. Here's a map of how the territory should be split. It will cause the least amount of tension between the people who live there, and will eventually become a peaceful border. It looks like Germany is winning, but having France trying to hold the territory will be more trouble than it's worth. Germany is getting some land, but France is shedding a perpetual headache. It's a fair deal and not worth having France overrun with German troops all the way to Paris."

"You know all of this for a fact," asked Moncrieff?

"Let's just say my understanding of the strategic situation has a sound basis," said Gallagher. "We will build a modern road from Berlin to Paris as a way of smoothing out the tensions between the two countries. You both get something you need, and it will buy us the time to begin making real improvements in both countries."

The French and German leaders shook hands on the deal.

"I wish all our problems were going to be so easy to solve," said Gallagher. "Just know Europe is going to be overrun with American engineers and workers for the next ten years, putting in roads, power plants and building steel mills, the components for a basic infrastructure. However, we will put a bunch of your people to work and give them a good wage. None of them are going to complain. The 'Most Favored Trade Status' the members of the United Nations countries are getting from us will ease the cost of your imports, as well. The rest of the world will pay the full price."

"By the way, before you ask," said Gallagher, "I will tell you two what I've told the others. It would be a little hard for you to put a million dollars in gold into your carry-on bags for the airplane. The gold went out on one of the Destroyers, this morning. They will be in London by the end of the week, and in Calais a day or so later. The gold is being transported to each of you personally by a detachment of Rangers. They are travelling by Humvee. That ought to attract a lot of attention from the local folks who have never seen such a vehicle before. It's our way of saying 'Hello, the United States is here'. There is no purpose in our hiding out in North America anymore."

"It will make our jobs easier, too," laughed the Kaiser.

When the banquet was over, President Gallagher jumped up on the stage and the band stopped playing.

"Ladies and Gentlemen, boys and girls, Americans and Europeans, Friends and comrades, this is a great day and the dawn of a new future for the planet Earth! God has blessed us with his wisdom and grace this past month and nothing will ever be the same again!"

There was a thunderous applause as every person in the room rose to their feet and gave full throat to their joy and happiness. Gallagher let them vent their feelings for several minutes. At last he held up his hands and the noise slowly died down.

"I believe we can say we have done a great work here and the long period of isolation and preparation for us has finally come to an end. We are now and will continue to be your friends. We are the even-handed, generous supporter of all free people wherever they are. We will freely share our bounty with all, and especially for the new organization we have forged that stands for peace, prosperity and the pursuit of happiness for all. Raise your glasses and join me in a toast for the greatest creation of Mankind, our United Nations!"

Americans and Europeans rose as one and lifted their glasses, "To the United Nations."

"This is our final night together. Tomorrow you will be flying home. Try not to be sad for your fellow citizens and what they don't have when you get there. Know we are coming home with you to fulfill our pledge of sharing all we have with our partners in the United Nations.

"We cannot let you go home without giving you the opportunity to say a personal goodbye to the guides who have been with you this last month. So, here they are."

Into the room marched a column of guides. They were wearing the dress blue uniforms of Rangers. The Europeans gasped. They had no idea the men and women who were their patient companions for the previous month were part of the most feared military force in the world.

Gallagher said, over the noise, "When I invited you to come, I promised you would be safe. What better way to do that then to surround you with Rangers, over 500 of them. They were your bus drivers, your cooks, your baggage handlers, and your guides, who have come to pay their respects now."

Cary came to the Gladstone family, smiling. He was wearing the stripes of a master sergeant, and he had medals galore over his left pocket. Gladstone was overcome with emotion and hugged the young man. The whole family took turns hugging him. "It was wonderful for you to volunteer for such a humble assignment," said Gladstone.

"Humble," said Cary, "I had to beat 25 people in the martial arts ring for the privilege of getting to do this. I hear congratulations are in order." He shook hands with Herbert and gave Andrea Marie a little hug. "Best of everything to both of you," he said.

"His Majesty, Leopold of Belgium tells me his fellow Europeans have a parting gift for us. He says it is uniquely American, as it should be," said Gallagher.

Leopold jumped to the stage, and spoke into the mike. "Fellow members of the United Nations, places please."

The Europeans jumped to their feet and took their positions on the ballroom floor. Leopold jumped down to his spot. The quartet of singers came to the stage and the musicians took up their instruments. The opening bars rocked the room, then on cue, the Europeans began their line dance. All 320 of them began dancing in unison, with a single plop of shoes, smacking of hands and Yehaws. None of the Americans had seen this before and they cheered and clapped their hands with the music. After dancing furiously for ten minutes, the song came to a melodic stop, and the Americans fairly mobbed the Europeans in appreciation and joy.

Chapter 52
Going Home

London, England

Leaving America was a sad experience. The Gladstone's gathered up their luggage, now filled to overflowing with practically nothing European. Their shoulder bags, once flat and nearly empty were just as full. They wandered around their rooms, fingering all the wonderful devices they knew were not yet a part of life in Europe, and looked out at the city of Washington on the deck for the last time. Then they took the elevator to the lobby and slowly walked to bus #2. Cary was there to meet them. He was wearing his green fatigue uniform. He put their luggage in the bus bay and got on with them. The buses pulled out and headed for the airport.

The big plane was sitting there waiting for them. The group had time to say their goodbyes to their guides while the luggage was being loaded on the plain.

"This has been a wonderful experience, the best of our lives, of course," said William. "We could not have managed without you Cary, uh Sergeant."

"Just Cary, William," said the Ranger. "It's been quite an adventure. I hope this isn't the last time I ever see you."

"We're coming back as special representatives of England, as soon as we can," said William. "How do we find you?"

"I'll find you," said Cary. "I'll take Herb to his room at the University. I guarantee it's not as swanky as the Resort."

"Thank you, I'm sure he'll manage." William turned to his son, "It's a strange thing leaving you this way, but I'm happy for you. Charlene hugged her son and Henry did the same. "Take care, brother. I wish I were staying here with you."

Then the family turned and walked up the stairs. Herb and Cary waved goodbye as they disappeared into the plane.

It was late night when the plane landed in Normandy. There were many coaches and carriages waiting as the plane taxied to a stop on the tarmac. The group said their goodbyes on the plane and now walked down the stairs and on to their carriages. Gladstone recognized the American Ambassador, and went over and shook hands with him. "I must say," said Gladstone, "if I ever needed a spy who could keep a secret, I would want you."

The ambassador laughed, "You wouldn't have believed me if I had told you."

"Good point," said Gladstone," now we have a whole country to tell."

The trip back to London was tedious and tiring. First the bumpy ride in the carriage to Calais with the smell of sweating horses, then the crossing of the channel, which was rough and choppy, then the ride through the streets of London to the Gladstone residence. London was more crowded and grubby than Gladstone remembered. The soot from the East end factories filled the air and the whole city had an unpleasant odor about it.

The house was musty from being closed for over a month. The servants got a month off, with pay. They had only returned that morning to put the house back in order.

As they came in the housekeeper greeted them and asked, "Where is Herbert?"

"He stayed in America," said Gladstone.

"My goodness," said the housekeeper, "who would want to live in that backwater frontier." All three of the Gladstone's laughed.

"Matilda, you have quite an education ahead of you," said Charlene, "America is the best kept secret in the world, as you and the rest of the country is about to learn."

Everything about his previously comfortable home was a pain. No switches to turn on lights, no refrigerator to keep drinks cold, no radio, no television, no phone, no beautiful view. When they went to bed that night, Charlene said, "I can't imagine us sleeping in this little, lumpy bed all those years." Gladstone just grunted and fell asleep dreaming of America.

The following morning Gladstone really missed his shower. He didn't even have running water in the house, just a hand pump from the well in the kitchen, and he was considered fortunate. He put on clean clothes and had his carriage take him to his office. His arrival was jovial by his staff. It was a good staff and he liked and trusted them all. The problem today was they all smelled. Gladstone had never noticed it before, and didn't let on there was anything wrong. He just greeted his people and sent messengers off to get an appointment with Queen Victoria, contact his parliamentary whip, and send for a reporter from The Times.

On the way back from France, Gladstone, and the ambassador made their plans. He learned that, at great expense and moaning and groaning, the ambassador had booked Prince Albert Hall for three months, beginning in three days. He said the techs were moving the equipment and the enormous big screen into the Hall that day and would be ready for screenings on Friday night. The program was just under two hours long.

The messengers came back. The Queen could see him that afternoon. The Whip came back with the messenger. Gladstone took the Whip into his office and closed the door. "Jack, I don't really have time for a lot of chit-chat. I want you to get in touch with every member of parliament, both houses and tell them I have just returned from America and have a vital message to show them on Friday night 7 pm at Prince Albert Hall. Nothing is at stake here, Jack, just the future of the entire British Empire."

"Good Lord, William, did something happen in America?"

"I wouldn't know where to start," said Gladstone, "but yes more happened than you can possibly imagine. You'll have to wait and see for yourself Friday night. Go get started." The Whip left.

A secretary put his head in the door, "The reporter from The Times is here Prime Minister.

"Send him in,"

The reporter who came in was the senior writer for The Times. That suited Gladstone. He knew him pretty well, and he was a friend to the Party.

"Come in, Alex," said Gladstone, coming around his desk to shake hands with the reporter. "Thank you for coming so promptly."

"Prime Minister, I would have brought the entire newsroom here if I could have. Your sudden disappearance for over a month has caused quite a stir."

"I announced I would be on Holiday in June."

"Yes, but you seemed to vanish and none of our contacts anywhere in Europe could find you in the places you normally go."

Gladstone had to chuckle, "That's because I wasn't in Europe. We went to the United States."

"I don't understand Prime Minister, "said Alex Hawkins, "an ocean voyage would have taken you at least a month to make the round trip."

"Yet it only took eight hours to reach Washington, D.C."

"I beg your pardon?"

"You do recall I announced before I left the government had received a message from the United States with an invitation for all the heads of state to come to America?"

"That was well known," said Alex, "and that is the strangest thing of all. None of the European leaders have been seen for a month. It's caused something of a sensation throughout the continent."

"Then I would imagine every other leader in Europe is sitting in front of a befuddled newsman at this moment."

"The subject of the United States has been one of the greatest mysteries for many years. They send amazing products to every country in the world, at bargain prices, but nobody has ever been able to find out any substantive information about that large, dark continent. The fact, Alex, is the United States has been reinventing itself for the last hundred years and chose this time to drop the mask of secrecy. For example, our passage to the United States for my family and over 300 other European leaders and their families actually did take eight hours, because we didn't sail on a ship, we flew on an airplane."

"That's preposterous," sputtered Alex.

- 366 -

"It's nevertheless true, as the continent is finding out today."

"America is a place of such wonders, I can't even begin to describe it. However, I can prove it."

"How are you going to do that," asked Alex?

"On Friday night at 7 pm, the members of Parliament and the press, including you, are coming to Prince Albert Hall, where you will see, with your own eyes, the stunning world of the United States."

"Is there going to be some demonstration of products, or a representative of the United States to give a speech?"

"In a manner of speaking," said Gladstone. "I'm sorry, Alex, I'm not being secretive or purposely concealing anything from you, it's only the story is so big it will be the only topic of conversation in Europe from now on."

"I must say," said Alex, 'you certainly have my attention."

"We'll have the attention of everyone starting Friday night. After you have seen the two-hour presentation, Prince Albert Hall will be open 24 hours a day for the next three months for everyone who is interested in seeing America for themselves. That is what I want you to print. Make you headline something like, 'Astonishing America Revealed', or words to that effect. Report everything I've said here, and tell all of London from now on, our lives will be forever changed, and changed for the better."

"That's quite a bold statement to make without any facts to back them up."

"Trust me, my friend, if you don't cover this story in exactly the way I've described, you will be playing catch up with every other paper in Europe. I've just handed you the biggest story in history."

Hawkins left the Prime Minister's office very confused. Gladstone had always been frank and honest with him. He was certain Gladstone was sincere. He couldn't see he had any choice but to do as the Prime Minister had said.

Gladstone had much the same conversation with his Parliamentary second in command. He said he would get right to work in getting the word out. Gladstone was glad he didn't have to try and give more detail. He didn't think that approach was going to work with the Queen.

He arrived at the palace 15 minutes before his appointment and waited half an hour. Then was ushered into the familiar office where he and Victoria had enjoyed many good conversations. He approached and bowed politely, "Your Majesty." He said.

"Good afternoon, William," said Victoria, "Please make yourself comfortable."

Gladstone sat in his favorite chair and looked at the queen. "Ma'am, I hope you have some time. I'm going to tell you a story that will simply amaze you."

"I'm not easily amazed after all these years, but go ahead," said the Queen.

Gladstone started at the beginning with the invitation from President Gallagher. He'd brought it with him and he handed it to her."

She read it, and looked up, "I take back my doubts of being amazed. Tell me everything."

For over an hour Gladstone spoke rapidly and sincerely about what he had experienced in America. Victoria interrupted him several times to ask more about some specific instrument or technology. She seemed moved by Gladstone's description of the Sabbath in the United States.

When he finished the detailed description of America's titanic industrial strength and their wiliness to share it all under a set of controls, he pulled out his copy of the United Nations Charter and handed it over to her.

"Are you of the opinion all of this is in the best interests of the British Empire, William?"

"I am, ma'am," he said. Then he told her about the fabulous big screen he was installing at Prince Albert Hall, and said, "Just the demonstration of the technology to show these images will confound every scientist in the country. The content of the video, as it is called, will create a storm of debate throughout the realm."

"When can I see it," asked Victoria?

"Our first showing is Friday night at 7 pm. It's for Parliament, the major departments of government, and the press."

"No," said Victoria, "When can *I* see it?"

"If you will just give me a minute, I can answer that question." Gladstone pulled his phone out of his bag and dialed the ambassador, who answered immediately. "Ambassador, I'm with the Queen and she would like to know the earliest moment in which she can see the video."

"It's ready now," said the ambassador. "We just finished testing the picture and the sound."

"Hold on," said Gladstone. He turned to the Queen and said, "You may see the video at your convenience, ma'am. It's ready to go."

"Then we shall go straight away," said the Queen. She rang a bell, and a butler came into the room. "Get my carriage ready to go to Prince Albert Hall, immediately."

Gladstone spoke into the phone, "The Queen and I are leaving now. We will be there in half an hour."

"You got it, William," said the Ambassador," we'll be ready."

"That instrument you have there, is it another piece of American magic?" asked the Queen.

"It is," said Gladstone.

"Who can you speak to?"

"Anyone who has a phone like it," he said.

"Could that possibly include the President of the United States?"

"Yes ma'am it could."

"Then contact him, I wish to speak to him."

Gladstone pushed the buttons for the President and in a moment the phone rang, "Gallagher here, what's up William?"

"Mr. President, I am with Queen Victoria, alone in her office. She wishes to speak to you."

Gladstone handed the phone to the Queen.

"President Gallagher?" asked the Queen,

"Speaking," said Gallagher, "I gather William has told you the whole story and you have some questions."

"I'm going around to Prince Albert Hall to see this video of yours. I think your presentation will only cause me to have even greater curiosity. As the Queen of my people, I think I should be able to speak about your wonders with some first-hand authority. Do you think it would be safe for me to come to the United States?"

"Excuse me for asking, ma'am, but do you have any medical conditions that might be aggravated by a change in altitude? Or any medical conditions at all?"

"I'm an old woman," said Victoria, "but I still go riding every day."

"In that case I don't think an airplane flight will harm you," said Gallagher.

"Then by all means send one of your contraptions."

"Madam, the only airstrip we have in Europe right now is in Normandy. The trip to catch the airplane might be more dangerous than the flight."

"I can endure a channel passage," said Victoria. "I have to smooth some ruffled feathers Friday night and could not leave London before Saturday morning."

"Then let's say Monday morning at 10 am. I will come myself and escort you back to Washington."

"That is most kind of you, Mr. President. Goodbye."

She handed the phone back to Gladstone, who was looking at his Queen in wonder.

"Don't slouch, William. What did you expect the Queen of the British Empire to do after hearing such news?"

"I'm very happy for you, ma'am. I can't begin describe what a wonderful experience this is going to be for you."

"The fewer who know about this the better. Now let's go see your presentation."

When the final notes of the closing music ended, Victoria had tears in her eyes. "Unbelievable, simply unbelievable," she said. "I really must see those geysers."

"They are beautiful," said Gladstone. "The whole country is beautiful."

"I will be the hostess for the Friday night showing," she said. "You're right, William, the technology just to make this presentation boggles the mind."

"I'll tell the press," said Gladstone. "You being here is bound to bring out the most skeptical Member of Parliament."

"Now that I have seen this, with its countless marvels, I am more anxious than ever to make the trip. By the way, William, I'm proud of you. It looks like you have found a way for all of us to live in peace from now on. That's a great achievement for any man."

Chapter 53
The Queen Takes Charge

London, England

Friday night came, along with the simultaneous arrival of 5,000 people. The news the Queen was serving as the hostess, swelled the ranks of those who were anxious to see this oddity from their Prime Minister. It must be worth seeing if the Queen herself was coming.

When everyone was in their seats, Gladstone stepped onto the stage with a long tube in his hand. "Ladies and Gentlemen," he said. Of course, the state of the art sound system amplified his voice to the farthest corner of the big building. It caused every person to jerk. No one had ever heard an amplified voice before. "As you have read, I spent the last month in the United States. I am back today to show you an America hidden behind a veil of secrecy for over a hundred years. Their emergence into our world is going to change our world in profound and stupendous ways. We are going to show you that country tonight. The very technology used to make this presentation will be a mystery to you in itself."

"Now it is my distinct honor to present to you, our beloved Queen Victoria. She has already seen what you are about to see, and has something she wants to say about it."

The Queen walked out on the stage and all stood and bowed in respect. Victoria took the microphone from Gladstone and said, "Please be seated."

"My fellow countrymen, in the past 20 years has England seen great changes and the introduction of modern developments in our Age of Industry. We can be proud of what we have accomplished. We can also appreciate improvements in technology when we see it. Tonight, you are going to see what the United States has been up to the last 100 years. I believe after you see it, you will begin to understand the significant changes in store for us. With this technology will come a new political age for Europe and the world. I'm sure you are going to enjoy this, and am honored to be the first to share it. Thank you and enjoy the show.

The lights went down and the curtain parted. On the stage was a huge silver frame. Music began to play. It was rich and triumphant music. Suddenly the screen lit up and the picture of a great mountain range with snow-topped peaks came into view as the music rose to a crescendo. Every person in the room jumped when the music started, and then grabbed their seat arms when the picture came on.

For the next two hours, Londoners were spellbound by the scenes they saw, the incredibly sophisticated technology displayed, from the huge streams of molten steel pouring from huge cauldrons, to trucks and trains running across the wide plains of the mid-west with thousands of miles of lush crops, and huge machinery harvesting it.

When the show was over, there was no applause, just the soft sound of humbled feet as they exited the theater.

Even the newspapers the next morning were somewhat subdued. The show at Prince Albert Hall was the greatest thing anyone had ever seen, but the British ego was severely damaged. To have been bested in such a spectacular way, brought grudging admiration for the Americans and a deep hunger for the United States to keep its word and start bringing this world to the English countryside. Only the members of Parliament truly understood the price this glittering world would cost. On the surface, the United Nations looked like a concept that would work, as long as America let it work.

The reaction in the other capitals of Europe was much the same. Otto von Bismarck was dumbfounded his Chancellor knew his plans in detail and even more perplexed when he produced a completed agreement between France and Germany. "No sense in wasting lives, when a little diplomacy works as well," said the Chancellor, and laughed when Bismarck left the room.

As it turned out, Queen Victoria's visit to America was more than just a great thrill and wonder for her. President Gallagher had the foresight to bring along a couple of doctors, nurses and a lot of medical equipment.

After they were in the air, Gallagher mentioned as gently as he could it was important the Monarch of the greatest empire on earth be kept in perfect medical condition and got her approval for a fairly extensive examination. A doctor gave her a shot with a mild sedative and the Queen slipped off to sleep. The doctors went to work.

An hour before they landed she awoke. She smiled and said, "I have not felt so good in 30 years." She enjoyed a delicious and healthy breakfast. She watched with beguilement as the plane skirted down the east coast, to see New York and the other cities from the air was a thrilling experience. President Gallagher kept a running commentary as they flew closer to Washington.

The plane made a low level pass over the city to give Victoria a complete view, and then landed at the airport. During the visit by the European leaders, Gallagher realized he needed some kind of official car to haul dignitaries. He consulted with Arcadia and she described the general outline of a limousine. The vehicle in shiny black was waiting on the tarmac, along with two young women and a driver. Gallagher opened the door and the 51-year old Queen stepped easily into the car. "I have no idea what your doctors did on the voyage here," said Victoria, "but I feel wonderful, like a school girl again."

Gallagher did not miss the opportunity, "Imagine all of the people in England having the same feelings?"

"That would be quite a gift," agreed Victoria.

"You have also been vaccinated against, measles, mumps, influenza, yellow fever, whooping cough, and tuberculosis."

"Really," said the Queen, "You have cures for all these diseases?"

"And many more," said Gallagher. "You have arthritis and gout, a form of arthritis that affects the joints. Your freedom of movement is largely from the treatment we administered for that."

"This vehicle...I saw vehicles like it in the video, what is the source of power for it?"

"It's called the internal combustion engine, and it runs on refined petroleum. Victoria now turned her attention to the two women who had gotten in the limousine with them. "I would like to introduce you to the two young ladies who will be caring for your needs while you are with us," said Gallagher. "This is Holly and Shannon."

"I am pleased to meet you both," said Victoria.

"It is our honor," said Shannon.

"Where are we headed first," asked Victoria?

"To your quarters where you will stay while you are with us," said Gallagher, "The sudden change in time zones from Europe to Washington creates something called 'jet lag'. This is a temporary thing proper rest will cure while your body resets it's biological clock."

"William told me something about his quarters. He said they were quite remarkable."

"You are about to find out for yourself. Your guides will stay with you and help explain everything."

They were pulling into the curved driveway of the Resort at that moment, and people came running out to handle the luggage.

"Is it always so hot here?" asked Victoria fanning her face with a handkerchief.

"It's summer," said Gallagher, "the clothing you're wearing is making it much worse. We have better clothing for you in your rooms."

Victoria had the same reaction to the interior of the resort as the others. She greatly admired it for a moment.

"This is where I leave you for a while," said Gallagher, "I hope you will accept my invitation to dine with us tonight at the White House, our Executive Mansion?"

"It will be my pleasure," said Victoria.

After Gallagher left, Holly and Shannon escorted the Queen to the elevators, which she thought were ingenious. They went to the corner suite, and inside. For the next hour, the guides explained all the appliances of the big suite. They gave Victoria her badge to wear around her neck and explained all it did. The Queen marveled at the sheer opulence of the rooms and the lovely balcony wrapping around the corner of the building, giving a truly spectacular view of Washington.

The guides opened the closets and brought out truly elegant clothing. The garments had the advantage of being light to wear and were far more comfortable than the mostly wool clothing worn by Victoria.

"You must feel very soiled and uncomfortable from your long trip," said Shannon. "Let me introduce you to the one thing you are going to enjoy the most about your rooms." They led her into the bathroom and demonstrated how the shower worked. Victoria giggled at how ingenious it was.

"Why don't you give it a try, suggested Holly?

They helped Victoria undress and covered her with a huge soft towel. She learned about the soap, shampoo, and conditioner dispensers. "Step right in and enjoy washing yourself from top to bottom, "said Shannon. " Wash your hair, and use the conditioner. It's very healthy for you, and we can fix your hair beautifully when you are finished."

It didn't take Victoria long to see what a relaxing convenience the shower was. She lingered at it. When she came out, the girls wrapped her in a soft towel.

"I can see where one would want to do that often."

"As a matter of fact, ma'am, almost everyone in America takes a shower every day. It cleans the skin, opens your pores, and promotes better health."

With that, the women started to take Victoria's now very soft hair and arrange it beautifully for dinner. She chose an elegant gown and some very ornate jewelry from the selection her aides offered. She would never again wear the clothes she'd brought from England. The girls discreetly disposed of all her stinking garments.

Gallagher left the resort and went straight to Arcadia's Georgetown home. "Well, she's in the resort and safe. Our docs fixed her up pretty good on the flight. It probably added 20 years to her life. Now, the question is, how do we make the most of the opportunity?"

"She's an invaluable asset, of course," said Arcadia. "The opening session of the United Nations is in less than a month, I would like her to be here for that. It could have a pacifying effect on our number one troublemaker, Kaiser Otto von Bismarck. Chancellor Wilhelm promises he will be on the plane of leaders who come here"

Arcadia sat and thought for several moments. Then she said, "Chuck, the seeds of the modern world with all its problems come out of the next 30 years in world history. The first problem is the intricate, complex, and continuously changing diplomacy of Bismarck. We have to use the United Nations to neutralize him and nudge the principal powers of Europe into peaceful coexistence. I believe they will be unwilling to give up the many improvements we will make to their countries. The trouble is it's not going to happen overnight. It takes time to build railroads, highways, and power plants to create an electrical grid,"

"The reason why there is all this turbulence in Europe is because the Ottoman Empire, which has existed for over 600 years, is on the ropes. From the 12th to the 17th centuries, it was a formidable nation. It conquered and ruled half of Eastern Europe, almost all the Middle East, and North Africa, including Egypt. However, today, the Empire is much weaker, and all of Europe is nibbling away at the Ottoman presence in the Balkans. This is where the flash point for World War I, will occur. As you know, we've been dealing with the Ottomans separately and caused them to rethink their position. We'll have to be very careful of our neutrality here. We can't afford to directly confront a Muslim country and produce the kind of animosity the results in our catastrophe in 2030. We need to establish an excellent relationship with the country emerging from the Ottoman Empire. We have had our best people working on this for years. It has been your successors pre-occupation for a decade."

"Poor Tony," said Gallagher, "you've worked him a lot harder than you worked me before I took over."

"We had the luxury of time in those days," said Arcadia. "Now events will start coming at us fast and furious. We would not be where we are today without your own hard work and inspired leadership, Chuck."

"Thanks for that" said Gallagher. "Arcadia, you might be immortal, but I am not. I have served this country for 30 years. If you want to know the truth, I'm ready to retire."

"I know, Chuck, and I love you dearly. You have been the greatest and brought us a long way, but I know burn out when I see it. You've got Tony Carter warming up. Do you think he's ready? He's 30 years younger than you are."

"More than ready," said Gallagher, he's already running more of the country than I was when I took over."

"I agree," said Arcadia, "he and I have spent a great deal of time together, especially on the Ottoman problem. The plan is coming together. However, for the moment, you are the face of America to the Europeans, and when they get here, I want you to get some of the credit for the coup we have on the front burner. You have to stay long enough to get through the next few sessions of a much different United Nations. When Tony puts the finishing touches on the grand plan, the Europeans are going to need a lot of handholding. After that, Tony Carter will be the fair-haired boy and you can retire.

"Are we still proceeding as you have told me?" asked Gallagher.

"We are working out the final kinks in the endgame with the Jews," said Arcadia. "We need to establish a Jewish state now, not 70 years from now after 6 million of them die in the holocaust. The Ottoman Empire currently controls all that land down there, including Syria, Lebanon, and Palestine. We think money will be the key to that problem."

"What are you going to do," asked Gallagher? "I thought you had all this figured out in 2030?"

"Wrong!" said Arcadia. "My angel only told me the solution to our catastrophe in 2030 began in 1770. He never told me how to work it all out. I pray all the time and seek guidance. So far we've been able to get an advanced society dominating the world and a reputation for being a neutral, problem-solving country whose intentions are only for peace and prosperity."

"Will membership in the United Nations, for the Ottoman's get you closer to solving the future problem?" asked Gallagher.

"It will if the plan works. However, there is the little problem of Sharia law, based on Muslim religion. The Ottomans are about to toss it out in favor of secular law, but I seriously doubt they are going to give the franchise to women, unless they have to. The trick is to make it seem like their idea."

"How do you intend to get them to do that?

"A dose of reality, I think," said Arcadia

Chapter 54
Romancing The Ottomans
Constantinople, Ottoman Empire, 1869

Vice-President Tony Carter hung up the phone. He and the Ambassador to the Ottoman Empire were making final preparations for "Operation Turkey" which had been in motion for years.

When Arcadia first came to Carter with the scheme, he was very doubtful of being able to do it. It did not have the luxury of being able to deal with a relatively civilized society, such as was present in Europe. He was dealing with a Muslim country as corrupt as they came, and one with a built in animosity against Christians and Jews. The law of the land was Sharia law, based on religious principles.

The ruler of the Ottoman Empire was Abdul Hamid I, who was extremely pious and devoted to Islam. Surrounding him was a court of viziers who often exercised independent authority in matters of state.

Into this cauldron of chaos, marched the United States.

The first thing Carter needed to accomplish was to establish diplomatic relations. Even this was difficult. America was a long way from Constantinople and the Ottoman Empire had done things in their part of the world pretty much as they pleased for 600 years. If you were to ask most people in the capital, they would tell you the Ottoman Empire was as powerful as ever. This Carter knew was not true. The Ottoman Empire had been in serious decline for the past 50 years, and their influence in Europe was under assault by Russia, Austria-Hungary, and the Germans. The Ottoman Empire had not kept up with modernizing their army, and was suffering defeats regularly.

Carter was not about to arm the Ottomans with new weapons. That would have been a violation of everything the United States stood for. Instead, in a bold and super-secret action with a team of Rangers, Carter captured the Ottoman Empires' public enemy number One. He was a notorious brigand and pirate who had raided Ottoman commerce for years.

With a couple of Rangers to protect him and handle the brigand, the American Ambassador padlocked the crook to the gates of Topkapi Palace, left an American flag attached to the pirate and casually walked away.

That did the trick. Two days later Carter was invited to the palace to be thanked for his service, by Abdul Hamid I. He surprised the Sultan by responding in fluent Turkish and asked permission to show the Sultan a video, in Turkish, of the United States. This marvelous piece of technology was so impressive to Hamid, he began to be interested in everything American. Carter complied and over a period of several months, was able to provide the Sultan with the wonders of American technology.

The Sultan was dumbfounded to learn the United States was the biggest country in the world. He was further surprised to learn America was the greatest trading nation on earth. He began to suspect the Europeans were causing his Empire so much trouble because of the advanced technology they were receiving, even though Carter stressed, very often, America was a neutral country and never took sides in disputes, and absolutely, never supplied weapons to anyone. Carter began to plant the seeds of a deeply held Religious ethic in the United States. Even though, America was Christian, it humbly followed the will of Allah in all things and practiced peaceful relations with each other and with other countries. In the end, the Sultan and Carter became close friends.

A stream of luxury goods and practical tools began to flow into the Capital. The modern steel ships caused a sensation whenever they appeared. Carter would only said these were normal samples provided to all countries when beginning a trade relationship. In return, America was accepting pistachio nuts and several tons of raw opium, which became high quality morphine for American medicine.

A year went by. In 1870, a letter was received by the Sultan from President Gallagher. It was an invitation for the Sultan to actually, visit the United States. The Sultan knew America never invited anyone to visit the super-secret United States. He had corresponded with other leaders and found such an invitation was unprecedented. The Sultan was to come alone, his safety was guaranteed, and he would receive a grant from the United States of a million dollars in gold. Not only that, but the United States would provide unique transportation.

Try as he might, the Sultan could not lure Carter to disclose what "unique" meant. The mystery grew when a huge cargo ship docked at the harbor in Constantinople and a line of heavy machinery came pouring out. In less than a month, the Ottoman Empire had a beautiful new mile long road starting a mile outside the north gates of the city. Then the equipment went back into the cargo ship and the ship sailed away. The workers didn't make a single contact with the people of the city.

Carter visited the Sultan, "Your highness, we have now completed the preparations to provide your transportation to the United States. We are ready to take you there at your convenience."

"This road you have built has something to do with the transportation?"

"Yes sir," said Carter, "you should plan to be away from the capital for one month. It will take at least this long to acquaint you with America. It's a big country."

"How much luggage shall I need," asked the Sultan?

"Almost none, Your Majesty, we will provide for all your needs. The climate this time of the year is challenging."

"How so?"

"You will be accustomed to the heat, but not the humidity."

"If that is the case, then we may leave as soon as your transportation arrives."

"Your transportation will be ready for you, the day after tomorrow at 10 am. I will be accompanying you."

It was a bright Tuesday morning when the opulent carriage of the Sultan pulled out of Constantinople's north gate and proceeded across a rough road until it came to the asphalt slab shining in the sun. The carriage went the entire mile and then stopped at the edge of the highway.

At exactly 10 am, the Sultan could begin to hear the roar of something resembling thunder. As he stood there, the noise grew louder. Carter pointed into the air, and the Sultan saw the shape of a bird getting closer. As it got closer, it got bigger. It touched down about a quarter of mile from the other end of the runway. It was roaring even louder as the huge bird slowed and came to a stop 50 feet from the Sultan's carriage. The horses were jumping and terrified. So was the Sultan.

"Your transportation, highness," said Carter with a big grin. The door of the plane opened and a set of stairs came auguring down from the fuselage. A person jumped down the stairs, bowed to the Sultan, and hauled his bag aboard.

"What in the name of Allah is this," cried the Sultan?

"Just the beginning of what is bound to be the greatest month of your life, after you, your highness."

The Sultan labored up the steep stairs and looked into the cabin of the airliner. It was filled with seats, but there only appeared to be a few flight attendants. Carter led the Sultan to the front of the plane and ushered him into a seat. He sat down himself and showed the Sultan how to fasten the seat belt.

The big jet spun around and started to accelerate down the asphalt. The Sultan caught his breathe as the plane left the ground and flew over the city of Constantinople. He could see people running into the plazas to see the airplane. This was by design. Certainly, the departure of the Sultan would be seen by all the palace dignitaries, viziers, and the Harem. There would be no doubt in their minds this magical bird was part of the wonders of the mysterious United States.

"Do you mind if our doctors examine you, highness. First time flyers sometimes have reactions and we want to make sure you are comfortable. The doctors moved in and started an IV on the Sultan. They made an injection and the Sultan was unconscious in seconds. Then the doctors did a much more complete examination, including taking blood, doing a chest X ray, and much prodding and squeezing of the sleeping Sultan.

"He has arthritis, emphysema, what looks like a tape worm in his colon, and is in generally poor health because of his weight. Still, there's a lot we can do to make him feel a whole lot better."

"Do it," said Carter. "How long will it take?"

"Couple of hours," said the lead doc, "Make sure you get him to the lavatory as soon as soon as he wakes. He'll need to dump that tapeworm."

When the Sultan woke up three hours later, he stirred, expecting to feel the pinch of stiff joints and a continuous ache in his abdomen. When none of these symptoms appeared, he looked around. Carter was smiling at him. "Did you have a nice sleep? I'll bet you could use the lavatory. Come this way. The Sultan almost bounded out of his chair. He felt wonderful, but he thought the need to relieve himself was a very good idea. Carter showed him the equipment and the Sultan shed the strange clothes he suddenly found he was wearing, and had a prolonged bowel movement. It felt he had shed ten pounds. He pushed the button, he was shown, and found there was more in him. Minutes later, he used the soft paper provided and stood up. He fumbled with the strange pants, and was pleasantly surprised at the zipper. The pants were loose and very comfortable, so was the short sleeve shirt he was wearing with buttons down the front.

"How long was I asleep?" he asked.

"The docs worked on you for a couple of hours. You still need some more treatment we can't do here, but we have given you medicine, for your arthritis, we think you should be breathing better and you just flushed away an unwanted guest in your gut."

"I feel wonderful," said Sultan Hamid.

"Glad to hear it. How about something to eat?"

"Oh yes, Please."

The Sultan got three rings of pineapples, a sliced papaya, and an avocado dip with low calorie chips, for a drink he got a sugar free Coke. He had never eaten any of these things, so he polished them off and felt full.

Land finally appeared far below. After the endless ocean, it was a novelty. Carter pulled out a large book with a soft paper cover. He opened the atlas and showed the Sultan where they started, and traced the line of flight across the Atlantic Ocean to the east coast of the North American continent. The Sultan looked with wonder at the enormous country. Carter pointed to a city on the coast. "This is Washington, our capital city.

An hour later, they were on the ground. A much better set of steps came to the open door, and the Sultan stepped out into a blazing day, dripping with humidity. He was immediately grateful for the comfortable clothes. At the bottom of the stairs stood a tall man who was smiling in front of a small group. Everyone was wearing exactly the same clothes as the Sultan. The only difference being the colors of the shirts. The man was older but looked very fit, and had a full head of brown hair. He stepped up and said in perfect Turkish, "Welcome to the United States, Sultan Abdul Hamid. We hope you will enjoy your visit to our country. I am President Charles Gallagher."

The two bantered only briefly before Carter said," This is long enough in this heat. We have transportation to your quarters. The Sultan only saw a long, black shape, but then a door opened, and a young man jumped out. "Hi Sultan, I'm Raff. Come on in out of the heat." The Sultan stepped into the limousine. "Does everyone in your country speak Turkish?"

"Would you prefer Arabic," asked Raff? "Or perhaps, Farsi? You don't happen to speak English do you?" He spoke each line in that language. Hamid understood everything except the English.

"Quit showing off," laughed Carter. "Raff will be your guide. We have a rather full itinerary for you, but if there is anything you want, Raff will get it for you."

The limousine pulled away from the curb and headed toward the center of Washington. The Sultan was deeply impressed with the gleaming city.

This was just the beginning. Sultan Abdul Hamid was the first guest, since his mission would take the longest to accomplish. Nevertheless, he got the same opulent rooms the Europeans would get in the near future. He saw the same industrial centers, the same factories, assembly lines, and row after row of equipment ready for shipment to far ports. He learned about computers.

He also got something the Europeans didn't get...a Ranger firepower demonstration. The show left the Sultan shaking, and he was only partially convinced when Carter told him this was strictly for self-defense.

The Sultan also got some advanced medical treatment. His teeth were terrible, so they were all replaced with implants. He lost 30 pounds in a liposuction treatment. He underwent a medical procedure that removed spurs from his backbone and cut out a benign but substantial tumor from the Sultans' abdomen. He got lectures from the doctors about his diet, translated enthusiastically by Raff. He ended up being convinced he should eat better if he wanted to keep the good health the Americans had given him.

When he recuperated, he got a wonderful ten-day personally guided tour of North America. He saw Yellowstone, the Tetons; the Grand Canyon…the list was endless.

After a month, the Sultan was on a first name basis with everyone, had learned a fair amount of English, and thought America was the kindest, most wonderful, most devoted to God, country in the world. He had never cared for Christians, but the Americans were a different breed of Christian and the Sultan was impressed.

When everything was handled, Tony Carter sprung the trap. He came to the Sultan's quarters ostensibly for lunch and a conversation about opening trade with the United States. Carter smiled and began telling the history of the Ottoman Empire, in detail from the days of Suleiman the Great. Carter went on and on, pronouncing the names correctly and identifying every major date and event in the glorious, 600 -year history of the Empire.

Abdul Hamid I was impressed. Even he didn't know the history of the Empire as well as Carter. As Carter came closer and closer to the present, the picture began to change and the reality of the futility of the realm's position became obvious.

"You paint a bleak picture of my beloved world, Tony," said Abdul.

"Yes it is bleak, and it will only get worse while the major European powers drive you out of Europe and the Balkans. The fact is you are not strong enough to defeat them. However, with our help, you can still be the leading power in the Middle East, and you can stay that way for a long time. You need to abandon the north and concentrate on the south."

"What are you suggesting, "asked Abdul?

Carter pulled out a map and spread it out on the table

"Pull back from the north to a position that straddles the Dardanelles in both Europe and Asia. This gives you a bargaining chip with Russia, who needs a warm weather port. Establish a country for the Kurds along your border with Mesopotamia, but continue to hold the rest of the land all the way down to the Persian Gulf. This will give you effective control over a large percentage of Middle Eastern oil. Your country will run from Constantinople to Persia, and Baghdad, along the Tigris and Euphrates Rivers. Give the Syrians their own country, the Palestinians their own country here, "Carter pointed at Jordan, "then gradually begin to negotiate your way out of Arabia as the circumstances arise in the next century."

"What about this land along the Mediterranean," said Abdul pointing to Lebanon and Israel?"

"It is our belief that this should be a homeland for the Jews," said Carter.

"That would not make me very popular with the other Muslim countries."

"Granted," said Carter, "that's why you sell the land to the United States. Over the years, we will make living in Jordan more attractive than Israel, and we will buy out the Palestinians to make it possible to move to Jordan and buy new land. Gradually, over a number of years, we will make it possible for more and more Jews to move into their ancient homeland. However, that's on us, not you. Simply, don't object."

"You are asking the Ottoman Empire to cease to exist," said the Sultan.

"If you do nothing, a great war between the major European powers, basically fighting over control of the Balkans, will result in you supporting the wrong side, and the Empire will be carved up the way the winning Europeans choose. Any smart man, like you, Abdul, can read the signals coming out Europe with all those interlocking alliances. You just step away from the conflict and don't worry about it until oil becomes more important. By holding on to Mesopotamia, you will own a significant fraction of world oil reserves. You will be rich."

"You have spent a lot of time telling me what we will lose," said the Sultan. "Tell me what we will gain?"

"You like America," smiled Carter?

"Very much, as you well know," said Abdul.

"In that case, you can have it all, or at least a duplicate of it in your new country. You can have a seat in the United Nations, which by charter guarantees your sovereignty. More importantly, when the Persians decide they are going to take some of that oil rich land along your border with them, away from you, an appeal for military aid by the United Nations will be approved. That means you get the Rangers.

"There are other reasons to pull out of the Balkans. You make sovereign nations of Bulgaria, Romania, Serbia, Bosnia, Croatia, Dalmatia, and Montenegro. You make a lasting peace with Greece, by giving them Thrace and most of the islands of the Aegean Sea. You give independence to Cyprus. If you do this before the Europeans have a chance to rush in and take over these countries we will admit these countries to the United Nations, adding additional security for you. We pull the fuse out of the coming World War in Europe, and continue to share all our technology with all, as long as they don't violate the charter of the United Nations. America continues to be the big neutral country it is, and everyone wins."

"I'm sure there are unknown problems to this brilliant proposal, but, at the moment, I can't see what they are, "said the Sultan.

"Then let me continue to be the neutral, fair broker we are, and tell you what the biggest problem, socially, you are going to have."

"I'll be glad to hear that," said Abdul.

"We know you are planning on giving up Sharia Law in favor of Secular Law."

"Absolutely, religious law is not compatible to the way most of us live," said Abdul.

"You need to read the entire charter of the United Nations. Among the rights it guarantees is equality for all people, which mean, no slaves and the voting franchise for women."

"I would imagine the Europeans are having a lot of trouble with that," said Abdul. "For us it may be less of an issue, than you might think. The women of the Harem are very active in politics. Making it official is not such a big step."

"As a good trader," said Carter, "this is the time when you ask for the sale. Will you approve this proposal?"

"How much money for your land along the Mediterranean," asked Abdul?

"How about $10 million in gold?"

"This is valuable land and seems to be critical to your planning. We will need at least $20 million."

"Will you split the difference and accept $15 million?"

Chapter 55
Sealing The Deal

<u>**Europe to America, 1870**</u>

When the videos started playing in the great capitals of Europe, people poured in to see it. On the same day, 100,000 men and all of their heavy equipment came off the big, waiting cargo ships in European ports, and went to work like possessed men.

The first thing they built were more air landing strips in England, west of London, in Hungary, outside of Budapest, and in Germany, north of Munich. This made the commute to an airplane departure point a lot more convenient. The engineers and contractors then turned their attention to building a starter steel mill in each country, and pre-assembled power plants. They also built the beginning of modern rail transportation, and a small network of roads around the big cities. Nothing was finished, except the landing strips, but the people turned out by the tens of thousands to watch the work. The Americans hired many thousands of new workers and put them to work. They had no skills, but were eager and the Americans paid well in silver coins.

When the time came for the delegates to the new United Nations to leave for America, almost all the same people came to the landing strips as before, but there were many new additions. This time Franz-Joseph decided to come. Particularly since Victoria was already in America. Wilhelm of Germany gathered Bismarck and his family. The Greek Monarch came. All the heads of state of Norway and the other Scandinavian counties came. This time it took three planes to bring the group. They were not all full, but the size of the delegations had grown from 320 to well over 700. The people, who'd made the flight before settled in, fastened their seat belts, and relaxed, which made it much easier on those for whom this was a new experience.

Still, the thunderous take off made all catch their breaths and put their noses to the windows to see the earth falling away.

Eight hours later, the planes came skimming over Washington, doing two passes to let both sides of the plane see the gleaming city of Washington, before landing one after another at the airport.

William, Charlene, and Henry Gladstone looked anxiously for their son. They spotted him standing next to Cary, and rushed forward for a happy reunion. "Have you actually grown, Herbert?" said his mother.

"I have been working out with Cary," said Herbert, "so I've gained a few pounds of muscle."

The routine for gathering luggage, getting the guides assigned to the new people, and giving them their badges went smoothly, even though there were twice as many buses.

They made the grand circle of Washington getting to the Resort and the Gladstone's got their old rooms back.

"Where's the Queen," asked the Prime Minister?

"The last I heard, she'll be in on the afternoon train. She's been out west visiting Yellowstone."

"Really!" said Gladstone, "I would not have thought her up to such a trip."

"A word of advice, Prime Minister," said Cary, "Don't offer to wrestle Victoria two falls out of three. You'd lose. We're very proud of your Queen. She's in the picture of health and having the time of her life. Very nice lady."

"She comes sometimes to watch Cary and I practice," said Herbert. "She laughs when I get splattered, which is every time."

"How's the video running in London," asked Herbert?

"Jam packed audiences around the clock," said Gladstone. Everyone is anxious to start having all the things on the video, but, of course, it takes time. Nobody is complaining about how hard the Americans are working, however, and they have hired many thousand Brits to work with them. A few of them can keep up."

That night was the first dinner of the bigger group. It was cafeteria style. The crowd was excited. The returnees were happy to be back and have all the luxuries. The new people were overwhelmed with them. Seeing them on a video was a poor substitute for the real thing.

The crowd was in a jovial mood. Even Bismarck softened a little, and chatted pleasantly to the others at his table.

The big hit of the evening was the entry of Queen Victoria. She was actually wearing blue jeans, a sort of light shirt, and baseball cap. She shrugged her shoulders and said, "I would have changed, but the train just got to Union Station. I've been traveling to see more of this wonderful country. No matter what you see while you're here, just know it's the very tip of the iceberg. America is the most modern country in the world, and is capable of doing anything. After all, if you can send men to land on the moon, it tells you unbelievable things are coming to the members of the United Nations, of which Great Britain is proud to be a part."

President Gallagher came to the stage as the meal was ending. He welcomed all the newcomers and greeted the returnees warmly.

"As you know the opening session of the United Nations is the reason we are here. For the observer nations, this will be your chance to watch as we wrestle with the problems of peacekeeping in the halls of diplomacy. We consider this infinitely better than wasting the lives of your sons in a series of never-ending wars and tension. The members of the United Nations have pledged not to engage in any hostile action with any other member, but to bring grievances and disputes to Washington for resolution, or in the case of a lack of agreement to accept the arbitration of the United States, as a fair and neutral broker. You also know we're keeping our word of bringing the many improvements to your countries as a part of this United Nations charter. We now have over 100,000 men, engineers, and contractors in all your countries, working to establish the infrastructure for a better quality of life for all."

"For your information, we'd already been working on a new headquarters of the United Nations, even before your last visit. I'm happy to announce this is now complete and we will have our first session there beginning on Thursday morning. Please have your prepared matters of discussion turned in to my vice president Tony Carter before then."

"In the meantime, we have a few days to let the newcomers see some of the very things being built in member's countries right now. Tomorrow we will be travelling to one of our industrial sites to view what a complete complex looks like. We also want you to enjoy

Washington, so that will be on the schedule as well."

"One last item of business, in our initial organizational meeting, the delegates voted to extend the voting rights to all persons over the age of 21. I certainly hope you women have been doing your homework and getting educated on international politics and economics." With that, a large number of women stood up and cheered. Otto von Bismarck looked disgusted. Wilhelm pretended not to notice.

"Excellent," said Gallagher. "I'm sure you'll make a valuable addition to our discussions. Now before I stand aside and turn it over to the band, I am happy to introduce formally the vice president of the United States and my successor. I've served this country for 30 years. Tony Carter has served as my vice president for many years and is more than qualified to take over. He will be active in the debates this session." Carter, came to the stage, and bowed and waved. He received a healthy round of applause.

"Time to relax and enjoy yourselves," said Gallagher. "See you in the morning. The buses will pull out at 9 am."

Herbert brought Andrea Marie and her parents to the dinner, and they were the first on the dance floor. Gladstone thought they made a handsome couple.

The next morning, after a delicious breakfast, the big group got on buses. The smaller children and young people were excused from the work trip and were separated to spend a day at the National Zoo, and the new amusement park.

The convoy of buses pulled out and sped south toward Three Rivers. The visit was a repeat of the first time. They saw the huge steel mill, the power plants, the oil fields, and a tour of some of the assembly and construction buildings in a ring around the mill. One of the assembly plants was building heavy machinery to be used for putting down asphalt paving. There were ten of these machines in progress and as they walked along, they could see them in more and more completed condition. Outside a fleet of 20 machines was lined up in a huge yard and being prepared for transfer to the cargo ships for their journey to Europe. All the Europeans, new and old, just shook their heads at the amazing ingenuity of the work.

Part of the next day was devoted to seeing Washington. It was a beautiful city and the big group was broken into smaller groups to tour the Capitol, The White House, the Washington monument, and the Arcadia memorial. They also saw the National Museum and the Archives where the original Declaration of Independence and Constitution was housed.

The afternoon was open and all the women descended on the big Emporium and its companion exclusive shops with their magic badges. They wondered back to the resort and many of them tried the swimming pool or at least sat in the hot tub.

During the day President Gallagher, Vice-President Carter, and Arcadia were in Georgetown putting the finishing touches on their two-year plan, Carter had negotiated with the, soon to be former, Ottoman Empire, and the new country of Turkey.

Carter had completed several trips to Constantinople to consult and negotiate with other decision makers in the Empire. The leaders of the proposed new countries in the Balkans were also included. All them came to America to see what they were going to get. Meanwhile, an ever growing flood of goods, products, technology, and advanced medicine was flowing into Constantinople and people were getting very used to having electricity, indoor plumbing and especially air-conditioning. Every shipload made the original deal Carter had struck with Abdul Hamid I more secure. The now, much healthier Sultan, was regarded as a modern hero.

Super-secret deals were made with all the new countries, which would emerge from the stunning announcement planned for the session of the United Nations, by the Ottomans. Small, but effective governments were formed. These included Poland, Bulgaria, Romania, Serbia, Bosnia, Montenegro, Cyprus, Syria, and Kurdistan. Croatia and Dalmatia decided to join as one country with the name Croatia. The Greeks give up claims on Cyprus in return for the territory of Albania, and a number of disputed Aegean Islands. All ten new countries had delegations in Washington, ready for the UN assembly. Greece was already a member, and was ready to support the Ottoman proposal. The Ottomans were also present with a delegation representing the new country of Turkey with its proposed boundaries. All the delegations were told, in no uncertain terms, unless this secret agreement stayed secret, the United States would withhold large portions of trade.

"Well, Tony," said Gallagher, "this has been your baby for years. Are we ready?"

"The question, Chuck, is, will the existing members of the UN stand for this. A lot of them have been drooling over getting new territories from the Balkans. Now, in one fell swoop, you pull the rug out from under them."

"We've been adding workers in each country in which we have our big crews working to build power plants, railroads, highways, and telephones. The extra jobs are very important locally to people and they would certainly riot if their own government did something to take that work away. In addition, we are operating schools in small towns, which previously did not have one. It functions as a day care center, so both parents can work and double their income. The big powers in Europe can see the trap closing, but I hope they think of it as a snug nest."

"My experts tell me we have reduced the likely-hood of a major war in Europe in 40 years by 77 percent," said Arcadia, "these are the same experts who told me 50 years ago the chances of preventing World War I, were zero. However, we aren't out of the woods yet. The major European powers still have both practical and nationalistic reasons to continue colonialism. I guess that's a battle for another day. I will thank the Lord if we get through this session."

The morning of the official first session of the United Nations dawned and the delegates, men, and women boarded buses to the new headquarters building while the guide staff organized the kids into a daylong adventure.

The building was built as a dome with two wings of offices and conference rooms going off to the side. The entryway led to a ramp leading to the main chamber. There was a large silver screen in the center of the room with a podium for a speaker beneath. The delegates were organized in wide seats with desks in front of them, and the name of the country on a plate in front. Delegations were organized alphabetically in a ring facing the podium. The American delegation was in a row beneath the podium. The flags of all the countries were displayed to the left and right of the screen.

There was a row of windows at the top of the assembly seats, divided into cubicles. It was here the translators sat. The official languages were English, French, German, Italian, Spanish, and Russian. The delegates had headsets to listen to a speaker and hear the translation in his ears.

President Gallagher gaveled the session into order and made a stirring speech about the noble cause on which the great powers were embarked. He reviewed the progress American work teams were achieving in all the countries.

Then he threw the first punch. "Ladies and Gentlemen, I ask we suspend debate of our agenda, to hear a major proposal from the representative of the Ottoman Empire. It is my pleasure to introduce Madam Vivienne Anthrapokis"

Gallagher thought it was a stroke of genius on Tony's part to have the proposal introduced by a rather attractive woman. She was dressed in a colorful but demure gown that covered all her body. Her hair was done up in a swirling ring and was highlighted by a large broach that matched her necklace. Best of all, she spoke in English, so most of the delegates could understand her without the headset.

"Ladies and Gentlemen, a wise man once said if we do not learn from the past, we will be obliged to repeat it in the future. This is the conclusion the Ottoman Empire has made in presenting for your consideration the following proposal."

"For over 600 years the Ottoman Empire has ruled over a considerable portion of the earth. In the early centuries, we found our culture, and advanced technology appreciated by the less developed people under our umbrella. However, times have certainly changed more than ever in the past 50 years."

"We believe the time for a major reorganization in our sphere of influence has come. We no longer share a common culture or traditions with many of the people in what is known as the Balkans, and other parts of the Empire. Therefore, in consultation with the leaders of the various Slavic groups, we would like to announce the formation of new and independent nations who may seek their own futures as they desire."

On the big screen behind her, the revised map of the Ottoman Empire was revealed. The delegates leaned forward in their chairs in stark shock. The woman Vivienne paused for effect, than continued. In total, we propose 10 new sovereign nations. Actually it's 11 nations since the Ottoman Empire will be dissolved and replaced by our own home country, which we shall name Turkey."

"A delegation representing all these new nations is present in the assembly today and asks an opportunity to address you one by one to pledge their allegiance to the charter of the United Nations, and ask you to ratify their membership. We also ask you accept the country of Turkey with our amended borders as indicated on the map. Thank you for your attention and we hope this great new world organization will favorably receive our proposal."

She bowed politely and left the podium. Gallagher was at the microphone instantly, "The delegates can now understand why this business was presented first. It represents a major political breakthrough.

"Mr. President," said William Gladstone, "I suggest a recess so delegates may consult with one another in private on this rather remarkable proposal."

"We will reconvene after lunch, at 1 pm." With considerable, noise the delegates filed out of the room.

"Chuck, wait a minute," called out Gladstone, who was accompanied by Queen Victoria, "a moment of your time."

"Take all the time you need," said Gallagher, "Let's slip into the lounge."

Gallagher brought a fresh pot of coffee over and three cups. "OK, here we are. How did you like the show?"

"You aren't going to seriously tell me you didn't know about this," said Gladstone.

"This morning was the first time I'd ever heard of lady Vivienne, let alone meet her. However, you have to understand we trade globally and our traders and ambassadors are listening to new ideas all the time. The first I knew the complete details of this proposal was yesterday afternoon."

"I can't speak for William, or the government, for that matter," said Victoria, "but I think the Ottoman proposal is pure genius."

"It does fill a lot of holes, dash a lot of hopes, and confound the greedy, doesn't it?" said Gallagher.

"Is the United States going to support the membership of these new countries," asked Gladstone?

"Why not?" said Gallagher. "As long as they take the pledge before God to honor the charter and follow the rules, there's no more reason to exclude this bunch than there was to exclude Great Britain."

"It really does take an enormous pressure off us," said Gladstone. Bismarck is running around making all sorts of alliances. However, the alliances are all based on some kind of gain in the Balkans. If the Balkans are all countries of their own and voting members of the United Nations to boot, he is marginalized."

"Exactly, the great European powers might go to war with each other over another European country, but it will be a lot harder to get public support over a dispute of who owns South Africa," said Gallagher.

"Of course, none of the members of the United Nations are willing to start doing without the wonderful innovations pouring out of America," said Victoria.

"There is that," agreed Gallagher.

It became obvious after the General Assembly reconvened after lunch, considerable debate had occurred between the delegates, and most of them had concluded the Ottoman proposal was inevitable. The big worry was the Russians, but the delegates did not know Madame Vivienne had searched out the Russian Czar and told him effective immediately after the proposal was approved, the Russians would have access to passage through the Dardanelles. For them it was a huge concession and sealed the deal for them.

In fact, it was the Russian Czar, Alexander, who rose and asked to address the general assembly first. Gallagher recognized him. "Fellow members of the United Nations I rise to support the proposal of the Ottoman delegation and move, subject to verification, this body approve the question."

A female member of the Greek delegation seconded the motion. Debate began including an impassioned speech by Otto von Bismarck saying such a revolutionary alteration in the stability of Europe was a dangerous precedent with many unforeseen consequences.

Most of the women in the General Assembly could see it was crystal clear this would reduce tensions and make it less likely they would have to sacrifice their sons in war. They said so, one after another. The delegates were getting used to women speaking up, and pleasantly surprised to find them to be reasonable, well informed, and articulate.

The debate lasted for two hours before it came to the vote. In Georgetown, Arcadia and Tony Carter hugged each other, as the vote came in with overwhelming support.

Chapter 56
Growing Threats

The turn of the 20th Century was upon them. President Tony Carter, now 65 years old was on a teleconference call with Arcadia, and President-Elect Susan Moore.

Arcadia was saying, "In the 30 years since we established the United Nations, we have negotiated many disputes and in Europe, not a shot has been fired in anger. The United States has had to arbitrate only one quarrel. All the historians said it couldn't be done, but we have definitely prevented World War I, from happening. With no World War I, there won't be a second phase of that War in 1939, because Germany never falls into a depression, and Hitler will not get a foothold."

"The Europeans are enjoying their higher standard of living," said Susan. "They have a strong middle class and the prosperity they've enjoyed from drastically reducing their defense budgets allows them to function a lot more like we do. The smartest thing they've done is to copy our educational system. They have smart people over there and four times the population, so they are beginning to develop new products on their own, or at least reverse engineer our stuff."

"True enough, "said the President, "they have nearly enough steel mills to handle their own needs, which is good for us, we can concentrate more on helping other countries, and doing some things in America we have postponed. The Germans have specialized in building power plants, which they are now exporting. They have 90 percent of our efficiency, but that it because nobody is close to us in micro-circuitry, computers, and other electronics requiring such a high level of sophistication. The power plants are clean too; they are running on natural gas. The Russians have big pipelines crisscrossing Europe."

Arcadia nodded, "Just what we wanted. Each country is specializing in what they do best and trading freely with other countries. They have become so interdependent, cooperation and good will are the order of the day. They have highways, excellent public transportation, buried utilities lines, especially the electrical grid. Almost every home has electricity, running water, flush toilets, and a supporting sewer system not polluting their rivers and streams. We still have to do most of the heavy lifting since the recycling centers use computers and chemicals they still don't have. However, their telephone system is exploding. Everyone wants to talk to friends and relatives across the continent. Radio broadcasting is a big business and some of the big cities are trying to get television broadcasting up and running."

"Another big problem we can check off our list is the rise of Communism in Russia, "said Susan. It never got a chance to get up a head of steam when Alexander announced he was becoming a constitutional Monarch and let the people decide what kind of a country they wanted. We were pretty proud when they adopted our own Constitution almost word for word.

The world is starting to use a lot more oil," said Arcadia. "So the majority of oil exports come from the U.S., Russia, and Turkey. The smartest thing you did, Tony was to redraw the boundaries of the Middle East so Turkey got Iraq and Kuwait. The rest of the Middle East countries know they have a lot of oil, but without the technology to produce it, they are way behind. It's just too bad we have not been able to admit them to the United Nations because of their stubbornness to recognize women's rights. They go to a lot of trouble to stay isolated to keep their women from finding out they are getting a lousy deal. That is in our best interests too since it has not allowed the rise of radical Islamic factions. We have kept a hands off approach to interference of any kind in Muslim affairs and there are not a lot of things they can complain about, since we freely trade with them along with the rest of the world."

"That's not entirely true," said Susan. "Since I have been concentrating on world affairs in preparation for taking over when

Tony retires, and have studied the old timeline of history in the 20th century in depth, I see some problems."

"I'm sure not all-knowing," said Arcadia, "What are you seeing?"

"We have two major problems we are going to have to solve. One of them is the Persians in Iran. They are a Shia nation and deeply resent not being able to sell, their oil. They hold an historic resentment for Christians and Jews. They honestly believe the Quran tells them specifically to kill all of us if we won't voluntarily convert to Islam. They also are looking across the border at Turkey and coveting their oil reserves."

"The other problem we'll face in the next 20 years is our relationship to China and Japan. They have been the hardest in which to establish normal trading relationships, because of their isolationist policies and suspicion of western culture."

"I would imagine," said the President, "both of those are critical, the Muslim issues are not more important, just more imperative. Remember we own a large piece of real estate on the western coast of the Mediterranean, and have spent 30 years buying the land of the Palestinian owners and relocating them to Jordan. That project is now nearly complete. We've poured money and improvements into Jordan to give them the best quality of life in the Middle East, except for the Turks. Our latest numbers show a 90 percent approval rate by the Palestinians of the United States. We have managed not to antagonize them by keeping the number of Jews moving in, small and low key. Moreover, it's our land, and the Jews who live there are actually renters. The Jewish people in America understand the go slow process and how it will take a number of years before we are ready to hand the land over to them."

Tell me more about the threat from Iran," said Arcadia.

"If the Iranians decide to invade Turkey, it will be a violation of International Law, and in conflict with the Charter of the United Nations," said Susan. "We have flooded Iran with Farsi speaking spies who physically resemble the Persians. They own businesses, shops and work in the government. We will know it in advance if the rhetoric of the Iranians turns to violence. Then we might find ourselves with a mandate from the General Assembly for the use of the Rangers. All our spies are actually Rangers in disguise."

"Can we move to something a little less gloomy?" asked the President. "Like how I have labored like a galley slave for almost 30 years, with almost no thanks for the amazing things we have accomplished."

Both Arcadia and Susan laughed, tickled and hugged Carter at the same time. He pretended to be severely wounded and ended up laughing and hugging the girls back.

"Oh Tony, "said Arcadia, "you are such a goofball. You know perfectly well how much we both love you, and how often we say you'll go down in history as one of the best!"

"That's better," said Tony, "I just wanted to keep the record straight."

"Speaking of grandiose," said Arcadia, "I haven't heard lately about your big and expensive project to bring oil and natural gas down from Alaska without poisoning all the caribou."

"Ah, the Main Line," said Tony. "You will be happy to hear the pipeline is finished. We ran it through the oil sand lands in Alberta and built a really giant refinery out in the middle of nowhere. The fracking systems plus the crude oil makes for a gusher of oil. We pre-refine a lot of it on-site in good weather and send it through a bigger pipeline to a warmer weather refinery site in Chihuahua, and then store most of it in those huge caves we discovered down there."

"I'm very glad you wanted to put a higher priority on the space program," said the President. As it turned out, that program is resulting in some astounding breakthroughs in technology."

"Necessity is the Mother of Invention," said Arcadia.

"Well, it worked," said Tony. "We've developed a system to mass produce really compact circuit boards. They're going into all the new laptops and a dozen other places along assembly lines and the like. Best of all, those mother boards have lowered the mass and size of the packages we are lifting into orbit. We've replaced all the original communications satellites. We did bring one back in a shuttle to make sure we hadn't missed anything in the 2030 model, turns out, we had. However, our new micro-processors are better than yours."

"They were last year's models, anyway," commented Arcadia.

"What's the name of that guy they call 'The Invention Machine'?"

"Franklin," said Arcadia.

"Really. Any family history there?"

"Nope."

"Anyway, Franklin turns out technology before we know how to use it. However, his new laser bore got immediate attention. His super laser can iris down to as small as a pencil and open up to as big as a house. Boy, does it cut, and it seals the edges of the hole stronger than before we started. We started out using it to cut new subway lines in the cities without subways. Then we got the idea to see if we could cut a really long tube. Franklin wanted to know what it was for and we said we wanted a high-speed underground train. You know what he did. He made a modification in the design and the laser bores left tracks at the bottom of the shaft, smooth as glass and very strong. We can even run a current through the tracks. Voile', we have an instant, high speed underground train."

"Obviously we aren't in much of a hurry to share all these goodies with the rest of the world," said Susan. "In fact, I am employing a hundred people in a special department to assess the level of development for every country we do business with, both imports and exports. The trick is to keep it fair. Not all nations need the basic infrastructure systems. They either are producing it themselves, or have a completed system. The rage right now is communications, meaning basic telephones, radios and a few television services for the bigger cities. The network idea hasn't occurred to them yet. We provide a long list of useful consumer products, but we have to think a long time before we make a major jump. The microwave oven, for example, will change the society, so we haven't given it to them yet."

"The main problem, as you know, is finding things a country can use as exports to cut the cost of their imports. The main things we need are the exotic metals, like titanium. We have good supplies of it in North America, but Norway is also a good source, as is Russia and Australia. They have no idea why we want shiploads of seemingly worthless rocks, but they don't care. They are happy to supply it. Since all of those countries are part of the United Nations and get 'Most Favored Trade' status, it works out profitably for both sides."

"We still export about five times as much as we import. We extend credit when we have a small or underdeveloped country, giving loans to their banks at low interest rates. We use the trade system to manage the world economy. Tony didn't have a single recession in his entire career."

"I haven't asked lately," said Arcadia, "what is our financial position?"

"Our flat tax has been steady at 10% for 30 years. It brings in enough money to fund the government, the Rangers, all our research, the schools, and most of the space program. Our balance of trade excess from other countries is as big as our tax income. Last year we ran a $500 million dollar surplus. We are currently holding about 700 tons of gold and silver and close to a trillion dollars in diamonds. Money is not a problem."

"You two take this for granted because you have never known anything else," said Arcadia. "In my time the dedication to the will of God was a relatively new thing. Our country gave lip service to religion, but didn't really believe. Then the Lord gave us the Park, and all the animals ran free. It produced a religious revival that changed our lives."

"When the few hundred of us came back to 1770, all were very strong Christians. The attitude of the times, more or less matched our strong beliefs and we used our influence to make sure the country stayed that way. Neither of you would even think about working on Sunday. Except for the most vital services, which we can't automate, the whole country is closed on the Sabbath. We all spend the day being thankful to God for our many blessings. We are well and truly, a Christian country and the whole world knows it. One of reasons we get along so well with the Muslim populations within the United Nations is we practice what we preach. We are kind, honest, loving, generous, and fair. When we talk to Muslim nations, we emphasize our devotion to Allah, the same God they have. The fact we believe Jesus is our savior and the one who has given us the promise of eternal life through his sacrifice on the cross to forgive our sins, is not emphasized to the Muslims. The populations of Islam in Turkey, India, Bosnia, and some of the African nations who have accepted the United Nations statement all people are created equal and extended equality to women, seems like a small price to pay for our continuing generosity and good will. We are very careful about choosing our presidents, and they generally serve for a long time. Susan here was picked from thousands of candidates. I'm very glad the person at the top of the pile this time is a woman. It reinforces our position in the United Nations and encourages other nations to do the same"

"We are still a very private country," continued Arcadia. Even though we now have a population of nearly 200 million, it doesn't travel internationally very much. Once they come in, they seldom go out. This is partly because we have limited international air travel to official business; however, it is also because of the absolutely superior life they live in America. They are not going to rub their good fortune in the faces of friends and family. The screening process we employ for our immigrants only solicits the best a country has to offer. However, even this is fair and open-handed. We have no less than a million Muslims in the United States. It balances out because we have a large number of Jews in the country. Of course, we are going export most of them to Israel when the time comes, but so far, the neighboring Muslim countries have not made that connection. We own the land that is Israel and Lebanon. The fact the population grows every year is viewed as Americans moving in, not Jews."

Tony and Susan remained quiet throughout the remarks. Arcadia did not give speeches very often and the two were happy to sit quietly while she covered a range of subjects. They always contained information helping the chief executives set the agenda for their administration. Both of them would agree the real Arcadia was just as wonderful and inspirational as the carved, marble image of her in the memorial at the end of the reflecting pool on the mall. Arcadia herself didn't bother to hide out in her Georgetown mansion anymore. Nobody really recognized her.

The General Assembly of the United Nations was in session. It now was meeting for three weeks every six months. The delegates from the 47 member nations figured out the main business for the body usually took about a week, and meant they and their family had a couple of weeks to visit and explore the huge country of America. They would scatter and go off on some new adventure

This was not the case for every delegation. Invariably there would be several countries, which had disputes to hash out, or wanted to talk with the President directly about some pressing need. President Moore was always busy throughout the General Assembly.

However, this General Assembly was different. Turkey was deeply concerned about a possible invasion in the south, near the province of Kuwait, by Iran. There was a considerable troop build-up along the already heavily fortified border. Of course, this was not news to the United States. Three spy satellites watched Iran for months and could see what was going on. The spy network had buzzed for a year.

President Moore took the podium and provided the Assembly with the grim facts. "The basic situation is this. Iran has gotten plans for a steel mill and is turning out heavy weapons, mostly artillery, but also some fairly sophisticated mobile artillery and heavy armored tanks.

"They also have armed their troops with the latest model of rifle available in the world and sold commercially. Their soldiers are equipped with helmets, knives, some hand grenades, and can carry up to 200 rounds of ammunition. Perhaps most ominously of all, their army is over a million men. They have moved toward the border with Turkey for three weeks and our estimates are they will be able to launch an offensive in less than a month. We believe this is what they intend. Their newspapers and radio are filled with propaganda they are on a Holy Jihad, to crush the Turkish heretics, who have turned away from the true faith. They further swear they will sweep across the whole of the Middle East and capture all the oil reserves. They say their Syrian allies are ready to attack our property in old Judea, Samaria, and Lebanon, and slaughter all the American Jews who happen to be there."

"My fellow delegates," said the President, "This is the very thing we have worked ceaselessly for 130 years to prevent. The world is at peace, secure, prosperous, and happy because the threat of war is banished from our lives. Now we have a country who claims to have the right to attack us on the basis of Religion. In this body, we have Christians, Muslims, Hindus, Buddhists, and Jews, all living in peaceful co-existence. Does Iran believe their own narrowly interpreted view of our Creator is the only correct vision of God?"

From the assembly, someone called out," Tell them the Rangers Are Coming!"

President Moore cried back, "The United States is neutral. We cannot invade another country, no matter the provocation."

The delegate from England stood and Moore recognized him. "Madam President, does not the charter of the United Nations say if the peace of our countries was threatened, we would be able to command the Rangers to face any threat in the manner determined by a vote of 60 percent of the delegates."

"It's true the Rangers may be ordered into action by a super-majority of this body. Exactly what do you want the Rangers to do?

"Destroy the threat!"

"Wipe out their Army!"

"Bring Iran to its knees!"

"Kill all the Persians!"

That was just a sample of what Susan Moore heard. "We will not mindlessly kill innocent non-combatants, including women and children, "she said. " If it is the will of the General Assembly, and the vote must be unanimous, the Rangers will repel the attack at the border, destroy Iran's capability to rearm and attack again in the future, and force their surrender. The United Nations may demand reparations of Iran by confiscating all their oil production for a period to be determined by the Executive Committee when the operation has been completed."

"Madam President," said the Turkish delegate, "I move your plan be adopted by the United Nations!" There were half a dozen seconds from around the room.

"Very well," said President Moore, "will any country with a dissenting vote please stand.

Everyone looked around the room. President Moore said simply, "Consider well, my fellow delegates, the carnage will be more terrible than you can imagine."

No delegate rose to his feet.

Moore said, "May God have mercy on those who are about to die."

Two weeks later, General Compton, the Commander of all the Rangers was on a video conference call with Arcadia. "After the United Nations vote, we started moving all the heavy weapons. We now have Humvees, Bradley's, and our Artillery on the ground in Basra, which we are using as the headquarters and staging area. The Black Hawks and the Huey's were broken down and loaded into C-130's. The Chinooks are hopping across the Atlantic with extra fuel tanks aboard. The troops will come last in the 130's. It will take a week to move all three brigades. The entire command will be in place and operational in 24 days. During the past several years, we've built more Humvees, Bradley's and three more batteries of 105 howitzers. We have a hundred bunker buster bombs available for use. They have a yield of 100 kilotons. When the entire force is ready, we'll have 25 Blackhawks with two mini-guns each, firing 3,000 rounds per minute. They also launch Rimfire missiles. We have 40 Huey's all with mini-guns. We are moving our entire arsenal of drones. We have several hundred of them. Our basic tactic will be vertical envelopment using company-sized forces from Chinooks and working in close cover with the Black Hawks and Huey's. Artillery will engage at 10 miles and begin walking through the main force toward the envelopment firebases."

"We estimate the Iranians will attack along this route," he put it up on the screen "we believe they will march along a 20 mile front with 20 motorized divisions. They expect to use their artillery in advance of their ground assault, but we will use our own artillery to neutralize them before ground troops begin their assault. I'm positive the Iranians have no idea they are walking into a trap."

"When the retreat begins we flank their army in a pincher and link up at the center. We then wipe out their forces and follow up with airstrikes on their entire military infrastructure located around the country."

"I wish I could say I understood everything you said General," said the President, "I'm sure Arcadia took it all in. The only question I have is this, if the Iranians really send a million men across the border, how many will be killed?"

"Practically all of them," said Compton.

"Oh God," said Susan.

"We've been pleading with the Iranians for a month to call off their invasion and have told them their losses will be horrendous," said Arcadia. "They just don't believe us."

"We'll record a complete record of this operation from the beginning to the bitter end. It will be shown on television worldwide. We think it will be very instructive to help people understand how terrible war actually is."

"Not to mention bringing home the line 'The Rangers Are Coming' to graphic reality," said the President.

Chapter 57
Unity and Purpose

Washington, D.C., 1905

Video receivers were on all over the United States to see the Ranger operation in Iran. Nobody had ever seen the Rangers in action. The same was true for the rest of the world. The Rangers had a mystique and a reputation, but none of the countries of the United Nations, who ordered the Rangers to battle, had ever seen them.

Arcadia and President Moore made live, real time coverage available for every country in the world. Most of the population would see it, and the leaders certainly would.

Kaiser Wilhelm II and his senior military staff were grouped around a large, LED screen showing very clear high definition pictures. They watched as the massive Iranian army poured across the border into Turkey. Wilhelm's practiced eye told him there were at least twenty divisions in the initial assault. He wondered where the Iranian artillery was. He got his answer as the scene shifted to the masses of artillery batteries behind the lines in Iran. Suddenly they begin to blow up. Wilhelm could not see the source of the fire, but it was devastatingly effective. The advance Iranian divisions were on their own.

Suddenly Black Hawk gun ships were flying along the Iranian line spreading death. Ranger artillery opened up. The rounds did not hit the ground, but burst above the Iranians mowing them down by the thousands.

Humvees and Bradley Fighting Vehicles moved into the thickest concentrations of Iranians and left the battleground littered with bodies.

Iranian troops who were still in formation suddenly found themselves surrounded by Chinook helicopters from which Rangers flew out and closed with the Iranians. Their weapons were deadly in the hands of the camouflaged Rangers. They moved with astonishing speed.

The gunships, artillery, and clusters of Chinooks with companies of Rangers repeated the maneuvers over and over. In some cases, the Rangers fought hand to hand with the Iranians. They were all short bloody fights with the Rangers performing complex personal movements almost faster than the eye could follow.

The slaughter went on for a week. The Rangers literally wiped out the lead divisions and were now carrying the fight into the Iranian rear and all the waiting divisions. The pictures cut away now and then to see gunships and strange looking flying craft, using rockets and bombs destroy the factories where the arms were built. A dozen Chinooks flew in from high altitude, over the steel mills and the big military complexes and dropped bombs that were the biggest explosions anyone in the world had ever seen. Destruction spread out from these explosions for nearly a mile.

In three days, there was nothing left for the Rangers to fight. The Iranians used their radio stations to signal they were surrendering and for the death to stop. General Compton ordered an immediate ceasefire.

Over the next month, the Rangers planted millions of mines across the access to the main Iranian oil fields and pumping stations

An Iranian secretary of one of the departments, the only living senior official in the entire government, met with General Compton and heard the surrender terms. The United Nations would supply humanitarian aid to keep the civilian population from starving. The army and all military installations were disbanded and closed. The curtain of steel surrounding the oil fields would be monitored. Any person coming into the field would be killed. All of Iran's oil reserves were confiscated by the United Nations and used to provide reparations for the damage caused by the Iranians to Turkey and to the Ranger force, for a period of ten years. Moreover, the Iranians would be required to clear the battlefield and dispose of all the bodies.

The entire world watched and saw the most lethal military force in history. The devastation, firepower, and destruction the Rangers could inflict was now a known fact. The personal effectiveness and precision in which the individual Rangers could function became the stuff of legends.

The final tally turned out to be a death toll for the Iranians of approximately 1 million men and all their equipment. The Rangers lost 150 dead and 275 wounded.

For the Iranians, the strangest thing of all was a huge cadre of men and machinery moving into Iran and constructing an airport and a highway all the way from Basra to Tehran. When the construction was finished, thousands of American citizens poured into Iran with food, clean water, medical supplies, and doctors. They all wore armbands with a Red Cross on it. The only Farsi they could speak was *"Please, Thank You, How can I help, and We are sorry for your loss"* When they were asked why they were doing this, the answer was always the same, "Allah has commanded us to render aid, treat you with kindness, and respect." A great many of the first responders were women and did not hesitate to tell the Iranian women the conditions under which a majority of the women in other countries lived.

The Americans rebuilt the destroyed government buildings. They constructed two new very large power plants. A pipeline of natural gas was tapped in the oil fields and brought in to power the plants.

It took two years to complete the work, and to the credit of the Iranians, not a single American was ever attacked or abused, despite the fact the Ayatollahs screamed the American invaders should be killed and thrown out of the country. The public could clearly see the Americans were not invaders, but angels of mercy. The power of the clergy was broken and the resulting secular government that took charge made it clear the clergy's job from now on was to tend to the religious needs of the people and stay out of the government.

When the work was completed, the Americans left without ceremony or fanfares. However, they'd made many friends and the country was clearly better because of their efforts. Crowds cheered them as they departed

The United States returned to the quiet neutrality marking their existence since 1770. There was one very large outcome to the relief effort the Americans had done in Iran. Other countries, struggling to pull themselves out of poverty, disease, and a lack of modern improvements, began to ask the United States for a repeat of the humanitarian effort accomplished in Iran. President Moore talked it over with the American people and a referendum was held to find out if there was an interest in doing this. It represented a kind of violation of the neutrality stitched into the minds of all 200 million citizens from the Panama Canal to Dutch Harbor in Alaska, so it was not a matter to be approached lightly.

Susan Moore consulted Arcadia on the subject. "I did the Iranian relief effort for entirely different reasons," she said, "it was just one more way to keep Islamic Terrorism from getting a place to start. It frankly never occurred to me it would produce an outcry from third world countries for aid."

"It's not without precedent, you know," said Arcadia. "Somewhere in your old world history books you must have run across an effort by an American President to do exactly what is being asked. It was called the Peace Corps and it was a stunning success from the beginning. We would just give it a lot more firepower."

The referendum by the voters of the United States was overwhelmingly in favor of establishing a Peace Corps.

The President took the proposal to the next meeting of the General Assembly of the United Nations, now 88 nations strong. The United Nations was a true force in the affairs and politics of the world. With the partnership of the United States and the clear means of backing up their decisions, national governments routinely came to the United Nations to solve disputes and to referee issues when one country had a problem with another country. The final arbitration by the United States was seldom employed. There were few countries or people willing to go back to the chaos of the previous century. The United Nations was perfectly happy to continue into the future with the stability of America's steady grip.

The General Assembly considered what to do with that part of the world thus far beyond their reach, The Pacific Rim, principally, China, Japan, Korea, and Southeast Asia, minus Burma and Thailand, who had joined the United Nations. The hands-off policy adopted by the European countries beginning in the 1870's, toward other countries left a huge vacuum in China and Korea. They were mostly isolationist themselves. China was still ruled by an Emperor, as was Japan with a strong group of Shoguns, or feudal lords, which fought ceaselessly with each other. They had sailed into the 20th century with big populations of very poor people and a ruling class that liked it that way. The only nationalism China had contemplated was a massive invasion of Russia. All thoughts of that dissolved when the Chinese watched the Rangers in action in Iran. Of course, they never disclosed such a plan was being deliberated.

When the United States proposed a Peace Corps to render aid and assistance to poor countries, and asked if they could expect some help from other modern countries in their noble effort, the General Assembly approved the plan on the spot, put the United States in charge of implementing the details and recruiting volunteers.

Susan Moore was pleasantly surprised at the large number of people from other countries who signed up to help. With the help of a staff of experts, some of which were Arcadia's, she started mapping out a plan of training, logistics, and decisions on what should be provided to each country, based on their needs.

Arcadia cautioned restraint, "Be careful what you give these people. They aren't ready for computers, cell phones, and video players. I would send in an advance team with leaders from their country and inventory their needs. That's what you provide. Make sure not to do the work for them. Work with them. When some fellow comes up with an idea, things would be better if his people had such and such, that's when you make it available. Small steps. Don't give them a tractor when what they need first is a good shovel,"

The initial advance teams went out to the countries who had asked for assistance. Arcadia breathed a sigh of relief when China and Japan joined the group. It was only 1920, plenty of time for everything to go wrong.

There were 50,000 volunteers, willing to donate two years plus of time, from countries outside the U.S. Arcadia was happy to see a nice contingent of Iranians. They started shipping them over in converted cargo carriers with 3,000 passengers per ship.

In the United States over 150,000 people volunteered. They carved out a space for a big camp in Nevada. It was pretty barren, but close to water, power, and one of the big underground shuttles. They threw up clusters of Quonsets' big and small for quarters and services, and the training began. Everyday more people arrived and soon the Peace Corps camp was a bustling enterprise.

Within a month, teams were heading out to some of the most remote places on earth. The Chinese contingent was actually going to be ten teams scattered out over a hundred square miles in the province of Guilin in the south. Chinese officials did a good job of clearing away the bureaucratic underbrush, so the flow of supplies and equipment could flow freely. The farmers had irrigated their terraces of crops in the same manner for generations. It was a system that worked. However, the team set up one of the small, mobile power plants, capable of providing enough power for a village of 300. They replaced the bicycle type pumping machines run by hand with a rotary wheel, filled with large scoops and running all by themselves, the farmers stopped resenting the encroachment of their time-tested ways and embraced the new technology. Soon the village was a veritable beehive of industry and innovation. When the time came for the harvest, the yield was three times the average. Similar results were achieved in adjacent villages.

The Peace Corps movement gained steam. The Europeans, who once competed for colonies to dominate and exploit, now competed to see how much good they could accomplish in underdeveloped countries. The explosions were in China, Japan, and Korea. Peace Corps teams from all over the world flooded those countries. The practical, pragmatic Chinese government had never been influenced by Communism and raw socialism, since it had never developed in Russia or other countries. It was very hard for them to object to clear progress in all areas of their lives, despite the fact it came from foreigners.

They learned fast and among the first things they found out when they stuck their heads out the holes they had been hiding in for centuries was the fact of the United States of America. They learned this country, the biggest in the world, had been neutral for nearly 300 years and had developed a society with wonders beyond the most impressive dreams imaginable. They learned America freely traded these wonders, fairly, with any country wanting it. The prices of these commodities were reasonable to a fault. They learned America only asked in return the materials, natural resources, and products, which were in abundance within the borders of the trading country. America never interfered with the internal politics of any country.

One of the most notable characteristics of the Americans was their unshakable faith in God. Simply by using good examples and applying love to all situations, the Americans found themselves planting churches all over the Pacific Rim.

Arcadia could hardly believe the rate at which the Chinese embraced Christianity. Once, the movement started, it grew so quickly the Chinese started sending observer delegations to the United Nations. President Moore made sure the delegations were quite large and included the most influential people in China. They got much the same treatment as the Europeans had received 50 years before, and the effect was equally as profound.

When the Chinese experienced the totality of the American society and its endless marvels, they realized how far behind they were. After an intensive month of observation, travel, mixing with the ordinary people, visiting the centers of research and development and seeing how all of this was applied to a steep curve of progress, the Premier of China asked for a private meeting with the President Moore.

Susan Moore expected this request, and anticipated the nature of the agenda the Premier had in mind. It amounted to, "How can we acquire all you have, and how much will it cost?"

The Premiere came into the Oval office and bowed low before the President. She was already around her desk and interrupted the Premier in mid-bow, instead shaking hands with him and smiling, "I realize your bow is a sign of respect and gives me honor, but it is more than I require. I much prefer we speak with one another as equals. Please be seated and we shall have some tea."

The President poured the tea with her own hands, and then sat down. At 57 years old, she was still a strikingly beautiful woman. Her lifetime of public service and 25 years as President gave her a gravitas that was palpable.

"Why don't you just tell me what you want for the Chinese people?"

The Premier was very impressed with the insight and directness of President Moore, and said, "I believe I should ask, how much of your astonishing world can be acquired by China?"

"An excellent question," said Moore, "We have many, many years of experience in delivering improvements to the quality of life of the world's people. It has been our practice to provide assistance to people only at the rate in which they can understand and apply it to their lives on a daily basis. We could certainly transform all of China into a duplicate of America, but the shock is simply more than your people can absorb. We did not achieve all you have seen overnight. We had to take small steps to allow our own people to grow accustomed to some new innovation. It will be the same for you."

"That sounds very wise to me," said the Premier. "The question I have is what do you expect from us?"

"What do you expect for yourself," countered Moore?

"Your counsel, your advice, and your wisdom on how China can assume a place of respect in the world."

"If that is the case, let me show you the standard which the majority of the world regards as the proper position of their country in the family of nations." She pushed a button on a controller. A Chinese women came on the screen and used a pointer to highlight the charter of the United Nations. She explained in detail what each point meant in the daily life of a country. At the core of the charter was that the Creator had given each person certain inalienable rights, which must be respected by each government. She talked about a government only having power at the consent of the people. She explained what this meant in real terms for the citizens of the whole country, including universal suffrage. She concluded her presentation by enumerating what the people should expect in the Bill of Rights.

"I must admit the Chinese form of government is authoritative in nature. Moving to a system like this would take a long time, indeed," said the Premier.

"Do you find our Peace Corps teams are making a material improvement in the morale, productivity, and quality of life of your people," asked the President?

"There's no question about it. The phenomenon has the entire government talking.

"If that is the case," said Moore, "then may I respectfully suggest your upper class requires an adjustment in their attitudes. You see,

Premier, our trade of advanced products and technology improves the entire country. It's like the principle of rising water raising all ships. You're going to start having real problems with your working class if they are being significantly more productive, but the government still takes the same share as always. The people will reasonably say, 'you had no part in our increases, why should we not keep more of what we have earned?'"

"We already are," said the Premier.

"If that is the case and you wish to stop it and go back to the way things were, then we will remove all our Peace Corps volunteers from your country."

The Premier of China left the Oval office a very confused and frustrated man. It was much the same for Japan.

Another year went by. The President let some selected technology and modern products slip into China. It only made the government's position more untenable. A very big shake-up occurred in the upper ranks of the Empire. The old leaders were replaced by younger, more practical men, who had spent a considerable time in America. Their attitudes were simply they actually had nothing to fear from a vibrant and active middle class. They saw it as a way of increasing revenues without arbitrarily raising taxes. Meanwhile, the Peace Corps teams were penetrating all the strata's of life throughout the country.

The great triumph of Susan's Moore's presidency, as far as she was concerned was the day both China and Japan applied for membership in the United Nations. It had taken a lot of soul searching, and there was bloodshed in some of the top ranks of the most independent provinces, but the reformers prevailed. Some of them had become Christians, saying the teachings of Confucius led to that kind of outlook on life all the time.

The enterprising Chinese spotted, what they thought, was the secret to America's success...the schools. They were right. With 300 years of bringing in students demanding they think for themselves, and knowledge was not an end to itself, without innovation and growth added to the total body of wisdom, the schools thrived. Students were tested continuously as the educators looked for the areas in which the young people could make a contribution to the total society. There were now over 2000 universities and all of them had advanced research centers attached to them. The gifted students went right to the place where they could make the biggest impact.

Arcadia's goal was always to stay at least 100 years ahead of the rest of the world. The schools exceeded that standard in a great number of areas. Medicine was one of the greatest triumphs. No longer were the physicians who had come from the future the teachers. They were now the students. The DNA genome was manipulated to prevent birth defects, Down's syndrome, Alzheimer's disease and a dozen other diseases and conditions. Transplants of every organ was routine. The cure for cancer was discovered, and grafting of limbs was a standard. Moreover, the life expectancy of the normal human shot up to over 100 years old.

The soul of the country was its dedication to seeking to live lives as close to a life of Faith as possible. Of course, there was still sin and behaviors God would never honor, but people worked at it. The Peace Corps teams were always respected in whatever society in which they were placed because of their pure love, patience, and sincere giving hearts.

The result of this was that the world's religions lived in harmony with one another. Each was tolerant of the differences and every person was free to exercise their expression of faith in whatever fashion was right for them.

Very quietly, the U.S. worked diligently on their space program. There were now enough communications satellites in orbit to handle whatever load might come in the future. Every American had an advanced cell phone. A substantial space station was constructed and used to build a band of solar receivers, which increasingly beamed power to the surface connected to the vast electrical grid built over the past 100 years. The Europeans noticed it first when the amount of natural gas needed to run the power plants dropped to zero.

Computers were now compact tablets, which connected to a number of public websites containing any kind of information anyone could want, transferred to other computers or printed out through the 3D, super high definition, LED screens of all sizes in every home. The keyboards on the tablets appeared whenever they were needed.

The United Nations was only 105 members. The trend for countries deciding their ethnic and cultural differences were not that significant, particularly when a larger country was able to make a better trading relationship with the United States, created fewer states. The organization was much superior than the one from Arcadia's time. It confined its business to resolving conflicts, keeping accurate records on the state of every nation in terms of health, wealth, quality of life, and overall satisfaction of the people. It had an Executive Council dealing with bigger issues, but membership was rotated between all the countries and nobody had a blanket veto.

Susan Moore stepped down in 1925, after 30 years of service as President. Unfortunately, the man who stepped into the Presidency was killed in a freak boating accident just a year later, and the process of selecting a vice president was still incomplete. Congress approved a compromise candidate named Tom Wilkinson. Arcadia had her doubts about him from the start. He lacked the discipline of previous Presidents. He increased the size of the Federal government and began issuing Executive Orders running contrary to the minds of the citizens who were accustomed to the government serving as a partner rather than an organization complicating people's lives unnecessarily. He lasted just one term. By that time Arcadia had picked five people who she thought were outstanding and started an intensive course in training. She made her choice of a brilliant, sensitive, thoroughly Christian man whose name was Arthur Curtis. His tribal name was translated as "Man on the Mountain" and he was a Lakota Sioux.

Curtis took office in 1936. His first actions were to reduce the size of government, and rescind all of the Executive Orders of his predecessor. He also took a hard look at the current fiscal health of the nation and wisely declared a tax holiday for the next year, the third such time that had happened. His popularity soared long enough for the country to realize what an outstanding President he actually was. He and Arcadia were great friends. She visited 'Art' at the White House often. No one ever suspected her true identity. They liked each other's company.

Curtis was the President who got to announce in a meeting of the U.N. General Assembly the completion of the solar band and tell all the countries of the world a simple antenna, tuned to the right frequency would interface with the electrical grids and gas operated Power Plants were no longer necessary. This came as something of a shock to most of the world. America had built the solar band from trading profits over a period of 40 years. Now, almost free power was available to the entire world. A very small surtax was added to the cost of outgoing trade from the U.S. and this maintained the Solar Band, making improvements, and repairs as needed. Nobody complained.

His second big achievement was to announce the nearly 15 million Jews who lived in the land America owned in the Middle East, had petitioned for self-government and membership in the United Nations. Not even the Syrians or Iranians objected.

America started to unload a good deal of its backlog of modern technology to the world. Curtis was careful to hold on to some of the more exotic developments, but the world didn't really notice. They were busy soaking up the improvements for their own countries, and life became very pleasant, indeed.

The world population was actually decreasing. The need for big families to maintain farms and do work was eliminated and most families were having only one or two children. In many cases, they had none at all. By 1950, the population of the earth hovered just below 5 billion. The populations of China and India fell to under 750 million each, owing to a concentrated policy of encouraging birth control.

It became fashionable for the United Nations to initiate projects involving the whole world. These were things everyone could support and receive the fruits of the labor. One of the "Global Projects" involved weather control. It turned out to be possible after all. The scientists erected entire fields of giant ionizers to generate waves of negative ions, which rose into the lower atmosphere and attracted dust particles. The dust particles, in turn, attracted condensation from the ambient air, and when enough condensation was achieved, the clouds couldn't hold the water anymore and a downpour of rain was unleashed.

The first practical application of the principal was in the Sahara Desert. In a few years, enough rain was falling every year to turn that enormous barren wasteland into a rapidly growing number of vast farms. It worked the other way too. The Americans set up ionizers that produced a counter storm near tornadoes and hurricanes and caused them to dissipate. This reduced damage and loss of life that had been a way of life for the east coast and Caribbean, and for Tornado Alley in the Midwest.

Buoyed by their success and public approval with weather, the United Nations became fascinated with space travel. The U.S. had a huge foothold in space and used it to expand the space station extensively. From it, regular missions to the moon were started and a permanent colony was established there. In 1956, the combined scientists of Earth built a vehicle to go to Mars. With a crew of eight, the roundtrip took three years. The whole world followed the flight, landing, and exploration of Mars and the return flight like it was a television series. Every week planet Earth tuned into the Mars program. It was the most popular program on television.

In 1976, Arthur Curtis stepped down after 40 years in office. He was a very healthy 75 years old. His replacement was 35-year-old Thomas Frost and he served longer as President than any of his predecessors, owing to a rapidly expanding life expectancy, there was nothing odd about him serving into his 80's. His Presidency lasted for 50 years, and was considered the Golden Age of America specifically and the world in general.

The major accomplishments for Frost was to see the moon colony top 100,000 people and the colony on Mars grow to 10,000 people. Missions were sent to the Jovian moons and the think tanks in America announced they were working on a radical new propulsion system that could send ships from Earth to far planets at multiples of light speed.

Another major step by Frost, in cooperation with the United Nations and the approval of the United States was to make the Ranger force an international police force. The expanded Ranger force recruited from many nations using the same rigorous standards the Rangers had always maintained, and set them up in scattered locations, never more than an hour from any place on Earth. Their installations were off limits to the public since the Rangers were now using technology far advanced over anything in the world. They were just as efficient and lethal as some factions learned, but were loved universally by all people. Being a Ranger was the most prestigious profession to which a man or woman could aspire.

Chapter 58
The Circle Closes

<u>Georgetown, 2016</u>

Arcadia had not been active in the process of selecting new Presidents for many years. It was a nearly seamless system promoting the best and brightest to the Office of Chief Executive. So, she was not surprised when Thomas Frost came to her Georgetown home with the choice for his replacement some ten years before his expected retirement in 2026.

"I'm happy to say I have chosen my successor."

"I suppose you intend to appoint this person as vice-president at the next election?"

"I do, and I'm looking forward a great deal to seeing his face when he meets you and the secret of our masquerade is revealed. I recall my shock very vividly."

"These days we are doing a lot more revealing of history which didn't happen, then an uncertain future we faced with fear and indefinite outcomes. Who is this lucky guy?"

"His name is Max Portner."

There was only the sound of Arcadia's teacup as it fell to the floor.

"Something wrong?" asked Frost.

Arcadia put both hands to her face, "I'm incredibly stupid."

"I beg your pardon?"

"You do remember thirty years ago when the Lord caused Isaiah's prophesy to come true, and the Animal Park in Missouri came to be?"

"You mean, the Holy Park? Yes, of course. The whole country, indeed the whole world regarded this miracle as a gift of God. The very idea a place would appear where the lion would lay down with the lamb was overwhelming. Suddenly we had a thousand acre park, filled with animals of all types, living in peaceful co-existence with one another. It's the number one attraction in the world. The lottery for tickets to visit, are the most prized possessions anyone can receive."

"I should have realized the Lord was telling me my journey is coming to an end. It's been so long since I thought of it, I wasn't listening."

"I'm sorry, Arcadia. I'm lost."

"No doubt it will come as a shock to you, but I grew up in the Park."

Now it was the turn of the President to be without words. He stammered and finally said, "Your personal history is one of America's enduring mysteries. Are you telling me you actually know the Park on a personal basis?"

"Born and raised there, Thomas. My mother and father did or do own the Park."

The President processed what he was hearing for several moments and then said, "Where does Max Portner fit into this?"

"Max was a good family friend and president of the country when we were bombed. The only reason he survived the blast in Washington was because he happened to be in Branson with us at the time."

"After all these years, I didn't think it was possible for anything to surprise me. What are you going to do?"

"I wish I knew." Arcadia stared out the window. For the first time in over three centuries, the path ahead was no longer clear. At last, she turned back to Frost, "I'm not going to solve this while you're sitting there, Thomas. Please excuse me. I'll let you know when I've figured it out."

The President left the house wishing there was something he could do for the person who had meant so much to America, but now seemed so lonely and helpless.

Arcadia went back to the kitchen and made herself another cup of tea. She wandered through the first floor of her townhome. It had always been a lot more than she needed, but she loved every square inch of it, all the way up to the third floor where she seldom went anymore. She sat down in her comfortable family room at the back of the house and looked through the windows to her patio and her lovely garden.

These days, there was no such thing as a backyard in a Georgetown townhome. Arcadia had it built in 1820, when land was not at such a premium as it was now. She supposed she was the only homeowner in Georgetown to have such a large townhouse, plus an enclosed yard.

As she sipped her tea, she resumed her conversation with God, which had run, more or less continuously for her entire life.

"The very fact I'm here must mean you have something else for me to do. Your dam on the fabric of time is clearly still in place. However, the circle must be nearly complete, since you are placing a known figure from my memory in the here and now. Please put a check in my heart if I'm not getting this right. My mind is telling me I need to complete the inauguration of Max Portner as president and insure he is well launched in what I hope is a long and successful term of office. There's nothing I can see in the future which would indicate anything like the tragedy of my time being even remotely possible. If all this is according to your plan and your will, let me feel your love and peace now."

Arcadia relaxed and a sense of peace and well-being washed through her soul. She smiled. There was still work to do. Still, for the first time in her memory she thought of Branson and the Park. She truly missed her family.

A full year passed as the gears of government ground away and the voters endorsed Max Portner as vice president and the presumptive successor to Thomas Frost. Arcadia did not waste a minute of the time. With relentless precision, she probed every intelligence source available to her, and these were extensive. They came from three centuries of building networks, contacts, and assets. There was not the slightest doubt in Arcadia's mind if there was anything to know about any clandestine operation of any kind, anywhere in the world, she would know it. It was a tremendous relief as she grew closer and closer to the time of the attack on the United States in her time that such likelihood was even possible in the alternative future time. It made her feel a lot better about bringing Max Portner into the tiny circle of individuals who knew the actual truth.

Thomas Frost was ready when his aide announced the vice-president had arrived at the White House. He rang over to Arcadia waiting in his private study next to the Oval Office. "He's coming. Are you ready?"

"Enjoy the moment, Thomas."

"I can promise you I will."

The door opened. "Mr. Portner is here, Mr. President," said an aide.

"Send him in."

Max Portner strode into the Oval Office, obviously in high spirits. He greeted the President warmly, "It's a great morning, Mr. President."

"It's entirely understandable you should feel as good as you do, Max. I know I felt the same on the day I came to the Oval Office, knowing I was elected vice-president, and would finally achieve my dream of becoming President. You certainly have a right to be proud of what you have accomplished."

"Thank you, Mr. President."

"I wouldn't be quite so fast to thank me just yet. There's more to say. How do you suppose previous presidents have managed to do exactly the right thing, at specifically the right time and with precisely the right tools?"

"Prudent planning has always been our strong suit," said Max.

"Actually, there is another reason. Its part of a thing called the Grand Conspiracy. I hope you can be trusted with the truth, keep it to yourself your entire life, except for your successor, and lead the United States forward in a long planned future.

"The truth is, what I'm about to tell you has only been heard by fourteen other men and women since 1770. Two of them died before they could take office and two others proved to be unworthy."

Max could hardly believe the enormity of words he'd just heard. His mind reeled. "I don't know what to say, sir."

"You can swear before God you will take this responsibility and never waver in the common resolve all of us preceding you have held as a sacred trust."

"I so swear, Mr. President."

Frost stared intently at Portner for a moment, "Very well, I believe you." He got up and walked around his desk to the couches, waving Portner to take a seat.

"Search your memory, Max and tell me the most important figures in our history."

"Well, there was Washington, of course, plus Jefferson, Madison,

Monroe, Hamilton, Gallagher, and Carter. We also had our mighty Rangers. There was also the woman, Arcadia, we revere as the inspirational Mother of our country. Of all the founders, we seem to know the least about her. I've watched many videos of her speeches and sermons. She was truly remarkable."

"I can tell you, Arcadia is much more than anything you can possibly imagine." The President smiled, "Tell me, Max, how do you suppose I've been able to anticipate so many critical events and prepare the country for them?"

"As I said before, long range planning is what we do best."

"Close in spirit, but wide of the mark. The reason I, and all my predecessors were successful is because we were being told what to do."

"By whom," said Max?

"By me," said a voice directly behind him.

Max turned in his chair and then jumped to his feet, shaking his head in shock.

"I'm Arcadia, Max. It's nice to meet you in person."

Hank looked at the woman before him. She was the perfect image of the Arcadia he had watched so often in the videos. She was tall, had flowing blond hair, and crystal blue eyes. She was young and beautiful. She was wearing the familiar silver/white, robe/dress that went all the way to the floor and there was a silver belt around her trim waist.

Arcadia came across the room and shook hands with Max, "Relax, my friend, everything is going to be okay. She said it with a smile, and motioned Max back to the couch, while she sat in one facing him.

"The truth is," said Arcadia, "I arrived from the future. In my world, it's 2030. Foreign enemies attacked the United States with weapons beyond your wildest dreams. 150 million Americans are dead, our greatest cities are shattered and we are about to face an army whose sole purpose in life is to kill every Christian on earth. I prayed to God for an answer to this tragedy, and He sent an angel and told me our God did not want this to be the fate of America, and sent me and a few hundred of my friends back in time to undo the damage and save our country. The correction in the time path had to begin in 1770. We brought all our modern weapons from the 21st century with us, and the rest, as you have read, is history."

"But it's almost 2030 now," said Portner, "and nothing of the kind could be evenly remotely possible."

"That is the case, Praise the Lord. However, three hundred years ago the outcome was a good deal more uncertain. All our previous presidents, were brought into the Grand Conspiracy, and told the truth of what was happening, as you are now. Together we built the America you have today."

"You lived through all these centuries, unchanged?"

"That was the will of the Lord, but I'm very happy to tell you the journey is almost over."

"There must be some reason why you know this."

"It's actually quite simple," said Arcadia softly, putting her hand on Max's. "In my time, when the bombs exploded, you were the President of the United States. You survived the carnage of Washington because you were in Branson, with my family. You were a dear friend with my mom and dad for many years. You loved the Park and came as often as you could. To me, you were my 'Uncle Max'. My folks thought you spoiled me all the time."

"I'm very sorry, ma'am, I have no memory, whatsoever, of any of the things you're telling me."

"That's because God has not released the time dam. I believe that when the past meets the future He will restore everything to the proper order."

"And what will that be?"

"I can't tell you, because I don't really know."

"Well," said Max, rubbing his eyes and running his hand through his hair, "this was certainly nothing like I expected it to be."

"It never is," said Thomas, "It was the biggest shock of my life. My predecessor enjoyed it a great deal when I went through it, as I have today with you."

"In any case, Max," said Arcadia, "You have a lot of work to do before you take office. For you it will be studying history that was rather than what is to be. It won't be any easier, but I'll be here to help you. We still have ten years before the timelines intersect."

❖

Arcadia had gone to bed somewhat late. She had no trouble in falling asleep. As she slept, a long procession of vivid dreams began to fill her mind. It was as if all the memories of the past three centuries were blurring by at blinding speed. Suddenly there was something sounding like a muffled explosion and she instinctively knew her timeline was different.

She opened her eyes and her familiar Georgetown bedroom was gone. She was actually sitting on a bench in the Emerald Cathedral, wearing jeans and a blue Park polo shirt. The angel David was sitting next to her. He looked exactly the same as he had when she last saw him. Arcadia stared into his eyes and asked, "Is it over?"

"Just about. There is one last thing to be done. You have served the Lord very well. The fabric of time can be restored. Because of your faithful service, our Father wishes to grant you a final choice."

"What's that?"

"Do you wish to retain all your memories of the last 330 years, or do you wish to step forward into the new age you have made, allowing each day be an unknown adventure?"

Arcadia was instantly conflicted. She knew it was because of her knowledge and deep well of experience developed over centuries the present day was possible. Giving it up would not be easy. Still, if she was going to live her life as God intended, a day at a time, she could not live on a lifetime of memories.

At last, she said, "Heavenly Father, I pass the test. I will leave the past behind and remain Arcadia."

"You are as practical as you are wise," said David.

"In my opinion, God can open the gates of time and let them run freely. My guess is no one will notice any difference in their lives."

"You could certainly put it that way," said David, "and you would be right."

"So, the cities of America intact and are our people alive?"

"You would know better than anyone else," said David. "The world outside is the one you created. The memories of the America you created have replaced the ones they used to know. It's the same all over the world. God has released the dam of time he put in place in 1770. The past they used to know, is wiped out. It says so right in their history books. From their point of view, the future you created is the way it's always been.

"You'll now live out your normal life, although I would say it will be anything but normal. I promise your life will be beautiful, exciting, and filled with many adventures. Your Presidency will be long and prosperous. Lead the world as you have. The Golden Age of Earth has truly begun. He stood up and gently kissed her on the forehead. Have no fear. The Lord is with you always. Now close your eyes, so you may awaken."

Arcadia closed her eyes and the hand of God washed across her mind. When she opened her eyes again, she looked curiously at David, "Hello there, I thought I was alone."

"I didn't mean to interrupt you. You seemed to be in deep thought. I will leave now. By the way, I think your family is holding lunch for you."

Arcadia Martin left the Emerald Cathedral and walked back up the hill to join her family for lunch. As she came in, her father, Jacob said, "There you are, we were just about to start without you."

"Sorry, Dad," said Arcadia, "I must have had a lot of things to think about."

"Come to any big conclusions," asked her mother?

"Nothing special."

"Well, I've got something special for you," said a voice from the other room.

Arcadia turned as President Max Portner came bustling in, "Hi, Uncle Max, when did you get here?"

"While you were out dawdling in the Emerald Cathedral. I've come on a special errand."

"What's that?"

"All your test scores are complete from the national computer. You've been selected to begin studies at the University of Political Science in Washington, next semester. I had nothing to do with the selection, of course, but I'm thrilled a super sharp mind like yours will now be directed toward a career, which I fully believe will make you a leading candidate for senior government leadership. Who knows? You could end up having my job."

"That sounds like something to look forward to," said Arcadia.

Meet Phil Walker

A lifelong career for him began when he was only 13 years old, as a radio broadcaster in his hometown, Fort Collins, Colorado. He says this was the year his voice changed. Over the next 58 years, he continued a much-celebrated career at radio stations in Colorado and Nebraska. He received recognition by state broadcaster's associations, for forty straight years, culminating in him chosen as Colorado Broadcaster of the Year in 1997.

Writing began early. He estimates he has written 10,000 radio commercials, and several million words of news copy. His first book, a non-fiction work on American Western history was the best-selling book in Fort Collins for nine years and reprinted seven times. To this, he added eight, hour-long CDs with music, sound effects, multiple voices - sweeping sagas of history. Over a hundred thousand CDs have sold to date.

Serious writing of fiction novels began in 2002. Six more books comprising the *Starlight* Series joined his first book, *The Galilee Foundation.* Phil admits writing in the genre of religion and science fiction was something of a tough way to crack the market.

Then came the critically acclaimed *The Black Angel, Crusade of the Black Angel, The Rangers are Coming,* and the latest book, soon to be released, *The Magic and the Misery.*

Phil Walker lives with his wife, Verna, a nationally known artist, in The Villages, Florida. When he's not writing, he loves the days in his garden.

❖

If you have finished reading this book, I would like to hear from you. I don't want to know what you liked about the book, although that would be nice, but rather what you didn't like about it. Please feel free to send your comments to my email address: walkhouse@yahoo.com

Enjoy these books by Phil Walker

The Black Angel
Crusade of The Black Angel
The Rangers are Coming
Lions and Tigers, and Bears, OH GOD!
Out of the Emerald Cathedral

The Starlight Series

The Holy Mission
The Galilee Foundation
The Galilee Garden
Island of the Angels
Terra Rising
Heaven's Angels
The Galactic Quest

Coming December 201
The Magic and the Misery

Non-Fiction History

Visions Along the Poudre Valley
Modern Visions Along the Poudre Valley

Made in the USA
Lexington, KY
15 December 2017